THE VEIL OF VIOLENCE

MARILYN MARKS

For my ferocious Erica,
Who read this book top to bottom, provided support during my many frantic phone calls, rooted endlessly for Jack and Addie, and in general is a pretty cool baby sister.
I still want my sweatshirt back though.

THE VEIL OF VIOLENCE
MARILYN MARKS

Once upon a dreary summer, two lonely children met in a meadow.
And thus they swore on love and blood that nothing would keep them apart.
Not titles.
Not magic.
Not time.
Not even death.

ONE

JAEVIDAN

Language studies were dreadful.

Everything Scholar Rindaw taught was dreadful, but I hated languages the most. We never left the kingdom of Gerenstad, and I knew the common tongue well enough. So I could not understand why we spent endless days in the library learning Leontish and Tearachan—or worse, the human tongues—when there were much better things to do. Like sword training.

"Am I lulling you to sleep, Prince Jaevidan?"

I sat upright, wiping the drool on my work scroll away. Scholar Rindaw used his wooden paddle when I fell asleep. "No."

"Hm." His beady eyes fell on me, the same color as his leafy skin. I once asked Donvidan if the scholar was always green, to which my eldest brother called me an idiot. I thought it was a good question. Scholar Rindaw appeared high fae, but I had never seen one his color. When I asked my teacher himself if he was cursed or if it had been a spell gone awry, his only answer was the wooden switch.

"Your studies are of the utmost importance, my Prince."

"I know." I did not know but would not say as much. That earned me a sharp rap to the knuckles.

He sighed in the way that meant he was tired of my foolishness. He made this sigh often, which I often ignored. "Your studies are concluded for the day."

I leapt to my feet, nearly departing before remembering our silly formalities. I gave him a curt nod. "May the fates bless your day, Scholar."

He waved a breezy hand. "And the Bogorans, my Prince."

I ran like sprites nipped at my ankles. The sun brushed the treetops, which meant if I were quick, I still had time to play outside. Mother forbade me from leaving the grounds after dark, and I did not like to dally in the courtyard where so many eyes watched. It was always more of the same—*This is unbefitting of a royal son, my Prince* or *Is the Queen aware of your presence, my Prince?* Every day was spent with studies and formalities, so when they concluded, I wanted to do fun things. Like use the dagger Scholar Dreshen gave me or play with my puppet. Kalvidan called it a doll, but Kalvidan was an idiot.

I hoped to retrieve my things from my bedchamber before someone asked questions. Unfortunately, my brothers were at the royal apartments when I arrived. We each had our own bedroom, but Mother insisted we share a parlor. Donvidan lay across his favorite settee, sharpening one of his beloved knives. Kalvidan sat opposite him, playing with his most beloved item—Periwen.

The dryad smiled from my brother's lap. Kalvidan yanked her dress down over her brown hips. "Oh, look. A third prince has arrived."

I froze.

Donvidan did not look up from his knife. "What are you doing, Jaevidan?"

Shuffling, I murmured, "I came to get—"

Kalvidan perked up, a mean smile forming. "Your doll?" he asked.

My cheeks burned. I shook my head. "My knife."

"And why would you need your knife?" Donvidan drawled. It meant nothing. He always sounded bored. That made him far more terrifying than Kalvidan. My middle brother showed all his emotions, and I knew when he was about to be a brute. But my eldest was always indifferent, and I could never tell when he was about to strike.

"Leave him be," Periwen said. She laid a hand on Kalvidan's shoulder. "We all know he only came to play with his puppet."

I glared at her. At first, I thought she was nice, but that was a lie. She only pretended to be nice. Whenever Periwen became involved, I ended up in trouble.

"Why would you need your knife?" Donvidan repeated.

I swallowed. "I wish to play outside."

Periwen smiled, her sharp teeth cutting into her lower lip. "How sweet the little princeling is."

"A little idiot," Kalvidan said. He did not look at me but at Periwen, running his fingers down her cheek. He nipped at her lips. "Perhaps we will be fortunate and the Dearg will eat him."

My blood ran cold. "Dearg?"

"She was reported outside the grounds this morning," Donvidan said. His knife flashed in the low torchlight. "Mother asked me to hunt it this eve."

For once, I was interested. My brothers rarely did exciting things, spending most days drinking wine or playing with women who only liked them because they were princes. I was never sure how I was the only one to notice. Since I could not partake in these things, and had no desire to anyway, I spent very little time with them. I chose to believe that was why. Not because they preferred each other's company over mine. "May I help?"

Kalvidan and Periwen laughed, my brother saying, "Do let him go with you, Donvidan. It would be so pleasant having one less brother in the hunts."

Donvidan scowled. I recoiled, wondering if I had time to run away. He was always indifferent until he was not. And when he was not, it was never good.

My eldest brother's cold, green eyes fell on me. He got them from Mother, but his dark hair was entirely Father's. Or so I had been told. He was slain shortly before my birth, and Mother had had all his portraits removed from the castle. "Why would I let a little runt accompany me?"

My tongue turned heavy. "I could help."

Periwen stifled a giggle.

"You will only get in the way." He no longer looked at me but at his knife. "Besides, the Dearg will likely eat you, and Mother would be most upset should you die before she does." He paused. "And I would be most upset should you die before I could kill you myself."

My hands balled into fists at my side. "Not if I win the hunts."

They all laughed, even Donvidan. Periwen sighed, draping herself across Kalvidan like she posed for a painting. "He really is so sweet. Could you truly kill him when the time comes?"

Neither of my brothers answered. None was needed. They had both made it exceptionally clear when Mother died and the three princes joined the hunts for the throne, I would be the first to meet their blades. The only question was if they would kill each other. Periwen thought not, but I knew they would.

They all ignored me, so I slunk into my room and retrieved my dagger from the wall. Nine empty mounts stretched out beside it. As I moved up in my training, I would receive new weapons. So far, I had spent six months trying to reach the second tier. Donvidan had reached tier five by my age, something he reminded me of every day.

With the dagger secured to my scabbard, I quietly dug through my toy box until I found Lesther. He was not a doll. He was a hand-painted marionette given to Mother when I was born, and he was my closest friend.

I held up his wooden crossbars and tugged the string that moved his mouth. A Scholar had enchanted him so he could speak to me, but he only had so many answers. I did not mind. He always agreed with me.

"My brothers do not like me," I whispered.

Lesther's wooden lips creaked. "Would you like me to dance, Prince Jaevidan?"

I sighed. "I do not know why. I only wish for them to play with me."

A whirring sound left his back. "Shall we sing a song together?"

Nursery rhymes were for babes, and that I was not. "Do you enjoy my company, Lesther?"

The puppet's glassy, black eyes fell on me. "That is my favorite ballad."

I frowned, shoving him back into my toy chest. Maybe when he said *favorite*, he spoke of me.

DONVIDAN HAD WARNED ME about the Dearg, but even without that, I was forbidden from leaving the castle grounds on my own. But I was a prince, and princes could do whatever they wanted.

By the time my brothers left the parlor, the sun sat low. Pink and orange and yellow took the sky, with the full moon peeking its head above the trees. It would be dark soon, but not so bad with the moon's light to guide me. I snuck through the castle and courtyard, avoiding everyone for dark corners and secret corridors only the royal family knew of. The gates loomed ahead with several guards, but they were all drunk, and I was small and quiet. I did not think I could win the hunts by hunting, but even Donvidan agreed I excelled at one trick—it was very hard to find me when I did not wish to be found.

The guards did not notice me, and Scholar Rindshaw had taught me how to sneak through the wards. I crossed our castle's infamous bone bridge as quickly as possible. *Not* because it scared me, but so I would not be spotted. Nothing scared me, just like nothing scared my brothers. When I reached the end, I dared a peek over the edge just to prove it. Hundreds of feet below, the Draith River cut through the rock. Crystals stuck from the water like thorns. My palms grew sweaty, but that happened often. I was not afraid.

The opal castle glistened behind me, absorbing the full moon's light. It was important the walls were washed and cleaned every moon cycle because it drew power from the light, and we only had the moon three nights of the month. Our world did not have its own moon, so each month, there were twenty-eight days of darkness, then three days where we borrowed one from the human world.

The Darkwood loomed ahead. The treetops stopped any light from pouring through, and fog blanketed the ground. Thankfully, pale blue will-o-wisps bounced through the thicket and along the low road. Anything likely to eat me would avoid their glow. I kept telling myself that, not daring to glance back at the safety of my home, perched on its lonely mountaintop surrounded by the ravine. I knew if I turned, I would see the silver candles in my bedroom window and be tempted to turn back. But I was not a *feerg*. I did not know what this word meant, and Mother forbade me from using it, but Donvidan always said it to describe a coward.

I brandished my dagger and walked into the forest.

Sprites chittered in the trees, and low fae ducked into the brush. In the distance, the rumbling song of the temple drifted on the breeze. I yawned and rubbed at my eyes but pushed onward. With each step, I grew angrier.

Why did Donvidan think he was so special, anyway? He was a master of blades, sure, but he was a brute. And according to the scholars, Kalvidan was *frivolous* and *pampered*. I did not know what these words meant, but I knew they were insults. There was no reason I could not win the hunts. My brothers were eighty and eighty-three years older, so of course they were better trained than me. When I grew up, I would be just as fierce. No—fiercer.

By the time Mama joined the darkness, I would be the best prince to ever live. And just to prove that, I would even spare my brothers in the hunts. I would simply gash out their eyes or remove their fingers. Then I would tell them they had no choice but to like me, because kings can tell everyone what to do, even princes.

But first, I had to prove myself.

It was not my plan to hunt down the Dearg, but the more I thought about it, the better an idea it seemed. Once I killed it myself, no one would call me *little prince* anymore or tell me I was a silly child. I would advance to tier five of blade training instantly, and Mama would hold a feast in my honor.

I quickened my steps, dreaming of all the scholars who would ask for my blessing and how I would have Rindshaw's paddle burned in my Calamity fire. Donvidan would fall at my feet, begging for forgiveness and offering to complete my blade training himself. Periwen would stop calling me sweet, and Kalvidan would give me my first sip of wine.

There were fewer will-o-wisps in this part of the Darkwood. I had never ventured this far, even with an escort. It did not matter. I had to find the Dearg. I stomped on, not caring my feet slapped against a dirt path or that the sprites had gone silent. It was not until I met a dead end I realized I was lost.

I turned around, but the low road was gone. Somehow, I had ventured off the path and into the grasses without realizing. Sweat trickled down my neck. If the Dearg was hiding anywhere, it would not be along the road, so this was fine.

Just to be safe, I ventured back the way I came so I could find the road when the time came. A thick forest of brambles rose from the grass that I did not remember. My palms grew wet, but it was nothing to be worried about. The forest moved on its own all the time. The Darkwood probably thought I was a silly child, too, and placed the brambles here to make me think I was lost. I grinned, knowing I had outsmarted it. The road must have been on the other side.

I pushed through the brambles, hissing when they smacked me in the face. My sleeve snagged on a thorn larger than my head and drew a thin line of blood. Tears dripped down my cheeks, but I angrily wiped them away. Only children cried when they were injured. I trudged on, not stopping until I was covered in cuts and emerged on the other side.

The low road was not here.

My right hand clutched my dagger, and my left wiped at my eyes. I reminded myself I was not afraid of anything, but the treetops were thick and the darkness heavy. I could only see a few feet ahead, and not very well. I hated the dark. I hated it more than I hated my brothers, more than their insults, more than the wooden paddle or anything else. I sunk to the ground, drawing my knees to my chest and shivering. It was cold here, and I was hungry, and I wished I had at least brought Lesther to keep me company.

Something moved in the brush. Something big.

I leapt to my feet and ran. I stumbled over tree roots and rocks, not caring that I wept as a gash appeared in my thigh. The dagger fell from my fingers, but I was too scared to stop and find it. When my chest ached and my head pounded, I fell to the ground and sobbed like the stupid boy I was.

A soft breeze curled around me, and with it, the low sound of crying.

I wiped my eyes. A meadow lay ahead.

I scurried for it, not stopping until my feet touched soft grass and the human moon shined above. The Darkwood rumbled behind me, laughing. As much as I wanted to go back and prove it wrong, I preferred the moonlit field instead. White moonlilies glowed everywhere, and the ground was soft enough to sleep on. I yawned, tempted, when I heard the crying again.

They were ugly and . . . girlish.

But there was no one in the meadow. Could it be the Dearg? My heart raced, but nothing came forward to eat me. I searched the grasses, wondering if I could find a weapon, when I noticed the trees.

There were two of them, so tall their highest points brushed the stars. Their thick branches reached for one another, forming an archway between their glowing trunks. And between them was something . . . strange.

It almost looked like a painting. It was a field, but not the field I stood in. Pee-yellow grass swayed in the breeze with ugly pink and purple flowers. Compared to my meadow, the one between the trees looked like it was dying. The sky was also different, a darker black with stars that looked too far away. In the distance were barren, rocky mountains.

It had to be an illusion, but I had never seen glamour like that. Maybe it really was a painting, but the grass moved, and besides, it was hideous. Shuffling forward, I squinted and attempted to make sense of the vision. A large gray rock came into view between the trees, and beside it, a girl.

I stopped, ducking behind one of the sky-high trees. Magic hummed between the oaks, the image of the little girl rippling like a pebble dropped in a pail of water. She wiped her face and buried her face in her knees. The awful crying came from her.

I walked behind the image, but it was only more of my meadow between the trunks. When I came around the front again, I could see the little girl once more. She was too busy crying to notice me.

Or maybe she could not see me.

No one had ever taken me to the human world or even to one of the breaks in the Veil. But I heard stories of fae crossing the archways and visiting. I wondered why. It looked disgusting.

I stared at the girl. Her dress was plain gray and torn everywhere. She had no shoes, and her feet were black with mud. Her small hands trembled around her knees, and dirt caked her fingernails. Her hair may have been blonde, but it was too dusty to tell.

She looked up.

And shrieked.

I shrieked with her, stumbling back and tripping on a rock. My backside hit the ground, and she scrambled against the boulder. "Do not eat me!" she screamed at the same moment I yelped, "You can see me?"

She spoke in a human tongue, and it took a moment before I recognized what she said. Obviously, she did not speak any fae languages. She continued to shriek and clamber on her hands.

I pushed to my feet. Her watery image flickered behind the Veil, her skinny hands held out in front of her. I thought hard back to Scholar Rindshaw's lessons of Welsh. "How can you see me?" Then, frowning, I added, "And why would I eat you?"

Her eyes were green like dirty water, ugly and too large for her face. They widened. "Are you not of fair folk?"

Whatever did that mean? I shook my head. "No, I am a sidhe."

Now, she frowned. "But sidhe *are* fair folk."

It must have been a silly human term. I took in her ripped dress and dull skin. Her ears were round and useless. Even on this side of the Veil, the smell of dying flesh and muck made me want to vomit. Was that what humans smelled like? No wonder I had never been taken to the Veil. She reeked.

"High fae do not eat humans, but even if we did, I doubt you would taste good." I sank to my knees and prodded the Veil. It felt . . . cold. "Are you glamour-touched? Scholar Rindshaw says only glamour-touched humans can see through the Veil."

She shook her head, lower lip trembling. "Who is that?"

I did not answer. Scholar Rindshaw was boring and old, and I was more interested in this hideous human. She looked close to my age, maybe a little smaller. Her owl eyes followed my finger along the Veil, tears dried to her cheeks.

"Why do you cry?" I asked instead. Not because I cared, but I wondered if she would be punished for it. If her human family beat her for these things too.

This time, she did not answer. It was very annoying. She tucked her face into her drawn knees, one eye following each of my movements. "Everyone in the village says the fae will kill you if you see one."

"They must be stupid," I said. Humans crossed the Veil all the time. Usually, they were made into servants, and they never really lived long, but they were only killed sometimes.

"So you will not hurt me?" she asked.

I thought of Donvidan, wondering what he would do. He would probably kill her for not answering, and Kalvidan enjoyed making anyone beneath him obey his will. But I had no reason to kill her or enslave her. I was simply . . . curious.

I shrugged.

Maybe she was curious, too, because she got on her hands and knees and came closer. I stiffened as she poked the Veil, right over my finger on the other side. The magic rippled out from our fingertips, but we did not touch.

Her eyes widened. "Can someone cross it?"

Yes, but I was forbidden to do so. And if she came here, I doubted it would be long before something really did eat her.

"Only very powerful fae," I lied.

Her head tilted. "So, can you?"

I was annoyed all over again. My brothers, my mother, Scholar Rindshaw, Periwen . . . everyone already doubted me enough, and now this silly little human girl.

"Of course I can. Are you dull?"

Her eyes narrowed. "Never mind." She stood and collected her bag from the ground, turning away.

I leapt to my feet. "Where are you going?"

"Away from you."

She meant it too. She was already past the boulder when I yelled out, "Wait, come back!"

Stopping, she threw her hands on her hips and glared at me. "Why would I?"

"Because . . ." I thought of anything that did not admit she intrigued me, or that there were no children at the castle, or that no one else ever bothered to talk to me.

She rolled her eyes and kept walking.

My hands balled into fists. I made sure no one was watching me. The meadow was silent, as if waiting to see if I would break one of the rules. I crossed the Veil.

It was cold, and then it was colder. The chilled air of the human world shook me to the bone, but I stomped forward anyway. When the girl realized I was following her, she froze like a sprite caught in a trap.

My teeth chattered. Loudly. "You are very impolite."

Her skinny hands balled into fists. "Me? *You* are the horrid one."

Horrid . . . perhaps that was a good thing. Servants whispered that word about Donvidan all the time.

I grinned. "Thank you."

She stared at me like I was a fool. "And weird."

I did not know this word, but I took it as another compliment.

In the distance, torches from a small village flickered in the dark. The little girl was shaking in her dirty dress and bare feet. She had a bag with her, though it seemed mostly empty. My nose wrinkled with the stench of moldy bread.

An idea came to me, something that made her much more interesting. "Are you running away?"

"Why does it matter to you?"

I shrugged. "I am bored."

"Then maybe I am."

I sat cross-legged on the ground, picking the grass. "Why?"

"My papa died." She joined me on the ground, adding yellow blades to my pile. "My mama cannot feed all us children, so she sent me to live in the convent and left for Cardiff."

"What is that?"

"A place where unwanted children go." Her voice grew low and sad, wispy as her hair. "Do you grant wishes?"

I shook my head.

"I thought so." Something about her disappointment bothered me. As a faerie prince, I should have been able to grant her wishes. Instead, I could barely make it to tier two of sword training.

"You could come back with me," I said. Having someone my age to play with would be nice. Someone who was not Lesther and could speak more than twenty words.

She laughed. "Your faerie tricks will not work on me."

"It is no trick."

"Of course it is." Her head cocked to the side, massive eyes making her look like a bird. "What would I do in Faerie?"

"Well . . ." What would she do? More importantly, would Mother be angry if I brought home a human pet? Probably not—she had plenty. "We could play all day. And we have plenty to eat, but you would have to hide whenever my brothers came around because they are cruel and like to break my toys. But you could stay in my room."

She shook her head. "But boys and girls cannot share rooms. Not unless they are siblings or when they grow up and get married."

This word was new to me. "What is 'married?'"

"Oh, it is when . . ." She frowned. "Well, I am not really sure. But if two people love each other or have a baby, then they make vows before God and live together until one of them dies."

I did not love this human girl, and I was too young for babes, but I desperately wanted a friend. "So, if we married, you could come stay with me?"

She burst into a fit of giggles. I frowned, but she only clutched her stomach, falling back on the grass. "We cannot get married, silly. Only adults can!"

Ugh. Only adults ever had any fun. I lay in the grass beside her. "How old are you, then?"

"I am not sure, but my mama said around six or seven years."

How could someone not know their age? Were all humans this stupid? "I am eight summers."

Grass crunched under her head as she nodded. "Then we cannot get married, and we are not siblings. So I cannot come with you."

I rolled to my side. "I could steal you."

Those strange eyes fell on me, her voice a whisper. "If you did that, I would hate you forever."

My brothers would steal her anyway, but then I thought of the women they fancied. All the ones who only pretended to like them because they were royal. Fake adoration was not as satisfying.

"Maybe when we are older?" I asked.

She considered it, tapping a finger on her chin. "Hm, how about when we are older, you may *ask* me?"

I squinted. All I had to do was ask? But there was no guarantee she would say yes.

"And if I decide I like you until then," she said, "then I promise I will agree."

That seemed more fitting. Magic thrummed in the air around us, ready to seal a bargain. "When can I ask?"

"When I am twenty," she said without thought. "Twenty is very old, so that should be enough time."

Twenty? But that was years away. I was bored right now.

My stomach hit the grass, and I cupped my chin in my hands. "I cannot change your mind?"

She grinned, shaking her head. "I am no fool, little fae boy. When I am twenty, you may ask to marry me. And until then, we can be friends. I have none anyway." She frowned. "But you will have to woo me when we are older."

Bogorans' wrath, this only got worse. "Woo?"

"Yes," she exclaimed. "Like the knights do for the ladies. With flowers and songs and poetry. And when all is done, you must get on one knee and declare your desire for me."

I gagged. "Ew."

She burst into another fit of giggles. "Now, do you still want to marry me?"

Not even a little, but I liked the idea of being friends in the meantime. I liked that she had no friends either, so I did not feel so odd. And she had a pretty laugh, even if she smelled like human.

"You must go to your convent, then," I said. "We cannot be friends if you run away from your village."

Her smile wilted like moonlilies in the sun. "I would have to go anyway. It was silly to try and run away."

No, it was silly for me to try and hunt the Dearg. We were both fools.

"I should find my way home now." She stood, brushing the dirt off her very dirty dress. "When I see you again, may you bring bread?"

Fae food would enchant her and make her my slave, but I could probably find something. If it guaranteed I would see her again, then I would find a way. I reached for her sack, finding the molded hunk she must have stolen from her convent. My glamour was not very good yet, but it would make it taste better.

She clapped her hands, squealing. It was only an illusion—the bread was still moldy—but she did not know that. Throwing her arms around my neck, she planted a kiss on my cheek and whispered, "I adore you already."

My cheeks turned red, but it was too dark for her to see. I was too flustered to notice her skipping away. "Meet me here on the next new moon. That is when the Veil is thinnest!"

"I will!" she called back.

Her skirts swished over the crest of a hill when I realized something. Something important. "Wait!"

She stopped.

"My name is Jaevidan," I said. "What is yours?"

She smiled, her eyes crinkling in the corners. Like that, she was actually quite beautiful.

"Annwyl," she said.

TWO

ADELINE

I WOKE WITH A start, head slumped against the back of my chair.

The ocean pounded the shore outside the window. Gossamer curtains fluttered on the cold, wet breeze, dousing me in early morning mist. In the tattered bed beside me, Tommy was still fast asleep.

My hand clutched the diamond around my neck. It glowed an iridescent silver, but as my blackened fingertips slipped away, it returned to its normal state. Just like Jack's memory fading from the forefront of my mind.

On the edge of Cardiff, the early morning was slow to begin. Seabirds squawked over the waves, and the early risers roamed the streets. Fresh bread wafted from the kitchens of our inn, and bicycles trilled along the sidewalk below. Peaceful, but we couldn't stay here for long.

So far, I knew this:

One, Estheria had given me these memories. How many there were, I did not know, but I had a feeling this was the first of many. And for whatever reason, they were important.

Two, the wraith was surely in love with Jack, but I was more sure she was gone forever.

Three, somehow, the Morrigan had bested us. They'd managed to disguise themselves as Knights and fake their headquarters in Ildathach, the world of fae. I fought them off, and we managed our escape into Wales.

Four, I was made into something else. Something we did not understand. My fingertips were black as night, my scream one of death and destruction.

Five, the man I'd spent the last few months with, the man I trusted with all my heart, the man who took me to bed and brought forth my powers and promised to always be there for me—the man who was my supposed *soulmate*—had made my designated term of endearment a dead little girl's name.

I was going to be ill.

I brought my fist to my mouth to suppress a scream. Behind me, Tommy stirred from sleep.

"Were you there all night?"

Taking a placating breath, I nodded.

The sheets rustled behind me, and his bare feet hit the floor. Outside, waves crashed against the foggy beach. "You should have said something." He ran his hand down his face, then groaned and held his head in his palms. "Whatever you did to me . . . that traveling thing . . . god, I feel like shit."

"Third time's a charm," I murmured. Estheria's diamond glinted in the early morning sun, small and unassuming where it lay in the palm of my hand. I clasped the necklace around my throat and stood on trembling knees. "I need a moment."

Hiding in the powder room, I held my hands on the sink and drew deep breaths. It could have been nothing. *Annwyl* was a term of endearment in Welsh, after all. *Like darling or sweetheart or, on occasion, a woman's name*, he said. Or Jack could be an obsessive, psychotic immortal, attempting to recreate memories of a dead human girl from his childhood.

Or there was a third option I hadn't thought of yet.

I mulled over what the wraith had told me, but that left more questions than answers. She said she'd found her remaining pieces but not where. She said she could move on now but never specified how. Now, she was gone, and it was too late to ask.

Then, there were the Morrigan sisters to worry about.

Were they dead? Or simply regrouping? They didn't seem like the sort of creatures to leave loose ends. They hadn't come after me yet, but that didn't mean they wouldn't. If they did, it would be soon.

I stared at my reflection. My smooth skin with the subtle immortal glow beneath. All but my hands, which remained blackened at the fingertips. *Beansidhe*—that's what the wraith said I was now. Vaguely, I recalled Arthur explaining them once. Explaining as much as he could because, according to him, not much was known about them. Only that they were tied into human fate and death, they came from wraiths, and there were always three.

Now, I was one of them, and I hadn't the faintest idea what that meant.

The Morrigan, the Knights of Templar, and now this new twist, whatever it meant. I craved Jack's guidance, his centuries-old knowledge, even the infuriating way he pulled all the strings while myself and everyone else were none the wiser. At least he had plans. Without his scheming, I was utterly lost. Worse, I was no longer sure how I fit into his grand design.

Friend, foe, lover, tool . . . obsession. I was one of them to him, but I couldn't say which.

Tommy knocked on the washroom door. "Everything jake?"

I splashed some water on my face. "I'm fine, just a minute."

And what the hell was I going to do with my brother?

Tommy sat in the chair when I reentered the room, drumming his fingers on the windowsill. Before he could make mention of it, I pulled on my gloves and sat on the bed. He tracked each movement, taking note of the subtle changes. I'd spent weeks practicing how to move more like a human again, but it was a work in progress.

Silence drifted on the breeze, long and arduous before Tommy broke it. "We should keep moving."

I nodded. Moving was good. Moving felt like doing something, even if there was no direction. If the Morrigan was alive, they were hunting us. The Knights, if their existence wasn't a farce created by the immortal sisters or they hadn't killed them off, would be hunting Tommy. And if Jack was alive, he'd be hunting me.

My silence was agreement enough because Tommy spurred into action, collecting his few remaining items and taking stock of our weapons and ammo. We still had the swords from the Knights' headquarters, which weren't discreet but better than nothing. The guns were more helpful, but our ammo would deplete soon if we couldn't replenish it. Money could buy anything, but I doubted Cardiff was in ready supply of iron bullets.

"We'll head east," he said, removing a city map that had been stuffed in the inn's nightstand. "There's fewer breaks in the Veil on the continent. And after that . . ."

Silence, apparently. I wondered if he was waiting for me to fill the gap in his plan, but one look at his face told otherwise. I recognized that look. It was soldier Tommy. Big brother Tommy. Man of the house Tommy. All of his worries and fears were hidden behind a stoic mask, worn by someone who felt they had others depending on them but had no answers. He pretended to study the map while I pondered options myself. If he knew what I was thinking, he didn't let on. The truth was, there was nowhere in this world one of our enemies couldn't find us. My father had already tried that, and look how it fared for him.

A knock sounded through the room.

Tommy's good eye widened, face taut. He brought a finger to his lip and grasped the gun, slowly rising to his feet.

He stepped forward. I grabbed his arm, silently mouthing, *No*, and gesturing to the mirror. If there was danger on the other side, I could shade us away.

Indecision played on his face. The choice to hand his little sister the reins or play his usual role in our dynamic. The latter won. I made a move to grab him and shade away, but he was fast. Before I could furiously whisper to stop, he was at the door, gun drawn.

Another knock permeated the tension. Tommy stood beside the door and flattened against the wall.

I slunk lower in my chair, snatching the remaining gun off the coffee table.

"Hello?" someone called. A man's voice, high and reedy. "Anyone here?"

Tommy sighed with relief. I didn't. That voice could belong to an innkeeper or one of the many shapeshifting creatures of the fae. His hand edged toward the knob. I jumped to my feet. "No!"

The door swung open. I raised my gun, Tommy froze, and a man in . . . sheets stood wide-eyed and trembling.

He pushed a pair of spectacles higher on his face, raising his hands in the air. His dress reminded me of the Greek tales Tommy used to read, a loose linen toga of white held at the shoulder with a golden clasp. I didn't recognize the man, but I recognized his scent. Earthy and deep with the faint tang of metal that accompanied magic. A perk of my new status as a *beansidhe*—recognizing the common undertones that followed certain species. I'd scented this on Arthur many times.

The druid lifted his trembling hands higher, sweeping into a hasty bow. "Lady Fate, I come to serve you."

THREE

ADELINE

TOMMY GAVE ME A blank stare. I returned the favor.

"Excuse me?" I asked.

The druid lowered his trembling hands. A terrified expression oscillated between me and Tommy, settling on the weapon I held in the air. "The Guild heard your call. I was sent to escort you."

Tommy looked truly lost. I wondered if the Knights knew of the druids' existence or if he thought the fidgeting man was as human as him. As a human, I'd been unable to tell the difference between myself and them. Either way, he sensed the threat, grabbing the man by his shoulder and shoving him forward. He frisked him for weapons and ordered the man to sit.

"You are currently Adeline Colton, are you not?" the druid asked.

Currently. What a strange choice of words, though if Arthur was anything to go by, the druids were strange people. "Why do you ask?"

"As I said, the Guild heard your call." He gestured openly with his hands, like this explained all. "You may call me Morris. I'm afraid the constellations speak of very little time, and the insects whisper of crows among them. I may take you to safety, but we must leave now." He sent a foul look in Tommy's direction, who still grasped him by the toga. "Unhand me, human."

"The human is with me," I said. "And forgive me, but what call?"

Tommy raised his working brow. "Birds and constellations?"

"I will explain along the way." Morris stood, dusting off his strange attire. Neither my brother nor I moved. "Will your human be joining us, then?"

Tommy cleared his throat. "Addie, can I have a word?"

I looked between the two men. "Morris, I would prefer some explanation now, please."

He frowned. "Are you or are you not the newest of the *beansidhe*?"

I supposed I was, not that I had any idea what that meant. But the Guild did.

"I am," I said slowly. "What does this mean to the Guild?"

Morris made a face like I'd asked him to drink blood. "We are at your service, my lady."

This made less sense as we went along. I doubted it would make any within the next few minutes, but Tommy and I had come up with no solutions, and one may have fallen into our laps. Assuming this visit was friendly.

"Why are you at my service?"

"This is the way things are done," the druid said, joining us in confusion. Good, we were all on the same page. "The Guild has always answered to your service, you and your sisters."

"I don't have any sisters."

He squeaked in horror. We were getting nowhere.

"I'm in danger," I said, leaping straight to the point. "Others are looking for me. Can you take us somewhere we will be safe?"

Dipping into another sweeping bow, he said, "It would be my honor."

"Alright, Addie, we need to talk." Tommy grabbed the druid by his toga and dragged him out the door. "Five minutes," he said, slamming it in the protesting man's face.

Tommy turned around. "No."

I took a deep breath, debating our options. We were fresh out of them at the moment, and while I didn't entirely trust this new development, it was the best one we had. As far as I knew, the druids were harmless. We'd thought Delsaran was an outlier, but it turned out he wasn't a threat at all. It had all been the Morrigan. They were scholars and librarians and historians, not fighters. If I had to choose any magical entity to put my faith in, it would be the ones that were once human.

Deep in thought, I hadn't noticed Tommy rambling the entire time. "—it's the wrong move. Shade us out, now."

"Please, be quiet," I murmured. I needed a moment to think. A pounding had gone off in my head, incessant and throbbing. It reminded me of something, something I couldn't quite place my finger on. I brought my hand to my temple and rubbed the aching spot.

"You can't be considering this," he said.

"Druids are notoriously neutral," I said. "And you heard him—he knows what I am and is willing to protect us."

"*Serve* you."

I waved a hand. "They're not from this century, Tommy. Take the language with a grain of salt."

"We're on the run from god knows how many devil-folk and humans, and your first thought is to trust a man that mysteriously shows up at the door? Really, Addie?"

It was like being a child again, except this time, I had equal experience in this field, and my head was on fire. My patience withered to twig-like proportions. "I think he's telling the truth."

"*Think* isn't good enough with the sheer volume of people trying to kill us." He ran past me, wrenching the curtains closed. The room plunged into darkness, and he gathered our remaining weapons. "We're leaving."

I sat down, ignoring him. I needed another moment. Another three. Tommy was used to battle, quick decisions, split seconds that meant life or death, but I could hear the druid's timid breath behind the door, and he wasn't going anywhere. We had a moment to discuss this. To weigh pros and cons.

I wanted to understand what I was. The Band of Banished had offered no insight, but apparently, the Guild could. And if the Guild could, it would give me more information about those I left behind. Arthur claimed to have no knowledge of the *beansidhe*, but he'd spent time with his brethren before. If he was lying—more importantly, if he was lying for *Jack*—that answered more than a few questions about how much I could trust Jack and his crew. That was knowledge we desperately needed right now.

If I knew more about what I was and what I could do, even better. What I did in Ildathach to the Morrigan was enough to save our skins once. If I knew how, I could do it again. And if the Guild offered to hide us in the meantime, it solved at least a few of our looming issues.

"We have nowhere else to go," I said, calmly and plainly. Tommy's energy was frenetic, his wild stare taking my memories to darker times. Nights spent with his screams through my bedroom wall. He was trapped, and he knew it.

"No."

"If it goes badly, I can shade us away again. All I need is a reflective surface, which I've learned the world is abundant with."

"It's too risky."

"What is our other plan?" The words came out harsh, more than I had intended. Despite everything these past few months, this was all new to me and Tommy. The shifting changes in our relationship, in me. I was no longer the scared little girl under his care. I was a woman, a powerful woman embroiled in something neither of us understood. He didn't expect me to fight him so much. Truthfully, neither did I.

"We head east," he said.

"And then?"

"Then I'll do what I always do. You will be safe, we will be far away from this godforsaken place, and we'll hide as long as we need to."

I shook my head. "That's not a plan, Tommy."

"It's better than this." Insecurity lined every syllable. He tried to hide it by reaching for my hand, but it was too late. I noticed. It was amazing what happened when you grew up. You realized the adults in your life were just as clueless as you.

"I know what you're doing," I murmured. "I know you want to fix things, be the man like you always have, but this time, I need you to trust me. This isn't a great option, I agree, but at the moment, it's our best one."

He said nothing. We hovered like that, me in the chair and his hand outstretched toward me. I was so used to taking Tommy's hand and letting him lead the way, it was almost instinct to follow suit. But not this time. Not with everything at stake.

"I'm letting him back in," I said. I brushed past my brother. He flinched. Behind the door, Morris offered a strained smile. "Ready?"

"Tell me what you can do for me, then we'll go."

MORRIS CHOSE TO EXPLAIN along the way, like he said earlier. Tommy wasn't happy, but as soon as I learned *along the way* meant traipsing throughout Cardiff and not the fae realm, I was more inclined to agree.

The old city hustled and bustled as we strode through a crowded intersection. The old world and new clashed on every street corner—horse-drawn carts filled with vegetables and fruits beside shiny new Fords, stone taverns from the Middle Ages sharing space with cafes in the art deco style. People milled past us, ignoring Tommy and me for our eccentrically dressed companion. The number of sniggers behind gloved hands reminded me why I'd left human society in the first place.

All the while, Morris rattled through a stream of nonsense consciousness. The crows and constellations weren't explained but joined by more cryptic statements about planet alignments, whispers from the local flora, and a shift in the Pool of Time. The only thing remotely familiar was mention of the shade—which, according to Morris, had been disturbed in some way. Early on, I cut him off to ask exactly where we were going. He looked at me like I had three heads. "To the Guild, of course."

While I knew what the Guild was, it never occurred to me it was an actual place. Arthur only ever described it to me as the coalition of druids, not a headquarters of sorts. Unfortunately, Morris was unwilling to describe where this location was, citing something about the trees always listening.

After what felt like ages, we turned down a street corner to a quieter part of the city. Here, it was easy to tell how old this city was. Where the main squares boasted modern advancements, this section appeared straight from the storybooks I'd read as a child. Narrow, cobblestoned streets stretched between squat, stone buildings. Wooden signs hung from iron posts, declaring what each business was. Diamond-paneled windows shimmered with candles on their sills, and clothing hung on drylines crisscrossing above our heads. Flower boxes bloomed with weeds, and chickens clucked through the streets. We happened upon a crumbling gray building with a wooden door, faded and sagging. The name of this establishment had been carved directly into the stone—Oracle Books.

We stepped inside. Despite the dreary exterior, it was warm and cozy behind the stone walls. A wooden floor ran beneath our feet, covered in colorful, overlapping carpets. Candles burned around the room and within sconces. In lieu of lights, gas lamps flickered to enhance visibility. Armchairs huddled around a smoldering stone oven, and a cat with one ear slumbered near the heat. Every wall boasted floor-to-ceiling bookshelves filled with leather-bound tomes. Baubles and curiosities decorated any remaining space—of which there was very little—obscuring the wilting old woman reading behind a desk.

She set her book down, peering over wire-framed glasses. Wrinkles molded her face into an endless sea of soft ripples, but nothing about her ice-chip eyes seemed kind.

"Is this her?" she asked.

Morris nodded. "Yes, Sibyl."

Sibyl observed me like a vulture circling dying prey, waiting for its meal.

"You are young this time," she said. "Though I suppose you are every time."

I pressed my lips together. Another strange comment, similar to Morris's *currently*. I recollected the few things Arthur had told me about *beansidhe*. They were always women, and there were always three. When I was little, Tommy told me stories of knights who would forsake their names upon joining an order, assuming a new identity and adopting the place bestowed upon them. Perhaps this was similar. My new status as a *beansidhe* meant I not only changed, but I assumed the role of something else. Something ancient and well-known.

To be completely candid, I didn't love the sound of that.

"Twenty summers," Morris informed her. A shiver raced down my spine. They knew an awful lot about me.

Tommy thought the same because he snatched my elbow and pulled me back. "We're leaving."

Sibyl cocked her head, much like the bird I had associated her with. "So soon, Thomas?"

He paused, all but his fingers twitching against my arm. "Have we met?"

"No." A garish grin stretched her face. "But I know all about you. Here, we know all about many things."

Tommy nodded slowly. "Sure, whatever you say. I don't think we require your services anymore."

"Don't you?" The words were laced with venom, the snap of her tongue like vipers. "What will be your plan to outrun the Morrigan, boy? You, a human.

Only thirty-one summers. A child. Or the Knights of Templar that seek your head. Their leader is still alive, you know . . ."

I shook my head. "Their leader never existed. It was Babd all along."

"Babd was only that man for a short time. Just long enough to grow close to you. The real man is alive and well. Hunting." She tsked. "The Guild has long been in service to the fates. We will educate and guard Adeline without question and with undying loyalty. As a display of our unwavering fealty, we extend this offer to her companion as well." Hawkish eyes raked over Tommy. "I see your devotion and your loyalty. You are made of it, too much, it seems. It is your strength and weakness, son of flesh and blood. Do not let it bring harm upon your heads now when there are better ways to obtain what you both seek."

I stared at Sybil, wondering what lay behind that face creased with time. Her scent was those of the druids, but her words, what she could *sense*, were like nothing I'd seen before. But Arthur was my only basis for comparison, and he'd admitted many times he wasn't exactly the best specimen the druids had ever produced. The entire reason he fell into Jack's circle.

If Tommy was rattled, he hid it well. "I want assurances we will be safe. That you have her best interest in mind."

Sybil nodded. "I do not understand your distrust, but I know well the ways of human men. The stars created you as protectors, for long before. When cruel beasts roamed this world. It seems it has never left your kind." A faint smile touched her lips. "We cannot make vows or bargains as our high fae brethren can, but I can give you my word and honor. If I fail to meet expectations, you may end me yourself. Are we in agreement?"

Tommy eyed the old crone. I didn't like this either, and these new druids unsettled me just as much, but all of Morris's ramblings made some sense with Sybil's warnings. The Morrigan was alive and searching. The Knights were searching. And . . .

"Jack," I whispered. " Or Jaevidan Valdivia, however you know him. What about him?"

Sybil stilled. "He seeks you too."

"Is that a warning?"

She shrugged, peering at me with unsettling curiosity. Like I was one of those many fizzing vials strewn across Arthur's living room. An experiment. "Once you are settled, we can decide."

FOUR

ADELINE

MORRIS BROUGHT US TEA while Sybil did what I could only describe as witch-craft. The four of us sat around the smoldering fire, watching her work in silence from her floor cushion. She cut a complicated concoction of herbs and flowers, thrown into a bubbling cauldron at paced intervals. Mumbled words danced on wispy breaths, but the few I could hear were in another language. An old one.

"Is the tea agreeing with you? Any unpleasant side effects?" Morris asked.

Tommy dropped his cup. I frowned down at mine. "Should there be?"

"It's very unusual, but some . . . concerning reactions have occurred in the past." He grinned. "Nothing to worry about though. It's merely to make the trip more comfortable."

"As in motion sickness?" Tommy asked.

"As in—" He fluttered his hands. "Well, the shade is unsettling at first. I presume you've used it?"

The last question was directed at me. "Yes, and so has he."

"Very similar feelings, but we won't be leaving the shade this time. Until a tolerance is built, our destination can cause illness, especially to humans. The tea will prepare your physiologies for the long-term effects."

Tommy picked up his cup again. I took a long sip of mine. "How can one remain in the shade?"

"Silence," Sybil hummed. Rhythmic swaying joined her chants, along with a book she produced from her violet robes. A book I would recognize any-where.

"That's a Dianomican," I murmured. The Dianomican was a book created by the Bogorans, containing all their ancient rituals, secrets, and spells. Before the gods went extinct, they split it into ten volumes and scattered them across the worlds. I'd had the unfortunate adventure of shooting a dragon in the face to acquire the second Dianomican, which contained the ritual to seal the parallel bond.

It was never confirmed but unanimously accepted that the books were cursed. Bad fortune often fell to those who possessed one, and many of the rituals resulted in grisly ends without a Bogoran's powers to guide them. If I remembered correctly, the druids owned two volumes. I'd only seen two of them myself, the one Agent Rodney—or Babd, disguised as him—showed me and the one I retrieved. I had hoped to never see one again.

"Of course it is," Morris said, as if that explained everything.

Magic hummed in the air, seeping down my skin like sludge. Like the book wanted its presence known now that I'd identified it. Like it was searching me.

"Is it safe?" I asked.

"Of course," Morris answered, but it lacked confidence.

"We're ready," Sybil said. Morris retrieved her gnarled walking stick, and she gestured toward the cauldron. "You may enter now."

We didn't move.

"It only remains open for ten minutes," Sybil snapped. "Move."

Tommy braced an arm before me. "I'll go first." He stood there. "What am I supposed to do?"

"Step into the cauldron," she said, like this explained it all.

"Alright," he murmured, inching closer. The cauldron's smell overwhelmed me, earthy and metallic like the druids but sickeningly sweet. "Anything else I need to know?"

Morris grinned. "We'll handle the rest."

Tommy shot me a final look and soaked his shoes in the bubbling material.

He disappeared.

I startled, gripping my teacup so hard it shattered. "Was that supposed to happen?"

"Quickly, now," Sybil said, guiding me forward.

I peered down at the sludge, a ghastly green color.

I stepped in.

Morris lied. This was far worse than normal shade travel.

Darkness enveloped me, and I fell. Down, down, down, at speeds no human contraption could create, at a velocity that should not exist. My stomach hit my throat, and my limbs scrambled for purchase, but there was only inky nothingness in each direction, gleeful laughter of creatures enjoying my descent into demise. I screamed and thrashed my limbs, grunting when I hit a marble floor.

Just like my early days of shade travel, I vomited.

"Here, have some more tea," Morris said, shoving a cup into my hands. Tommy wretched something awful beside me. I shoved the druid's hands away.

I froze.

An open room spanned out in every direction. There were no windows, but in the center, a pool glowed with golden light from a massive light source floating above it. Cool, white marble ran beneath my splayed hands, thick with black and teal veins. A dozen archways pockmarked the circular wall, leading to shadowed hallways where blue will-o-wisps bobbed. The room buzzed with noise, light and sound, all from the hundreds of druids milling in colored robes.

All at once, the noise stopped. They stared, open-mouthed, at where Tommy and I were splayed on the floor.

They bowed.

The only sound was fabric swishing on the floor. Knees hit the stone, and foreheads pressed to the ground. My heart stalled in my chest, a dull thrum echoing in my ears. The spell broke with another round of Tommy's sickness.

"The third fate," Morris announced. Pride filled his voice. "You may all rise."

The druids pushed to their feet, resuming their tasks with straight spines and nervous glances. Tommy's fingers fluttered against the floor as he reached for me. I took his hand and spoke to Sybil. "What is this place?"

"The Guild," she said, as if that explained all. Tommy jerked on my hand, drawing my attention. He'd gone red in the face, a feverish light igniting behind his dark brown eyes. I recognized that look.

"Are you hurt?" I asked, but that worsened his panic. He released me to fumble with his hearing aids, spinning the little dials over and over. Strange sounds came from his throat, and I knew immediately what had happened. So did Sybil.

"Human technology does not work here," she said.

I leapt to my feet. "You didn't think to mention that?"

"There was no time," she huffed.

I dropped to my knees beside Tommy. *It's okay*, I mouthed slowly. It did nothing to quell his panic. Curse his wretched stubbornness and refusal to learn sign language. I turned toward the druids. "Is there something you can do?"

"I believe we can find a temporary solution," Morris said, growing quiet as Sybil frowned.

"After we have you settled," she amended

It was too late for that. "Now," I demanded, gesturing around. "Where do I take him? I'm not going anywhere until we fix him up."

Sybil released a wary sigh, shooting a look at Morris like this was all his fault. "Come with me."

Grabbing Tommy's hands, I mouthed, *They are going to help you*. He didn't move, stubbornly shaking his head and pointing at the ceiling. I got the message. He wanted to return.

I shook my head. *Trust me.*

His expression dimmed. He was sick, exhausted, and had just lost one of his senses. Worry gnawed at my stomach, wondering if he would have another meltdown. The shell shock hadn't affected him in years, but I knew all the signs. He teetered on the edge of a precipice. It was written all over his face like words in a book.

"Find me pen and paper." I had no idea if I was in a position to make demands, but Morris scurried away like his robes were in flames. Sybil watched us with a pinched expression. Unease coursed through me.

Morris returned, and I wrote a note explaining the situation. Tommy looked no less pleased, but his demeanor calmed, his human scent less intense as the perspiration dried along his forehead. He still looked green, but with a little maneuvering, Morris and I brought him to his feet.

"He will show you to the infirmary. When that is done, we must speak," Sybil said.

Ignoring that, I threw one of Tommy's arms around my shoulders and followed Morris down one of the halls.

There were fewer druids here, but their reactions were pronounced. A steady mix of slack jaws, open curiosity, and narrow-eyed suspicion. Warning bells went off. We'd been told they were trustworthy and here to serve me, but outside of Morris, no one seemed pleased about it.

After traversing the labyrinthine halls, we found ourselves at a set of round doors. Gold inlay swirled through the wood around a heavy, golden knocker. Morris rapped it twice, and the door ripped open.

At first, I saw nothing, and then my gaze slipped down to the tiniest woman I had ever seen. Soft, brown skin and full cheeks gave her a youthful appearance, but her dark eyes spoke of centuries. She wore similar robes as the other druids, the color liquid gold. Unlike the rest, she wore her hair in the current human fashion. Short, black curls framed her face in perfect ringlets.

She cocked her head. "What is this?"

"The third fate has arrived," Morris said, giddiness bubbling through each word.

"I meant him."

"Oh, a human. Lady Fate requests his affliction be remedied during their stay."

She looked no less pleased than before but opened the door wider. "I will do my best, but I remember little of human physiology."

I made a mental note to ask Arthur how different druid physiology actually was. Then, remembering my current situation, I shoved the thought to the back of my mind.

Morris bowed. "I will be outside if you require me."

Following the petite druid inside, I observed what I could only guess was an infirmary. Several brass beds stretched out in a row, none occupied. Clean, white linens were tucked with military perfection around the corners, and above each station hung a shelf with apothecary bottles, small surgical trays, and gauze. The standard hospital items ended halfway through the room, replaced with long wooden tables covered in laboratory equipment, notebooks, and herbs left out to dry. A feathered quill scribbled notes of its own accord atop a sheet of yellowed parchment.

The druid made a hasty bow, pointing to one of the beds. "My name is Guinevere. Place him there."

I guided Tommy to the bed and urged him to sit. It wasn't long before he turned green again. Guinevere retrieved a surgical tray and deposited it in his lap, which he made use of about three seconds later. I sat next to him and rubbed his back, watching the tiny creature flitter around her workstation, collecting items. The contraptions were similar to their human counterparts but odd enough to make me question their use. I squinted hard at a stethoscope covered in owl feathers. A reflex hammer that jiggled and changed shape when lifted.

Guinevere sauntered closer, hands on hips. "Just some shade illness?"

"That and his hearing," I said. "He usually wears aids. They're these human devices—"

"Understood." She returned to rummaging through her equipment. From the back of the room, she called, "I will give him something for sleep."

I penned a note to Tommy, who nodded once and closed his eyes. Sweat dripped from his hairline, and he was pale, but the vomiting had improved. Guinevere returned with the largest syringe I had ever seen, but Tommy hardly flinched. A quick pinch and drop of blood later, he crumpled unconscious to the sheets.

I frowned. "Is that safe for him?"

She shrugged. "Most likely."

That didn't inspire confidence, but it was too late now. I remained seated on the bed, where Guinevere fussed and worked around me. A full hour had passed when she said, "So, you are the newest fate."

I brushed a strand of hair from Tommy's eyes. "That's what they say."

"I have never met one. I expected you to be more . . . intimidating."

I fought the Morrigan single-handedly. I wielded the shade in ways no other had before. I transformed without a Bogoran and shot a wyvern with a tommy gun. I didn't need this woman's approval to know I was capable of far more than I once believed.

Her first comment stuck out more. Guinevere looked young but must have been centuries old. Her manner of speech and an ancient accent confirmed it, along with the depth of her stare. It must have been a long time since a fate had come here.

"I thought you served the fates?"

"There has not been a new one for a very long time. Not in my lifetime, at least, and they never leave their domain."

She had pored over a little workstation, taking notes and mixing herbs beside Tommy's bed. It was all but forgotten as she took in the diamond around my neck. "Interesting object you have there."

My hand dropped from my throat. I'd been holding it without realizing. "It was a gift."

"Quite the gift." She stood. An apothecary bottle filled with bright, glowing blue rested in her hand.

Silently, she placed several drops in each of Tommy's ears. "Hopefully, this works. Either way, it will only be a temporary solution, I'm afraid."

"That's fine. Thank you." I was sure Tommy would desire permanent hearing again, but I wouldn't speak for him. It would be his choice if the option ever arose.

"When he wakes again, we shall see." Guinevere set the bottle down. "If you would indulge me, I would love to know how you acquired your *gift*. The stars and the *beansidhe* tend to remain . . . separate."

My curiosity piqued. Sibyl wished to speak more with me, but I didn't entirely trust her. Answers from more than one source were preferable so I could cross-compare, see if someone was lying or withholding the truth.

"I'll tell you the story if you answer a question of mine."

She laughed. There was no humor in it. "I see you have been spending time with the fae."

I gave no answer. After a long moment, she added, "I'll bite."

"What are the fates?" I asked.

"That would be a very complicated question."

"You'll receive a long story in return."

"I sure hope so. As I am sure you know by now, the fates, or *beansidhe*, are a group of three women. Similar to a Morrigan, if you have heard of them."

"I've heard of them," I said dryly.

"They are called banshees in your tongue. We do not completely under-stand them, for we were never meant to, but we know what they do. Think of them as preservers."

"Preservers?"

"Of fate, time . . . death." Her head tilted. "They weave threads, determin-ing everyone's path and, ultimately, their end. But your sisters will explain more once they call on you."

A shiver raced down my spine. "Call on me?"

"It is a rare thing indeed for a fate to be replaced by a new one. As I said, this is the first I have seen it in my lifetime. I cannot say when they will ask for your presence. These things are a mystery to even the druids."

I'd hoped for more. "How is a new fate chosen, and why?"

"There are many rumors, though some say fates are only allowed their position for an allocated amount of time. Others say a fate will choose to move on when they feel ready to. As for how they are chosen . . ." She shrugged. "From what we know, they begin as wraiths."

Wraiths were something else I had far too much experience with. One in particular. "Then I suppose I am a rare exception."

Guinevere squinted, words forming on the tip of her tongue that she ultimately swallowed. "Tell me about the artifact."

I launched into an abridged tale of my visit to Estheria. "I needed a blessing, so a high sidhe took me to visit a star. She was . . . intrigued by the two of us and my path in particular. She gave me this as a gift."

"And what does it contain, exactly?"

"Memories."

"Whose?"

"The sidhe who brought me to see her." I was being intentionally vague, but Guinevere pushed for more.

"Why would a star do such a thing?"

That I had an honest answer for. "I don't know. I haven't figured it out yet."

In fact, all I had were more questions. Jack's last memory played in my mind. A sense of familiarity hit me in a wave. It was both tangible and blurred, the memory of a dream slipping away after you wake up. I could remember the feeling, the sense of proximity, but nothing strong enough to understand why.

Especially because of the memory I'd seen. How that was relevant four hundred years later, I couldn't say, but if anything, it offered more insight into Jack. I wasn't sure what to do with the information. It was possible I didn't want to. Jack's obsession with me was never a secret, but I always thought it was his desire to claim his parallel, then make his Morrigan. But what if it was something more nefarious? The similarities between myself and that little girl were glaring. Both blondes, both orphans, both called Annwyl by a certain sidhe. If Estheria wanted to show me his dark fae nature was fixated on a human from the sixteenth century, then what was my role? A replacement?

The room felt colder than a moment before.

"Who was this sidhe?" I jerked at Guinevere's question, forgetting she stood beside me.

Sybil already knew. It was only a matter of time before the remaining druids learned. "Jack Warren."

"I do not know this name."

"It's his human pseudonym."

"And his true one?"

"Jaevidan Valdivia."

Guinevere stiffened, her only movement a thick swallow. "Oh." With that, she retreated to her laboratory in the back of the room.

I followed her. "You know him?"

"I do," she said curtly. I didn't miss the visible shake to her demeanor. "It may be too late now, but a word of advice for the future. If a sidhe becomes obsessed with you, it is never a good thing."

My eyebrows furrowed. "What does that mean?"

She ignored me, asking an even stranger question. "Does he still work with a druid who goes by the name of Arthur?"

I frowned. "Yes, but—"

"How is he?"

"Um, doing well the last we spoke."

"Ridiculous as always, I presume?"

"Ridiculous as always." She said nothing else. Crossing my arms, I searched for something to keep this conversation from dying. I still needed answers. "It's funny, you know. That you two are friends and named Guinevere and Arthur."

She chewed her lip. "It's not."

I let it rest. Arthur had admitted he didn't leave the Guild on the best of terms. I should have known the topic wasn't safe to broach.

"So, Jaevidan," she continued. "I have heard whispers over the years about what he did but never paid them much mind. But now that you are here, living proof and a fate of all things, you must forgive me if I ask an invasive question."

"What question is that?"

Her voice lowered, the tone firing warning signals. "How did he do it?"

"Do what?"

She tapped the back of her neck, indicating the birthmark I'd recently discovered. The one Babd told me was on every woman Jack became entangled with over the years.

"I'm sorry, I'm not sure what you're asking." I paused. "Is it an aftereffect of the parallel bond?"

A long moment in silence. I could see words on the tip of her tongue, a debate. "It hardly matters," she said, gesturing to a bed. "You should rest. Your companion will not wake for many hours."

After spending the night in a chair, rest sounded wonderful, but I wouldn't sleep while Tommy was poked and prodded by a stranger. While I still couldn't say if we were safe here.

Guinevere sensed my unease. "I swear on myself and the Guild, no harm will come to either one of you. For better or worse, you are both safe here."

"For better or worse?"

A shrug. "I would take the opportunity if I were you."

Only because there was little space, I left Tommy's bed and sat against the headboard of an adjacent one. Subconsciously, my hand drifted to my throat, the diamond hanging from its delicate chain. Another hour passed while Guinevere gave Tommy different medicines, crushing them with a mortar and pestle bedside before sending them through syringes or rubbing salves on his lips. Another hour passed, my eyes drifting open and shut while she ground pastes at her workstation. Darkness tugged the edge of my vision. The room grew warmer. I fell asleep and, with it, plunged deep into Jack's memories.

FIVE

JAEVIDAN

"You. Are. Late!"

I huffed. "Am not."

Annwyl stood with hands on hips, face a berry red. Behind her, the human sun was just beginning to set, throwing pale pink and dull orange across the dying hills. I visited every full moon for the past six months, but I never got used to how . . . drained the human world looked.

The one bright spot was always Annwyl, though she was very displeased right now. Clucking her tongue, she pulled a long, threadbare piece of fabric from her satchel and draped it around my shoulders. "Eyes," she said.

I had been practicing for months, ever since Annwyl announced the faire would cross through her village mid-summer. Everything she described seemed boring to me—we had plenty of jesters and singers and food at the palace—but she was so excited, I pretended to be as well. The only thing that piqued my interest was that Annwyl and the other peasants were allowed three days off from the fields. So more time to play together, as long as I could sneak away from my brothers' watchful eyes.

The only problem was I would need to pose as a human to attend the faire with her. If only my glamour would work.

Annwyl frowned. "Try just one more time."

She always said that, and it never worked. Not for lack of trying. It seemed like all I did anymore was attempt to coax my powers out. I could use it somewhat a few months ago, but suddenly, it stopped altogether. Kalvidan accused me of being a *lurgga*—magicless.

"I shall keep the hood low, I promise." I tugged the dark cloth over my brows and cast my face down, just to prove it. In the ratty cloak with my eyes and ears covered, I looked just like a human beggar. "See? No one will know."

Through the thin fabric, she frowned. "Be careful, please."

I grinned. "When am I not?"

She rolled her eyes, but her little smile said she did not mean it. Grabbing my hand, she skipped through the primroses and cowslips and bluebells dotting the hillside. I could not say the names of wildflowers in my own world, but Annwyl had a gift for memorizing all the plants, their names, what tasted bland but was safe to eat and what looked delicious but was terribly poisonous.

Torches went up all around the village as darkness crept over the hills. Even from here, the scent of sugary sweets and rowdy laughter overwhelmed me in its humanness. At home, laughter was always accompanied by the tortured screams of the current entertainment.

I preferred Annwyl's version of fun to my family's, even if all the human scents were like a kick in the face—dung and sweat and the never-ending decay of mortals. It was worth it, though, because Annwyl shrieked with joy at the bottom of the hill, tugging me faster than my faerie legs could carry me.

"First, you must try the marzipan tarts. Mother and I saved a groat every year to buy one."

I nodded, sounding out the word in my head. Mar-zi-pan. My Welsh had improved since my time with Annwyl, but it was still all too often her words made no sense to me.

She tugged me to the side, unfurling her hand to reveal two small, dirty coins. Leaning close, she whispered, "I stole them from the convent. No one can know."

I frowned. If I had glamour, she would have no need to steal at all. I could pluck a few flower buds or twist some grass and produce all the perfect shillings in the world . . . until we were too far from the vendor to catch us when he realized what he had.

Instead, I was useless. Again.

"You should not steal from the convent, Annwyl. What if they make good on their threats this time?"

She shrugged. "I can take the beatings. And if they throw me out, I still have you." She grinned. "It will be worth it, I swear to you, Jaevidan. Come now, they are best when fresh!"

I followed her through the thick crowd of humans, grimacing. Maybe Annwyl could take the beatings, but her arms were already covered in black and blue from the nuns. And if they truly made her leave the orphanage, she would have nowhere to go. Nothing to eat. I would never risk taking my only friend back to Ildathach. My human would not last a day.

Annwyl had no care in the world but for one, hopping from foot to foot before a sagging stall filled with sweet treats. It all looked the same disgusting brown to me, but Annwyl selected the best one and gave him her groat, receiving three pence back.

We found a quiet alley where no one celebrated. I could see in the dark well enough but had to guide Annwyl around piles of human waste and holes in the packed dirt. We sunk against a stone hut and bit the tart at the same time. Annwyl made a noise of delight. I tried not to gag.

"Is it not the best thing you have ever tasted?" she asked, tearing the treat in two. She offered me my half, and I nodded, still attempting to swallow.

"Delicious," I finally choked out.

She beamed, finishing off her piece within seconds. I offered her the rest of mine, saying I was full from supper. I would have eaten it if it made her happy, but I knew she was hungry and wanted my piece too.

After that, she dragged us from stall to stall, oohing and ahhing over the molding treats and merchants' wares. One man loudly declared the textiles he carried were ancient artifacts from the Persian Empire. I asked Annwyl what that meant, but she could not say, so we moved on.

A circle formed around a man in colorful clothes performing tricks. Annwyl excitedly whispered he was a royal jester, sent from the castle by Lord Beynon himself just for the peasantry. She laughed when he contorted his body into strange shapes and yelped when he breathed great plumes of fire. I grew bored within moments but grinned whenever Annwyl glanced at me, seeking my approval.

The jester released another ball of fire into the air, lighting the night sky. Behind him, a crowd of children sat cross-legged on the ground before a tiny, rotting stage. I pointed to it. "What is that?"

"Oh!" Annwyl squealed and clapped her hands together, fire-breather forgotten. She trotted to the growing crowd, blonde hair glowing gold in the torchlight. We sank to our bottoms, and she whispered in my ear, "The puppets are my favorite."

They were all her favorite, but I was intrigued. It had been months since I'd removed Lesther from my toy box to play with. He was old and dull anyway, and Annwyl was far more interesting. Still, I wanted to see what human puppets would be like. If they held enchantments like the one I had at home.

Not that I wanted many reminders of home. Annwyl was my best friend, and I liked visiting her, but I also liked the hours spent away from the castle. My brothers. The more I faltered in my training, the worse their jests became. Worse, Mama had begun to agree with them. When I could not advance in sword training, I went to bed without food. When I failed to show magic, she no longer spoke to me or showed me any attention at all. Everything I did became a mistake, a wrong, and when words and taunting failed to make me better, my brothers turned to endless beatings.

I eyed the bruises dotting Annwyl's arms. At least we matched.

I could not understand the humans, but I did sort of like them. They were poor and hungry and smelled very, very bad, but they were much happier than the faerie court. Donvidan never smiled, and Kalvidan only to be cruel, but Annwyl smiled at everything. Even disgusting sweet treats and magicless jesters. Even me.

Patched curtains spread apart, and everyone clapped, Annwyl loudest of all. She elbowed me in the ribs, and I disguised my wince of pain by clapping even louder than her. Two men dressed in silly clothes lifted puppets behind the wooden window. None of them were enchanted, but their clothes were fine, and they had been painted well. Faerie craftsmen used magic, but these had to be done by hand. The first was a knight with real metal armor. The second was a beautiful blonde doll with a little crown. The last one had been painted green and black, with pointed teeth and . . . ears.

A puppeteer moved the princess, singing in a girlish voice. "Once upon a time in a kingdom of snow, a princess once lived of fair hair and rose glow."

The princess shifted, tiny wooden hands waving to the crowd. It was too dark for the humans to see the strings, but they glowed like sinew to my sidhe eyes.

All the children leaned forward.

"In her castle on high lived the princess by day, for with dangers untold, a maiden must stay."

"How do they move them so? Do you think it is magic?" Annwyl whispered. I laughed. "Maybe."

"But the lovely girl aged, and the older she got, the more restless she grew, for a ronyon, she was not."

Everyone giggled, but I did not know the word. I glanced at Annwyl, but she was too taken with the story to notice.

"Good knight!" the puppeteer shrieked, waving the princess's arm. The second puppeteer trotted the knight closer, waving a flag of green. "Good knight," the princess repeated. "A favor I must ask. For I am trapped in this tower, a quest is your task. A beast roams the wood, and if you give me his head, upon your return my hand you shall wed."

A chorus of delight rippled through the children. Annwyl turned pink.

The knight sang next. "I accept your quest, and the beast I shall seek. Worry not, fair princess, I'll slay the sneak! In your tower on high, you will no longer be stuck. And when my task is complete, be ready to . . . duck."

The adults laughed around us. I could not say why, but human humor was odd.

The puppeteers made clopping noises as the knight rode away. Someone behind the set held up a painting of trees, showing the puppet entering the woods. The third puppet, the one with pointed ears, rose from the dark.

"Watch out!" the smaller children yelled, pointing to the creature. The knight puppet swiveled, pretending not to see what they spoke of. "Watch out! He is right behind you!"

The puppet moved so its steed reared back. "Whoa, there!" the knight cried.

The ugly one sang in a nasally voice, "Good morrow, little knight, on your flesh I shall feast. You entered my forest and now face the beast. I planned for your princess, but you will do well. Raise me your sword and join me in hell."

The puppets engaged in combat. I yawned, glancing around for something better, but Annwyl was enraptured. The hood slipped atop my head. I yanked it back into place.

"Back, you demon, on my sword you will lay. I know of your kind and your wicked way. My flesh and my fear are not yours to snatch. Die, evil faerie, for you have met your match!"

Frost prickled my skin as the puppets battled. A little boy stood, yelling, "Kill it! Kill the evil faerie!"

"Yeah, off with its head!"

"Rip out its heart!"

A drunk man stumbled behind me, sloshing drink onto my cloak. "Come on, then, you heard the children. Kill the little bastard."

I shrank down, trying to appear small. Annwyl took my hand, whispering, but I could not hear her over the human's cries.

It is only a puppet show, I thought, but excitement rippled through the crowd. Even the adults were yelling now, the drunk ones screaming for increasingly gruesome violence and laughing about it.

Remaining low to the ground, I slunk back through the gathered humans' legs.

"Kill the little whelp!"

"Cut off its ears!"

I backed into a woman, stumbling on her skirts. My chest hit the ground, and tears burned my eyes. She kneeled beside me, cooing, "Oh! Do not fret, little one. It is only a story."

The hood fell back to my forehead, and my snake eyes met hers. She jumped with a startled scream.

Other adults noticed. I scrambled to my feet and broke into a run. Tears blurred my vision, running down my face. Donvidan would beat me if he saw. I wiped them away, racing for the darkened meadow as shouts of alarm raised behind me. I refused to stop. Not when my legs burned, not when I wept too hard to see, not as I found the meadow and a ferocious wind nearly bowled me over. I struggled against the gusts, collapsing against the boulder near the Veil. I could not return like this, not until I stopped blubbering like a babe. I gripped the sides of my hood with both fists, shredding at it as I cursed myself for being such a fool.

"Jaevidan!"

I pressed against the rock, hidden by shadows. It blocked the wind some, but I was shaking.

"Jaevidan, where are you?"

I ignored her. Did Annwyl know? Was this her plan all along? Lure me to her silly faire and reveal what I was, then let the adults tear out my heart and cut off my ears? I knew the humans were scared of fair folk, but I did not think they *hated* us.

Worse, I thought Annwyl was my friend.

A whimper left my throat. She appeared from behind the rock, hair blowing around her head. "There you are."

I scrambled back on my hands. "Go away!"

"But why?"

"I know what you did. I know you wanted them to hurt me." The more words spilled from my mouth, the truer they felt. Of course Annwyl never liked me. Of course she wanted to be rid of me. Everyone did.

"Oh, Jaevidan." She fell to her knees. I inched away. "I am so sorry. I did not think . . . It was not supposed to be like that. I would have never shown you if I knew."

"Liar," I spat.

Her lower lip trembled, tears brimming her lashes. It was too dark for her to see my expression, but I could see everything on hers. "I swear to you. I do not lie."

"Just go away." My voice broke on the last word. I hated how it sounded. Weak.

My brothers always said weakness was the worst thing a man could have. That people only liked you or wanted you if you were powerful. And it was true. Mother no longer wanted me because of my uselessness. My brothers beat me for my insolence. Power was the only way to protect yourself. Power was the only way to make friends.

"It is okay to be scared," she said.

I snapped my teeth at her. "I am not scared! Do not speak such daft things to me, human. Perhaps I should cut off *your* ears. Or better, your tongue."

Silent, she crouched in the yellow grass. The wind picked up, freezing our skin.

Quietly, nearly drowned by the wind, she whispered, "What does it say of me that you are still my closest friend?"

My words were good ones. Strong ones. Ones my brothers would use and approve of. But a strange feeling sank into my gut, one I had never felt before. Something bad, a notion I had done something very wrong. But not the sort of wrong where I displeased someone, so they punished me. The sort of wrong that I had said something I should not have. That I hurt her when she did not deserve it.

"I cannot say." Bringing my knees to my chest, I fought not to weep again. Suddenly, I feared Annwyl had not plotted against me at all, but my threats assured she now hated me forever. "I . . . apologize, I suppose."

She laughed, the sound wet with tears. "You suppose?"

I nodded, unsure of myself. It was a weak thing to do, but Annwyl was so different from me. I never knew the right things to say to her.

"I know." She crawled closer, her human scent filling my nose. Usually I hated it, but it did not bother me now. Her arms wrapped around my neck, and her warmth pressed against me. "I know. I forgive you. And I still love you more than anyone."

I swallowed. "What is that?"

"What?"

"Love."

She pulled away. I tried tugging her back, but she would not relent. "You do not know what love is?"

No, and I had the sudden urge to lash out at her again. Curse her for making me look dim-witted. Instead, I shook my head.

Her head cocked to the side, confusion touching her brows. "But your mother and siblings must love you, no? Do not they tell you this? Or do you not know the word in Welsh?"

If we had that word in my tongue, I never learned the translation for it. Annwyl went on to describe it to me, convinced it was a barrier of language. I sank into myself the longer she prattled on. No, in Ildathach that word, that idea, did not exist.

Her eyes were wet again. I wondered why—because I did not know some silly word? The way she looked at me was worse. She did not cry for herself but for me. I had never heard of someone crying for another.

"Stop that," I said.

Wiping the tears away, she mumbled, "I understand now."

"Understand what?"

She approached again, holding us close and laying her cheek on my chest. I was glad she did it without me asking. I liked the feeling more than I thought. "If no one loves me and no one loves you, then I suppose we just have to love each other most."

I wove my fingers through her hair. It was soft and silky, soothing the pain in my chest. "Love each other most?"

"More than anything," she murmured into my shoulder. "To make up for all those who do not."

I liked the sound of that. I liked Annwyl forgiving me even more, that I had not lost her after all. I squeezed her against me, tucking my face into her hair against the violent wind. A storm brewed around us, but I did not care. It felt safe and warm here. "Okay. Then I love you most."

SIX

ADELINE

GUINEVERE WAS SLEEPING AT her workstation when I awoke. Tommy was fast asleep in the bed beside me. My fingers clutched the diamond at my throat, a swarm of emotions vying for attention.

There were no clocks or windows in the Guild, but it was safe to assume night reigned. I slept so little since my transformation, but druids maintained human sleep cycles. It would be hours before anyone rose. The wisest course of action would be to stay here, keeping an eye on Tommy, but I no longer wanted to sit in this room. Couldn't stand the silent dark.

After a cursory check on Tommy, I slid out the doors. Morris could go to sleep if he still stood watch, and I could use the time to explore my surroundings. I doubted anyone would stop me.

Instead, Sybil's ancient eyes met mine.

"It is late," she said. Her fingers clutched a pipe, thick tendrils of smoke swirling from her lips. Tobacco filled the narrow hall.

"I don't sleep much."

"Neither do I." Taking a long drag, she leaned forward on her cane. "Walk with me, dear."

The sentiment didn't sound forced. Even with her robes, she appeared every bit a wise elderly woman in this moment. Grandmotherly, in a way. I wondered who she was in her human life, her experiences before becoming a druid. Immortality had certainly hardened her, but not like so many others. It made me wonder if men like Henry Foster—the druid we'd encountered over the summer, whose house had been taken by a phooka—were born wrong, instead of made that way.

Sybil was strong of will and mind, but her body was feeble. I looped my arm through hers, helping her across the marble. "Where are we going?"

"I have not decided." She glanced at my arm. Smooth, pale skin against her aged. "To be transformed so young is a gift."

I hadn't decided if being transformed in general was a gift. Right now, it felt like a curse.

"But we have much to discuss," she continued. "I assume Guinevere has spoken to you?"

"She did, but she wouldn't say much."

"Because she does not know. Neither do I."

I frowned. "If you are sworn to serve the fates, how can you not understand what they are?"

"Because, my dear, some things are not for us to know." Smoke drifted into my face from her pipe. Sybil watched the curled vapors like they held answers. "We know you are weavers. We know you installed the histories we pass to new generations. And we know you are to be protected and worshipped. This is what the stars spoke to us, so this is what we do."

That was less helpful than the few words Guinevere offered me. I tried a different approach. "Guinevere said the other fates would call on me. What does this mean?"

Sybil shrugged. "You will know."

Wonderful.

"If I could answer your questions, I would," she said. "The fates have long since been a conundrum to us. An empty book in a sea of our knowledge. Many have tried to glean more, and many have failed. As I said, this is not for humans, or those who were once human, to know."

Her words reminded me of another life, a small, pious town in the Appalachia. My family never followed the bible like others, but one thing was always the same—divinity was beyond human understanding. God's plan was not for human minds.

"What is more important is the here and now. Your current dilemmas. Until your sisters call on you, you must be protected."

"From the Morrigan?" I asked.

"The Morrigan, the Knights . . . others." We came to a stop at the end of the hall. An intersection flickered with faerie lights, more doors like the ones to the infirmary lining the hall. Sybil gestured to the nearest one. "Let's go here."

Behind the doors was a library. An enormous one. Marble stretched across the floors, covered in ancient carpets. Tables and chairs scattered the main floor while two sweeping staircases entered a second level, rife with endless bookshelves. Between the two staircases were wall-to-wall rows of books, stretching so high a ladder was needed to reach them.

It was beautiful, a reader's dream, but I could only think of my time with the wyvern. The library I nearly died in trying to reach the second Dianomican.

"Only a select few are allowed in this one," Sybil said. "It is a secret, of sorts. A library of our rarest and most dangerous information."

A secret library. One that contained books the ancient druids deemed too valuable to share. It brought me no comfort Sybil wanted me to see it.

"You have something to say," I told her.

She nodded. "I want to reiterate to you that the druids will bring you no harm. We are sworn to protect the fates, and that we shall. Fae and humans are both beneath our mission. We live to serve, to pass on history, and obey the stars." Her arm left mine, cold gaze sweeping my face. "When I say we will do anything to uphold that, these are not vapid words. Our vows do not wither like smoke. Here, you are safe from the Morrigan. Only those who have been permitted to enter or druids with knowledge of our gates can access the Guild. This place is not within Ildathach, nor the human world, but somewhere in between. Suspended within the shade. It is impossible to find on one's own, and no one can be detected inside."

Suspended within the shade. I wondered how that was possible, and then it became clear. The Dianomicans they possessed. Tommy said the Knights had done something similar, creating tunnels with access points between their bases. It was how we got from New York to Cardiff within the night. The druids must have done something similar, but with their own magic to utilize, more advanced.

Fascinating. I'd been told time and time again nothing could survive for long within the shade, but somehow, the druids managed it. No wonder some of them became so powerful.

"With this, your brother will also be safe from the Knights," Sybil added. "As will you. But there is one other who seeks you, one that may be more difficult to keep away."

"Jack," I whispered.

She nodded.

I didn't like how she lumped him in with the Morrigan and the Knights, as if he, too, were a great threat. I'd never thought of him that way, even in the early days when I was terrified of the fae. But that's what made him the most dangerous.

I had followed Jack. I had fought for Jack. I had trusted him, let him into my life. I may have even loved him.

It was impossible to tell what was truth. Disguised as Agent Rodney, Babd told me our parallel bond was a farce. Worse than that—a bond Jack had created to enslave me to him. It could have been a lie, but she showed me the ritual from the Dianomican itself. I could lie and hold on to foolish hopes that he had never used it against me, that it was all a large misunderstanding, but I would never know if any choices I'd made were of my own free will.

Then, there was everything else. The other girls, ones who shared my birthmarks over the centuries. They had all died young and, according to Babd, often in parallel rituals led by Jack. I still didn't know what the mark meant. I didn't know why the star Estheria chose to give me the memories she did, ones of Jaevidan and a little girl whose name he called me by mere days ago.

I knew the truth, but accepting it was another matter. If Jack had lied, if he were truly as evil as all the signs said he was, the consequences were too much. Beyond what they meant for myself, there was the world to keep in mind. I formed my own Morrigan with him. I made him more powerful.

Sybil analyzed me, expression shifting as if she could read my thoughts as I produced them. "What is he to you?"

I shook my head.

"I can't say either." She drew from her pipe, silence drifting on the smoke. "I cannot speak for your supposed parallel bond. I have never seen the spell, so I cannot attest to its nature. There are many rumors about what paralleled pairs mean, but the fae often lie. This you must not forget."

I would never forget again.

"I also do not know what you were told by the Morrigan when they possessed you. We only knew they captured you after your abilities awoke. They spoke to us, even from across worlds. Your own Morrigan is very powerful, likely the only reason you survived. So I do not condone Jaevidan's actions, but I must be grateful for them. That power saved you where we could not, and we have the parallel bond to thank for that, evil as it may be."

"So it was a lie? He's not my soulmate, or however else he framed it."

Sybil frowned, eyes glossy and pensive. "That depends on what you know. Has anyone ever explained the birthmark on the back of your neck?"

Ice shot through my veins. "A little."

"And you know it has appeared on quite a few women before you?"

The files flashed in my mind. The names, the dates, the portrait of Jack with a French duchess. "Yes."

"But you do not know what this means." She tilted her head, thoughtful. "To this day, I have no theories on how he did it. It is one of my life's greatest mysteries."

It was eerily similar to what Guinevere had said, but I wasn't leaving without answers this time. "How he did what?"

She ignored me, hobbling to a table and scribbling on a card. "This is the location of our own files on that birthmark, all those past women we have managed to find. Only three of us know of it. If others discover the truth, they may be inclined to use it themselves. The consequences would be devastating if that knowledge fell into the wrong hands. It is a blessing from the stars Jaevidan has only ever used it for you." She shoved the paper into my sweaty palm. "I cannot tell you whether or not he is a threat. That is only for you to decide. Find me when you are done."

With those final words permeating the air, she disappeared into the hall.

The druid's filing system was immaculate, allowing me to find the leather-bound tome she spoke of in no time. I stood between the shelves on the second floor, staring at the indiscriminate spine. Between its covers was the truth. All I had to do was open it.

But did I really want to know?

Jack's character still hung in limbo, suspended between the scant knowledge I possessed. There was everything he told me, what I wanted to believe, then all I'd learned in the last two days. Whatever truth Sybil gifted me with would determine him one or the other. Friend or foe. Soulmate or master. Lover or enemy.

A year ago, I would have said ignorance is bliss, but I wasn't that woman anymore. Truth catches up with us all, even if we pretend it doesn't exist.

I took the book downstairs and settled into a chair. The first page was much like the one Babd had, a list of dates and names, though this one was far more comprehensive. The file from the Knights had gaps and question marks to fill in the spaces. Thirteen women were listed here, with my name and date of birth at the bottom.

You are the thirteenth, the wraith once told me. Thirteenth what, I was about to find out.

The next pages were information on the women. My eyes caught on a few. Sabina Costa. Clara May. Zahra Emad. I skimmed past them. I had no desire to read about these other human girls without understanding why they were included.

Toward the end were someone's fevered notes. Sybil's, I guessed. They discussed theories about how they were all connected, why they *mostly* died young. One woman in India lived all the way to sixty-eight.

That pushed me forward. I skimmed the pages, searching for anything that spoke of my mark. After a hundred pages of nonsense and conjecture, I finally found it. Sybil had drawn the strange shape, two downward crossing swords, and underlined her conclusion three times.

Reincarnation, it said.

I stared at the word, numb. Reincarnation. Reincarnation. *Reincarnation.*

Someone rapped on the door.

The book fell from my lap, loose pages scattering the floor. The ominous knock echoed through the library, repeating itself against the ancient marble walls.

Something familiar settled beneath my skin, an arcane sense of darkness, a being. I stood, my chest constricting with each step forward, the air thickening the closer I drew to the entrance. Someone waited behind it, and they weren't a druid.

The scent hit me too late; I had already opened the door. I stilled, paralyzed by the view before me and a familiar wave of memories. Oleander and rain. My dark prince.

Jack leaned against the doorjamb, serpent eyes flashing. "Hello, my love."

SEVEN

ADELINE

THE LOW FAERIE LIGHTS pronounced the gold in his eyes and cast his face in shadow. His rumpled suit looked worse for wear, and he was missing his jacket. My fingertips trembled at my sides. With the room suddenly too small, my mind still racing and a fresh note of panic lighting my veins, I did the only thing I could think of.

I slammed the door in his face.

Then I found the nearest mirror and pressed my fingers to the glass. I had no indication of where to go, but anywhere was better than here. Jack's rumbled "Annwyl?" was the last thing I heard as I entered the shade.

The main room of the Guild opened wide around me. At this hour, only a few druids remained. I didn't think, didn't question my decisions as I ran down the nearest dark hall.

That word, reincarnation, bounced around my skull like a thimble in a sewing box. Joining the cacophony were the warnings from Guinevere and Sybil—never trust the fae. If a sidhe became obsessed with you, it was never a good thing.

Jack was never supposed to know I was here. I was supposed to be protected and hidden away. I didn't think I would need it from him, but now I wasn't so sure. What was I? *Who* was I? If my birthmark meant what that book said it did, then what did Jack want with me now?

Nothing good. The thought came unbidden, followed by a twinge of fear. The truth I had been ignoring for days, weeks, maybe even months now. I wanted to trust Jack. I wanted to believe I had something real with him.

But the parallel bond wasn't real.

Everything he told me about Papa and their bargain, none of that was real.

And now this mark on my neck, the biggest lie of all.

I didn't understand what all of this was for, I didn't know what was real anymore, and I certainly couldn't trust him.

I raced down hall after hall, burying myself deep into the bowels of the Guild. But I couldn't run forever. I needed a way to hide. I needed a way to escape. I needed to find Tommy.

The thought brought me to a screeching halt. *Tommy.* I couldn't leave him behind, not with the druids and certainly not with Jack.

I turned on my heel when the scent hit me.

My forehead clipped his chin, and then my back hit the wall. Jack had one hand around each of my biceps, holding me captive between his body and the stones. Breath sawed from my lungs, and I opened my mouth to scream, but his lips pressed against mine.

"It's me, it's me," he murmured, taking no pauses for breath between mumbled assurances and assaulting my lips. I remained still, fighting the rising heat at his proximity. At the familiarity of his warmth. My body reacted on instinct, a muscle memory so ingrained in me I didn't have to think about melting into him.

He swiped a thumb over my cheekbone. "I'm sorry, I should have sent word ahead."

My brows furrowed until I realized what he meant. He thought I ran away because I believed him an illusion. Either as an aftereffect of the phooka, or he knew I met the Morrigan. That they had shape-shifted into Agent Rodney and used that to gain my brother's trust.

He didn't know I ran away from him.

Something shifted, and his demeanor changed all at once. "Were you hurt?" he asked, answering his own question by running his hands up and down my sides. The bruises and bumps from my trip to Ildathach had already faded, but that didn't stop his relentless perusal. His thick leather gloves ran down my arms, pulling my silk ones down. He paused as my blackened fingertips met open air.

"Annwyl," he said softly, each letter laced with concern and remorse and too many other emotions to sort through. But I no longer heard it as an intimate Welsh endearment. I heard it for what it truly was. A first name.

My name.

That shook me from my stupor. I yanked my hands back from his, flattening against the wall. Hurt flickered through our bond, my *slave* bond, but I shoved the emotion away. He stepped forward. I searched for the nearest reflective surface.

"I'm sorry this happened. It should have never happened, and I take all the blame. I should have protected you better," he said, once again misinterpreting my reaction.

The entire foundation of our relationship was built on lies. Secrets. But now I had my own as well. He didn't know I knew the truth, just about the only advantage I had.

The wraith never said whether or not I could trust him, but her hatred for him was clear enough. That was, until the very last moment I saw her, when she appeared more conflicted than anything. That all made sense now too. She said she couldn't move on until she found the rest of herself and had the help of a banshee. I thought she needed me to glue her back together or something, but that wasn't what she needed me for. She needed *me*. The rest of her.

If the wraith was me—pieces of me—then I should do what I had always been told. Trust my gut.

But Estheria's whispered words still haunted me. *You must always trust in Jaevidan. This is the only way to remain in the light.*

I needed time to think. I needed to stall. If I couldn't outrun him, if I couldn't conceal myself from him, then I needed to hide in plain sight.

I threw my arms around his neck, burying my face in his sweat-soaked collar. I ran my hands down his back and sides, checking for weapons. He didn't need them, but a gun poked my hip where I pressed against him. He had at least one dagger hidden against his thigh.

The distraction worked. An audible sigh of relief heated my hair, and he embraced me like I'd been gone for years, not days. His lips crashed against mine again, and this time, I was too confused to hear his mumbled words.

Love. Anger. Fear. I gave it all back to him, letting him mistake all my actions for exactly what he wanted to see.

The dagger Tommy stole from the Knights heated against my own thigh. Iron. I hadn't taken it off since our departure from Cardiff.

Tears burned the backs of my eyes. Tears of anguish. Tears of rage. "I was so fucking worried," Jack breathed, and I was torn between agreeing or damning him to hell. Two voices screamed inside my head—one to fall blindly, the other to protect myself.

My fingers twitched against my leg. To grab it, or not. To trust him, or not. All my emotions heightened with him so close. The taste of him was the perfect poison I remembered. I wanted him. I wanted him so badly I would risk everything, including my own life, including the world subjected to his power, to keep him. And that was exactly why I couldn't.

I wouldn't kill him, but I could hurt him enough to get away.

My fingers closed around the hilt concealed beneath the folds of my dress. I dragged the hem to the apex of my thigh. Jack responded like a man ensorcelled, kissing me harder, panting faster, pressing me so deeply against the wall I hardly had room to breathe. His hands went beneath the dress, between my thighs, his hardness pressing into my stomach as he gave a quick glance up and down the hall. One hand entangled in my hair, and the other undid his belt. Each kiss, each swipe of his tongue, each desperate moan plunged my heart further into a blackened abyss.

I slipped the dagger from its resting place.

He moaned my name against my lips.

I ran my fingers up his back, careful to never touch him with the weapon.

He told me how much he wanted me, how much he missed me.

I tipped the knife point toward him, trying not to scream, wondering if I really wanted this, if it was something I was capable of.

I decided it wasn't when someone clicked their tongue. "None of that."

Jack whipped toward the intrusion, and the dagger dropped from my fingertips.

The clattering echo of iron against marble reverberated up and down the hall. Jack looked at the offending object, me, then the weapon once more. He licked his lips, hands trembling as he took a slow step back. Down the hall, Violet *tsked*.

"How would you two survive without me?" she drawled. Heels clicked against the stone as she strode closer, peering down at the weapon with distaste. Harold poked his head from her hair and hissed.

"Adeline . . ." Jack started. I wouldn't look at him. I couldn't. But my eyes lifted to his anyway, knocking all the air from my lungs. The hot tears against my eyes finally spilled over. The anguish, the *betrayal*, written all over his face was too much to bear. I wore the same expression myself.

Violet scoured my disheveled state, frowning. "Clean yourself up. We need to talk."

EIGHT

ADELINE

WITHOUT A BATHROOM OR any notion of where I should be, cleaning up simply meant returning my dress to its proper place and flattening down my hair. Jack stalked off before I could say a word, leaving me with no one but Violet and Harold for company.

The former appeared bored, and the latter twined up and down her torso, flicking his tongue at the untouched dagger every so often. When I'd calmed myself enough, I reached out for the arm she proffered. She nodded her head at the weapon. "No use in wasting that."

I didn't want to, not after what just happened. Pragmatism won out in the end.

She handed me a postcard and a compact emptied of powder. Only the mirror remained behind. "Shade us here."

I'd never shaded anywhere based on a photograph or anywhere I didn't know of, for that matter. But if I could picture a place in my mind and land there, I didn't see why this couldn't work. "Is this in the Guild?"

"No."

"But—"

"You've been given access to roam back and forth as you please. And unlike the druids, you don't need to waste your time with potions and brews to use the shade." She lifted an eyebrow. "Ready, then?"

No, but I was strangely grateful for her presence. Violet and I had a tumultuous relationship at best, but one thing had always remained certain—she never lied to me. Not once. In fact, she spent most of her time warning me away from this entire mess. The same mess her twin had lovingly dragged me into.

We were in the shade for seconds. I blinked at a canopy of stars and a long row of streetlamps battling the night. Exhaust perfumed the air, and laughter echoed from around the corner. The door from her postcard gleamed cherry red, a shimmering number 8 embossing the surface. It was polished just enough to cast a reflection.

I stumbled from the cheery alleyway, bumping my hip against a wrought metal chair. Around the corner, a sea of them stretched across a plaza, each filled with a dazzlingly dressed human sipping cappuccinos or wine.

An automobile honked for me to move out of the street. Violet stepped up beside me, grinning.

"Where are we?" I asked.

"Paris."

"But—"

"The Guild was built below it. An extension of the catacombs, plunged into the shade." She produced a silver case and lit a cigarette not meant for human consumption. "Though it's a well-guarded secret, so don't go spouting off about it."

Yet, Violet knew. Surely, Jack as well. Most likely that information came from Arthur, the only druid in our little circle.

She looped her arm through mine. We crossed the plaza, passing beside an enormous fountain carved with merwomen and copper embellishments. I gave it a wide berth, well accustomed by now to treating all things reminiscent of magic with wariness. The world was never what it seemed.

We passed several shops, all closed down for the night. Mannequins sporting hand-crafted suits and cases filled with leather bags gleamed in the lights reflecting off the windows. Everywhere were hand-painted signs written in swirling French, often adorned with caricatures of beautiful, lithe women. Despite the hour, whatever it may be, the streets were filled with chattering people.

Violet eventually brought us to a crowded street teeming mostly with men. The signs here were flashier, golden stage lights instead of hushed streetlamps. A long line formed outside a club, but Violet nodded at the doorman, and he let us through.

Cigarette smoke rolled through the low, sensual lights. Candles flickered on dark tabletops like a sea of stars, stretching through a crowded hall buzzing with excitement. A stage with drawn velvet curtains loomed in the distance. Behind us, a mahogany and crystal bar.

Despite the human atmosphere, I knew Violet had brought us here for a reason. The metal tang that often accompanied magic coated my tongue, sharp and bitter. As far as I could tell, we were the only non-humans present, but glamour still concealed those who did not wish to be seen, even with my new and improved eyes.

I quickly realized another reason she chose this venue. Every inch of wall space to our right and left was covered with mirrors. Small ones, large ones, ones inlaid in golden frames, and others speckled with silver stains. They crowded on top of one another from wall to wall, all the way to the vaulted ceiling, where a large circular one loomed down from above.

"This place ain't human-owned," I said. It wasn't a question.

Violet snorted. "What gave you that impression?"

A flustered waiter arrived at Violet's beckoning, leading us through the dark labyrinth of tables to a secluded spot beside the wall. We took seats, and Violet continued. "Jack has an arrangement with the owners. It's the safest place to chat outside the Guild."

But only safe for so long. The unsaid message wavered between us. She lit another cigarette, and I made a gesture for one as well. I'd smoked twice in my entire life—both occasions with Jack—but I had a feeling I would need it.

"Did you know?" I asked.

She blew out a roiling cloud of smoke. "Which part?"

Where did I even begin? "Annwyl," I said.

"Ah." She snapped her cigarette case closed with a loud smack. "I wondered how long it would take you to piece that one together."

"How long does it usually take me?"

She shrugged. "Usually, you don't."

I wanted to ask what was different this time, but I already knew. *I* was different. Changed. No longer human. Mostly because of the parallel bond but partially because I was born glamour-touched. Maybe the other times, I hadn't been. And according to Babd and Sybil's notes, I'd already passed my average age of death.

"Does everyone know?"

She shook her head. "Only me and Jaevidan." I wondered what prompted the sudden use of his true name.

"But how?"

"Some have suspected it. The druids, of course, because they're brown-nosing little shits. But it's not supposed to be possible. No one else has ever done it."

I would return to that in a moment. "But Lillian, Will, and Arthur have been with you for centuries."

"Time is less of a concern for us, in case you've forgotten. If Jack disappeared for a few years, or even ten or twenty, no one concerned themselves in the meantime. We always found our way back to one another."

I had a hard time believing that. "And the parallel bond?"

Another puff of smoke and a vehement shake of her head. "That particular spell has been hidden for millennia. The only place it's been recorded is in the tenth Dianomican, which as you know has been missing for centuries."

"But it's not. The Knights of Templar have it. Or rather, the Morrigan has it now."

"Babd and Nemain have it. You killed Macha," she corrected. Frost trickled into my blood, vision darkening. I knew there was a chance, but it was different hearing it. Having it confirmed.

Violet eyed me, continuing. "But in the hands of the Knights, it was good as gone. Jaevidan didn't know what it contained when he requested it from your father and found it by sheer luck. He didn't know what it was, because most of us don't. As you've heard a thousand times, parallel bonds are incredibly rare. Both because the spell is rare, and those who used it created a myth surrounding it."

"Why?"

"Because it gives one power, obviously. If you could tie yourself to glamour-touched human siphons, would you want anyone else to seek it out and do the same?" She raised an eyebrow. "Likely some bastard from a thousand years past came up with the idea to tell others it was a unique soulmate bond, something found rarely, if ever, in nature. Not only do they keep that rare source of power to themselves but send everyone else on a manhunt to the human worlds, attempting to find a match that doesn't exist. Quite ingenious, actually."

"Then how do you know?"

"I know all my brother's secrets," she said, gazing off into the shadowed room.

The silence between us filled with a loud round of applause from the room. The chime of bells and drums echoed between the thousand mirrors, the velvet curtains lifted from a stage washed in deep blue light.

A woman entered from stage left, bare feet sliding across the floor. Her body moved like the tide, all rolling hips and sweeping fingers. A headscarf covered all but a few dark curls, dripping with coins and jewels that trapped the light. A long skirt brushed the floor, but it was far from modest—both of her bare legs peeked through slits beginning at the waist. Her midriff was bare, and in lieu of a corselette, nothing but long, sparkling tassels hung from the nipples of a buxom chest.

"Don't you just love Paris?" Violet asked, delighting at the scarlet filling my cheeks.

"Why didn't he tell me?"

Her attention left the stage. Despite the oppressive dark of the club, I could see she had dropped her glamour. Golden serpent eyes, eerily similar to her twin's, narrowed on me.

"Would you have believed he was only trying to keep you alive?"

"Not the parallel bond," I hissed.

A long moment passed before she answered. In the meantime, the woman engaged in a sensual dance, eliciting excited jeers from the men crowding the room.

"You asked him not to."

I barked out a laugh. "I did no such thing. In fact, I distinctly remember screaming at him across Times Square to tell me everything."

She tugged back the collar of her dress, revealing a mark I had never seen before. The thin lines of an intricate scar wound around her collarbone. A vow mark. "Not in this life."

I stared at the laurel pattern of her mark. I would have noticed it before—it was impossible to miss—unless she had been intentionally glamouring it from me.

"You asked him to never tell you who you were or about all the other lives. So he took a vow mark and asked me to do the same." She released the fringe of her dress, letting the collar fall back into place.

I thought of all the times I'd seen Jack's bare chest. Enough to memorize the intricate tattoos that loved to shift across his body, to trace the endless scars crisscrossing his skin like a map. I'd never seen a vow mark. He could be hiding it like Violet did, but I also wondered for all those moments the facade of his glamour cracked away. When it flickered by in moments of anger or lust or sadness, when it dulled to nothing but a shimmer in the air as he fell asleep . . .

It would have taken an inordinate amount of power and concentration to hide it as long as he had. But that had never stopped Jack before.

"Why would I ask that?"

A lofty round of applause reverberated around us, and the dancer gave an elegant bow. Within moments, she was replaced by another equally scandalous woman.

"How should I fucking know?" Violet blew a puff of smoke into the air, admiring it. "That remains between you two."

Something dawned on me, a strange thought I'd never entertained before. Violet knew. Violet knew *me*. Likely, for a very, *very* long time. I thought of all the warnings she imparted on me. How angry she had been at Jack that first day he brought me back to the hotel. *You've had your time*, she had said to him, something I never understood until this moment. I always assumed she hated me, but perhaps it was the opposite.

"Were we always close?" I asked. It wasn't meant to be sarcastic, and Violet's silence answered the question for me.

She looked anywhere but me. "It grew rather . . . cumbersome to bury someone so many times."

My heart thumped against my ribs. No wonder she had been so cold. Callous. From the moment I arrived, she sought to send me away, and not because of who I was, because she grew tired of mourning. Watching her brother do the same and watch it tear them all apart.

"You won't be getting rid of me now," I said.

She snorted. "And how unfortunate that is."

"So, why?" I asked. "Why all this effort for some human?"

"It wasn't my choice," she grumbled. "But as for why, I know what Jack has told me. I know what I've seen of you. But in the end, it's not for me to say." She tapped the mark over her collarbone. "Estheria didn't give you the memories on her own. It was Jaevidan's suggestion a long time ago. His way to explain what happened without breaking his vow."

Involuntarily, my hand drifted to my neck. The diamond hanging in the hollow of my throat. The answers were in the memories, something I had been told many times by many creatures. I just couldn't understand what it meant until now.

But so far, the only memories I had seen were of two lonely children. And Jack hadn't exactly been a warm and loving companion in the first one. His interest in Annwyl had been little more than wanting to fill an unoccupied space in his short life. He threatened to enslave her, for god's sake.

My pulse stopped at the realization he had.

"He doesn't love me," I said. "I don't know what it is or what his reasons were, but this isn't love or friendship or whatever he wishes to call it. You don't enslave people you love with a bond. You don't commit them to death over and over again. You don't lie to them, you don't *ask* them to lie for you with a vow. That's not love. It's obsession."

"Let us be clear about something," she said slowly. "I am in no way defending any of his actions, nor his methods, but I know my brother better than anyone else. I know what he is. I can't say whether his intentions have always been pure because what love is to you and what it is to us are very different things. You forget how long we have been among humans. Your experience with other fae has been limited, so you don't understand how we truly are. We may often look human, may even act it, but we aren't. So if you want me to give you a tidy answer wrapped up with a bow, I can't. The only people who can decide what this is—if it has all been worth it—are the two of you."

Another round of applause. Silence descended between us in the deafening noise, trapping me with my thoughts. To trust him, or not to. I had asked the wraith. I had asked the druids. I had asked Violet. But I hadn't asked myself.

I didn't know. There were four hundred years of history to sort through. One lifetime hadn't been enough. Apparently, several lifetimes hadn't been enough.

"You said it was supposed to be impossible. Reincarnation. If that's true, then how did he do it?"

She visibly cringed. An ugly feeling bubbled in my gut. In all the time I had known Violet, at least in living memory, I had never so much as seen her squirm.

"Remember what I once told you about prices?"

I couldn't forget. It was only a few weeks ago but felt like a lifetime. Violet said there were prices for everything, most of which weren't worth the cost. In the same conversation, she told me a grave secret, something I knew without doubt was her biggest regret.

"That's why he killed the Bogoran." I wasn't sure if it was aloud or inside my head. With the rush of blood pounding my ears, it was impossible to tell.

Not just any Bogoran, the *last*. Violet said she and Jack killed it together. It was the reason she didn't use the endless cache of magic she possessed. All power had a price, and while I still didn't understand what Violet's was, I knew what it was to Jack. The cost was the extinction of an entire race. Of *gods*. And the price had been . . . me.

The crowded room grew unbearably hot, the raucous cheering pounding against my skull. I wanted to scream, I wanted to ask her if it was worth it, but I already knew the answer. How wretched did someone need to be to genuinely believe it was? To think their existence was worth the complete extinction of an entire race. That a successful annihilation was a fair price to pay for their own life, for the life of someone they loved . . .

I needed air. Violet locked my wrist to the table before I was halfway up from my seat. "Sit," she ordered. It wasn't like her usual snark, which only increased my need to vomit.

"Whether you like it or not, you have power now, do you understand?"

I couldn't speak, couldn't bring myself to so much as nod.

"I don't know why, but they made you a Fate. You have real power, real control in ways none of us understand yet. Even with that aside, you are the third piece of a very powerful Morrigan. The only one to exist as of two days ago."

Because I had killed one of the triplets. My path of destruction was limitless.

"My advice to you?" she continued. "Make it worth something. I don't care if it's with me and Jack or entirely on your own, but you have a responsibility now. You didn't ask for it, but that changes nothing. So make a choice. Make them every day. I'm not asking you to forgive Jack, or be with him, or trust him, but I need him right now, you need him right now, and humans need him right now."

My voice came out a trembling whisper. "But is that true? Are we actually on the right side of things, Violet?"

Her answer didn't come for a long time. Not until the show completed for the night with a lofty round of applause.

"None of us are."

NINE

ADELINE

SLEEP FADED INTO WAKEFULNESS, and for a moment, I completely forgot where I was. The bubbling flasks were the first clue, the tiny druid the second. Guinevere glanced up with a scowl before resuming her work.

After the brief adventure in Paris, Violet retreated into the labyrinth of the Guild, and I resumed my post in the infirmary. She never said how they arrived in the Guild or if they were even welcome, but I feared that inquiry would lead to where Jack was. In the middle of the night, after hours of revelations and my own thoughts consuming too much space, that was a problem I wasn't ready for.

In the bleary morning, it still wasn't. Tommy was asleep beside me, but the color had returned to his cheeks. His breathing had evened out too. I shifted from my cot and sat beside him, smoothing out his hair like he used to do when I was a little. Guinevere wore a curious look and collected her things, retreating from the infirmary before I could ask her any questions.

"I don't think she likes me too much."

I startled at Tommy's voice. He ran his hands down his face, blinking sleep away. It was strange to speak to him without his hearing aids, but he responded to my voice, so Guinevere's potion must have worked.

"You look better."

"Could certainly be worse." He jerked his chin toward the door. "Since we're both still alive, I assume they've been treating you right?"

"Fine." I tucked a strand of hair behind my ear, trying not to fidget. I had to tell him and knew it was better to get it over with, but I'd really hoped I would have the morning to ruminate alone. And with Jack's latest memory still on my foremind, I only felt more inclined to avoid the topic.

"You think they got anything to eat—"

"Jack is here."

Tommy blinked. I picked at my nails—an unladylike habit Papa had always tried to break me out of.

"Jack Warren?"

I nodded.

He chewed his lower lip. "Is that bad news or good?"

It occurred to me I hadn't exactly defined my relationship with Jack to Tommy. Between the Morrigan attempting to kill us, escaping the faerie world, and being escorted to the Guild of the Druids, my romantic endeavors hadn't been priority. A few days ago, the answer would have been simple. Today, I didn't know where to begin.

The one time they had met wasn't the best circumstances either. Granted, Tommy admitted he had been undercover for the Knights and hadn't meant a word he said, but the vitriol felt a little too real to be a complete fabrication. And as far as Jack knew, it was.

After a moment of deliberation, I settled on "I'm working on it."

Tommy's eyes narrowed. "Is he going to be a problem?"

"It's complicated," I said, shooting him a smile that didn't reach the eyes. "But let me worry about Jack. We have far more important things to dwell on at the moment."

"Well, now I'm going to dwell on it." He pushed back the covers and sat up. "He ain't scaring you or anything, is he?"

The sentiment was sweet, but what I really wanted to say was it hardly mattered. It wasn't like Tommy could protect me from the sidhe, even if I wanted him to.

I squeezed his shoulder and hopped off the bed. "You really oughta find more things to worry about than me. Remember, I'm practically invincible now."

His eyes scanned me up and down like he was noticing all the subtle changes for the first time. The truth. I may have looked human, but I wasn't. Not anymore. A few days ago, he said it didn't matter, but with the small frown he wore now, I wondered if he would always feel that way.

A knock rapped on the infirmary door. The bond surged inside my chest, alerting me to who it was before I had the chance to stand. The door swung open to reveal Jack.

If possible, he looked more rumpled than yesterday. Purple half-moons lay beneath his eyes, golden skin sallow in the wan infirmary lights. The weariness only lasted moments, sharpening into knifelike attention at my brother in the bed beside me.

Silence echoed between the three of us. Jack still didn't know the truth about Tommy's double-agent status, and judging by the look on his face, hadn't been informed of my brother's presence either.

Jack leaned in the doorway casually. I'd spent enough time with him to know it was anything but. He spoke slowly and with exaggerated pronunciation, assuring Tommy could read his lips. "Are our druid hosts aware of your allegiances?"

"He's with us," I said, not entirely sure which one of them I spoke too.

Tommy pushed out of bed, days of illness, injury, and travel all but forgotten. "I'm with Adeline," he corrected.

Tension thickened the air. Jack stepped forward. "Adeline as she was or as she is now?"

My teeth ground together. "Tommy knows what I am, and if he hadn't, it wouldn't be your place to inform him."

His eyes flickered to me. Through the bond, I felt the faint sense of displeasure. Betrayal. "I know you may find this hard to believe, but I'm only trying to maintain your protection."

"I can protect myself." The words came low, unsure. Violet hadn't seemed to think so, and not with her usual vitriol but the pragmatic assessment of what we faced. That I may have faced one of the Morrigan sisters alone, but that didn't mean I could handle the problem on my own.

Tommy stepped in front of me. A useless, stupid action, but old habits didn't vanish overnight. "My sister and I need to talk. In private."

"You said that the last time I saw you. If I recall, you were also wearing a certain talisman," Jack crooned.

"Enough." I stepped between them. "Tommy, stay here. I need to speak with the druids, and Guinevere didn't say whether you were well enough yet to leave. Jack, come with me."

Neither man seemed thrilled at the prospect, but I gave neither time to argue. The infirmary door clicked shut behind me, the last thing I saw Tommy's silent, mouthed words. *Scream if you need me.*

I wondered when it would finally dawn on Tommy he needed me to safeguard him and not the other way around. That line of thought died as Jack and I stood across one another in the doorway.

Druids streamed back and forth beside us, pretending to ignore the uneasy moment. "Can we speak somewhere?" he asked.

"I don't want to stray too far from my brother," I said. It was only half the truth.

He sucked hot air in between his teeth. "Addie, I don't know what he has told you—"

"We can discuss Tommy another time."

Jack looked like he wanted to argue but let it lie. Obviously, he had come here to speak with me about something else. I didn't care for what that something else was at the moment, but knowing Jack, I wouldn't have a choice in the matter.

"How did you enter the Guild?" I asked.

"I have my ways."

"No one but druids can enter without Sybil's permission."

"Well, I suppose it's a good thing I have a druid on retainer and no regard for the law."

We stared at one another.

"Does she know you're here?" I asked.

"She's aware," he murmured, distracting himself by adjusting his watch. "We have a little agreement going as long as I cause no trouble."

"That will be difficult for you."

"Undoubtedly."

Glowering, I looked anywhere but Jack. The tension leaked from him all at once, replaced with an exhaustion too heavy to name.

"Are you well?" he asked, an echo of last night, but this time, he made no move to touch me. The space between us became its own entity.

"I'm unharmed."

"That's not what I'm asking."

A kernel of guilt seeded deep in my chest. He thought I meant to kill him less than twenty-four hours ago, yet his concerns still remained on my well-being. His last memory made an unwelcome appearance. Jaevidan as a little boy, faking his enthusiasm for the happiness of a little human girl. The lengths taken by a child to provide a friend tiny moments of happiness and the stark relief when that friend was there for him in return.

But Jaevidan was no longer a little boy, and that little girl, Annwyl, was long dead. The two children finding solace in each other in the Welsh countryside were not the same people standing in this darkened hall.

"Violet and I talked," I said, refusing to answer his question.

"What did she tell you?"

Everything and nothing. Enough to know Jack may have had my best interest in this moment, and perhaps he believed he always did, but there were too many strikes against him to know for sure.

"Nothing you can speak of." I turned down the hall. I couldn't do this, not right now. I needed to talk with Sybil. I needed to know more about the fates, what they knew of Babd and Nemain, and if the druids could actually protect us until a better plan was formed. Jack reached out, faster than should have been possible for a living thing, and grabbed my wrist.

"What do you know, Annwyl?"

My heart thudded against my ribs. "That's not my name anymore."

Shock crashed through the bond, followed by a strange coil of relief. He concealed his end of the bond before I could learn more.

"I swear, I wouldn't have kept it from you—"

"I know." I shook free of his grip. "I know about the vow mark. I know about the parallel bond, and I know about the Bogoran."

Fraught silence pulsed between us. Two druids shuffled past. Jack waited until they were out of sight to reply. "What do you know about the Bogoran?"

I blinked. Of all things, that was what he was most concerned about. That I knew the atrocity he had committed? "I know you killed it for me, or Annwyl, however you think of it." My voice rose high, anger mounting with the neutral expression he donned like a mask. The bond was sealed so tightly there was no hope of gleaning anything from it. Just like that, I knew he withheld another secret from me. An important one.

A sardonic laugh choked my throat. "You're a monster."

Two whispered words, heavy with a past so soaked in blood the stains could never be removed. "I know."

"Do you?" I breathed.

"I—" He froze, seized by that preternatural stillness that always unnerved me. My lips parted, but he held up a finger, shifting his head to better hear down the hall. It was moments like these I remembered how *other* he truly was. Gone were the excessive little tics he performed to maintain his human facade. He moved through open air like a drop of ink unfurling in liquid.

Slowly, without tearing his eyes from the empty darkness down the hall, he reached back and clasped my upper arm. He stepped back, prompting me to do the same. Lower than a whisper, he murmured, "Where did you and Violet go last night?"

"What's going on?" I asked instead. It dawned on me how silent it was. Gone was the steady patter of druids' feet through the halls. The echo of murmured voices through the thick stone walls. Even the fae lights dotting the walls waned, dimming to a sickly glow.

"Where?"

"She gave me a postcard to shade to. A residential street beside a plaza, then we walked to a club several blocks away. One of the racy sorts."

"With all the mirrors on the walls?"

"That would be the one." I attempted to tug my arm free, but he could have been made of stone. "What are you—"

I was thrown against the wall. He pressed against me and locked a hand over my mouth. My eyes widened with rage, but he glanced down, warning me to be silent.

His hand slid away. *My brother*, I mouthed, shooting a furtive glance across the hall. A moment of hesitation, and then the infirmary door disappeared from my view. Glamour. *Strong* glamour.

Hold your breath, he mouthed back. Footsteps slapped against the stones. The steady drip of water pattered beside the squelching noise, joined with heavy, creaking breaths. I sucked in a large gulp of air, trying my best to remain still.

Jack's eyes widened with an insistent look. He was full fae now, not a hint of human glamour remaining. The tattoos along his neck fidgeted in a chaotic dance. The snake usually wrapped around his arm slithered up his throat, flicking a furious tongue in the direction of the noise. The battle scene along his side had shifted upward, the tips of crashing swords swinging above the collar of his shirt.

My chest ached with stale air, but I didn't move. The sound grew closer. Beside Jack's shoulder, a thick shadow grew along the floor.

I withheld a scream as the creature came into view. The body shape vaguely resembled a beaver, but the similarities ended there. Not only was it five times larger than the human version, but every inch was covered in scales. Kelp and slime plastered it in a shimmering coat, water dripping from a thick maw lined with hundreds of needle-like teeth. Its rattling breath blasted us with hot air as it ambled past.

My lungs were on fire. My body twitched, and my hands shook, demanding oxygen. Jack maintained his heated stare, a warning. His thumb smoothed over my shoulder, attempting to still the tiny convulsions.

A tiny breath hissed past my lips, barely enough to intake air. The creature halted in the middle of the hall.

It was close enough to brush with my outstretched hand. The rotten stench of bog and something necrotic burned inside my nose. It swiveled its massive head, two beady eyes pointed at my face. A steady stream of saliva formed at the corner of those needle-like teeth. It splattered against the ground and splashed my bare ankle.

Jack's hand twitched against me, preparing to grab the dagger at his hip.

The beast glanced up, hearing or seeing something I couldn't. It broke off into a galloping run, faster than any creature of its size should be able to, and disappeared down the hall.

I gasped, sinking against Jack as I hyperventilated. One arm threaded around my waist, and the other freed every weapon hidden in his clothes.

I wanted to ask what that thing was. What was happening. Before I could, a loud crash emanated from the direction of the main room and the thrum of heavy footsteps.

Then, the screaming began.

TEN

ADELINE

JACK WAS ALREADY IN motion, dragging me on stumbling feet down the hall. "Tommy," I gasped, straining against him for the infirmary. He rambled something incoherent when another voice joined the fray.

"What the fuck is happening?" Violet asked, flanked by Arthur and Lillian. Gosh, were they were a sight for sore eyes. *And don't know anything*, I reminded myself. While they were loyal to Jack, they had no idea about the true nature of our bond or why it existed in the first place.

"Thank the stars," Lillian gasped, throwing her arms around me. I swayed with the weight of her tall form and squeezed back. Arthur fidgeted in the corner of my vision, cleaning his glasses with a sweat-soaked handkerchief. I couldn't explain why the nervous habit filled me with warmth.

"Where's Will?" The last time I saw him, he was bleeding out from iron bullet wounds on a rooftop.

"In New York. He's still recovering."

The happy reunion was over before it began, squashing further questions. Jack turned to Violet. "I think they found her."

There was no need to confirm who *they* or *her* was. Somehow, the sisters had discovered I was in the Guild and, despite Sybil's assurances, had infiltrated it.

"That shouldn't be fucking possible," Violet snapped. The statement was contradicted by a fresh round of screams, then a wet gurgling that rolled my stomach.

"Maybe Tharonnen betrayed us, I don't know."

"The bastard," Violet hissed. "I'll peel the flesh off his bones and feed it to his dancing cunts."

That was extreme, even for her. I could only guess Tharonnen was the owner of the club we'd visited, but it hardly mattered. If Babd, Nemain, and followers were here, we needed to be anywhere else.

"We don't have time for that," Jack said. "Lillian, shade Violet and Arthur to the backup location. Addie and I will meet you there."

"What about Tommy?"

They all stared at me. Clearly, no one had informed them about my brother.

Jack sighed and jerked his head to the infirmary. "Take the brother. Watch him closely."

Lillian gave a jerky salute, and the three of them disappeared. I had no time to ponder what reflective surface she used as Jack broke into a run.

I stumbled with his hand locked around my arm. My shoes clicked against the stones, deafeningly loud despite the chaotic noises rising around us. Our stretch of hallway was empty, but I feared that wouldn't last much longer.

"Why did we split up?" I panted. Even with my new form, Jack moved at a pace I could barely maintain.

"We need something." He pulled us left and gave a wide berth to something against the wall. I chanced a glance back, bile rising in my throat. Two druids, or what used to be, slumped in a tattered, bloody pile.

"We need to find Sybil," he said, wrenching me past another pile of corpses. The screams grew louder, the voices clearer. Whatever was happening, we were running *toward* it.

The pathway retched us into the main room. The brilliant, sunlike light high in the glass dome had been extinguished, leaving nothing but frantic will-o-wisps for light. They washed everything in a sickly blue, illuminating flashes of carnage before they were extinguished and the scenes plunged into darkness. There were several more of those creatures we saw by the infirmary, teeth shredding flesh like melted butter. I recognized red caps from my encounter on the train all those months ago. They scuttled across the floor, picking across the debris and dousing their cloaks in pools of blood. There were more, creatures I had no name for or hope to describe. Jack yanked me forward, practically lifting my feet off the floor with each hard pull to the left or right to avoid another obstacle. But when a heap of bloody rags beside us groaned, I ground us to a stop.

"They're still alive," I said. In the recesses of my mind, I knew we couldn't stop. That pausing too long in this room meant certain death. But the chaos flooded all my senses and overwhelmed any remaining reason. There was no room to think, to plan, just get to the next step. My thoughts came in a rapid series of orders. Person. Alive. Help. Run away.

Jack pushed me forward, but I'd already launched into action. I grabbed the druid's tattered robes by the shoulders. Their face was too bloodied to recognize anything beyond a whimpering person. My new immortal strength allowed me to drag them along, but even I noticed how much it slowed us down.

Jack screamed something, then lifted the druid onto his shoulder, shoving me forward. In the brief flash before a will-o-wisp died, I saw strands of puffy, white hair through the blood. The muted grimace of an elderly woman I'd met the day before. Sybil.

There was no time to alert Jack of who we found. More of the creatures poured into the room, but in the flickering darkness, I couldn't tell from where. He shoved me down a hall nearly obscured by fallen bodies, and I was given one more opportunity to look back. Some of the druids had weapons, but even those wielding armor and swords were overwhelmed by the mass of creatures. We should have helped. We should have done something, but deep in my soul, I knew they were already dead.

A group of will-o-wisps cowered together in one last effort. Their faded glow was enough to illuminate something stretching up the wall, a blot of darkness rising dozens of feet to the ceiling. I followed the blackness higher until I noticed the eyes, two great, burning spheres of red looming down from the ceiling.

The remaining will-o-wisps extinguished, the last of the light becoming perpetual shadows.

Jack pulled us onward, knife swinging through the flesh of monsters crouched against the walls in wait for their next meal. A cluster of will-o-wisps moved with us, but their light was just enough to visualize the next horror ahead. We retreated deeper into the pit of the Guild, the floor sloping with a decline. We didn't stop until a light brown hand reached out from the darkness, and Jack skidded to a halt.

Guinevere wasted no time, pulling Sybil from Jack's shoulder and blotting her wounds. Screams echoed in the distance, far less than we'd heard earlier. The adrenaline coursing through my veins muted all the horror and anguish I knew I would feel later.

"Sybil," Jack said, kneeling beside the healer and joining her efforts to staunch the bleeding. It wasn't enough. For every wound they patched, another appeared. Blood pooled around her like a growing halo, expanding on the floor in a crimson ring of death. Her fading eyes found me and pooled with relief. Guilt. I would feel it for the rest of my life, but not now.

"You will help her," she whispered. I couldn't tell if it was a question or an order.

"Where is it?" Jack asked.

Sybil didn't answer, looking to Guinevere. Solemn resignation filled the healer's face, and she nodded.

Jack and Guinevere stood. The latter bowed her head and recited something in a foreign tongue, the tone indicating they were last rites of some kind. Sybil reached out with trembling fingers, and I took her hand. Blood stained her teeth and choked her throat, but she managed a few scratchy words. "Remember the druids, Lady Fate. Protect them."

Tears. I couldn't feel them, but they dripped off my chin and mingled with her blood. "I will."

Someone pushed me forward, and the will-o-wisps moved ahead. Sybil had minutes, maybe moments, left, but she would leave this world alone in the dark.

Time moved slowly and all at once. Eternity could have passed as we ran, but each moment bled so perfectly into the next it felt like seconds before I was jerked to a stop. Guinevere produced a knife and grabbed my hand, scoring my palm with a deep mark. She shoved my flattened hand against the wall before pain had a chance to reach my brain.

The spot was indistinguishable from the remaining wall, but it indicated something because my blood took effect immediately. A deep glow arose from the droplets of red, rolling down the wall like tears. The ruby streaks ignited into fire, burning and racing along the marble at angles defying gravity. A door formed from the crimson glow, and then the section of stone pushed inward and separated behind the remaining wall. Jack pushed me inside, and Guinevere followed close behind, mumbling a few words that sealed the stones again behind us.

The will-o-wisps that squeezed in sank to the floor, exhaustion stealing all but the faintest of their light. A hall stretched forward, too narrow for more than one person at a time. Darkness pushed in, and the stale fog of mold, but a golden glow illuminated ahead. Jack nudged me forward with a gentle push, a ghost of the violent maneuvers from moments ago.

I walked. It couldn't have been more than twenty feet, but it felt like miles. The glow separated into three solid gold figures huddling beside each other with hands outstretched. Three women, all but their mouths and arms concealed by rippling gold cloaks. Six upturned palms formed a bowl, the light source contained within their fingers.

"What is this?"

Guinevere answered. "A sacred place. The druids were tasked with protecting it. Only an appointed few know it exists."

An alcove expanded around the statues, just enough for three people to stand before them. I stepped to the side so Jack could exit the passageway, who did the same for Guinevere. "We don't know what it is, but in the event a *beansidhe* made their presence known, we were tasked with bringing you here. Only the blood of a fate can open the door."

I glanced at Jack. "How did you know?"

"I didn't," he said. "Sybil informed me I couldn't spirit you away before she bestowed an artifact to you. She said it was a matter of life and death."

I leaned forward, just enough to peek over the crested hill of the statue's fingers. Inside was . . . a candlestick.

Frowning, I craned my head to see if I had missed something. It was just the candle—stout, white, and glowing with a normal yellow flame. It stood upright with no holder. The wax had been carved with symbols of red ink, all but a smooth rectangle stretching down one side.

"You don't know what it is?" I found that hard to believe. The druids were curious by nature, their sole purpose to find and record knowledge. I doubted they would possess something for so long without at least attempting to uncover what it was.

Guinevere frowned. "We have theories." Succeeding silence said I would hear none of them.

"I don't—"

A resounding boom rattled the walls, raining dust onto our hair. Sinister silence followed, nothing but our uneven breaths filling the room.

Jack glanced up, then behind him. "I think we should—"

Sizzling erupted down the passageway. I couldn't see around the corner, but Jack and Guinevere both whipped around, eyes wide.

He yanked her forward by the robes. "I thought only her blood could open it."

"If her blood remained on the wall, they could have used it," she wheezed, clawing fruitlessly at his hands. "You need to leave."

Jack dropped her and jerked his chin at the statues. "Grab the candle. We're getting out of here."

"Wait!" she called, but it was too late. Jack had produced a women's compact from his pocket, and my fingers snatched the candlestick. I'd barely lifted it from the statue's outstretched hands when Jack grabbed my arm, fear permeating every muscle of his face.

I looked up.

The statues stared at me. All three of them, their necks suddenly craned in my direction, mouths twisted into scowls. For the space of a breath, there was stillness. Nothing but Jack's heated warmth against my skin, Guinevere's ragged breaths, the sizzle and crackle of fire lancing stones down the passageway. Then, the middle statue grabbed me by the collar and lifted me skyward.

"*Jack!*" My feet dangled midair, kicking wildly. My heel hit solid gold, and pain shot through my bones. The statue grabbed me with its second hand, hoisting me as if to get a better look. The other two crouched down and produced knives from the sheaths of their golden cloaks.

Guinevere screamed, and Jack scrambled back, hitting the passage with a grunt. I looked back to see him jump to his feet, fingers already pressed through the surface of his rippling mirror. Behind him, twenty feet down the hall, fiery light formed the outline of a doorway.

The statue nearest Guinevere grabbed her cloak, dragging her closer. "Do something!"

My mind erased. I didn't know what to do. I barely knew what a fate was. Jack screamed something behind me, and a golden dagger whizzed past my ear. A curse erupted before shattering glass, followed by the shifting stones down the hall.

"*Adeline*," Guinevere screamed. A statue had its golden arms locked around her chest, squeezing the life from her. "Do something, anything," she rasped.

The third statue darted around me, melting and reforming a section of its cloak into another dagger. Another grunted curse from Jack, then the sound of the stones slamming into place. Gleeful laughter followed it.

Terror infiltrated all my senses. I could recognize that laugh, the empty chill of it, anywhere.

"Stop," I ordered the statues. "Stop, *stop*, I'm a *beansidhe*."

The statue wrenched me closer. Its golden eyes were covered, but it inspected me, flaring its golden nostrils wide to take in my scent. Its lips curled back in a sneer, revealing rows of sharp metal teeth.

Screams rang out behind me. The clash of metal and cries of fury. It was too late. We were surrounded. We were going to die. I was going to die. *I was going to die.*

Would you like to know what we have become? the wraith had asked me. I was bleeding, desperate, looking death down the face in that moment too. The same creatures behind me had cackled as they broke Tommy's bones. As they reveled in the delight of my pain.

Then scream, she had said.

Golden talons lifted to my neck. I inhaled a deep breath.

This time, there was no gust of wind. A maelstrom of poisonous white petals didn't pepper the air. There was nothing but silence, complete and utter silence. Even as the stones shook around us. Even as I convulsed in the statue's grip. Even as blood splattered my mouth as I screamed myself hoarse.

Metal hands sprung open, and I crashed against the floor. The statue holding Guinevere stood, and they both faced the passageway.

My eyes craned up. Looming larger than life, black hair floating around her like a halo, was the face of my nightmares.

Babd's eyes met mine. Behind their glassy surface lay nothing but death.

Three things happened then.

Babd lifted a glowing dagger and threw it down the hall.

The golden statues leapt forward, crawling along the walls and ceiling past me, past Jack, into the darkness beyond.

And Jack threw himself forward, a shard of the remaining mirror jutting from his bloody palm. His hand connected with my ankle, and I reached out for Guinevere.

Babd roared in the distance, but the scream was no match for my own.

My fingers brushed the glass in Jack's palm. The last thing I saw before the shade was an iron dagger inches from my nose.

ELEVEN

ADELINE

I DIDN'T KNOW WHERE to send us, so I pictured the brassy number eight from Violet's postcard. The three of us landed in a heap on the front stoop. Across the alley, a little boy in church clothes screamed and ran for the plaza.

"Is everyone jake?" I asked. Jack leaked blood from too many wounds to count, but thankfully, most of them were already closing. Guinevere shook like a leaf in a storm, but she offered a little nod. Jack ripped the glass from his hand and threw it to the ground. It shattered into sparkling dust against the cobblestones.

Voices—human voices—echoed from the plaza. The boy was still screaming, the pound of adult footsteps matching his cries. Jack grabbed us with bloody palms, and we disappeared.

Instantly, we landed in another alley. "*Fuck*," he spat, kicking a nearby garbage pail. The metal lid clattered against the ground.

He sank to his knees, pressing a hand to his shoulder. Blood spurted forth with the beat of his heart, red blossoming on his shirtfront at an alarming rate. Guinevere jumped to her feet, tremors erased as if the familiar task set her back to rights. Jack slumped against a brick wall with ragged breaths.

"How many are iron?" she asked. He pointed to his shoulder, then another spot between his ribs. She ripped strips of cloth from her robes and tore open his waistcoat and shirt. Buttons plinked against the fallen garbage pail and bricks.

He craned his head up with great effort, watching me where I stood behind the druid. His glamour was completely gone—a side effect of the iron. If any humans peeked out their windows or entered the alley, we'd have a lot more trouble.

Guinevere had the same thought. "Hold these bandages for me, quickly," she called back.

Hesitation. Jack's serpent eyes honed on me, narrowing the world to two black slits. A question lay within them. A raw plea.

I dropped to my knees before I could question myself. He sucked air between his teeth as I dug the scraps of cloth into his wounds.

Guinevere tore a row of stitches in her robe, and vials clanged to the street. She sorted through them, settling on a small concoction that perfumed the air with sulfur when she popped the stopper. "This will slow down the bleeding, but it takes time."

He gritted his teeth and nodded. Guinevere shoved my hands away and poured several drops over each wound. Smoke rose from his skin, and he screamed against the closed wall of his lips. Nothing happened for a moment, and then the bleeding slowed from pulsatile gushing to a steady trickle.

"Did it work?" I asked.

"He'll live." She recorked the vial and glanced up and down the alley. "We need to move him."

"Meeting location," he ground out.

"Can you shade?" I asked.

He shook his head, scowling at the thought. His glamour was still shot, then. "How far is it?" I asked.

"Several blocks."

"He can make it," Guinevere said. She shrugged her arms from the ruined robes, leaving her in nothing but a thin slip. She'd stand out, but at least it touched the tops of her bare feet.

Jack grunted and gripped the wall for support, pushing himself to stand. Taking the cloth from Guinevere, I draped it over his head and wrapped it around his bare midsection.

As I tugged the top down to cover his eyes, déjà vu struck me. Not for my own memories but for his.

"Keep the hood low. No one will know," I murmured.

Jack tensed. I couldn't read his expression with half of it covered, but I felt him through the bond.

His voice came in a soft whisper. "Marzipan grew on me, you know."

A sad smile lifted my lips. "Ready?"

He nodded. I ducked beneath his good arm and helped him straighten. He swayed dangerously and nearly toppled me with his weight, but thank the stars for immortal strength and the last vestiges of adrenaline.

"Go slow, and be careful not to open the wounds. He needs a few days of rest, but I doubt either of you will get it."

I gawked at Guinevere. "You're not coming with us?"

"Some of us are still down there, in the Guild." She swallowed, looking away as the first wave of emotions finally hit. "I don't know what will remain of the druids now, but my people need me. It will take a long time to rebuild, if we ever can."

"If there is anything, anything at all we can do—"

She shook her head. "Protect yourself, Lady Fate. The druids need me. Everyone else needs you." A small bow, and then she glanced up once more, unsure of herself. "When you see Arthur, tell him I say hello."

I nodded. "Of course."

"If you change your mind, my door is always open," Jack said. "And the druids will always find refuge in New York. On my own flesh, I vow it."

Magic pulsed in the air, the metallic tang of it coating my tongue. Jack leaned heavier against me, a small grunt in the back of his throat as a wound etched itself onto his neck.

Guinevere shifted at the fresh vow mark. "I may just hold you to that vow, Prince Jaevidan."

His mouth curled up in a smile. "I hope you do. Although you should know, they call me King of the Banished now."

"If we only we could all change what we are." She gave a passing glance at me. "May the stars bless you both. And don't forget to tell Arthur." Then she was gone, running down the alley and out of sight.

I nudged Jack with my shoulder. "Come on."

"Do you have the artifact?"

I glanced around, having completely forgotten about it. The cursed candlestick had rolled against the bricks. Propping Jack against the wall, I knelt and shoved the damned thing in his trouser pocket.

The walk was slow. Jack did his best to direct me through less crowded areas, but we received alarmed stares from the few Parisians we crossed. One poor gentleman went white as a sheet at the fresh blood staining Jack's makeshift cloak. He rattled a monologue off in French, attempting to dislodge me from Jack's side and help him sit. Jack exchanged a few foreign words before the man relented, mumbling anxiously as we shuffled on.

I nearly asked when he'd learned the language but remembered a detail Babd had enlightened me to during my captivity. One of those women Jack had been acquainted with—a woman with the same mark on the back of her neck as me—had been a French duchess.

I peered around, soaking in the Parisian streets. The ancient cobblestones and stained-glass churches of centuries past. The little shops with dried meats or wine in the window and the wafting scent of hot pastries and cappuccinos on every corner. Part of me should have been familiar with it. Not my body, but the soul that had once seen this city. It should have evoked some emotion. But my surroundings were as foreign to me as the first time I saw New York.

We found our destination in a rougher quarter of the city. Here, two bloody people elicited nothing but closed window shades and downcast eyes. Jack motioned toward a squat building nestled between two abandoned ones. A weathered sign creaked from a trash and piss-soaked breeze, declaring the structure a hotel.

The dark and musty lobby was small enough to touch both walls. Gray light washed a shabby staircase from a barred window, and a shabbier man slept beside a wall of keys. The wood groaned beneath our feet, and he jerked awake.

"*Non, non, non, non, non! Je ne veux pas des problèmes ici.*" He shoved his hands against Jack's chest wound and us out the door.

Jack rambled back in French, but the man only shook his head, pointing at Jack's bloody cloak. I glanced upward, wondering if I should call down for Violet.

They exchanged a few more words, and Jack murmured, "Darling, do me a favor and get my wallet from my back pocket."

I raised a brow but completed the task. "Give the gentleman a hundred dollars," he added.

Blanching, I pulled out several fresh American twenties. The man paused, deliberating, before swiping the cash from my palm and spitting a few more words at Jack. I was fairly sure all of them were curses. At least one on his mother.

We only made it to the second-floor landing before Jack needed to rest. He slumped against a patch of peeling wallpaper, shrugging off Guinevere's cloak. Between sweat and blood, it was drenched.

I sank onto the stair below him. "Do you know where the others are? I'll get them to come help you up."

He shook his head and waved a hand for good measure. The bleeding had finally stopped, but the wounds were vicious. He hadn't just been cut—he'd been stabbed. Deeply.

I played with the hem of my dress while he held his head in his hands. After a long moment, I whispered, "They all died for me. It's becoming a habit."

Face still covered, he shook his head. "Neither the Bogorans nor the druids were your fault."

The Bogorans, maybe, but the druids weren't up for debate. I wondered if Arthur knew yet. If he would ever speak to me again, knowing I was the reason his old friends and colleagues were now dead.

"Look at me."

I didn't, far more fascinated with the frayed cloth around my knees.

"Addie, look at me."

He leaned forward, and I vaguely worried he'd topple sideways down the stairs. He reached into his pocket, presumably for the candlestick that proved the druid's allegiance to me, but only produced a cigarette case. "I think we deserve a little indulgence."

"Did you not just get stabbed in the lung?"

"This is just another Tuesday." He lit a cigarette and offered me the case. I sighed, taking it from him.

"Better," he said, blowing out a puff of smoke. It wasn't tobacco, I could tell that much by the smell alone. My own drag came away with the flavor of something sweet, followed by magic's trademark metal. Serenity rolled through me like a storm.

He held his cigarette to a stream of watery light. Dust swirled around the glowing ember. "You know, I have this blend smuggled in by a veil crosser."

"From Ildathach?"

"The very place."

My appetite for the vice disappeared, but I wasn't one to waste something expensive. The woman may leave poverty, but poverty doesn't leave the woman.

"That cost you a lot?" I asked.

"Too much."

"Why bother, then?"

He shrugged. "I don't know. I like the familiarity, I guess. My immortal habits peek through every once in a while."

I blew out a stream of smoke. "Does that go for women as well? You like the familiarity?"

A long moment passed, the air thick with smoke and remorse.

"No," he said carefully. "I do and have always loved my wife."

My head shot up. Before I could speak, footsteps pounded down the stairs.

"Look at you two," Lillian exclaimed. Her dress was a pale spring green, her glittering jewelry the antithesis of the surrounding walls. "On the fucking fates."

Jack extinguished his smoke. "Fairly sure I'm the only one fucking Adeline."

"I'm fairly sure no one is currently fucking Adeline," I snapped, just in time for my brother to appear on the landing.

In that moment, I was incredibly grateful for being doused in blood. "Holy shit." He leapt over Jack's outstretched legs, already tearing strips from his shirt.

Jack raised a brow. "Awful lot of blasphemy going on here."

I ignored him, pulling Tommy down beside me. "Calm down. None of it's mine."

He wasn't convinced. I patted myself over my dress, murmuring, "No wounds."

Satisfied, his stare roamed to Jack, who grinned. "I wouldn't mind some of your valiant efforts."

Tommy ignored him. Like brother, like sister. "Come on, there's food and a bath upstairs."

"A *very* large bath," Lillian added, winking. "There's an en suite connected to me and Violet. We'll put you and Jack up in there."

"I'll stay with Tommy." I nodded at Jack. "Do you need help, or can I wash all this off?"

Lillian frowned. Surely, this was not the fiery, passion-fueled reunion she had expected. I needed to hide all her romance novels.

Tommy went rigid beside me, laying a gentle hand on my back. Jack remained silent. We didn't need to speak with words—we had a bond for that. But even without the artificial status of our souls, I knew him more than I wanted to admit. He didn't need my help getting up the stairs, but he needed my help in other ways.

"Whatever she wants," he finally said.

I stepped past him for the third floor.

TWELVE

ADELINE

I DIDN'T SOB UNTIL I washed all the blood off, which I considered a small victory. Sensing I needed privacy, Tommy left the room and ate dinner with Lillian and Violet. I somehow managed to avoid my sister-in-magic-law for the afternoon. While her harsh commentary was often gospel, it wasn't what I needed right now.

I tried sleeping, but each time I closed my eyes, I saw the dead druids, scattering the once beautiful halls of their home. I thought of abandoning Sybil to die alone in the dark.

I thought of Arthur's quiet sobs through the powder room door when I walked inside. Worse, how he cleaned up and acted like everything was dandy as I stood there, coated in the blood of his brethren. He'd patted my arm, said, "I'm so relieved you and Jack are safe," and shuffled into the hall.

"Guinevere says hello."

He'd frozen at that, rooted to the doorway. "Is she . . ."

"She came out with me and Jack. We offered to bring her with us, but she wanted to find the others."

He'd nodded, never turning back. "Right. Good. Thank you for letting me know." And that had been that.

In the evening, I finally joined the others in the *large room*, as Lillian called it. No one quite knew what to make of Tommy, who stood cross-armed and stock-still in the corner. Arthur feigned a headache and went to bed for the night. Violet kept busy by applauding Harold each time he caught a mouse sneaking about the room, Lillian glanced between me and Jack, and the man himself slumped in a chair, coated in bandages, drinking a lowball glass of something tawny.

He swirled the liquid around and around. "I think I'll put her head on a pike."

Only Violet responded. "Babd or Nemain?"

"Haven't decided." Tommy's mouth twisted into a scowl as Jack knocked back the entire glass but remained silent. "Is there any way to avoid a fucking boat?"

I rubbed at my temple, the forming headache behind it. "What boat?"

"The boat back to New York."

"Not too soon, I hope," Lillian chirped. We all glared at her. "Well, we've only just gotten to Paris."

"We're not here to shop," Violet said.

"But—"

"Adeline no longer dresses like a country bumpkin. You've run out of emergency excuses."

Lillian slumped in her chair.

"Why a boat?" I asked.

"The druid channels may still be open," Violet said quietly. "It doesn't hurt to look."

Jack grimaced. "I'm not risking that. Besides, the sisters will expect it."

"Why a boat?"

"What about the channel Thomas and Adeline used to get here in the first place?" Lillian chimed in.

"Why a boat?"

"You mean the *Knights of Templar's* channel? Are you out of your fucking mind?" Violet jerked her chin at Tommy. "Maybe he can use it. Do you still carry your card, darling?"

"I defected. They want to kill me as much as they want to kill you," he said.

"I doubt that," Jack muttered.

The pounding in my skull slammed harder.

"How long do you think it's safe for us to be here?" Lillian asked. "Will is holding things up well enough at home. The priority is hiding Adeline until we have a plan. Perhaps returning to New York isn't the best option for her safety."

Violet rolled her eyes. "You just want to shop."

Jack shook his head. "She's best protected in New York, hidden or not. All our wards, all our weapons, and all our allies are there."

"But—"

"Maybe—"

"*Excuse me*," I screamed. "Why a fucking boat?"

Violet looked at me like I were a simpleton. "The only channels capable of travel like that belong to the druids and, apparently, the Knights of Templar. Unless you have a magic broomstick, how the fuck else do you propose we get to America?"

I glared at her. "I can shade."

They all stared at me.

"Addie, darling," Lillian said slowly, "we appreciate the thought, but you can't possibly shade six people across the Atlantic. It's not possible to send a paperclip that far."

"I can do it," I said. I wasn't sure why, and I didn't know how, but I knew I could. I wasn't like them. Ever since becoming a *beansidhe*, I'd been drawn to the shade. In fact, I found it more malleable each time I used it. I couldn't glamour or use compulsion, but even they had to admit I'd done things with the shade they had never seen before.

Jack snapped, refilling his glass. "No."

I glowered at him. "No?"

"That's insanity. We aren't even going to attempt it."

"It's worth a try."

"It's not worth a try because if you fail, you're either trapped between worlds for eternity or drowning halfway across the ocean."

Tommy shifted against the window. "I have to agree with him there, Ads. Doesn't sound worth it."

I gave Violet a pointed look.

She rolled her shoulders back, sighing. "As much as I love the thought of never listening to you whine again, I have to admit, it's foolish to try."

"I can do it. You know I can do it."

She lifted one shoulder. "Honestly, you might. The benefits don't outweigh the risks though."

"Isn't that for me to decide?"

"It's for all of us to decide," Jack said. "We all need safe passage right now."

"Since when?" I snapped. "Since when is anything a group decision?"

He leveled with me, lowball glass forgotten. "We always act together. Always have. And if I make a decision on my own, the rest trust me enough to know it's the best for all of us."

"But you don't always know what's best."

He drew a breath through clenched teeth. "I'm not perfect and never claimed to be. But I can say with a fair amount of confidence risking your neck for the sake of proving a point isn't in anyone's favor."

"Then what was the point of any of this!" My hands balled into fists, red flushing my cheeks. "What was the point of killing that Bogoran, or the parallel bond, or my father's death, or our Morrigan, or all of Arthur's friends dying to protect me if I'm not supposed to do anything substantial? Why go through *everything* to become a fate if so far its only value is an immortal bed partner for you and a fucking candlestick?"

The room went deathly quiet.

"Sorry," I whispered, shaking. "Sorry, it's been a long day. I need some sleep."

The last thing I heard before shutting the door was Lillian's quiet whisper. "Bogoran?"

Tommy came into our shared room shortly after. "Addie? You awake?"

I remained quiet, eyes shut tight until he left me alone. He sighed. "I'm right over here if you need me."

The clock ticked away. I heard muffled voices from the room over, confirming our plans. After a few hours' sleep, we'd all shade to Dunkirk and catch the first ship to New York.

Hours passed. I still couldn't sleep.

When the sky was at its darkest for the night, a note appeared on the bedside table. I glared at the mirror someone had moved beside the bed and adjusted so moonlight illuminated the page.

Annwyl,

As you damn well know by now, I am ~~not always the best~~ fairly shit at saying the right things when I am supposed to. I'm unsure if this will be much better, but there was one point in time I often sent you letters and you always loved them. Perhaps you no longer do, but it cannot hurt to try. So, there are several things I think you should know.

Firstly, I truly believe there is a point. There is always a point, and it is not for your body ~~(which I think about quite often,~~ (Disregard—not important right now)), and it is certainly not a fucking candlestick. I wish I could say why you became what you did. I'll be honest, it is as much a mystery to me as it is to you. It was not a part of the plan, but the fates chose you for a reason. We may not know that reason yet, but I promise it is waiting for you. And for the sake of honesty, I will tell you the little I know of the beansidhe is this: it is not an easy destiny. I fear there is a long road ahead, and you may be forced to make decisions and lead in a way you do not want to. For that, I am deeply sorry, and I can never make it up to you if this is a path you would not have chosen on your own. I always wanted the best for you, but often our intentions are not reality, and I will never pretend I had no part in your fate. With that, I will say if anyone can do this, it is you. You are, and have always been, the best person I have ever known.

Secondly, Violet told me you know about the parallel bond. I can't say if I did the right thing. Only you can decide that, but there is something I don't think you know. It's true the parallel bond is not the meeting of soulmates most of us believe it is. It's also true I found the ritual to complete it in the tenth Dianomican, which was given to me by your father. Even then, I knew it takes an incredible man to fight against the beliefs he has always known for the sake of something virtuous. In that case, it was you. He cast aside many years of hatred for our kind to save his daughter, and for that, he will always have my greatest respect.

But he didn't trust me. With the vow mark, I could not explain what you meant to me or why I wanted to save you. And even if I could, I doubt it would sway his opinion. So I added something to our bargain when we struck it. Before I created the parallel bond, I took another vow. The exact wording is lost on me now, but it was that I could never use the parallel bond to force you to feel, think, or act in any way you did not wish to. You have and have always had complete free will. That is the true reason it took me so many years to find you, because without that mark, I could have made you come to me, even with all of your father's wards. But it was something I wanted to do because (and I cannot stress this enough) it was never my intention to hurt you or control you. I swear on my life and all our friends' lives if there was any other way to save you, I would have taken it. But as it was, the parallel bond was the best option. Jonathan did not trust me even with the vow mark, and truthfully, I do not blame him for this. So he hid you away for twenty years and died willingly to keep you that way. I know that will be absolutely no solace to you after losing him, but that is the ~~full and complete truth.~~

There is one more thing I should admit. I did lie to you, or at the very least, I withheld the full truth from you about the bond. I honestly cannot say if I ever would have told you. I've spent a lot of time deliberating it. It was selfish, because I knew if you knew the full truth, it would destroy all the fragile trust we had built. Because I took that vow and could not use the bond in the way it was intended to, even if I wanted to, I felt there was no harm if you didn't know. To you, it would be exactly what you expected it to be, and as long as you were happy, there was no point in ruining that. So I concealed both vow marks, the one that keeps me from discussing your past and the one for the parallel. But I will show you both those marks if you want to see them, and I'll swear thirty times in the Abstruse what they exist for and have Lillian pull my memories for good measure if that gives you peace of mind. I ~~don't always do~~ often don't do the right thing, and I don't really have an excuse for it beyond I'm sort of a rotten bastard. That is why you are so important to me. You remind me to stay in the light.

Thirdly, what happened to the Bogoran was not your fault. That rests solely on me and Violet and the thousands of others who killed them before us. We had reasons, and maybe one day you will learn them, but that is not a burden for you to carry. I hope one day you learn the truth, but that isn't something I can give you. It is not my story to tell, and I promise that is not some shoddy excuse. Just know it is Violet and I who will atone for it.

Thirdly and a half, the same sentiment applies to the druids. You cannot take the blame for what happened to them. It rests solely on Babd, Nemain, their followers, and, to the barest of extents, the druids. There was no deceit on your part. The druids knew exactly what you are, knew exactly who was after you and why, and they sought you out anyway with the sole purpose to protect you, knowing what the consequences could be. There is no justification for what happened to the Guild, and someday soon, I will make the sisters pay for every life they took. But I am forever indebted to the druids because, ultimately, they completed their task. They kept you safe. That is why I offered Guinevere a vow, and I truly hope she uses it. But the last person anyone blames is you. Even (and especially) Arthur. So please don't blame yourself. Honor them by being the fate they died to protect. That is the best thing you can do for them.

It is now well past three in the morning, and I realize I have written you a small novel. I also realize you may tell me to fuck myself and throw this in the rubbish bin. Additionally, I understand the possibility of you throwing this in the rubbish bin and telling me you read it anyway, so in that case, the password is "marzipan," and if you cannot provide that to me, I will be forced to repeat this entire disaster to you face-to-face, which I highly doubt either of us desires. Since we are about to have a long boat ride back to America with little to do and no means of escape, I sincerely hope you read this.

To finish off, I know I am not your favorite person right now, but I told you just a few weeks ago I would be here for you, always. And I always am. Maybe you don't understand why yet, but there are answers in the memories. I can't say if they will be answers you want to see or if in the end they will justify anything to you, but at the very least, I hope they help you understand. We still have much to talk about, but I'll save that for another night. Dream well, darling. I love you most.

Yours Truly,
Jaevidan

THIRTEEN

JAEVIDAN

"Guess who?"

Annwyl tensed, then released a giggle. I covered her eyes, leaping away each time she tried to reach back and push me.

"Stop being silly!"

"Not until you guess."

"Then I guess my blindfold is attached to one very meddlesome prince." She peeled my hands from her face and turned around. "Was I correct?"

"Partially, I am only reasonably meddlesome."

Her expression said she could not have agreed less, but she smiled anyway. The sun beamed down without a cloud in the sky, and it was unreasonably warm for the human world. It felt perfectly fine to me, but a thick sheen of sweat glistened on her forehead. Strangely, she wore a head covering.

"What is this?" I plucked the fabric from her hair. She scowled and reached for it, but I'd just had a large growth in height. I held it high over our heads, inspecting the thin, yellowed fabric.

"It is my coif, and I am required to wear it at all times now. Give it back, Jaevidan."

I frowned. "For what ridiculous reason? Do you feel the air today?"

"Because . . . I . . . need to," she huffed, jumping for the quaff or whatever she called it. She succeeded on the fourth attempt. "How did you cross the Veil so early, anyway? It is only midday."

I shrugged. "I cannot say, but it was thin enough. Perhaps because it is Lughnasadh."

I hoped she would not inquire why I'd tested the Veil so early. In truth, I had ventured out the moment I woke this morning, planning to twiddle my thumbs in the meadow until the moons rose for the night. Not only was

I anxious to see Annwyl—we lost a day last month when I was required to welcome the Court of Leonta—but I was avoiding the celebrations. I had little love for Lughnasadh. Everyone drank far too much wine, and no less than a dozen humans were burned alive. Besides, Lugh himself was fond of my mother and made a point of visiting each year. Donvidan practically worshipped him, but I thought he was rather an arse.

"What is Lughnasadh?" she asked.

I frowned. Scholar Rindshaw taught us all the humans across the Veil celebrated the holiday, but he was often wrong about these things. The humans lived and died so quickly, constantly changing. The sidhe stayed the same and were quite terrible at assuming the star's children did as well. In the few years I had known Annwyl, I'd seen plenty of humans keep the old ways, but many no longer did. Annwyl herself lived in a convent, which supposedly belonged to the Catholics. But just a few years past, one of their silly kings declared Catholicism no longer existed, and now they were something else. Something about how he no longer fancied his wife. I could not be sure. It was all too confusing, and faerie politics bored me enough without thinking of human ones.

Suddenly, I had a brilliant idea. I bowed at the waist. "Why, Lughnasadh is the most important day of the year. It is your birthday."

Annwyl laughed. "You foolish boy. I have no birthday."

"Of course you do. Everyone has a birthday, and I have declared that yours is today."

"Hm, can one do such a thing?"

"Of course I can. I am a prince." I beamed at her. "Today marks the eleventh birth year of Annwyl of Wales. And to commemorate such a day, we must celebrate. Beginning . . . now." I grabbed her hand and started past a row of bushes, leading her into the forest.

She shook free of me. "Jaevidan, I cannot simply leave."

"Of course you can."

She sighed, moving to brush a strand of hair behind her ear before remembering the quaff. "Lord Beynon requested at least six pails of blackberries by day's end, and I am hardly halfway done. I am to deliver them myself." She beamed with pride at this, and I remained silent. It had been a small point of contention in months past. On one of his visits through the village, Annwyl's lord had taken a keen interest in her. She claimed the reason was she had spirit and the fastest hands among the convent, but I worried it was . . . something else. He often requested she deliver correspondence between the fortress and convent or provided other tasks in addition to the ones the convent required of her. And for all this additional work, he offered little more than the occasional shilling, sweet treat, or pat on her head. Complete blandishing if you asked me, but Annwyl was convinced it was a good thing. That the lord may offer her permanent work at the castle, meaning she would no longer live in the convent. Or—worse, according to her—begin training as a nun.

It had caused another significant reduction in our time. And all she ever seemed to speak of these days was the lord and how greatly she wished to please him. I was not jealous, simply . . . annoyed.

"Then I will inform the lord he shall receive the wrath of the fair folk should he forgo offerings on the holiest day of our year."

"You should not speak ill of the good lord. He has treated me well," she said. "We will celebrate tonight, after I finish my work for the day."

The good lord. Blessed Bogorans, what hogwash. "Wait here," I said.

I donned a cloak and entered the village, searching for a reasonable hut. Magic tickled my nose beside one of the peasants' homes. After checking the quarters were empty, I slipped inside.

This family must have been richer than the others because not only did they have two rooms for living but a third one just for their animals. Their livestock was impressive for the poor as well—three swine, a skinny heifer, and a dozen hens. The hearth had been freshly swept and the beds stuffed with clean straw. A bowl of milk rested on the lone windowsill, free of dust.

I strode to the window, whistling, and tipped the milk onto the floor.

A shrilly squeak came from the walls, then a little brownie dressed in daffodil petals. She muttered curses and produced a rag for the spill. "The second offering this week, gone! Wretched humans. I can find a new home, I can find a new—"

Her eyes craned up to my grin. She fell into a low bow.

"Blessed Sidhe, forgive me. I did not hear your arrival."

"Forgive me for the milk. I shall provide more." I crouched beside her, lifting her fuzzy chin. "I am afraid I have a favor to ask. You see, I require a large picking of blackberries by day's end, but the human I employed is no longer fit for the task. What say you to work for the day, and perhaps for your friends as well, in exchange for a favor from House Valdivia."

Her eyes went wide. "Good Prince, I could ask no favor."

Annwyl would be displeased if I made the brownie work for free. "I insist." After providing direction and negotiating our terms of payment, I returned to Annwyl with a grin. Her forearms were stained with blackberry juice and blood from the bush's thorns.

"You are dispatched from your duties for the day, O holy Annwyl of Wales. Now, it is well past the hour to begin celebrating Lughnasadh, and I will accept no more excuses."

She gave me a sidelong glance. "What did you do?"

"Have no fear, nothing horrid." I winked. "Come on, I know a fine place to go."

We trekked through the forest, stopping whenever Annwyl needed a rest or she noticed something pretty. Imps darted between the trees, and flower pixies sang into the breeze. They delighted at a glamour-touched human and sidhe traveling their forest, but I had to intervene when a spriggan offered Annwyl a beauty charm in exchange for ten years of memories. Annwyl was already beautiful, and besides, the bargain would make her forget who I was. After that small hindrance, I hurried her to the place I'd found one night when she fell asleep and I procrastinated returning home.

"Oh, how beautiful!" she said. The trees ended at a small ravine, surrounded by purple rocks and pink wildflowers. The creek above cascaded down a mass of stones to a clear, blue pool at the bottom. I helped Annwyl down the rocks and smiled as she pointed out all the little fish. Not the most fitting way to celebrate a fire festival, but I preferred it to burning humans alive.

"What a lovely place. When did you find it?"

"The spring, I think." I unlaced my boots and cast off my tunic and trousers, jumping into the pool in nothing but my braies.

When I resurfaced, Annwyl stood on the shore, fidgeting.

I flicked water at her. "What are you doing? Get in. I think we can swim behind the waterfall."

She shuffled her feet, glancing around the empty forest for humans that were not present. "No, thank you."

"Huh? Whyever not?" Annwyl and I went swimming quite often in the summer months, though this new location was far nicer than the murky creeks we usually frequented. "No faerie creatures are here to drown you, I promise."

"I know."

"Then what is the problem?"

She sighed, gesturing to my clothes on a sunny rock.

"And?" I asked.

"I have nothing to swim in."

Was she going mad? "Swim in your underthings, like you always do."

"Jaevidan, *I can't*."

"Is this about your quaff?" I asked. "It looks silly anyway. I like your hair."

"It is a *coif*, not a quaff. And I told you, I must wear it all the time now. And I certainly cannot undress before a . . ." She waved at me.

I frowned. "Prince? Fair folk?"

"No, you fopdoodle, a boy."

She was almost certainly going mad. "We swim all of the time, Annwyl."

"Yes, but that was before. I am a woman now."

I laughed. "No, you are not."

"Yes, I am."

"Annwyl." I leaned my arms on a nearby rock, pulling myself halfway from the water. "I can assure you, you are not a woman. You do not possess, you know, *women* things."

She scoffed. "I do."

"No, women have . . . curvy parts, and they are taller. And breasts. You certainly do not have those."

Her face turned bright red. "I have breasts."

"Annwyl, you look like a boy."

That was very much the wrong thing to say. "A boy? A *boy*?" she sputtered.

"I did not mean it like that," I rushed. "You know, I just meant . . . well, anyone can see you are very pretty and look nothing like a boy, but you are still little and all, so if you cut your hair and perhaps rubbed some dirt on your face—"

"I do not look like a boy," she spat. "And I will have you know my bleedings began, so according to the nuns, I *am* a woman, and that is why I must wear this silly coif and why I cannot undress and go swimming because if I do, I will either be damned to hell or never find a husband."

I blanched. "Bleeding? Where are you bleeding?"

She threw her hands up with a groan. "From my lady bits, Jaevidan. Women bleed from their lady bits every single month, usually until they die."

I was suddenly, inexplicably, *very* distressed by this. "But that is foul."

"It is not foul. It is to make babes."

I grimaced. "But . . . not all women, right?"

"Yes, all women. What is wrong with you?"

There were several late-night, private thoughts about girls I desperately needed to revise. "So . . . you bleed from your lady bits, and that means you have to cover your hair and cannot go swimming?"

"Yes."

"Why?"

"I don't know, because humans are stupid." She sighed and slumped onto a rock. "I have to be good, Jaevidan. If not, I shall never leave the convent."

"Of course you will." I left my rock and swam back to shore. "Is the lord not going to offer you work? And even if he does not, you are brilliant, Annwyl. You will find a way."

"That is not how life works, not for orphaned human girls."

"But—"

"You do not understand, Jaevidan. You are a prince. A faerie prince who lives in a big castle and studies with scholars and practices with swords all day. You have a family and a crown. I have nothing, and I will never have more than that. Lord Beynon is the only man who has ever been kind to me, and everything rests on making him happy." She reached up, brushing a tear off her cheek.

"Am I not kind to you?" I whispered.

"No, of course you are, but . . ." She sighed. "I only see you during the full moon. And sometimes not even that because you are important and have important things to do, and I am not."

"I think you are important. You are the most important person in the world to me."

She gave me a watery smile, nodding. After calming herself, she said, "Let us forget this. It hardly matters right now."

I frowned. "But you are not happy."

"I am." Realizing how unconvincing that sounded, she cleared her throat and nodded. "I am, truly. And I would like to not waste my birthday on tears."

The day was ruined, anyway. Annwyl never recovered from her poor mood, shuffling silently through the forest back to her village. Not even a hint of a smile when a sprite hid in the folds of her dress, chittering a happy tune as we walked.

By the time she delivered her blackberries and night descended, she said she was tired and would see me tomorrow.

Journeying back to the Veil, I wondered what had gone wrong. Was it because I said she looked like a boy? I had apologized and even said she was very pretty. But perhaps after intervening with the spriggan, she was unsure, and I only made her feel worse. Or maybe it was Lord Beynon, and she was anxious to deliver him his fruit.

Ugh, Lord Beynon. He was likely old and boring and smelled of piss.

Or maybe the nuns with all their silly rules. Or maybe . . .

I stopped. The Veil lay ahead, grass blowing in a cooling breeze. Maybe she was displeased with me. Not because I called her a boy—because I had been utterly useless.

Stop, that is your brothers speaking. But the thought had already formed. Annwyl wanted to leave the convent. She wanted a life without wondering where her next meal would come from. Where people cared about her. I should have been able to give her those things. I fed her when I could, but faerie food was dangerous, and without any magic ability, it was difficult to steal or acquire meals in this world. I should have been able to visit her more, but without any power, it was impossible for me to cross the Veil until it was at its thinnest. And as far as taking her from the convent . . . I had offered once to bring her home with me, but that was years ago. I was eight summers old and her a mere six. Maybe she had changed her mind since then, but I had too. I could not protect her in Ildathach. I could hardly protect myself in Ildathach. I had thrown myself into sword training—actually outpacing Donvidan in something for once—but without magic and constant vigilance, Annwyl would be as good as dead.

I shivered at what Donvidan and Kalvidan would do if they knew she existed. Nothing I cared about ever lasted long in their hands.

So, I was a complete and utter waste of breath. I knew it, Annwyl knew it, and my brothers knew it. It was no secret the moment our mother passed, I would be the first to die in the hunts.

My hands balled into fists. Why? Why did those wretched Bogorans need to make me a *lurgga*?

Sighing, I marched onward back to my own world.

The familiar heat of Faerie wrapped around me. This time of year, the meadow was overrun with thousands of pale white moonlilies, glowing beneath the full moon borrowed from the human world. I stomped to the edge of the Darkwood, slashing my palms before reaching the first of the thorns. I discovered the secret by the time I was nine—as long as you offered the dirt a steady stream of blood, the Darkwood would take you wherever you wished. If it felt extra generous that night, it would provide a shortcut.

It must have been eager to belch me out because I walked for mere minutes before finding myself at the low road. Torches roared on either side to honor the fire festival. Most travelers had already found their way to Gerenstad, but several stragglers joined me on the walk. I pulled my cloak low over my eyes, not wishing to be recognized.

The gates lay wide open on this side of the ravine, saving me the hour or so it took to sneak through the wards. Bonfires dotted the castle grounds, battling the spires in height. Any holiday that fell on a full moon was celebrated with excess, and today was no exception. Mother had employed phookas to glamour the Draith River so it appeared a molten path of fire. Decor to honor Lugh covered every inch of the bone bridge, railings doused in eternal faefire. The pound of drums and strings of lutes lifted over the roaring water below, and above my head, dancers performed like a living ceiling until one reached the castle. Between the raging fires and full moon, the polished castle walls glowed in yellow and red, a miniature sun in the dark mountainside.

By the time I reached the castle grounds, I had been offered everything from a tonic that would grant true love, to a wreath of flame posies to wear on my crown, to the offer to join an orgy atop the south turret. I numbly accepted the second gift and mumbled I was only thirteen summers to the first and third.

A great beast roasted over the nearest bonfire, and revelers performed a ritual dance around it. My feet itched to join, and my stomach grumbled ferociously, but my brothers would be out tonight and likely sought trouble. I forced myself to keep moving, maintaining my disguise even as I entered the palace. The first floor was open to celebrants, but everything above was business as usual. I revealed my identity long enough for a guard to let me past and snuck through the corridors until I reached my rooms.

The moment I arrived, I would barricade myself behind my door, then double- and triple-check all my wards were in place. If I managed a few hours' sleep now, I would awake around the time most of the festivities continued in private rooms. It would be safe to find something to eat, then catch a few more hours of rest before rising for sword practice in the morning.

My ingenious plan was thwarted before it could begin. Periwen's chiming laughter drifted through the parlor door. Where there was Periwen, there was Kalvidan. And where there was Kalvidan, there was Donvidan.

I backed away, praying they were too drunk to scent me. No such luck. Periwen threw the door open. "Little prince," she crooned.

As of this summer, I far exceeded her in height, but I still felt small as she tugged me inside. At least twenty faeries scattered the parlor, most in various states of undress. An eternal bonfire sat in the middle of the room, and hundreds of candles floated along the walls. Crystal decanters outnumbered the revelers three to one, and one of my brothers had stolen a musician for a private performance. Most notably of all, a naked human woman danced to the ballad, offering kisses to any faerie who gestured for her attention. Her glassy eyes landed on me, clouded and empty behind thick layers of glamour and compulsion.

Periwen slammed the door shut behind me.

"If it isn't the little runt!" Kalvidan called, nearly toppling off a divan writhing with bodies. "Why is it every time you sneak off on the full moon, you return smelling like shit?"

Periwen giggled, laying her hands on my shoulders. "I find him quite enticing, do you not?"

Gagging, I shimmied from her grip. "Goodnight."

"Where were you, runt?"

My blood froze at the icy voice. Donvidan lounged atop a circle of furs, brandishing one of his famous knives to pick at his nails. A hawthorn dryad was in the process of running her hands across his bare chest.

"Training," I lied. It was my usual excuse and the only one anyone bought for my newfound excellence in swords. How could I possibly be good at anything unless I was practically enslaved to it?

"Liar," Donvidan drawled, lips lifting in one corner. "Every sword you possess remains in your bedchamber."

My face heated. "You entered my room?"

Kalvidan leaned forward. "Is that a problem, little brother? Hiding something from us?"

I loosened a breath. "I train with the swords in the armory as to not ruin my own. And as I will return first thing in the morn, I am retiring for the night."

Donvidan threw his knife before I could take a step. It cut across my forehead, leaving a line of stinging blood before flying through the fire and burying in the far wall.

I gnashed my teeth at him. "Would you go fuck yourself?"

"Did he insult you?" Kalvidan lilted.

"Naughty words," Periwen scolded, wagging her finger.

Donvidan smiled. "I believe that was an insult." He glanced around the room. "What say you, my dear friends. Did the little runt just insult me?"

Cackling rose up with the flames. The naked human woman stilled, then joined in with barking laughter.

"How should I punish him?" Donvidan murmured. "Blades are becoming so redundant, do you not agree? Perhaps we shall flog him and hang him from the turret."

"I say, it has been far too long since the whelp had a good beating," Kalvidan said.

"Or," Donvidan continued, "in honor of our revered guest, we uphold the spirit of this day with fire."

The room went deathly quiet, all but the human woman still laughing.

"What say you?" Donvidan whispered.

I ran.

My footsteps pounded down the hall. Whoops and cheers sounded behind me, gleeful laughter as others joined the hunt. I pushed myself harder, faster than I ever had before, trying to remember every entry into the secret passageways my mind suddenly forgot.

I should have stayed in Wales. I should have begged Annwyl for forgiveness. On the fates, I was such an idiot.

Blood pounded in my ears. My breath came in ragged pants. I could hide easily at the armory; I just needed to make it there. Just one more flight of stairs, just three or four more halls—

Something struck me in the face.

I fell backward, air exploding from my lungs as I hit the stones. My vision darkened for several heartbeats, and then Donvidan's face swam into view.

"Where do you think you are running off to?"

I grunted and kicked out, but he was already on top of me. Kalvidan joined the fray and a dozen other gleeful strangers. They clawed at my clothes and ripped at my hair. Someone grabbed my ankles and pinned them to the ground. Claws and nails and fangs tore at my skin.

"Hold him still," Donvidan grunted. Kalvidan grabbed either side of my face. I screamed, trying to push them off, but the weight of my attackers was too great. Donvidan's eyes sparkled with gleeful wrath, and I knew whatever he had in mind would be especially painful.

I did not think. I wrenched a hand free and swiped for his hip, stealing a knife and slashing it through the air. My brothers dodged it easily, but I kicked between Donvidan's legs and slashed up at the same time. Red splattered my face and coated my tongue.

I stopped moving. Breathing. Stars danced in my vision, blood roaring in my ears. What—what had I done? But the moment ended when Donvidan growled, squeezing a hand around my throat. Air squeezed from my neck, and a wound dripped his blood onto my face. Straight across the forehead. A wicked sensation arose, delight we now matched.

"You shit," he hissed. "You little fucking shit."

Someone struck my face. Then again. The jaunty laughter transitioned to outraged cries, and their hands were everywhere. Tearing, ripping, destroying. I was bleeding. I was in pain. I could no longer see. These were the only things my mind could process, the only thoughts that flooded my brain. Blood. Pain. Darkness.

"Get me a torch," Donvidan snapped.

Blood. Pain. Darkness.

Stop, I wanted to say, but I could no longer feel my lips.

"Come here, runt."

Blood. Pain. Darkness.

"I hope this fucking hurts."

Stop.

Searing heat touched my arm. I was too cold, too numb to register it.

Stop. Please. I am sorry.

I will never do it again.

I will never do it again.

I will never—

Above me were Donvidan's dead, ice-chipped eyes. "Open your mouth, runt."

I shook my head.

He grabbed me by the chin, slamming my head against the floor. "*Do it.*"

I was going to die.

The thought should have scared me more. I should have been terrified. My frozen limbs should have thrashed and fought against the inevitable. Thirteen summers. Not very long at all, but each day felt like eternity to me. I would never earn the highest tier of sword training. I would never finish my lessons with Scholar Rindshaw or fight my brothers in the hunts. Never travel to farther kingdoms or bed a pretty girl. My life ended before it began, but strangely, there was peace with it.

Donvidan pried at my lips.

I would never see the sun rise.

Kalvidan clawed at my face.

I would never see my fourteenth summer.

Donvidan snatched my jaw, snapping the bone in two.

I would never see Annwyl again.

My heart stalled. Someone rammed three fingers between my teeth, slowly wrenching my lips apart.

Annwyl.

Annwyl with her gray dresses and dirty feet. Annwyl, who loved jugglers and clapped with delight at every jester we saw. Annwyl, who picked flowers for other orphans at the convent and gave compliments like she breathed air. Annwyl, who did not fear the fair folk but came to love them with my guidance. Who sang with the flower pixies and left milk for the brownies whenever she could. The girl who picked blackberries until she bled to please a crusty, old lord. Who held me close in a violent wind and swore she would love me. Annwyl, the fiercest and kindest and silliest person I knew. My best friend. The person I loved most.

Annwyl, who would wake up tomorrow and never know I was dead. Who would wait for me the next full moon, only for me to never return. Annwyl, who deserved all the world's love and kindness but would be abandoned once again.

Donvidan tore open my broken jaw. Blood filled my mouth. The faeries laughed and chittered and screamed. Fire filled my vision.

I braced for pain.

Instead, there was darkness.

Not from outside but within. It filled my chest, starting as a tiny seed and blooming out of control. Pleasure rippled down my veins, and ecstasy coated my nerves. It consumed me. It ate at the last vestiges of my flesh, and it was not until the screaming started that I realized what it was.

Power.

Burning flesh met my nose. Cries of horror and a circle of black expanding along the floor. Kalvidan leapt back, but Donvidan was still atop me, eyes wide with fear. *Fear.* How many times had he provoked that emotion in my own eyes? How many times had he delighted when I wore the expression he donned now? Pure, unadulterated exhilaration filled me, and before he could flee my fucking wrath, I reached up and grabbed his face.

The more horror I inflicted, the stronger I felt.

The more bodies fell around me, the more I felt alive.

And the more my brother screamed, the more I loved it.

In that moment, I understood my fate. Without a single shred of doubt.

I would bestow gifts upon Annwyl. I would prove to her I was more useful than not. I would steal all the love she felt for her lord, and I would do whatever I wished, whenever I wished, because I had every means to conquer the world now.

And no one—*no one*—would harm either of us ever again.

FOURTEEN
ADELINE

A FOGHORN BLEW IN the distance, and I damn neared jumped out of my skin. Salt perfused the air, and seabirds squawked overhead. Ahead, a harbor teeming with passenger liners and freighters swayed with gray-capped waves. And behind us, the port city of Dunkirk alongside a boardwalk. Under different circumstances, I would have adored the eccentric little city. The buildings were all painted a different color, windows and balconies trimmed with delicate craftsmanship like a row of dollhouses all smashed together. The docks teemed with sailors and workers, welcomed with open arms by the cafes and shops lining the streets.

On the bench beside me, Tommy didn't fare much better. The tincture Guinevere made to help his hearing had worn off within the day. He'd removed his aids for some reason and had spent the last half hour bouncing his knee at an erratic pace. He strode off briefly to purchase a pack of cigarettes. I'd never once seen him smoke.

Jack was busy swindling someone on the dock. Violet lingered for a few moments, grew bored, and strolled the boardwalk, then repeated the cycle. Lillian and Arthur had gone off to buy everyone fresh clothes.

I tapped Tommy on the shoulder until he faced my lips. "What's the matter with you?"

He shook his head, returning to a very intense study of the ground. Jack appeared a moment later.

"Fucking rip-off," he mumbled, lighting his own smoke. There was an awful lot of that happening the last few days. Both the ripping off and smoking.

"When do we leave?"

"We have about an hour." He gestured at Tommy. "What has him all riled up?"

"Nothing, I just—I don't think he likes France very much. Bad memories," I said.

Jack frowned but accepted it.

My theory was correct because Tommy calmed down the moment we left the harbor. I'd never been on a ship before and instantly lamented dry ground. The choppy waves shifted the deck beneath my feet, and my stomach rolled like the first time I used the shade.

Chilled autumn rain came down in thick sheets, forcing everyone inside from the upper decks. The first-class lounge teemed with people in fine clothes. Even with Lillian's mad-dash shopping spree, our ragtag group stood out like sore thumbs. Oriental rugs scattered across real wooden floors. Red and gold wallpaper glowed under crystal chandeliers, and brass moldings lined the walls. Plush chairs surrounded perfectly set tables, dripping with ivory cloths and china inlaid with gold embellishments. It all seemed solid enough, but at my clear unease, Tommy reminded me he'd been on ships dozens of times in his military days. Still, I was old enough to remember when a certain White Star liner sank some fifteen years ago, the news screaming from every front-page paper, even in our tiny mining town. While the others situated themselves around a table for refreshments, I hovered near the window, counting lifeboats along the deck.

Lillian kept herself busy planning our itinerary for the trip. With little else to do until our arrival, we were free to explore all the amenities offered. Many of the first-class areas had strict dress codes, so she'd be in charge of handling our glamour—both to appear human and avoid social *faux pas*—while Jack recovered from his iron illness. I tuned out her rigmarole of appropriate tennis attire and ideas for dining gowns, fingers brushing the diamond at my neck.

Jack noticed. He said we were safe here—even the sisters had limits to their reach and magic, and we had little to worry about while in the middle of the ocean. But I couldn't shake a steady undercurrent of trepidation. I still had more questions than answers, still had no solution to the Morrigan or the

Knights, and no idea what would happen to Tommy and me when we arrived back in the States.

Those thoughts followed me through dinner and back to what would be my sleeping quarters for the next six days. For the sake of propriety, Jack registered us all as married couples, one to each room—Arthur and Violet on the second deck, Tommy and Lillian down the hall, and Jack and me one floor below them. I assumed we would shift around as we saw fit, but Lillian made a fuss over what other passengers and crew would think if they saw different men entering "married" women's rooms. We just so happened to be traveling with several well-known business associates of Jack's, along with an actual duke from Belgium and a group of diplomats from the United States. Also, I was highly suspicious she wanted Jack and me to have the privacy to kiss and make up from what she dubbed our "little rift after the stress of the last few days." I didn't have the heart or energy to explain all that happened, or if I even should. Of course, I wanted to talk to Lillian, but not knowing how it would affect her opinion of either myself or Jack was a gamble I couldn't afford to make while we were on the lam.

Violet quickly gave up and dragged Arthur off to their suite. When Tommy realized she wasn't joking and he would actually need to spend the next week sharing a bed with the woman, his face and ears turned bright crimson. After stammering something about how ungentlemanly it would be, he asked if I would be fine alone and announced his intentions to sleep on the floor.

That left me alone. One of the businessmen requested Jack for cigars, and he felt obligated to heed the invitation. After delivering me to our room and proffering the extra key, he strode off in silence.

The bedroom was even finer than the lounge or dining areas. Mahogany furniture and gilded paintings had been bolstered to the cream and gold walls. A single bed took up the center of the room, complete with brocaded comforter, embroidered sheets, and pillows that sat like fluffy, white clouds atop a glamorous landscape. I sighed and removed my jewelry, then my dress before realizing what Lillian had procured me for nightclothes. If I thought her previous purchases were scandalous, this was from another world.

I held up the sheer, lace-trimmed negligee and scowled. A little note fluttered from its folds in Lillian's sweeping script. *Now kiss and make up*, it said, except "kiss" was a much cruder word.

I changed into the new day dress and crawled into bed. The ocean swelled with the day's storm, rocking me inside the buttery soft sheets. It was blissfully dark and quiet save for the rhythmic waves breaking along the side of the ship. It was safe here. The first sleep I'd get in nearly a week without the fear of waking with a hand around my throat. But each time I closed my eyes, I returned to Jack's memory. Felt the stinging blows to his face and the heat of fire licking up his skin. Then that power. That raw, relentless poison, how it ate away from the inside out and how viciously he revered the feeling.

The rain stopped sometime after midnight. I donned silk slippers.

The upper deck was quiet and dark. Everyone remained inside, either fast asleep or staving off the chill while they indulged their vices. The only human was a young crewmember, tying up deck lounges for the night. He asked if I needed anything and departed down a service stairwell.

I leaned against the railing. The thick layer of clouds dissipated into clusters of puffy gray. They drifted across a waning gibbous moon, plunging the deck in and out of total darkness. Without city lights, stars flickered in brilliant arrays across the vast, open sky. I could tell it was frigid with the relentless November breeze, but my new form reduced it to a chill.

I touched the diamond again. Before I could think, I tore the chain from my neck and dangled it over the railing. The moon reappeared, illuminating the churning black water dozens of feet below. But even as I ordered my fingers open, I didn't move.

I had seen enough. Or I had no appetite to see more, I wasn't sure. There were too many conflicting emotions to make sense of it all. Why did Estheria think those memories were vital for me to know? *Trust in Jaevidan*, she had said, but these visions were hardly convincing me to.

Instead, they terrified me.

I recognized some grace was required. These were not the memories of a man but a lonely, tortured child. A child who simultaneously adored a human girl while seeking to covet her all for himself. Who didn't understand her or what she needed. I couldn't expect much more from a thirteen-year-old's head, but there was still the rest to concede with. Not just his love for power but *pain*. The euphoria of death and destruction. And who could blame him—this frightened boy who'd known little besides cruelty? But Violet had been correct, once again. The sidhe did not feel like we did. They were not like us. They reveled in wickedness, glorified disaster and ruin. It may have been all Jack knew at the time, but had he really changed, or was he simply better at appearing human?

I wanted to say no, he hadn't changed at all. He still resorted to violence, still wore a vicious gleam in his eyes when the moment provoked it. He still acted without thought and mercy, and often.

But he'd saved Lillian and Will. He left Tommy alone—for the time being, at least—despite not trusting him. He was adored by Arthur, one of the gentlest and kindest souls I knew. And he liked attending the cinema, writing letters . . . brushing my hair back in bed and whispering how beautiful I was until morning.

He once told me hard times defined us, that our decisions in those moments showed us who we truly are. But I couldn't decide who Jack was.

Slowly, I brought my hand back from the rail. The answers were in the memories, even if I didn't wish to see them.

Clattering came from down the deck. I froze, cursing as another cloud blocked the little moonlight. The clank of chains and a large splash followed.

Did someone fall overboard? It was dark, and the deck remained slick with rain. Panic lit behind my ribs. Surely, one of the lookouts could see if someone had taken a plunge, but it was dark as the shade, and they were high up in their roosts. The deck was completely empty. I was the only one who would know if someone needed help.

Gripping the railing, I hurried down the deck and strained my eyes at the ocean below. While I could see much better in the dark now, it was impossible to tell if anything was down there. Should I call for someone? Maybe—

A thin, hissing sound drifted from the dark.

My hand shot to my thigh, but I'd forgotten to stash my dagger beneath this new dress. I thought it'd be safe. Jack said it was safe here. Stupid, stupid, stupid.

I stepped back, breathing easier when the moon reappeared. Whatever it was seemed to be gone, and then the chains rattled, and a hand appeared on the slick railing.

Bogorans be damned, someone really had gone overboard. I rushed forward, realizing my mistake too late. The hand was joined by a second one, belonging to a creature I'd never seen. Slime-coated, dark, webbed fingers rimmed with thin, pointed claws. Scales covered its forearms, glistening beneath the silver moon.

I stepped back, shaking as the creature threw itself onto the deck. Scaly legs ended in flippers that smacked the floor. Delicate fins flared on either side of its smooth, bald head, and depthless black eyes found me cowering on the deck. It smiled, or something close to it, displaying long rows of serrated teeth.

"Lady Fate," the creature hissed, dipping into a long, ceremonious bow.

My heart stuttered. I whipped my head around, trying to glean if there were more of them, but the creature came alone.

"Fear not," the faerie breathed. Its voice was odd, a high-pitched whisper from the back of its throat. "I only wish to impart a message on thee."

"Who are you?" I asked, deciding, *what are you* may have been impolite.

"They call me Grillow, patron messenger of the Undersea." He swept into another overzealous bow. "I come on behalf of my masters, an emissary of the tides. They wish to extend their greatest gratitude that a Lady of Fate has chosen to visit our waters."

Well, how . . . horrifying. I looked to the ocean with unease. "Your masters?"

"Yes, the great Queens Tarelus and Syruna of the Atlantic, themselves." It paused, as if waiting for applause.

These damn fae and their ridiculous pride. "Truly, the great and noble queens? What an honor."

Satisfied, Grillow's mouth stretched into another gruesome grin. "An honor it is. This ship was marked for offering, but upon realizing who this vessel carried, my great queens refused to sink her. They hope you find this sacrifice pleasing."

"Yes, yes, very pleasing," I stammered. "No—not pleasing. A better word is in order for this. I am truly overcome by their generosity."

"You flatter the Undersea, Lady Fate. And now for my message, on behalf of my masters. Ahem." They cleared their throat with a rasping cough. "It is with great triumph we receive the Maiden Fate to our mighty ocean. May the tides soothe her, may the salt grace her tongue, and may the waters guide her vessel to welcome harbors. With your sincerest respect, we ask of her a blessing and good fortune in the years to come. Blessed be."

What in god's fucking name . . . "Of course. They have my highest blessing."

"Oh, blessed fate. Oh, glorious one." Grillow fell to their knees, webbed hands stroking my feet. "How could we thank you?"

"No thanks needed," I murmured, gently stepping from its grip. "If that is all . . ."

"Oh, but one more thing." They rooted through a strange patch of flesh, a pouch outfitted to their sleek body, and produced a golden coin. "Please accept this offering, bestowed upon you from the coffers of the Whydah Gally herself."

Grillow's webbed hand trembled around the coin. I truly had no desire to accept it but feared slighting the queens would be much worse than whatever magic leeched from the gift.

"Thank you," I said, snatching the slime-coated coin before I could change my mind.

Footsteps hit the deck close behind.

Grillow bowed. "May our names flicker from your ferocious candle. Until we meet again."

"Wait! You know about the candle?"

Too late. The . . . whatever it was dove over the railing and fell back to the sea.

Jack emerged from the darkness, hands stuffed in his coat. He looked me up and down. "I thought I heard voices."

Too stunned to speak, I shrugged and resumed my position by the railing.

"I brought your coat."

I glanced sidelong at the offered clothing. "Thank you, but I'm fine."

"Yes, but it's November, and we're at sea. Human women should be chilled to the bone by now." Without waiting for permission, he dropped the coat over my shoulders. "You can't forget we have an image to uphold."

I gripped each side of the fabric, pulling it close over my neck. "Sorry, I'll be more careful."

He hovered beside me. Inevitably, I would need to speak to him. We had at least six more days on this blasted boat, not to mention the shared bedroom. Just like old times.

"Did you read the letter?" he asked.

"Marzipan," I murmured.

His lips lifted in the corner. "So, was it shit?"

No, and that was the worst part. As much as I wanted to be angry with him, as much as I wanted to condemn him, he made it so damn hard too.

"I loved it, and you knew I would. But I still—"

Need you. Hate you. Want you. Blame you.

"I don't trust you," I said. "And honestly, I don't know if I ever can."

"I told you about the vow—"

I shook my head. "It's not about the parallel bond. It's everything." All those hard decisions in impossible moments. The ones he chose.

The breeze grabbed our coats, and salt water splashed our faces. I had the vague notion something listened beneath the waves but doubted there was much to be done about it.

"Annwyl—"

"Annwyl is dead, Jack." He flinched but didn't respond. "I don't know how or when, but she's no longer here. I know you feel that I am the same little girl you met in Wales, but I'm not."

He bit his lower lip, rocking back on his heels. "Your differences are only flesh-deep," he said, sounding each word carefully. It was the vow mark—the one I'd supposedly asked him to take in another life.

"That's not true." The longer I spoke, the more I realized what else had been bothering me. "What you remember of me, Jack . . . those things aren't who I am. I wanted to feel something when we were in Paris, but there was nothing. No notion at all I ever knew that language or visited that place. Those pieces of me are either dead and gone or locked up so tight it doesn't matter. You told me our choices showed us who we truly are, but I remember none of mine or anything from those lives. Even your memories are from your perspective, not mine." I leveled with him. "My name is Adeline Ruth Colton. I was born in 1906 and grew up on a farm in Georgia. I have one brother and dance ballet. I've had nearly twenty-one years of choices to make me who I am, and none of those could possibly be the same as Annwyl's or a duchess's or anyone else."

He nodded, refusing to look at me. "I understand."

"I'm sorry," I whispered. "I know this isn't what you wanted, but I just started figuring out who I am. I just started making my own decisions and finding my own voice, and I'm grateful to you and all our friends for showing me I could, but I can't be something that I'm not for you. You deserve someone to build new memories with, and so do I."

His voice drifted into the darkness, low and sad. "That's not true."

"You can't say—"

"This is exactly what I wanted," he said. "All I ever wanted was for you to be happy. To have the opportunity to live the life you never got to. I promise."

Somehow, I knew the life he spoke of wasn't this one.

"What happened to her? To Annwyl?"

"It doesn't matter. Like you said, it's all in the past. My past," he added. "So live whatever life you want, Addie. It's yours now to keep forever."

"Even if you're not in it?"

He gave me a sad smile. "Whatever she wants."

"Our bargain . . ." I started.

"Completed," he said. "You helped me find the Morrigan and were brought to the Guild. Magically speaking, we no longer owe each other anything."

So, that was it. He set me free.

I didn't understand him, but maybe that wasn't bad. I'd spent the past few days cycling through facts and information, placing things into neat little boxes of good and bad. Yes or no. Trustworthy or not. But I had his memories now and the truth. At least some of it.

"Babd and Nemain still live," I said slowly. "And with Violet, we still form a Morrigan. The Guild is gone, and besides, I didn't become a druid. I became this."

He nodded, hopefulness weaving through his expression.

"I want to rid the world of them, Jack. I want the same thing as you, for humans to be safe. And there is so much I still don't know, especially about myself. I started this with you, so let's end it that way too. But maybe as friends this time."

"I can live with that," he said.

But I wanted to be firm. I wanted to be sure he understood. "I mean that, Jack. No more secrets and lies, no more scheming behind my back. We don't have the unfulfilled parallel anymore, so there's nothing pushing for . . . more all the time. I'm not your girlfriend or your wife, but I'd like to try being your partner. But only if you can make those promises to me."

He lifted a brow. "You want another vow mark?"

"No vow marks. I—I just need your word. And for you to uphold your word without the threat of magic or espionage or anything else. If you truly want to rebuild that fragile trust with me, this is how you start."

He grinned, throwing an arm around my shoulders. It felt *right* in a way I couldn't explain. "You always have the highest expectations of me, don't you?"

"Only because a small, foolishly hopeful part of me believes you might fulfill them."

"Maybe so, but I'll do everything I can. I swear it. Though for right now, we should probably get some rest. I've been forewarned we have a long day of aquatic aerobics and tea parties tomorrow."

After days of endless turmoil, I knew I'd made the right decision. The past was the past, and the future was bleak, but so many of my best moments were at Jack's side. There was so much I needed to learn about myself and him, but I didn't need to give him up completely to do that. I could have both. I still didn't trust him, I didn't forgive him, and part of me was terrified of what lay beneath his skin. But for now, this was good enough.

So, we returned to our bedroom, and like a gentleman, Jack took the floor. The next day, we woke up bleary-eyed and joined a neurotic Lillian as she made friends with the entire lounge. The days passed slowly, then a little too fast when I began to think of it as a little vacation. A break from the ruin we left behind in Paris and all the chaos waiting ahead in New York.

I should have known better.

A twinge of disappointment arose as we pulled into New York Harbor. The Statue of Liberty glistened beneath the low autumn sun, and passengers spoke with fevered excitement around us. The moment we departed, it would be straight back to the hotel. Will needed to be relieved of his interim duties, and there was so much to do. The bootlegging business needed to resume, people needed to be interrogated, and a plan needed to be made to hide Tommy from the Knights and a new one made for fighting the sisters.

We packed our few possessions and joined the others in the lobby. The ship jolted as it docked, crewmembers running back and forth before allowing passengers to disembark. Jack stepped forward with our things, but the captain hurried down the stairs, calling after us.

"Mr. Warren! Just a moment, please."

Jack frowned. Tommy and Lillian had already gone ahead. Violet and Arthur hung back, mixing into the crowd to keep an eye on the spectacle.

"How can I help you?"

"Sorry, just a moment." The captain grinned, but it strained in the corners. "I was reviewing your papers, and—well, there was . . ."

Jack sighed. Deeply. "Out with it, man."

"Apologies. I only need a moment of your time." He reached inside his uniform, smiling at me. "And who is this?"

"One of your passengers. What was the problem again?" He signaled behind his back to Violet and Arthur, urging them to move on.

"Right, your papers. I just wanted to confirm a thing or two." He blathered on about a discrepancy that made no sense at all. Jack argued back while the ship cleared around us. Within moments, we were the only passengers left.

Sweat lined the captain's brow. "Ah, I see now. My mistake, Mr. Warren. I hope you enjoyed your trip."

"Sure." He grabbed my arm, and we left for the exit. "What was that about?" I asked.

"Nothing. Lad's getting too old for this job."

The moment we stepped on the gangway, I realized the issue.

Six cops waited on the dock, guns pointed in our direction. "Hands in the air!"

Jack side-eyed me, then slowly lifted his arms above his head. "Gentlemen, can I ask what this about?"

Two rushed forward and clapped him in handcuffs. From the dock, the captain said, "Jack Warren, you are under arrest for escape of lawful custody, obstruction of justice, and murder."

PART FIVE

JUDGEMENT

FIFTEEN

ADELINE

"ALL YOU HAVE TO do is go inside and show your face. It's impossible to fuck up, even for you."

Violet and I stood on the sidewalk while she finished her cigarette. Behind me was the police precinct for midtown Manhattan. After a flurry of frantic calls and a quick introduction to Jack and Violet's private lawyer—Mr. Theodore King, a human and, honestly, sort of a prick—I was washed, dressed, and sent here to "stand silent and look pretty." Instructions directly from the desk of Mr. King.

"Why the hell did he break out of prison?" I hissed, leaning close so none of the swarming officers could hear.

"He didn't *break out* of prison. It was jail. Enormous difference. And some circumstances led to the building setting on fire, so he used the opportune moment to leave." She blew a cloud of smoke in my face. "And as far as you know, which is *nothing*, you had spent that day shopping, returned to your apartment to pack for your trip, and boarded a liner for France."

"What if they ask for the ticket?"

"You act like we can't make shit appear from thin air." She threw her cigarette to the sidewalk and looped her arm through mine. "And stop fidgeting. It makes you look like a dunce."

I glared at her, then plastered a smile on my face as we entered the building. "Name?" a prehistoric secretary asked.

"Ms. Adeline Ruth Colton. I'm here for Jack Warren."

She glanced up, eyes narrowed over wire glasses. "Excuse me a moment."

I shot a look back at Violet, who returned her own that said something close to *do as you're told or I will kill you slowly*.

I mimed zipping my mouth closed and tossing the key.

The secretary returned and led me into the back. We passed several blocks of cells and officers who looked me up and down a little too slowly. Lillian had gone a tad overboard on making me presentable. We passed through another door, meeting with roiling cigar smoke and boisterous laughter.

"You're kidding," someone said, roaring with laughter.

Jack's voice. "Couldn't have made it up if I wanted to."

When we arrived at the offending sound, three cops lounged in wooden chairs, forming a semicircle around a cell. The prince of prohibition himself sat in that cell, leaning forward on his knees with his arms hanging out of the bars, a cigar dangling from his fingertips.

I swore this man was the fucking devil.

"Ah, there you are, darling." They all glanced up, mildly surprised at someone's arrival. Compulsion, obviously. Just a little to get them comfortable around Jack.

I gave them my demure Southern smile. "As you can see, I'm alive and well."

"I certainly can, ma'am," the youngest of the three said, too appreciatively for the moment. Behind them, Jack's eye twitched.

An older officer stood and held out his hand. "Officer Addams, and I'm sorry to ask this, but we need some confirmation."

"It's a pleasure. Adeline Colton." I held out a handful of papers from my pocketbook. "You will find my birth certificate and a news clipping of me and Mr. Warren in there."

The birth certificate was fake, as last I knew, Babd and Nemain had acquired my real one. The newspaper clipping wasn't though. It contained the picture of Jack and me at the ballet several months ago. The same paper Tommy recognized me in.

"As I said, alive and well."

Officer Addams donned a pair of reading spectacles and scanned the evidence of my existence. Satisfied, he laughed. "Well, I think we can say with certainty Mr. Warren didn't murder you."

Jack grinned in the background. "I am afraid I don't have the taste for it."

I shot him a look, then implored the officer. "Does that mean we can put this nasty business behind us? I don't know how this FBI fellow got such a ludicrous idea in his head anyway."

Violet informed me of the situation on the way over. The Knights raided the hotel the same day I ended up in Babd's clutches. They didn't find any booze—courtesy of lofty contingency plans Jack had in place—but needed an excuse to hold Jack in custody. Since I was officially missing, the excuse was me. My supposed murder, according to court documents produced by Agent Rodney. The real one.

The prison break was another story, but I was sure Jack had a plan for that.

"Since there was no murder and no contraband, I can say Mr. Warren was not legally detained. Even still, the courts may take issue with him leaving the jail. Especially since he was out of the country for several days."

If this spooked Jack, he didn't show it. I was already sweating, wondering how he would explain a round-trip voyage to France in less than a week. I highly doubted the local courts knew about druid channels and shading.

"If he didn't commit any crimes, then I don't understand—"

"Darling, don't worry yourself too much. These fine men are just doing their job, but this will all be cleared up soon." Jack winked, but there was a raw edge behind it.

According to Violet, the Knights were leaving for Chicago this afternoon. Agent Rodney wanted to process this case himself. Somehow, he had survived the prison fire and, surely, Jack's unchecked rage. I'd faced them before but still held tight to all the warnings I received of them. Those that fell into the Knights' custody never made it out.

The young officer piped up. "We're taking fine care of him in the meantime. No need to worry yourself, sweetheart."

Sure. When Tommy was a prisoner of war, the Germans had taken *fine care* of him too.

I gestured for Officer Addams to lean in, feigning great importance. Jack shot me a questioning glance, but I signaled through the bond to let me have this one.

"Look, I need to be honest."

Officer Addams looked to the other two cops, no longer in a humorous mood. "Go on."

"I'm sorry, it's just so . . ." I fluttered my hands in the air with a shaky laugh. "You see, what really happened was this. I'm sure you know by now Mr. Warren and I are sweethearts."

He blinked. "I was made aware."

"And he had this whole lovely trip planned because . . ." I leaned in, lowering my voice. "You see, he was planning on giving me a ring."

The officer nodded. "I see."

"And I will tell you, all of this stuff going on at the hotel? I had no darn clue about. I was at home with my brother, packing my things for our trip. And you know what else? They didn't even allow Mr. Warren a phone call because I assure you it would have gone to me. But I boarded that boat all by myself, and the moment we set off, I was convinced I'd been stood up. Can you imagine that? Hopping on a ship to France with no money, no man, and no way home?"

He raised his brows. "I can't say, ma'am."

"I felt like—well, excuse my language, but I felt like a damn fool." I pinched myself until tears sprang to my eyes. Behind the officers, Jack grinned. "Of course, Mr. Warren knew all of this. He also knew he didn't commit any crimes, so when the jailhouse burned down, he did what any concerned gentleman would do—left right away to find my sorry behind. Paid half a fortune for a private charter to get him over there as fast as possible. I was so relieved, but the moment he explained what happened, I knew he was in a world of trouble. We scrapped the whole trip and got the first ticket we could home. I thought we could just explain the mishap, but then all these men with guns appeared at the docks and . . ." I let a fresh tear roll down my cheek. Distressed, Officer Addams scrambled for a handkerchief. Jack silently laughed in the background.

"Oh, thank you." I dabbed at my eyes, smiling like a silly girl. "I'm sorry for this. It's all just been so stressful. But the whole way back, Jack kept saying he would clear this whole thing up with the police, no more than a few hours, then book us dinner at the Waldorf Astoria to make it up to me. I agree it was terribly foolish of him, but you can't really fault a man in love, can you? And the story ain't about to change when that ridiculous FBI man gets here. I mean, he thought I was murdered, for the lord's sake. I was in France!"

Officer Addams nodded. "I understand, ma'am, but—"

"And I forgot to mention this, but my brother, Thomas Colton—he's a war hero, actually, served in the 77th against the Krauts—he's in the FBI himself, the same unit that arrested Mr. Warren. He knows this whole story and would be more than happy to come down right now and sign off on the paperwork. Why waste the other agent's time, traveling all the way in from Chicago, when Agent Colton is right up the street?"

Officer Addams shifted. "Well—"

"The happiest day in any god-fearing woman's life was ruined for me." I let a fresh round of tears fall. "You seem like a fine, upstanding gentleman. You wouldn't want to be the one responsible for ruining it twice, would you?"

"REMIND ME WHY I pay a lawyer again?" Jack retrieved his belongings from the secretary, shooting her a smile that turned her red. I tugged him down the stairs.

"Beats me, but let's get the hell out of here before someone changes their mind."

Jack looped his arm through mine. The blinding sun shot down from above, stretching our shadows across the sidewalk. Violet had already left for the hotel, where we would meet everyone else. As soon as we got back, Tommy and Jack would make a brisk return to fill out the promised paperwork, then get out before any unsavory characters arrived.

Someone approached before we took two steps. The man was tall with stringy hair, his thin frame swimming in a tweed suit. A camera hung around his neck, and a notepad stuck out from his front pocket.

He double looked when he spotted Jack. "Mr. Warren, having a nice afternoon?"

"Swell," Jack said, pushing past him.

"What brings you to the police station?"

"Nothing. It was a misunderstanding that is now resolved." Jack pulled me forward, but a voice called out our names.

Officer Addams ran down the steps, waving paper in the air. "Mr. Warren, Ms. Colton. So sorry to bother you, but we need one last thing signed before you head off."

Jack sighed and met the officer halfway. The reporter turned on me. "A misunderstanding?"

"Just as Mr. Warren said."

"In your opinion, does Mr. Warren frequently have 'misunderstandings'?"

"No."

Jack glanced at the sheet without reading it.

"Interesting that a young lady such as yourself would take the trip down here with him."

I pressed my lips together. Jack jogged back to my side, shooting an annoyed look at the reporter. Officer Addams waved from the stairs. "Thank you. I hope you enjoy your evening, and let me be the first to say congratulations. You two make a fine pairing."

I cringed. The reporter vibrated with glee. "Congratulations? Are those wedding bells ringing in the distance?"

"No comment," Jack murmured.

"Why don't I get a photo of the happy couple?"

"Don't you—" Too late. Jack was halfway turned when a lightbulb shattered, a tendril of smoke rising from the camera.

"Great shot!" the reporter said.

"Get back—"

He took off, scribbling notes as he practically skipped down the street.

"Should we go after him?" I asked.

Jack shook his head. "I'll have Violet handle it later. We have more pressing matters at the moment."

I couldn't disagree, but unease swept through me. Not even a week after Jack and I agreed to be friends, I didn't need the announcement of our engagement making front-page news. An engagement that didn't exist.

We found a quiet alley and shaded to the hotel.

The study was just as I remembered it. Stones lay beneath an ancient carpet, and flora crowded every open space. The fire I'd come to be so familiar with crackled in its hearth, and the vines slithered protectively over the bookshelves. I inhaled a deep breath, savoring the comfort of my home these last months. We hadn't broached the subject of whether I would continue to live here yet. The Abstruse still existed if I needed it, but I'd all but moved from that room completely. Before everything changed, I spent every night sharing a bed with Jack.

The study was empty, all but for Violet lounging on a chaise with Harold.

"Where is everyone?" Jack asked.

"Congrats, you didn't fuck it up," Violet drawled, waving her hand in my direction. "Lillian went with Arthur to retrieve something from his apartment. Will is at home until we request him."

"And Tommy?" I asked.

She shrugged.

Jack closed his eyes, breathing deeply. "Please tell me he is with Lillian and Arthur."

Last I knew, he had remained with Lillian after she fixed me up at her apartment and sent me off with Violet for the jail. He wasn't supposed to leave any of the faeries' sides. "Maybe he went to visit Will," I said.

"Perhaps." But Jack sounded less than assured.

"I'll check with Lillian and Arthur. You check with Will."

"Addie, you shouldn't go off alone—"

I was in the shade before he finished that sentence. Arthur jumped at my arrival in his haphazard living room. Lillian lay across a table, dangling a cherry in front of her face. "Have either of you seen my brother?"

Arthur opened his mouth, but Lillian cut in. "He said he would wait for you at the precinct."

I reminded myself how much I adored Lillian and how awful I would be if I hurt her feelings. "And you let him go alone?"

"He insisted, and it's not like Babd and Nemain are after him."

That was highly debatable, and I didn't have time. "Let me know if you hear anything."

I checked the police station next, but no one had seen or heard from Agent Colton. Next was Will's; neither he nor Jack were there. Back in the study, Violet dully told me no one had returned yet.

Goddammit.

I tore at my hair, brainstorming anywhere reasonable he might be. Somewhere that wasn't a Knights of Templar cell or the bottom of the Hudson River.

As a last-ditch effort, I tried our old apartment.

It had been cleared out weeks ago, but it was right across the hall from Lillian, and maybe he'd left something behind. Relief coursed through me as I arrived through the powder room mirror. Tommy's scent drifted from his old bedroom.

Inside, he tore up the floorboards. He startled, calming when he realized it was me. "Good, you made it. We don't have much time."

I gaped. "What the hell are you talking about? And why are you here? Did I not say to stay with Lillian or Violet?"

He ignored me, sweat dripping off his face as he peeled up another plank. "It should still be here."

"What should still be here?"

"This," he said, pulling a sack from beneath the floor. Inside were two handguns, five hundred dollars, and three small cases of iron bullets.

"Really, Tommy?" I snapped. "We have plenty of guns and plenty of money. It's not worth you risking your neck out here alone."

"No, Jack Warren has plenty of guns and plenty of money." He donned shoulder straps and inserted the firearms, throwing his coat on. He held the cash between his teeth, mumbling, "They have a train leaving in fifteen minutes. If you can do your moving magic, we can make it."

"It's called shading, and what train?" Silence. I spun him to face me. "What has gotten into you?"

"We're getting out of here."

I stared at him. "Since when? Why?"

He stared back. Slowly, like I had missed something vital, he said, "I know you're not going to like this plan, but I have a way to keep you safe from everyone. You're right. We can't outrun those Morrigan women forever, and I think it's clear Jack won't stop either. So we're going to Chicago and waiting this all out."

"Waiting this all out? Waiting *what* out?"

"The sisters, Jack, all of it. The rest will be easy after that."

"Tommy, I have no idea what the hell you're talking about."

He placed both hands on my shoulders, like I was a child again and he was preparing to impart some great wisdom on me. "The Knights don't know I worked against them. That night was all an illusion by those fae, so as far as the Knights are concerned, I'm still one of their agents. Neither do they know what you are. No one has ever seen you face-to-face. A single, grainy photograph from the papers isn't enough to tell you've been changed. I know this is risky, but we saw how powerful those sisters were in the Guild. All those other magical creatures and even Jack Warren himself couldn't fight them off. But the Knights can, Addie. They've been doing it for centuries. As long as you conceal what you are and I keep up this charade a little longer, they'll protect you. Even better, they'll go hunting for those sisters and take down Jack in the meantime. Two birds, one stone. Once the outside is safe, we can make a run for it again."

Blood roared past my ears. "That's insanity."

"The way I see it, we don't have too many other options. We can't outrun or outfight the sisters, Jack, and the Knights at the same time. Something needs to be eliminated."

"I already handled that. Jack and I are on the same page now. He's not a threat."

"Jack is a lunatic from another world. How long do you think it is before he's unsatisfied with whatever bullshit you said to stave him off? And if he's already gotten into your head, that's more than enough reason to get you away from him now."

Crimson climbed my throat. "Gotten in my head? What does *that* mean?"

"I ain't calling you stupid, Ads. I'm talking about that bond thing y'all two have."

I waved my hand. "Forget about the bond. It's been settled."

"Sure it is," he murmured, backing me toward the door. "That would be exactly why you were so afraid of him before the Guild, then a few days together and suddenly it's all hunky-dory again."

I blocked his shepherding into the living room with two hands on the doorway. "I told you, we worked it out. And I'm not sure how this brilliant plan of yours would capture him anyway. It's not like the Knights have managed to hold him before."

"He ain't getting out in some freak prison fire this time, alright? The Knights got something else to take him off the cop's hands, then it's straight to Chicago for him. He won't be a problem anymore." He tried shoving past me, but I pushed him back.

"Tommy, what the fuck are you talking about?"

He ran his hands through his hair. "We don't got time for this."

"Tommy," I whispered, heat pouring from each syllable. "What did you do?"

"I took care of things. Just like I always do," he said. "There was a telegraph office in Dunkirk. I got a message off while you were sitting on the boardwalk so everything would be arranged before we arrived in the States. And now they are, so let's go."

I closed my eyes, counted to ten, and released a breath. "Thomas Colton, are you telling me that you contacted your old agency from France? That we were escorted off the boat at gunpoint on order of the Knights of Templar?"

His voice softened. "I know you don't like it, but I swear this is the best way to keep you out of harm's way. I can play along with them for a little longer while all else gets resolved, and they have no way of knowing what you are. I would have told you sooner, but I couldn't get you alone. I'm sorry this is all jarring right now, but we have a train to catch."

He pushed past me. I turned but realized too late. The scent hit me all at once, all-consuming. Rain and oleander.

Jack leaned against the wall, eyes flashing beneath his flatcap, hands stuffed in his coat pockets.

My voice came in warbling squeaks. "Jack . . ."

He sauntered forward and grabbed Tommy by the throat. "Don't worry, darling. I only want to chat."

They shaded from sight.

SIXTEEN

ADELINE

I GRABBED JACK'S ARM in the nick of time.

The shade rippled around us, dark and unforgiving. I'd never tried this before, tagging along for a trip I wasn't welcome to. There was no way to know where we were going. And from what I had been told, whoever entered the shade determined the location.

My fingers slid through the icy mist, but it no longer felt dangerously cold, like the liquid darkness invaded every space of my lungs. I thought of the study—the crepitus fire and slithering vines. All three of us landed there.

I hit the floor with a grunt, stars bordering my vision. Jack spent a moment gaping at me with deep confusion, and then my brother punched him in the face.

"*Tommy.*" The scolding was useless. Jack threw him to the ground and swung his own punch or three or ten.

Violet slowly set her book down, grinning.

Jack pulled him up by the shirt, snarling. "I knew you were still a fucking Knight."

Another round of swinging. "Stop it!" I fisted Jack's coat. "Stop it, he's fucking human, Jack!"

Tommy dodged a blow before taking one directly to the chin. "I ain't with the Knights. I'm with Addie."

Jack rattled him against the floor. "So you'll give her to people who want her dead?"

Lillian appeared with Arthur, the latter stumbling against the bookcases with the bloodthirsty scene. Lillian rushed forward. "Jack, on the fucking fates, what are you doing?"

Violet scowled. "Don't interrupt. We were just getting to the good part."

Tommy swung but missed by a mile. "I'm trying to save her."

Jack, "You'll get her killed."

"She has a better chance with them than she does with you!"

I tugged Tommy's arm while Lillian pulled at Jack. More violence, more blood splattering the floor, and Lillian was thrown against the desk. I clawed Jack's shoulders, begging him to stop.

Jack hit him. "Unlike you—" Jab. "—I'm not—" Jab. "with—" Jab. "—the fucking enemy."

Lillian paused. "What is he talking about?"

"I think Thomas here contacted the Knights," Arthur stuttered.

"Jack, stop," I screamed. "Fucking stop it, you'll kill him!"

"You enslaved her with the parallel bond," Tommy screeched. Blood ran from his nose and poured between his teeth.

Lillian paled. "Enslaved?"

"How many times has she died with you? How many times have you brought her back just to do it again?"

Arthur stepped forward. "Wait, he's not implying—"

"Stop it!" I wrenched Jack by the hair, but it was no use.

"The parallel bond—" Lillian started.

Arthur, "But reincarnation is not—"

"Just kick him in the prick," Violet said.

"*Stop it!*"

The room froze, painfully still and silent. Magic crackled the air, gathering like lightning in roiling clouds. Energy filled my chest, my limbs, floating me off the ground. A moment passed in this otherworldly state, the space between tranquility and violence. Then came the chaos.

Books flew off the shelves. The potted plants shredded, the vines flattening themselves against the floor. Chairs and loungers hit their sides, papers and petals whirling through the air. Thunder ricocheted through the room, and sunlight streamed across the floor where an entire wall had been blasted onto the street.

I collapsed to the ground. Someone groaned, and Lillian asked if anyone was harmed. Then, a seventh voice joined the fray, quiet and disbelieving.

Will stood in the foyer, gaping at the study doors hanging from their hinges. "You may all return to France now."

HUMANS SWARMED THE LOBBY, a sea of police and scribbling reporters. Flash powder and the thrum of chattering voices tinged the air. I pulled my shawl tighter around my shoulders, nibbling on my thumbnail.

The blast hadn't harmed anyone in the hotel or on the street, thank the stars, but had broken windows of adjacent buildings and scared the bejeezus out of everyone. Police cars blared outside within minutes, mixing into panicked voices and curious pedestrians. All our human guests had been evacuated while a bomb team uselessly swept each floor.

It was truly the crowning stroke of this marvelous day. After assuring everyone was alive and would remain that way, Jack and Violet went downstairs to deal with the police. Lillian was ordered to put Tommy somewhere *safe*. When I asked her to let me take him, she shook her head and said we would speak later. Arthur and Will did damage control with the frightened guests, and I had been told to wait for instruction.

Reporters approached me, but one side glare from Jack and they backed away. The police officers weren't as easily swayed. After the fifth one asked for "my version of the story," I feigned a headache and claimed amnesia.

Jack breezed through his performance. People swarmed him like flies to honey, utterly consumed by his narrative. "Not to make any heavy accusations," he said, "but after the jailhouse fire and my false charges, this does not strike me as a coincidence." They ate up the sordid tale like a final meal before the chair.

The chief of police himself offered a protection detail, but Jack declined on account of not wanting to frighten anyone nor take up any more of the department's time. When he asked if Jack had any suspicions of who would plant a bomb, he waved the police chief to a private corner and spoke in low whispers.

I edged closer.

"I think it is clear someone with great influence over that department set this up," Jack murmured.

"The FBI is a federal branch, Mr. Warren. You're accusing the United States government."

"I have it on good authority money has exchanged hands between Agent Rodney and a group in Chicago." If possible, his voice lowered more. "They've had it out for me for years. Convinced I'm cornering the New York market."

The police chief narrowed his stare. "I'm unsure what market you speak of, Mr. Warren."

Jack wore an empty smile. "Will you remember if I raise your cut to fifteen percent?"

I tuned out the rest, pleading some moral fifth. When all was said and done, Jack appeared somewhat pleased I blew up his hotel. The feeling was not mutual.

He appeared beside me, turning us away from lingering eyes. "Go over to the police chief, thank him for his diligence in solving this case, and say we would love to have him and his wife spend a night here, on the house."

I glared at him. "Where's my brother?"

He glared back. "Lillian will be keeping an eye on him. Offer to have tea with his wife while you're at it."

"I'm not your fucking dancing monkey, Jack. I want to speak with Tommy."

"No."

My teeth ground together. "You can't do this."

"I can," he whispered, leaning close. "Since I already told him he could speak to you after he indulged me. So far, he hasn't taken the offer."

Vitriol hissed past my teeth. "Probably because you beat him within an inch of his life."

"He should consider himself lucky I didn't kill him."

Steadying my pulse, I lowered my voice. "He ain't with them. I agree with you, what he did was foolish beyond reason, but he's not a traitor. He did what he thought was best for me, and it ain't like you haven't made some spectacularly awful choices for the same reason."

"This is not just about you. It is about me, and Lillian, and Violet, and Will, and Arthur, and every other that depends on me and all of this for protection." He waved his hand around our heads, distinguishing the *all of this*. "That little stunt would have cost a whole lot more than your life, which is more than enough for me to throw him off the Brooklyn Bridge without losing sleep. But out of respect for you, I will be keeping him *contained* until I deduce how to keep him silent without wringing his neck. Can we agree on that?"

When Jack was angry and wrong, it infuriated me. When Jack was angry and right, it made me damn near irate. I'd blame the bond, but I think he had a special way of getting beneath my skin. "Fine."

"Fine?"

I scowled. "Yes, darling. You may go finish playing puppeteer now."

He wanted to say more but, thank the Bogorans, bit his tongue for once. It was astounding how talented we were at making one another insane. How we were ever married was the eighth wonder of the world.

Several hours later, the bomb team declared the building clear. Despite the true source of the blast, I was honestly surprised they found nothing at all. The profit loss nearly made me vomit, but Jack glanced at the number Will proffered without so much as a twitch, then did his last rounds with the guests and police while I made my way upstairs. The destroyed wall had been covered with sheets until builders arrived to repair it.

The study was empty. With Lillian off wherever with Tommy for the night and the hotel handled, everyone else returned home for some well-deserved rest. My reunion with Will had been short and solemn—disheartening because I truly had missed him, but he promised we would meet for dinner in the kitchens soon. I worried about Arthur spending the night alone in his apartment, but Violet said he wanted solitude.

Aching loneliness swept through me.

It was alarming how quickly the Band of Banished became more than a circle of friends. I wanted to gossip with Lillian, hear stories from Arthur, trade quips with Violet, and torture Charlene with Will. Mostly, I wanted Jack. The version of him that didn't exist.

The study held memories. Too many of them. Moments and stories from what seemed like a lifetime etched into the walls and rippling across the air. The day I met this dysfunctional little family of mine. Where I discovered what I was for the first time.

Other less welcome ones too. Jack reading the paper across from me at breakfast. Jack delivering me flowers in the Abstruse. Jack undressing me on the carpet and painting runes across my skin. Jack kissing the hollow of my throat, sinking between my legs in the darkness of his bedroom.

But whether I liked it or not, those memories were mine, moments of *this* life. Addie's life. They were wounds, and like any other, the more I neglected them, the worse they would fester. The more I would be tempted to stave off the stress and anger and loneliness in ways that only served to hurt me. Starving myself had done no good, and neither had running away. Leaning on Jack wasn't an option anymore, leaving only one solution to move forward—cleaning the debris and bandaging the damn things myself.

I started with his room, returning my belongings to what remained of the Abstruse. His scent clung to every corner, strongest in the rumpled bedsheets. The last time he slept in that bed, I lay beside him.

Jack appeared while I dug for my shoes. His eyes followed my movements, face made of stone. "What are you doing?"

"Returning to the Abstruse."

If he was surprised or upset or felt any emotion at all, I couldn't say. "Stay here."

"We agreed to be friends, Jack. I won't share a bed with you."

"Then I can sleep on the floor."

"I won't make you sleep on the floor, that's absurd."

"The Abstruse is not structurally sound at the moment. That aside, it's safer if we are together. The Knights are on high alert, the sisters lurk, and while this place is warded to hell, the Guild was too."

That was a shockingly pragmatic point. My subconscious itched to agree, already deciding he was right and there were certainly no ulterior motives and we were two adults capable of sharing a room without crossing a line. We'd already done it for an entire week on the ship. But that room never belonged to us. Memories didn't cling to the bedsheets. Or floors. Or walls.

"I can sleep in the study," I said.

"Could we make things simple for once?"

If only, but simple wasn't a word in our vocabulary. Never mind the past looming over us; the future was grim enough. We still didn't know what my transformation meant, but I doubted it was anything good. One moment of me losing control and I damn near killed everyone in the study. It was a slim stroke of luck no one was on the street.

Jack had once helped me find my voice. Ironically, it was actions that now took it away.

I exhaled. "I'm not trying to start an argument. This isn't passive aggression and will go much faster if you help."

"Believe me, Annwyl, if there is anything I know about you, it's that you are more than happy to speak your mind."

Ignoring that little slippage of name, I continued. "I don't think it would be very smart of us."

He fell back on the bed, kicking off his shoes with eyes trained on the ceiling. "I am more than capable of behaving."

Unfortunately, I knew that. Neither did I want to admit *I* was the problem. That returning here dredged up old thoughts and feelings, and now I was confused. Turmoil thickened with his quiet voice. "I can't do this without you, Addie."

Ransacking the closet, I paused. "Do what?"

"Any of it."

"You've come this far and managed fine."

"If only." He scrubbed a hand down his face, pinching the bridge of his nose. "If it were just the Morrigan, they would be dead. If it were just the Knights, I would have a solution. If it were just this or just that, it would all be resolved, but it's as if the world has gone to shit all at once."

"It's always been this way," I whispered.

"Has it?" The hollow question sank between us. "I don't know what to do about the druids. Magically or legally, I owe them nothing, but I know I should do something, and I don't know what it is. And we still have fuck-all information on what you are or exactly when that will bite us in the ass, explosions notwithstanding. Lillian and Arthur are furious and full of questions, and I can hardly blame them. Will is still recovering. The sisters are hunting us down, the Knights are too, I have to glamour the goddamn apartment until repairs are done, and now I need a ten percent raise in profits just to pay off the fucking cops."

There was a common denominator to this mess. Jack said he couldn't do this without me, but I was the reason those problems existed. *We* were the reason. His love, obsession, whatever one wished to call it, had brought all this chaos to our lives. In our wake was nothing but destruction.

I lay down beside him, letting my feet dangle off the edge. "Do you ever wonder if we're the villains?"

"Do you want comfort, or do you want the truth?"

"You already know the answer to that."

His answer took long to come. "Sometimes we have no choice."

No, there was always a choice. We had just chosen wrong. He killed a god to keep a friend. I killed a sister to save a brother. He made a bond to save my life. I took a curse to keep it.

Ruination behind us, but the future could be altered. Jack was overwhelmed, and I didn't entirely trust his solutions anyway. "Give me something to do."

"You don't—"

"Would you hush for a moment?" I breathed. "You gave that fancy speech about how we make our decisions as a group, but let's be honest, Jack, it's you. You're always three steps ahead while the rest of us scramble behind, and since I can't expect you to change anytime soon, at least give me some direction. Let me ease the burden, please."

The bond flickered, him weighing his words beside me. "Write a letter to the police chief's wife."

I frowned. "Jack—"

"I raised the bastard's cut today because he actually has the guns and political means to intervene on our behalf. But he will only take the deal if I show him the refinery below the hotel, which I can only do after dark without risking the entire operation. But ever since his wife caught him in bed with her cousin, she won't allow him to spend the night away from home without her. And as she is infamously antisocial, I need another woman to convince her to make the trip. I make no excuses for the pure stupidity of this ordeal, but if we can get him on our side, I can hand him evidence that slows down both the Knights and my current competitors. It's not a permanent solution, but it removes several players from the board in the meantime."

A vine draped in moonlilies crept across the ceiling. We gave it our pensive attention. "How do you keep up with it all?"

He exhaled a long breath. "Nearly four hundred years of practice. Whiskey. You."

Those damn feelings again. They swam up from the deep, pounding against the surface for release. "I make your life far more complicated."

"Maybe, but you also make it much more enjoyable."

The diamond burned against my chest. I said before the past didn't matter, but that was wishful thinking. Jack would never segregate Adeline from all his memories of the past, and I wasn't realistic to ask him to. What I didn't remember was several lifetimes for him. The only reason I existed now was those memories. I thought we brought nothing but devastation, but Jack had a different perspective. One I could never understand with twenty years of living memory to his centuries.

My hand inched toward his on the mattress. When his fingers enclosed around mine, relief was instant. A sense of the familiar. Something like home.

I could blame it on the parallel bond, but that wasn't at fault anymore. It sat dormant in the background nowadays, only present when one of us called on or noticed it. But if my draw to Jack was more than magic, more than the moments of this life I was so unsure of, then where did it come from?

I turned, hair crunching beneath my head against the sheets. Jack flicked his gaze sideways, watching.

"I want to try something, but I still want to be friends," I whispered.

He didn't move. Even his lips remained still as he breathed, "Okay."

Propping myself on an elbow, I traced every curve of his face, his neck. Only his eyes moved with me, like he could glean my secrets by tracing my exploration of him. I swept a lock of black hair aside, a little too long without time to visit the barber. I leaned down, eyes closed, and brushed my lips against his.

The usual reactions—a fluttering in my stomach, heat across my cheeks. The bond snapped into sudden focus, roused by the little touch. But there was something else. Something partway between truth and the subconscious. The notion that without any doubt, I had done this a thousand times before.

My eyes fluttered open, but I didn't move. Stare locked, he whispered, "Find what you were looking for?"

Possibly, but instead of answering, I posed a question of my own. "How old was Annwyl when she got married?"

He couldn't speak about my past lives, but he had mentioned pieces in roundabout ways. I framed my question so he could do that now. It was another test. He never said when or where he had a wife, but I knew in my bones it was her.

"Twenty," he said, so low I had to read his lips.

A smile twitched but didn't break free. "So Jaevidan wooed her after all?"

He shook his head, jaw set. "Jaevidan should have left her alone."

Shifting out from under me, he knocked several pillows to the floor and sighed. "I'll take the floor. We have another long day tomorrow."

SEVENTEEN

JAEVIDAN

SCHOLAR RINDSHAW STOOD OVER me, frowning at the blank parchment on the table. The letter should have been written days ago, but the pounding in my skull kept me in bed. It was quiet in my bedroom nowadays—quiet everywhere I presently stood—but I had not released the magic in days, and when it built like this, it punished me.

I reached for the pen, knocking a pot of grimflower ink over in the process. With my new leather gloves, I fumbled with everything. With the constant hammering in my head, I did practically nothing. With my newfound powers, I was completely alone.

"Should I call for the healer, Prince Jaevidan?"

I gritted my teeth hard enough to chip. "No."

The scholar paused. A glance down told me why. Despite the gloves, darkness poured between my spread fingers, competing with the spilled ink. The parchment rippled and burned beneath my hands, the table beneath it scorching black.

"You must exercise more control, my Prince."

A shuddering breath passed my lips. The poison stopped, but the damage was done. I was only grateful for the moment of reprieve behind my eyes. The pain returned moments later, but significantly less.

"Have patience, my boy. You shall become accustomed to these abilities, same as your father had. But to be dust-marked requires fortitude and time."

The poison nearly lurched from my fingertips again. I did not wish for patience or fortitude. I did not wish for this affinity at all.

Father's portrait stared back at me from the library's west wall. They were all taken down after his death on Mother's order, but I requested one be exhumed after my awakening. No one dared argue with me about it either. Not anymore.

Father was dust-marked, or so I had been told. The man put me in my mother's womb and failed to live long enough for the birth. We all knew she'd killed him, but none of us spoke of it. Not a soul in Gerenstad or farther wept for his death. When the ancient basilisk's power found him, he used it to destroy everything and everyone he knew.

Mother had not seen or spoken to me since Lughnasadh. According to a sprite I threatened, she howled like a dying animal when they told her what I was.

Kalvidan never returned to the parlor. His private rooms were cleared the following day, and from what I knew, he now resided across the palace. Only Donvidan came back, perhaps to prove something, to show I was still a runt in his eyes. But whenever I examined the brutal scars bisecting his face, he flinched.

The days had been long and lonely. Longer and lonelier when I could not seem to maintain control of my affinity. The longer I held on to the poison, the more it tortured me. But if I released it, the consequences were worse.

"My father was an evil cunt among the most evil of all cunts."

The scholar smacked my head with his switch. "You will speak with respect to your elders. This is the barest etiquette required of you."

"But you do not deny it. Do you, old man?" I met his eyes, and for the first time since this nightmare began, a note of fear entered them.

On the fates, not him too.

I could not say why it became impossible to keep my mouth shut. The poison affinity was not the only change after my awakening. I was quick to anger, seized by more rabid urges than I had ever been before. Any sense of reason seemed to flee my mind. All I felt was the pain, all I acknowledged was the urges, all I wanted was release. The poison was my master and I, its violent servant.

I tried to feel remorse. Guilt. Anything. It only worked when I thought of what Annwyl would say if she could see the blood coating my hands.

I missed her.

Scholar Rindshaw rounded the table and took the chair across from me. His cane lay across his green lap, face bestowing me a long, green stare.

"May I speak freely, my Prince?"

I gestured for him to continue, though it felt wrong. He had never asked my permission before.

"This is the first time in your young life you were given the opportunity to survive. Have you truly comprehended this?"

I thought I had. The affinity saved me from Donvidan, and it finally gave me the peace to be left alone. But this was not what the scholar meant.

"All your life, we feared you a *lurgga*. This would be a death sentence for any of the Bogorans' children but an atrocity for one of your line. Not only a way to assure an early death but a tarnish on your great name. You see, our lives do not end when we join the darkness, my Prince. Like your father over there, a presence watching us even now from the wall, we leave things behind. For an immortal to die is a sadness, but to be forgotten is a tragedy."

He folded his hands on the table, robes brushing the new scorch mark. "We all know when your mother joins the dark, you will be the first they kill in the hunts. This has always been true. Your brothers were born too close in time and have always shared that bond, making you the most sensible choice before. This has not changed with your awakening, only that neither one of them can kill you on their own, but together may stand a chance. And because they were your dear mother's firstborn sons, she will stand by their sides. From this day forward, you have no more family, my Prince. You are completely on your own."

I scowled, scoring a sigil into the table with my dagger. "I do not want the crown."

"You can and may just be king one day, Jaevidan."

I would rather have brothers, but Scholar Rindshaw would not understand.

His hand brushed my gloved one, halting my brutal assault on the table. I froze. Even with the leather gauntlets, his fingertips left red and raw. He said nothing, hiding his withered hands beneath the table.

"You *will* become king one day, my Prince. This is not a debate nor a gamble. You are dust-marked by a basilisk. You carry the poison affinity in your blood. All you could ever desire is within reach, but you must take the steps now to acquire it."

All I could ever desire. Could my affinity give me loving siblings? Could the basilisk blood in my veins provide a father to be proud of? I did not want power or the crown or a dusty old scholar to tell me my fate. I wanted my mother.

I wanted Annwyl.

That last thought gave me pause. Scholar Rindshaw eyed me, sensing his words had snagged my attention.

"Anything?" I asked.

"Anything, my Prince."

I chose my question carefully. "What about a girl?"

A deep laugh rumbled from his belly. I had never heard the sound. "Yes, Prince Jaevidan. Any girl you desire. As *many* as you desire."

"I have a specific one in mind." Taking Annwyl to Ildathach had been out of the question before, but everything was different now. My brothers paid me no mind, nor did anyone else. I could protect her. She could be safe here. With my poison affinity, I could assure no one would ever harm her.

Then again, who would protect her from me?

I shrank into myself, flexing and extending my cursed hands. There were too many nights I woke with a ring of poison surrounding me. Belladonna bloomed where I walked, and foxglove rose from my half-finished meals. I was yet to touch any living thing without burning them.

It had been three months since my awakening, and I had not visited the human world once. I would not dare to leave the castle in the days after receiving my affinity, but when the next full moon arrived, I was still in isolation. One month later, I could contain the poison enough to leave my rooms, but only for a few minutes at a time. After the third full moon, I could leave as long as I was fully dressed and donned the gloves. Still, it slipped often.

The only reprieve I seemed to have, the only time the poison stopped to heed me, was after I fed it into the corpse of whichever poor servant I accidentally killed last.

Annwyl would never look at me the same if she knew that.

"Is this girl you speak of in the courts?"

No, she was a dirty human orphan who picked blackberries and bled from her lady parts. Instead of saying that, I shook my head.

He smiled in a grandfatherly way, the kind adults used when they thought you endearingly stupid. "Well, as I said, girls will certainly be in no short supply. Whoever this mystery girl is, you may have her, *and* a princess worthy of your title, and any others you desire. But in order to accomplish that, we must strategize now. Brute strength alone cannot win a throne, my Prince. You will need supporters, and you will need allies. This letter I have asked you to write is a fine place to start."

My nose crinkled. "Why?"

"To put it simply, the kingdom of Raiiash may be small, but they possess a formidable army, large caches of grain with the means to farm more, and the King's niece is a lovely maiden close to you in age. I received word from their emissary this fortnight past, and they are very interested in exchanging correspondence with the Poison Prince."

I propped my head in my hand, tracing the sigil I carved into the table. "Is that what they call me now?"

Scholar Rindshaw lifted a shoulder. "It is what you are."

SCHOLAR RINDSHAW RECOMMENDED I visit the armory after our lessons were completed. It was my usual routine, not that I abided by it much anymore. I hovered on the outskirts of the practice ring, shadowed by a dark alcove as I watched the soldiers below. Each clash of their swords, each swish of their feet against the dirt, only increased the pounding inside my head. I would lose control again, and soon. I left for my rooms without making my presence known.

But as I reached the parlor once shared with my brothers, I kept walking. I had no direction or aim, only that I could not spend another moment locked away. Only true monsters were locked in cages, and I had not decided if I was one of them yet.

There was no need to sneak through the palace anymore. Servants gave me a wide berth, and members of the court changed direction upon my steps. No soldiers halted my march at the gates to the bone bridge.

The Darkwood shuddered at my presence, brambles parting before I could spill my blood. The thorns shifted as it guided me toward the meadow. Deadly nightshade bloomed in my wake, and the Darkwood kept them, forming thorny cages around each flower I left behind.

Low fae skittered through the brush of the meadow, avoiding my path. The vibrant grass blackened beneath my feet. No moon hung in the sky tonight, and by my best measurement, it would be a crescent in the human world. The Veil was at its thickest this time of the month, but when I pressed my hand to the warbling gate, it gave no resistance.

Deep into the barren meadows of Annwyl's world, I finally screamed.

And screamed. And screamed. And screamed.

A circle of necrosis formed around me, some twenty feet across the grass. When the pain subsided enough, when the last of the poison fell from my skin, I walked.

This was a terrible idea. I had little control over my emotions or my affinity. One slip would reveal myself to the humans. But I kept thinking of that letter, finally penned at the scholar's request. Perhaps I should care more, but I could gather no regard for Raiiash and their grain stores. Or their soldiers or the King's niece. We had never met, and Scholar Rindshaw provided no details, but I hated her already.

I wanted to laugh. I had not laughed in months or so much as smiled. Nothing in Ildathach would bring me joy or any feelings besides pain and rage. So I did not think, did not calculate the costs, as I stomped onward to Annwyl's convent.

I had never been inside, but I knew which room belonged to her and the other orphan girls. She'd shown me one night before I returned to my own lands. But this proved fruitless information because when I stood beneath the iron-latticed window, her scent was absent from the mass of human bodies behind it.

A will-o-wisp bobbed in the dark, pale and blue along the forest's edge. I followed it.

We did not venture far. The will-o-wisps appeared more frequently, undulating to low humming. A copse of trees formed a faerie circle ahead, and in the center was Annwyl, eyes closed. She sang and danced to words she could not pronounce, but I recognized the melody. It was a song I'd always loved, sung by the snow spirits in the human lands. I'd taught it to her two winters past. She swayed to the sound, fae lights circling her like she was the center of all divinity.

I stayed far outside the circle. The wisps left me in the dark. She could not have seen much farther past the ancient trees, but when she turned and opened her human eyes, they landed on me.

She staggered back, from surprise or revulsion, I could not say. I glamoured my outward appearance well, but even the human world could sense it, how wrong I was. The grass stretched away from me, and the trees were happy to bend outward in the breeze. Only Annwyl remained still.

"I thought you were dead," she whispered.

Frigid wind cut through the circle, lifting her hair. The will-o-wisps flickered with warning. I shook my head.

"I thought you were dead," she repeated, louder. "I thought something happened to you, Jaevidan. I have wept every night since the first full moon. I tried to come after you, but the Veil would not let me through."

Blood drained from my face. "Annwyl, you can never—"

"Where you have been?"

I did not answer. Her hands balled into fists, bonier than the last time I saw her. "Where. Have. You. Been?"

I looked at my own hands, coated in dark leather. It was strange how quickly hands could change. Hers thinner, mine stained in red.

"Where have you been, Jaevidan?"

I stepped back. This was a mistake.

"And now you run from me?" Her lip trembled, eyes filling with tears. "You can no longer face me, you no longer love me? Which is it? What have I done?"

I swallowed, ignoring the pain erupting in my skull.

"What have I done, Jaevidan?"

"Nothing. You have done nothing, Annwyl."

Her cheeks bloomed red in the wisps' light. Fury, rage, everything I'd felt the last two months seemed to leave me and pour into her. It must have been part of my curse. I ruined goodness in more ways than one. "You promised," she spat. "You promised you would always come. You promised, Jaevidan. *You promised*."

Our breath formed icy clouds in the air. Her knees trembled, and mine locked. I wanted to apologize, I wanted to explain, but she would never understand. Annwyl was good, and lovely, and full of life. Even the will-o-wisps knew that, forming a protective circle around her.

I was nothing but a monster.

"I came to say goodbye." Each word scalded my throat, a destruction of my soul I would never recover from. "You were right. I am a faerie prince, and you are a human girl. I never should have entertained you so long. It was a foolish little game, and I will not be returning anymore."

Her lips pinched, nose screwed up between her eyes. "I hate you."

Poison leaked from my shoes and burned the ground.

"I hate you. *I hate you I hate you I hate you*." She threw a rock at me. "Go away, then! If that is how you truly feel, be on with it. I have shed too many tears for you, and I refuse to anymore. Just *go*."

The trees beside me groaned. Pain swelled behind my eyes, sharp and vengeful. I could feel the affinity leaking, the poison beating the ground in time to my pulse. I needed to breathe, or scream, or run far, far away.

I took another step back. I expected her rage—needed her rage—but she left forth a whimpering cry, tears cascading her cheeks as she sank to her knees. "You left me."

My vision blurred, Annwyl a streak of gold in the grove.

"I knew you were too good to be true." She hitched a sob, shoulders shaking. "I knew you would leave me just like everyone else has."

My chest cracked in two, a feeling like grief clutching my lungs. My vision worsened, and wetness streaked my cheeks. I was too broken to stand, let alone run. I fell to my knees in the darkness, both our sobs ringing through the forest.

The will-o-wisps drifted closer but remained outside the creeping circle of blight. The harder I sobbed, the farther it touched, only stopping at the faerie ring Annwyl occupied.

I wiped my eyes. The poison still left me, killing everything outside the circle. But where Annwyl continued her mournful cries was free of the plague surrounding her.

"Just go," she murmured.

I steadied my breath, grasping the poison inside my body. Pain flared with malice, but I could contain it.

"Look around you," I said.

She did. In the will-o-wisps' light, the destruction stood in full view. A stuttering breath condensed the air, and she stilled. "What is this?"

"Do you not see what I am, Annwyl?" A fresh round of tears heated my face. "They say I am dust-marked. A great basilisk once bred with my house, but his power has only passed through a chosen few. The cursed. It came to me three months ago, and it has made me *this*."

"You have magic?" She should have cowered in fear. But her voice was soft and thoughtful, bordering on hypnotized. The voice she used when she discovered something new and wonderful, like the flower pixies' songs or the benevolent brownies who slept beneath her bed.

"Corruption," I corrected. "That is what it means to be dust-marked. To be corrupted by perverse magic from outside our kind."

"You foolish boy." She shook her head. "You are anything but corrupted."

"Annwyl, you are not listening to me." Destruction spread, the tree nearest me crumbling to the ground. Its death knell echoed through the silent wood. "You think you understand magic and the fae, but you do not. I am *wrong*. Can you not see that? The very earth rejects me, both in this world and my own. I wish I could control it, but I cannot, and if you know what is good for you, you would not shed a tear. Turn away and never look back, *please*."

I needed her to see reason, to understand. I knew what I should do, but perhaps it was the dust taking residence in my body, corroding my mind and turning me into the monster I was meant to be. If I had the strength to walk away from Annwyl, I would.

Scholar Rindshaw's words haunted me. *From this day forward, you no longer have a family.*

For my brothers and mother, it was always true, even if I only realized it now. But the scholar was wrong about one thing. I did have a family—it was Annwyl—and I was too selfish to protect it.

She rose on trembling legs, peering into the darkness. At the ruination. But instead of retreating back the way she came, she stepped forward.

"Annwyl, don't."

She took another step, not pausing until one leather boot touched outside her grove. Then both feet. She continued.

"Annwyl, *stop*."

I yanked on the magic, screaming for the control to send it around her. Agony struck behind my eyes, and heat scored my chest. It would not listen to me, but she kept walking.

She did not stop until she kneeled before me.

"Go away," I hissed. "You stupid girl, *leave*."

She reached out and brushed my face. Through a mist of tears, her skin came away raw and red, prickles of blood spotting her fingertips.

"Breathe," she said. "Just breathe."

A ragged breath hissed past my teeth. I sobbed again, full-body, racking sobs. She brushed the back of her hand across my cheek. That time, her flesh returned unblemished.

"See?" she whispered. "Not a monster."

She reached out again, and I snatched her wrist. I wore my gloves, but that did not stop me from injuring the scholar. For reasons only the deep magic knew, they protected Annwyl now.

Softer than the breeze, than the delicate frost webbing the forest floor, she spoke against my ear. "I still love you most."

The poison stalled, neither sieving from my body nor worming its way across the wood. Neither did it punish me so much in its prison behind my skin. For the first time in months, I took a breath. A real breath, free of anguish. My hand shook around her wrist. I slowly lowered it to the ground.

She crawled into my lap, tightening her arms around my back and burying her face against my neck. Tentatively, I lifted my arms and squeezed her back.

"Never leave again," she whispered. "You are all I have."

She was all I had. More than that, all I truly wanted. More than all the crowns or land or armies in the world. My dirty, little human girl.

She deserved better.

But I kept that thought to myself. One day, she would realize, but not today. Soft, white snowflakes drifted through the trees, suspended midair like they held this moment in time. Snow spirits floated through the forest, summoned by Annwyl's song. I held her closer than ever before, only letting go when the sun rose over the mountains.

EIGHTEEN

ADELINE

"Wake up."

I could sense Jack already up and moving around, but my bleary eyes opened to a shock of red hair. Lillian hovered inches from my face, shaking my shoulders against the sheets. I rubbed at my eyes, brain not quite caught up with the rest yet. "Lillian, what time is—"

"Late. We have a small dilemma in the ballroom."

That sapped the last dregs of sleep from my mind. I rolled from bed just in time to see Jack disappearing into the hall. His rumpled pile of blankets and pillows remained on the floor.

Lillian glanced between me and his echoing footsteps, frowning. I needed to speak with her soon.

After donning my robe and slippers, I followed Lillian up the stairs to the ballroom. Thick layers of fog roiled as we emerged, only broken by our steps and the disorderly vines. While I avoided the top of the hotel—and the endless parties Jack hosted to keep the fae entertained—I had wandered here on occasion, and it always looked *human*. The last time it appeared this way was the night of Calamity, when I discovered what Jack was.

Apprehension settled low in my stomach, but when we arrived at the ballroom, only two voices spoke.

It was empty inside, save for Jack and . . . Guinevere, of all people, conversing in the center of the vast room. They spoke in hushed tones, the tension in Jack's shoulders indicating this conversation was not a pleasant one.

The druid noticed my presence and bowed at the waist. "Lady Fate."

"Is something wrong?"

She straightened, relieved I skipped pleasantries. "I was asked to deliver a message."

If it was more correspondence from the sea queens of the Atlantic, she could withhold it. "What is it?"

A perfunctory nod, and she began. "The remaining druids have been rebuilding. After you left, the Morrigan pursued you, as well as their followers. Several of our old channels remain intact and were reclaimed, allowing us to communicate with some of the other factions.

"I have reestablished contact with several of the prominent sidhe leaders on our continent." She produced a crumpled letter from her robes, smoothing out the creases. "This is the list."

Jack snatched it from her fingers, scanning the list no less than a dozen times.

She cleared her throat. "As I already informed Prince Jaevidan, news of your transformation and destruction of Macha has come to light, and there are some among the sidhe who are . . . displeased."

Jack crumpled the list into a ball, pinching the bridge of his nose. "How much time do we have?"

Guinevere shook her head. "They did not say."

"Time for what?" I asked.

The little druid gave Jack a pointed look, imploring him to explain. He was too busy rubbing his temples, muttering beneath his breath.

The latest memory came to me. All the poison brewing beneath his skin and the constant edge of pain. It had been nearly four hundred years since then, so it was likely he had learned how to cope with it by now. But the way he squeezed his eyes shut, attempting to breathe, warned me otherwise.

Everything else I knew of his power had been equally destructive. It was not very long ago he stretched himself so thin it was killing him. The cane and reading spectacles he required remained in the closet, forgotten now that our parallel bond and Morrigan had rejuvenated him.

I laid a hand on his back and gestured to Guinevere.

Her eyes flitted between us, narrowing. "To put it simply, there are quite a few factions looking to mobilize against you and Prince Jaevidan."

I paled. "Why?"

"Cowards and opportunists," Jack muttered.

"You must understand the Morrigan was the most powerful group in this world and the last for a very long time," Guinevere explained. "Many still fear them and hope to appease them and their wrath by giving them what they want. My people served as a fine example of what happens to those who defy their wishes."

Shame squeezed my heart. "And the opportunists?"

Lillian sighed. "Correct me if I'm wrong, but I believe what Guinevere means to say is when you killed Macha, you created a power vacuum."

Guinevere shrugged. "To put it informally, yes. Many think now that the Morrigan is broken, they stand a chance against Nemain and Babd."

"Shouldn't that work in our favor?"

"No," Jack said. His eyes fluttered open and found me. "Because now that you, Violet, and myself form a Morrigan—and a new, untested one at that—we are the next targets. Additionally, with you becoming a fate, many seem to think I have acquired more power than I should possess."

An old idiom Papa used floated into my mind. "Better the devil you know than the devil you don't."

"Exactly," Guinevere said. "The best scenario for most would be if Babd and Nemain destroyed you and the New York faction, and whoever is leftover kills them. Even if the sisters cannot be killed, the largest threat is still eliminated."

Lillian swore in her native tongue. Jack was faraway in thought. I asked the druid, "Why did they send you to warn us?"

"Not a warning. A formal intent of war."

On the fucking fates. "So what now?"

She frowned. "I cannot say. The druids would offer you continued protection, but I am afraid you are still safer here while we rebuild."

I shook my head. "The druids have done enough. Focus on protecting yourselves."

She bowed her head. "You are generous, Lady Fate. We have little to give, but I have some information that may be of use to you. It would appear that the sisters lost possession of the tenth Dianomican after you killed Macha. It fell back into the hands of the Knights of Templar. No one knows why, but it would appear they are collecting the old books and plan to steal the tenth volume back soon. They acquired two from us when they destroyed the Guild."

Chills racked my spine. Whatever the sisters wanted with the Dianomicans couldn't be good.

Guinevere continued. "My only other words of wisdom would be this—you have the means to kill the remaining sisters. I would do so quickly before they find you first. And in order to do that, the tenth Dianomican cannot fall back into their hands. It contains the parallel ritual, which as we all know is what gives you your power."

Lillian cocked her head. "I just don't understand."

We all looked at her.

"What is the point of all this?" she asked. "We know they used Delsaran's corpse as a puppet, sowing seeds of dissent against the humans. We know they are incredibly powerful, enough to bypass their banishment and reenter Ildathach. No matter how much technology develops in this world, they will be formidable. So why all the deception? Why attempt to collect the Dianomicans now, after all this time? And why kill Jaevidan and Adeline?"

I thought of my one horrible night in the faerie world. I had asked Babd why she was doing this, why she suddenly had an interest in human affairs. And what she said in return . . .

She does not know what we seek. She does not know what the poison prince did to her, let alone how.

She does not know what the poison prince did to her, let alone how.

What the poison prince did to her.

How.

"The Bogoran," I whispered.

Jack gave me a sharp look. The women looked on with furrowed brows.

"Excuse us," he said, leading me into the hall.

The door slammed shut behind us. "What are you doing?"

"That remains between me and you, do you understand?" He watched the doors, pointed ears twitching for sound.

"They already know what I am—"

"No one can know how." His voice became a fevered whisper, hot words brushing my lips. "Don't argue with me on this, Addie. Please."

My skin flushed with anger. "So no one knows what you did?"

"So no one tries to kill us for it," he hissed. "Very few who possess a Bogoran's power are still alive. They have long since been hunted down and the power split thousands of ways. The three of us may just be the most potent possessors of it alive."

Fear and disgust wormed beneath my flesh. "You want me to keep secrets from the druids sworn to protect me? From *Lillian*?"

"While their intentions may be true, information has a way of leaking the more people know. It is safer for the ones we care about if they do not possess that knowledge."

He had a point, but the thought of keeping our friends in the dark rubbed me wrong. "We can discuss that another time. My point still stands—the sisters knew, Jack. I don't know how, but they knew what I was, and they know how you did it. I don't think they're after me and you specifically. They must want the Bogorans' power."

He shook his head. "For what? To what end?"

I wish I knew the answer to that. Moreso, I wished Jack knew. While his constant puppeteering was the bane of my existence, I forgot to appreciate its value every once in a while. "I don't know, but whatever their plan is, they must need Dianomicans for it. Which one contained a ritual for resurrections? Maybe they seek to bring Macha back."

"That doesn't explain what their goals were before she died."

"No, but it may explain why they want Dianomicans now. So which one was it?"

He was silent for a long moment, stiff with tension. "It doesn't matter. If the book is with the Knights of Templar, it's as good as gone."

"But they managed to steal it once," I said. "And if they could steal it, so could we. Preferably before they get any use out of it."

He sighed. "Addie, the Knights of Templar aren't like Lorvellian. Besides, they have bases all over the world. There is no way of knowing where the book even is."

"No," I said, thinking. "But we may know someone who does."

At Lillian's insistence, Guinevere agreed to stay the night before returning to France. We offered her a hotel room, which I had a feeling she abandoned the moment we left. From there, Lillian led the way into the bowels of the basement, through several halls I suspected were not actually there to what must have been the nicest cell in existence.

Behind the bars was Tommy.

He didn't startle, meaning his hearing aids were off or malfunctioning with all the magic around. He sat with his back against the bars, fingertips coated in ink as he penned something into a journal. The cell itself was nearly as spacious as the Abstruse, with a thick rug covering the stone floor, a single bed with hotel linens, and a private bathing area behind a Japanese room divider. It was luxurious as far as prisons went, but still a prison.

I scowled at Jack. "Is this really necessary?"

He leaned against the stones, hands stuffed in his gray trouser pockets. Kicking one foot up against the wall, he shrugged. "I wanted something less comfortable. You may thank Lillian for the accommodations."

I had half a mind to throttle him but decided that could wait for later. I sank to my knees behind Tommy. He sensed the change in the air. His hand paused over the journal, and he turned. It was a mere second before his gaze flicked to Jack behind me.

Lillian settled on the ground beside us, legs tucked to the side and skirt smoothed. "We're sorry to interrupt you, Thomas, but your sister had a few questions."

He ignored her, attention entirely mine. His expression was guarded, but I knew him better than anyone. Anger and betrayal glinted through his mask.

Can you hear? I mouthed, tapping my ear. Mouth a thin line, he reluctantly turned his aids back on.

"I'm surprised he let you down here."

Despite the truth of it, I waved a hand. "Like I already told you, Jack doesn't control me. Are you doing alright?"

"Fine," he said, making the word sound anything but. "Is there a reason for this visit?"

It was now or never. "I need to ask you a question about the Knights."

He scowled. "Like I already told him, I ain't working for the bastards."

"It's not that." I paused, wondering if this was such a good idea. Jack would undoubtedly protest, but his concerns were the last thing on my mind. "Look, Tommy. We need some information, and if you have it, then we can do away with all this prison nonsense. It was just a precaution, anyway."

Jack stepped forward, but I let all my wrath barrel down the bond. His footsteps halted, his own anger and unease shooting back, but he remained still.

Tommy looked between us, perturbed. "You know, you never told me how that works."

"It's mostly based on emotions," I said.

"So he can't . . . I don't know, read your mind?"

I laughed. "I'm sure Jack wishes he could."

That answer didn't satisfy him, but he had nothing to add.

Lillian leaned her head against the bars, shooting him a smile that could thaw the Arctic. "Thomas, darling, I'm afraid something rather unfortunate has occurred with our allies. Just like you, all we care about is keeping our dear chicky here safe. But in order to do that, we desperately need some information about a certain book. The Knights have held it for a long time, so we were wondering—"

"No."

Lillian blinked. "But—"

"I don't know anything." He turned around, clicking his hearing aid off.

Jack approached. I shot him a scathing glare, flicking Tommy's aids on through the bars.

"Tommy, this is important."

"I don't know anything." He craned his neck, just enough to glare at Jack. "And even if I did, the last thing I'd do is hand it over to you."

Jack didn't move, not even a twitch. Like he was reciting the weather forecast, he said, "Lillian, take his memories."

"Nobody is taking anyone's memories," I snapped, the same moment Lillian whispered, "No."

We all stopped.

Her jaw clenched with a slight shake of her head. "Jack, you know I have always been loyal to you, but you are in absolutely no place to be making demands right now."

"It's this, or we try our luck with the Librarian," he said.

A frigid shiver raced down my arms. The last thing any of us desired was paying another visit to that particular creature, if it would help us at all after its last encounter with Jack.

Tommy paled. "What does he mean by 'take my memories'?"

"Nothing, it means nothing," Lillian said. "I won't risk it. Besides the fact he's Addie's brother, he is still only human, Jack. The risks of bringing him permanent harm far outweigh the benefits."

Jack's nostrils flared. "If he doesn't want to talk, that's his choice. Let him take the risk."

"I have a vow, in case you have forgotten," she snapped. "I do not harm others. I do not kill. And no one, not even you, will make me go back on that."

Tommy watched her with disquiet interest, like his idea of the fae didn't quite reconcile with the enigma of Lillian.

"I'm not harming him or taking anyone's memories," she said, resolute.

Jack released a long breath, imploring me. "I don't think this is a good idea."

"You're entitled to your opinion." I reached for Tommy. "I can't stress how important this is. Anything you know about where they keep it, any protocols they have for it, anything that can point us in the right direction is useful. We thought the sisters had it, but the Knights reclaimed it. They're going to steal it again, and if they do, the consequences will be severe. I know you think the Knights can take down any fae, but Babd and Nemain are different. If they want the Dianomican, they will get it."

A tic feathered in his jaw. Behind his eyes, gears of thought whirred with vigor. "I wasn't lying. I don't have much information. I never took vows and formally joined the order, so it was inaccessible."

Lillian perked up. "But you know something?"

"Not much," he warned. "All I was told was that the Dia—whatever you call it—was assigned a new guardian every twenty years or so. The book goes to their home assignment and is only removed for approved uses, which I doubt will happen much now that it's been stolen once. For the past ten years, it's been with Agent Rodney, so unless that's changed, it will be locked up at the North American headquarters in Chicago. Which is impossible to get into and impossible to get out of."

"Good. Glad this was a waste of our fucking time." Jack pushed away from the wall.

"Where in the headquarters?" I asked.

All three of them gaped.

Tommy shook his head. "It don't matter, baby. It's not like you can just waltz in and take it off the Knights' hands."

"They still think I'm human though. You told them as much, and as far as they're concerned, I'm expected to arrive in Chicago under their protection."

"Not to their *headquarters*. If all went to plan, you wouldn't be interacting with them at all. You would have lived under their protection but separate. There was an address set up for us, and it sure as hell wasn't anywhere near those freaks."

"But they don't know what I am," I pointed out.

"Addie, that place is warded straight to hell. They would detect it the second you stepped foot in the place."

"Which is exactly why we are burying this conversation," Jack said. "I appreciate the thought, Annwyl, but it's a no."

I ignored him. "But do they know what *I* am?" I asked. "Wards are specific. They can be made against the fae, or even subsets of them, but I'm not fae. I'm not a druid either. I'm something they've likely never encountered before. As long as I don't use magic, they wouldn't know."

"Addie, drop it," Jack said.

Lillian chewed her lower lip. "I agree, darling. It would be a foolish mission."

Tommy didn't answer me, but I could see the truth behind his eyes. Violet said she knew all her brother's secrets. Maybe that's what happened with a bond of blood because I knew I'd just learned Tommy's.

"You wanted me behind bars because I spoke to them, Addie. If they're that dangerous to you, then the last thing I think you should be doing is knocking on their front door," he said.

"I didn't want you behind bars. This was not my decision and never would have been. I trust you." My voice cracked on the last word, swelling with the emotion I'd kept locked inside. I was still so angry with him, but I understood his fears. He only wanted the best for me, and I for him. It was just a cruel fact of life it never worked out that way.

Chewing his lip, he said, "I know you do. And I know you and that you think this is something you have to do, but it's not worth it. You're not getting into that place and back out again. If the book falls into the hands of the sisters, then so be it. We'll deal with those consequences when they come for us."

That appeared to be the death knell in my plan. Lillian offered to watch Tommy at her apartment, but strangely, it was my brother who refused, stating he was fine and would stay in his cell for the time being. Despite never aligning with the Knights, I knew he still didn't trust the fae. I made a passing remark to Jack, who only said the safest place for him at the moment was hidden away in the hotel. Since no one else argued, we retreated upstairs.

Jack collapsed back to his floor bed and told me to get another hour or two of rest. But as I lay in bed and stared at the ceiling, sleep eluded me.

We couldn't kill the Morrigan—or what remained of them—yet. We had already tried, and our encounter at the Guild only proved they were still too powerful. If we had a moment to stop running and plan, our combined power would be enough, but they had effectively assured that was impossible now. It was not just them but a mass of banished sidhe we faced now. And whatever they learned from the cursed books.

Jack slept fitfully, turning and muttering in his sleep. It was a rare, unsettling sight. If this new, larger threat was enough to make him squirm, we were in enormous trouble.

I rose from the bed and paced the study.

We needed that book. We couldn't let the sisters have another edge on us. It was obvious Jack was spread too thin, and he would never request the help he truly needed. Everyone continued to remind me I was a fate—something special and rare and powerful, though it had done nothing for me so far. The other two had not yet called on me, and my powers had been limited to the shade. If I could not solve our problems with brute force or power alone, then something else needed to be done. Jack couldn't scheme his way out of this one. Not this time.

After assuring he was asleep, I made a quiet phone call in the study.

She picked up on the first ring. "Do you have any idea what fucking time it is?"

"I have an incredibly stupid idea, and you are the only one insane enough to help me."

Violet paused, only her quiet breath echoing across the line. "Alright, I'm listening."

NINETEEN

ADELINE

VIOLET HAD ME SHADE to her apartment. After packing a valise each of some basics, we made our plan. The next train to Chicago would be 6:00 p.m. from Grand Central Station. Even though I was positive I could make the jump, using the shade to enter the Knights' territory was a sure way to trigger some magic alarms, so we would travel the human way. After a day spent acting natural around Jack and company, we would sneak off and meet at the train station.

Violet smoked a cigarette as we waited on the platform. The mid-November wind barreled down on us, prompting the few other passengers to tighten their coats and hold their hats. I pulled the brim of my own well over my eyes, hiding my face from view in the scant lights along the dark railway.

"You sure about this?" she asked.

I shifted. No, I was not sure at all, but we were swiftly running out of options. We needed to keep the Dianomican away from the sisters. We needed to buy ourselves time while they rallied for an attack. And perhaps selfishly, I needed to prove something.

Everyone else had made sacrifices. All those who fell into my orbit seemed to suffer or pay for something I had not yet returned. It wasn't fair for everyone else to lose or risk their lives while I was shuffled into a corner. I owed this to the druids, to my friends, to Tommy, and even to Jack. Maybe to myself. I told him on the ship I'd just begun discovering who I really was, and after what happened to the druids and seeing the lengths Tommy went to to protect me, after my voice becoming a weapon and learning a god had died so I may live, a question was thrust upon me. Did I want to be a person who cowered and hid away, or did I want to be brave enough to do the right thing, no matter how hard—to earn the sacrifices everyone else made?

I thought of the letter I shaded into Jack's bedroom moments before, shattering my compact in the bathroom so he couldn't trace where it came from. Unlike his, it was short and sweet.

Jack,

As you know, my brother often read me Tennyson as a child. It was that very book in his chest pocket that saved his life. So while you were never one for poetry, I must leave you with this:

It may be that the gulfs will wash us down:
It may be we shall touch the Happy Isles,
And see the great Achilles, whom we knew.
Tho' much is taken, much abides; and tho'
We are not now that strength which in old days
Moved earth and heaven, that which we are, we are;
One equal temper of heroic hearts,
Made weak by time and fate, but strong in will
To strive, to seek, to find, and not to yield.

Dream well, darling. I will return home soon.

Adeline

P.S. The password is Ulysses.

By the time he found it, we would be well on our way to Chicago. I just hoped he wouldn't try to follow.

As we boarded the train, I thought over the last five words I had written. *I will return home soon.*

Home.

Once a farmhouse in Georgia, then an ancient study with a bedroom of gossamer, then . . . nothing. I was on the run, and all my past homes were ruined beyond repair. So, I couldn't explain why home became synonymous with Jack once again, written into his letter without thought like it was never a question.

It was that unsettling sense of familiarity again. The notion I had done something a thousand times, even if it remained outside my memory. A thirteen-year-old Jaevidan sobbing beside a copse of trees and a little girl with no family left joining him. A girl who liked to dance in the forest and feel her feet in the soil for no other reason than the pleasure of it. A little girl who was utterly alone, who came from nothing and had nothing—nothing, except for Jaevidan.

Right now, I had much more than her. I had a brother and friends and people ready to protect me. But in the end, emotions could not be wrangled by logic. What we felt deep in our souls was not a matter of choice or reasoning, no matter how much we tried to pretend it wasn't.

It was her dancing that struck me the most. Exactly how I used to sway to Papa's song, pouring salt around the farmhouse.

I buried the thoughts as a conductor in fashionable blue and gold showed us to our car. While both Violet and I had access to Jack's accounts, we couldn't leave a paper trail until our task was done. Violet had paid for our own tickets from her personal savings and, in typical Warren family behavior, got us first class.

My last train experience was on a dirty bench being attacked by red caps, so it was needless to say I hoped this venture went smoother.

Our room was small but far from quaint. Two luxurious beds sat side by side, separated by a small chest of drawers with golden knobs. Floral curtains had been drawn over the lone window, and a private powder room hung off the side. The luxury continued into the hall and the first-class dining area two cars ahead. Velvet couches of royal blue lined the walls, each with a small table set with ivory cloths and crystal stemware.

Violet and I settled down when a bubbly voice said, "Have room for a third?"

Lillian appeared, hands on hips.

I gaped. Violet settled back with a dangerous grin. "How did you find us?"

Lillian winked. "Violet, dear, did you already forget what sort of work I do for your twin?"

"We can explain—"

She cut me off. "No need. I want in."

Violet and I glanced at each other. "You do?" I asked.

"Of course I do. I couldn't very well let you two run off and get killed all by yourselves, now could I? How gauche."

Gauche was not the word I would use. "You told me it was a terrible idea."

She waved a hand. "All our ideas are terrible, darling. Besides, I had a long chat with your brother, and I do believe he gave me some intel that may actually save your necks."

I frowned. "But Jack—"

"Will be furious no matter what. It's only because he cares." She sank to the open space beside me, chiming a fork along her glass for a server's attention. "Besides, Addie and I have much to discuss."

Violet rested her head in her hand. "And you swear this is not some ploy to alert Jack where we are?"

"He already knows by now," Lillian answered. "I know you think he has me wrapped around his finger, but I do think as my own person now and again. I believe Adeline can relate."

Tension steeped the air. Since we met, there had always been some friction between Violet and Lillian, but with two centuries behind them, I never dared dig deeper into it. I wondered why it bled through now.

There was also guilt since I had had the exact same thought as Violet. Lillian was so loyal to Jack, often to a fault. And with her effervescent, loving nature, it was easy to underestimate her.

Our redheaded friend broke the silence first. "Violet, I adore you all the same, but you must remember you have your purposes, and we have ours. A soft-spoken woman is often the loudest in the room."

Violet scowled. "If you came here to lecture me, you can fuck off now."

"Just a reminder," Lillian murmured. The waiter arrived, and she gave him a glowing smile. His cheeks turned redder than an apple orchard. "Oh! How darling you are. Tell me, what can a lady find to drink on this fine evening?"

AFTER DINNER, VIOLET RETURNED to our shared bedroom for some privacy. I wasn't tired, and my new body wouldn't allow me to be for hours. So when Lillian requested I join her on the caboose, I was happy to oblige.

We stood on a platform overlooking the dark countryside. The metal rails were slick with earlier rain, the air thick with the scent of an impending storm. No humans ventured out with the frigid night air, leaving us to enjoy the rear balcony in solitude.

I leaned against the door, watching New York fade into the darkness beyond the rear lanternlights.

Lillian wasted no time. "Tell me about the bond."

"Would Jack not tell you himself?"

It was a hunch. I knew how close they were and that Lillian would have no qualms about interrogating him. Though I doubted he would relinquish that knowledge, what with how secretive he had been all along.

"No, he did."

I blinked. I had certainly not expected that.

"Then why ask me?"

"To get your perspective, of course." She grinned. "I always confirm my intel—it's the mark of a good spy. And besides that, I want to know how you feel. Your side of the story deserves to be heard too."

Bless the stars for people like Lillian.

I told her all I knew, everything from how I discovered the truth of the bond from Babd, then my conversation with Violet in Paris, and the letter from Jack. When I was done, she only said, "And the past lives?"

I had brushed over those parts but regaled that to her as well.

"Who would have thought?" she pondered.

"I would have told you sooner, but I was worried . . ." I hushed, wondering how to put this delicately, considering what had happened in the dining car.

She beat me to it. "How it would sway my opinion of Jack?"

I almost flinched. "You care about him so much, Lillian, and hold him in such high regard. I was only afraid to hurt you."

"And you were worried what it would make me think of you."

It wasn't a question, and it would be a lie to deny it. Deep down, there had been some worry that Lillian would not see my side of everything. That her childlike hope of me and Jack reconciling would overshadow all my concerns.

"I'm not upset," she said. "Truly, I understand. But I wish to make something incredibly clear—I know how I am with Jack. I'm well aware I often hold him on a pedestal after all he has done for me, but I am also well aware he is not without his faults. None of us are. I know he has done terrible things and made some horrid choices, but I have and continue to believe in him for the right ones."

I developed a sudden interest in picking my nails. "You make it sound so simple."

She laughed. "Nothing is simple, darling, people least of all. Look at where we are. Look at what we are doing. If the world was divided into good and evil, right and wrong, we would have had all the answers very long ago."

Somehow, it was both exact and opposite to Violet's advice in Paris. I asked her if we were on the right side of things, and she said none of us were. Lillian essentially said the same but infused with a hope and sanguinity only she could muster.

"More importantly, how do you feel?" she asked.

I gave her the only answer I could. "I haven't decided yet."

"I wouldn't have expected you to."

My thoughts rushed forward, driven by the dam Lillian had just shattered. "Maybe it's simple of me, but I think I've forgiven him for the parallel bond. I understand why he did it, but only time will tell if he sticks by his word to never use it against me."

She nodded. "I agree."

"It's the rest of it. These supposed past lives, the reincarnation. Everything it means, in the past, present, and future."

"I understand the present and future. I presume the past you speak of is both your former lives and the Bogoran he killed?"

Tensing, I raced to decide if I should confirm or deny.

"I figured it out, darling. You don't need to lie."

I sighed. "He asked me to withhold it, but it's nothing against you, Lillian. I swear it."

She snorted. "I've spent two centuries with the man—I know how he thinks. There's no need to placate me. Of course, I have suspected it for a long time now, anyway."

"And it doesn't bother you?"

"Of course it does, but what's done is done. One bad deed doesn't erase a million good ones, and I've always known if it happened, it was a very long time ago. He's grown and changed much since then. So have I."

"But you didn't kill the last god of its kind," I said.

She paused, lost in the darkness racing by us. "Addie, I murdered every one of my siblings for a crown I couldn't keep. We can argue all day, but to me, it will always be a darker stain to murder your own blood. And this is something you have never judged me for because I have proven myself time and time again. Our world and your world are two very different places, with two very different values. It doesn't pardon us from our evils, but our willingness to become something better should always be recognized. Without that, no one would ever change."

I knew little of Lillian's circumstances beyond the cold, hard facts, but I'd learned much of Jack's past. The beatings, the torture, death, and enslavement treated like party games. A much different world, indeed.

Still . . . "He killed it in cold blood. For me, or at least some past version of me. And while I understand our differences, I have a hard time understanding how someone could justify something like that. It's not devotion; it's obsession. Even if it was the former, it justifies nothing now. I'm a completely different person who has lived a completely different life. He loves Annwyl, not Adeline. I'm nothing but a mirage of what he truly wants."

Rain pattered down, sizzling against the heated rails. The horn blew from the front of the train, throwing us into deafening silence.

"But he does love you," she said.

I shook my head. "He barely knows me."

"That's not true, and you know it." She faced me, squeezing under the tiny overhang to avoid the fresh rain. "He wouldn't tolerate half our shenanigans if he didn't. He wouldn't stick by his vow to never use the parallel bond against you, and believe me, fae will find a way around anything if they want to. If he found nothing to love in who you are now, he certainly would not go to all these lengths to protect you, or train you, or spend all his free time at dance halls or the cinema with someone whose company he deplored. He actually smiles now, Addie, and it's been so rare for so long it's honestly strange to see. And if this was nothing but obsession, he certainly wouldn't have let you go. An obsessed man wouldn't watch you walk away from him to find yourself or decide what you want from life. Only someone who truly loves you would accept that pain for your happiness."

The train chugged diligently along into the night. Smoke stuffed itself in my nose, and the fresh scent of rain. Jack's scent, only missing the oleander. "Violet told me the sidhe cannot love like humans do. That you're too different."

Lillian shook her head. "That's Violet's opinion, and while there is some truth to it, it's not the whole truth. I respect her and adore her despite our differences, but she is very much her own person and always has been. Her perspective has been vastly skewed by her life and who she is."

"But you said it yourself, you and Jack grew and changed. Hasn't she too? Why shouldn't her opinion be the right one?"

Lillian sighed. "Growing and changing means different things. In many ways, she's come along, and in others, she hasn't."

"Why do you think that is?"

She gazed off into the distance, arms crossed. "I'm not sure, but time doesn't heal all wounds. Some just grow more complicated."

We stood in heavy silence.

"He loves you, maybe more than anything or anyone," she said, the declaration final. But it was the sadness threading through each word that gave me pause. Something occurred to me, a thought I felt utterly stupid for never having before.

"You're in love with him, aren't you?"

A conspiratorial sideways glance, a tight grin, and she said, "Would you hate me if I said I was?"

I shook my head.

"Emphasis on 'was,'" she added. "It was a while ago, and I've moved on since."

It was none of my business, but I wanted to know. "So, have you two ever . . ."

She laughed. "Blessed Bogorans, no. Not for lack of trying, but Jack was never interested in me like that."

It was unfathomable to me he wouldn't be. Besides the fact Lillian was gorgeous beyond comprehension, she was one of the loveliest people I knew. Not to mention, entirely loyal and devoted to Jack. Essentially, the opposite of myself.

"Not even once?"

"No, not even once." She licked her lips, thinking. "When we discussed your past, you know what my first thought was?"

I shook my head.

"That it all makes sense now." Another sad, little grin. "For all his charm and the persona he sells the humans, that man is the furthest thing from wanton I have ever seen. Let's be honest, women throw themselves at him—I was one of them—but he never bit. He crafted an image of it, sure, but never engaged. I thought he may have been hurt in the past, but there was something more to it. Like he was anticipating something."

It was so contrary to Jack's character I wondered if Lillian was lying to me. "I highly doubt he has been that loyal to me."

"I don't," she said. "In the early years with him, I tried to win his favor all the time, firstly to escape, then because my thoughts and feelings of him changed. But he was always so rigid, and then, of course, he would leave for years at a time. One day, he'd be there; the next, Violet would say he had gone off for a while. I always found it strange, but Jack is strange, so I stopped thinking much of it until about eighty or so years ago."

"Why?"

"He came back . . . not himself." She pursed her lips, a million words between them. "It was like the sun no longer existed for him. But whenever we tried to deduce what had happened, he pushed us all further away. Only Violet knew, but try getting her to talk."

"What do you think happened?"

"I can only guess, but I think you, or some version of you, told him not to come back." She tapped her collarbone. "Why else would he take that vow mark?"

Because he loves me. The thought came unbidden, without mercy or remorse. Because if I told him never to speak to me again, or of my past lives, or that I wanted a life without him in it, he would do it.

Still, it didn't explain the here and now.

"But he did come back. That's why I'm here, isn't it?"

She shrugged. "Only Jack can explain that."

Unfortunately, she was right.

I slipped my hand through hers. "I'm sorry for everything you've been through. And I know it's strange, but I'm sorry about Jack too."

Shaking her head, she smiled. "Oh, darling, never apologize for that. You know why I understand the difference between love and obsession? I've lived both. I wanted Jack because of what he gave me, because I was in a dark place and was still a dark person who became fixated on this one beacon of light. I didn't care that deep down I knew he had someone else. I only began truly loving him when I stopped convincing myself I was *in* love with him. When I wanted his happiness, and I wanted my own. And from that, we have had a long, prosperous friendship I wouldn't change for the world."

I leaned my head on her shoulder. "If I forget to tell you today, I love you to pieces, Lillian. And I missed you very much."

She threw her arms around me. "I missed you too."

We stayed like that, hugging and giggling like schoolgirls in the rain.

Grinning, she pulled away. "So, now that we have assuaged some of your concerns, that leaves only one predicament left."

"And that is?"

"Whether you love Jack too." She said it so airily I wondered if I had misheard her.

"Oh, is that all?"

"Of course it is, darling. We all know how he feels. The rest is your decision and what you decide you want in your life. And no matter what you choose, you will always be my dearest friend. No one else lets me play with their hair like you do."

I laughed, the sound drifting away as a thought surfaced. "May I ask you something?"

"Of course."

"When the wraith found me in New York, she gave me memories. But they were meant as a curse, and it went wrong, so Jack had taken me to see Estheria. But before that, he told me you had taken those memories away."

She nodded. "I did."

I picked through how to ask this. "I'm not sure how your affinity works, but something that has been bothering me is all these strange feelings around Jack. Like I know him, but I don't. And while I have his memories, I still don't have—"

"And you want to see it from your own perspective," she finished.

I nodded. "I think it would feel more real to me and maybe explain some things."

She bit her lower lip. "I don't know, those memories didn't mesh well with you last time."

"But I was human then," I said. "You just said to Jack and Tommy that this kind of magic can harm humans in ways it doesn't with others. Maybe that's what happened, then."

Thinking, she angled her head. "It's possible, but Addie, I'll be honest. Most of those memories were not things you want to see. I believe there were a few earlier ones, but most were of the deaths you lived. I think that's why the wraith of you was so—"

I raised a brow. "Angry and evil?"

"I was going to say eccentric, but yes."

It was risky, but Lillian hadn't swayed my decision. No matter how awful those memories were, they still belonged to me. I told Jack I was not those women from the past, and I still believed that, but I realized some part of that was how disconnected I felt from it all. All I had were strange nudges and notions, muscle memories of things I had done a hundred times before, no different than tying a knot or using a dinner fork. But Annwyl liked to dance in the forest. She learned the names of flowers and enjoyed farming. That could be mere coincidence, but if pieces of those lives still lived on in me, I wanted to understand them.

"I want to try. And if anything goes amiss, I give you full permission to yank them out of my head, no questions asked."

She sighed. "Alright, but I *will* remove them the moment something goes awry."

Violet was mysteriously missing from our cabin, so we decided it was as good a time as any. We sat cross-legged on my bed, Lillian's hands on my forehead. "Ready?"

I nodded.

The last thing I remembered was her bright, blue eyes, concentrating. There was the vague notion of falling asleep—my head falling back on the bed, mind overcome with too many thoughts to remain conscious. My eyes fluttered closed, and when I dreamed that night, visions of the past came to me.

But not Jack's.

This time, they were mine.

TWENTY
ADELINE

THESE WEREN'T LIKE JACK'S memories, vivid and linear. A true reliving. They came in short snatches, an image here or there, some of them longer and others nothing but a glimpse. Something beyond my control sifted through them, as if flipping through a book—backward, forward, and without reason, pausing once an intriguing chapter was reached.

The sun was fierce yesterday, drying all but a few of the clay—

And—

Smoke rolled through my home, a new blend of sandalwood and flowers I picked after the monsoons. I was sad to no longer see the drying flowers above my head, only the bare, red clay when I awoke each morning. Next year, I would pick more. They sold well, especially to the—

And—

Juice exploded on my tongue, sweet and rich. I suppressed a quiet groan, forgetting how much I missed the fruit. They were everywhere this time of year, scattering the ground in splashes of orange. But I wanted my first taste to be just right, restraining myself until the mango was perfectly ripe. The anticipation was worth it. I could not wait to share it with—

Then, a longer one.

A man stood in the entryway.

I had not heard his arrival, which was strange. I was usually attuned to these things, always wanting to be prepared when a customer arrived. I tugged my headscarf into position, hiding most of my face. It produced better sales among the men, obscuring my appearance. And, of course, had the added benefit of making them believe I was married. They were less prone to poor behaviors that way.

My newest blend filled the room with rich scents. Tea leaves and herbs formed a swaying, colorful ceiling above. The man stepped in from the glimmering sunlight, and I stilled with surprise. He did not wear a dhoti or the sherwani common among local men influenced by the West. Instead, his attire was entirely European, his skin a light bronze uncommon among visitors but still many shades lighter than myself or others from the village. He had black hair, and his eyes were a startling shade of gold. The British men seldom impressed me, but he was eerily beautiful.

I extended my hand toward him, bangles rattling along my wrist. "Hello, foreigner."

He seemed surprised I used his language. He bowed at the waist and replied in Tamil. "Did you make these yourself?"

Huh. That was a pleasant surprise. Pride filled my Tamil reply. "I did."

"They are beautiful." He lifted a clay vase from its shelf. It was one of my favorite pieces, a challenge that took me months to perfect. The design was etched into the clay, and I had spent many nights grinding fruits and minerals for the paint, wanting the colors to be just right.

"How much?" he asked.

Beneath my headscarf, I smiled. "How much do you believe it's worth?"

He set the vase down, looking at me. "For something as lovely as this, I am afraid it must be priceless."

Then—

"The foreigner has returned."

The man gave me a sheepish smile. It had been many months, but I would recognize his face anywhere. It was strange, as I had thought of him not too long ago. He had appeared in my dreams, cross-legged on the floor beside me while I painted. But when he spoke, it was not of any language I knew—

And—

"I brought you something, from my home." He extended a parcel wrapped in painted paper.

I beamed. "A gift?"

And—

We stood beneath the mango tree, his arms wrapped around me.

"We can try again," he said.

I shook my head, tears streaking my cheeks. "No, I could not bear this pain twice."

And—

He licked up my throat, thrusting inside me. My back arched against the floor, breathy moans filling the air.

And—

"What do you think? Am I Michelangelo?" He held up the portrait, a ridiculous caricature with stick legs.

I burst into laughter, tears blurring my eyes.

And finally, last of all—

Wrinkles and liver spots coated my arms. He held my hand, quiet breaths racing across my cheeks. I was surprised to wake again but grateful for the moment. His golden eyes searched me, bright and full of life. No matter how many years had passed, how much time had ruined my skin, he still looked exactly the same. As beautiful as the first day I met him.

His low voice curled around me, fingers smoothing back my hair. Hair that was once as black as his now white and withering away. "You can go, my love," he said.

A shuddering breath passed my lips. I was tired, so very tired. This body brought nothing but pain, far too many years past when it should have returned to the soil. But he was still here, bright as ever, and suddenly, I felt no peace with what would happen next. "I do not wish to leave you," I said. My eyes filled with tears, my hand clutching his as tightly as I could. If I held on to him, if I never let go, maybe we could stay together. His sacred blood would heal mine, or the gods would have mercy and carry him with me into the next life.

He kissed my cheek, wiping away my tears. When he spoke next, I knew my prayers had been answered. "Wherever you go, I will always find you."

I pulled our fists to my lips, kissing his fingers. "I love you."

Black closed around my vision, a last moment following me into the dark. His lips pressed against mine, releasing me with four quiet words.

"I love you most."

I WOKE UP IN the powder room.

My hands were submerged in the sink, liquid filled to the brim and sloshing over the side. But it wasn't water staining my—

I leapt back and fell to the floor with a crash. Pink coated my blackened fingertips and wrists, and I clutched my undershirt.

Red seeped from the fabric, dribbling from a wound that didn't exist in the cloth. The train lurched sideways, sending more of the watery blood across the tiles.

"Strange."

My head shot up. Violet perched on a shelf above the toilet, some six feet in the air. Something about her seemed . . . wrong. All her glamour had fallen away, but I was used to that by now. It was the air around her, pulsating like blackened lungs. The shadows condensed around her, darkness sticking to her skin like she drew it from every corner of the room. In the inky mist, her golden eyes gleamed like searchlights.

I blinked. "What the fuck are you doing up there?"

She cocked her head to the side. "Observing."

I pushed onto wobbling legs, trying to still my heart. I shook so hard the shirt fell from my grasp. "Why do you look like that?"

"Like what? Devastatingly attractive in a way you could only hope to be?"

I scowled. "The shadows and . . . darkness. It's creepy."

She frowned, jumping down in a smooth motion. "Glamour must be getting testy so far from Jack."

"Well, fix it. You know I can't." I ran a hand through my hair, staring at the mess across the floor. "What is this, some kind of joke?"

She snorted. "Do you think I would plan some elaborate scheme to bother you? I do it well enough on my own." She flicked a finger under my nose. "You rose from bed a few hours ago and lumbered in here. I assumed you had pissed the bed, but you just kept washing that bloody undershirt."

I needed coffee. "Were you watching me the entire time?"

She yawned. "I waited for it to get more entertaining, but even enchanted, you're a complete bore."

The smell finally hit me. Metal, cold, and tangy in the air. Magic. "Did someone do this to me?"

She picked at her nails. "I think you did it to yourself. Anyway, I'm famished. See you in dining."

AFTER CLEANING THE DISASTER in the powder room, I dressed and joined Lillian and Violet in the dining car. Smoothing my gloves, I passed through the rows of velvet settees and evened my breathing. Whatever had happened, it was likely nothing more than a strange side effect to Lillian returning the memories. The wraith had washed bloody clothes in the river beside our farmhouse and again in the Long Island Sound outside of Henry Foster's estate. If it was a habit or ritual ingrained in her, it made sense I would receive it with her memories.

Though, the clothes had always belonged to someone nearing death.

I thought of my bloody undershirt, long gone after I disposed of it outside the window. It was likely nothing. Perhaps a recreation of a past death of mine, a premonition in reverse.

That seemed the simplest explanation. I settled on it, heart winding down for the first time since waking.

The dining car was filled to the brim with excited travelers, refreshed after a full night of sleep. We had about two hours before arriving in Chicago, and the girls had already set to work without me. Notes scattered their breakfast table, heads pressed together in heated conversation. When I arrived, Lillian grinned. "Good morning, darling! How did you sleep?"

I looked between them. "Out with it."

Violet rolled her eyes. "Must everything be a conspiracy with you?"

"I'm fine," I said to Lillian. "Really. What's all this?"

She plastered on a smile, strained at the edges. "Just some things I wrote down from Thomas. But really, how did you sleep?"

My gaze shifted to Violet, who ignored me to feed Harold beneath the table.

"There was a strange side effect to the memories, but I slept fine. Truly, there's nothing to be worried about."

"Maybe I should—"

"It's fine, Lillian." I settled into the space beside her, smoothing my skirt. I wasn't sure where the protectiveness over the memories came from. I knew I should be rational—I'd promised Lillian she could reclaim them if anything went awry, and we had a dangerous task ahead. But I was worried if she took them now, she would never return them again. Despite the rude awakening, I felt curiously better. More complete, so to speak. Like I'd found something long missing, a photograph at the bottom of a shoe box or a beloved trinket I'd forgotten existed.

"Okay . . ." Lillian gestured at the papers. "Your brother was mostly restricted to the first and second floor, but he provided the best schematic from memory he could."

I pored over the first sheet, drawn in hasty charcoal. It showed a front door, a small security station, then a single hall leading to an intersection. From those two branches were six rooms each, most labeled as either an office or interrogation room. Additionally, there was a chapel, a room marked "Storage," and a second security station leading to a stairwell denoted "Basement."

The second blueprint was more familiar. When Babd tricked us into believing she was Agent Rodney, they had recreated the building in Ildathach, likely to not alert Tommy of anything wrong. I remembered the layout of those halls, the additional interrogation rooms, and the armory.

I pointed to the basement stairwell. "I'm assuming I need to go there."

Lillian nodded. "Thomas couldn't say what else was down there but knew there was some kind of storage space for classified files and artifacts. You'll be going in blind."

That was not comforting news. Especially after the last time I entered something's lair *blind*. I could still feel the heat of Lorvellian's breath moments before he nearly turned me to ash.

"This stairwell is under guard by four men at all times. There are two checkpoints to the entrance, two guards each, divided by an iron wall. The first point is manageable if you can convince the guards to let you through, but the second will be sticky."

"Why?"

"Warded straight to shit," Violet said. "And marked with every sigil under the fucking sun. Power blockers, power *trappers*, marks against malevolent intent, anti-compulsion symbols, anti-glamour, and the icing on this shit cake, an active curse."

My heart sank. A fool's mission, indeed. "Is that all?"

"No, it gets worse," Violet muttered.

Lillian frowned. "As you can see, this hall on the first floor leads to a dead end, and the second has an outside emergency door, also under heavy guard. There are no windows and no other means of escape. These two doors are the only exits."

I leaned back. "Fine, we've dealt with that before. The bank only had one exit."

"All the walls are one-way glass. You can't shade."

Fuck.

Violet raised a scathing, black brow. "Ready to cut your losses yet?"

It would be the smart thing to do, but unfortunately, no. I was a firm believer in the old idiom "If there's a will, there's a way." We simply hadn't discovered the way yet.

"And after all of that, you still won't know what lies beneath," Lillian added.

"Never mind that. We'll cross that bridge when we get there." I pointed to the stairwell. "Suffice to say, there's no way in hell I can break through all that on my own. Which means one of two things—I manage to sneak by with someone who has access, or I convince one of the Knights to take me down there."

Lillian worried her lower lip. "How would you sneak by?"

My first thought—glamour—was clearly not an option. Not only was Lillian's not strong enough to create an illusion like the one Babd possessed, but the anti-glamour sigil was a glaring problem. With only Lillian and me here, we were working solely with fae abilities, though it was safe to assume there were sigils and wards against druid spellwork as well.

"Fuck it. How can we convince someone to bring you down?" Violet asked.

I shook my head. "It'd be a whole lot easier if we knew what was down there."

"And we've come full circle," Lillian said, folding up the blueprints when a waiter sauntered over. It was the same boy from last night, fidgeting and red in the beam of Lillian's brilliant grin.

"Can I get you ladies something to eat?"

Lillian ordered an elaborate spread while I mulled everything over. I didn't know how long we could remain in Chicago without being discovered, but I gave it a few days at most. And that was being generous. I wanted to kick myself for becoming distracted last night with Lillian, but there was no way to retrieve the lost time now. From the moment we stepped off this train, we realistically had twenty-four hours to devise a plan. A plan that didn't involve my capture, maiming, or death.

Lillian patted my hand. "Let's eat, get settled at a hotel, and put our brains together, then."

The sentiment was reassuring but a farce. I knew exactly what she was thinking. This was a complete waste of a trip, and sometime tonight, when we realized how impossible this was, we would tuck tail and return to New York.

I picked at my food in sullen silence. Something Tommy said kept playing in my mind, a niggling afterthought I should pay attention to. *He ain't getting out in some freak prison fire this time. The Knights got something else to take him off the police's hands, then it's straight to Chicago for him.*

Straight to Chicago for Jack, but why? To interrogate him? That wouldn't last long, and eventually, they would need to dispose of him in some way. None of those rooms were labeled *chopping block* or *firing squad*, so what else would the Knights have done with him?

The thought pressed at me as we pulled into Union Station. A conductor took my valise and guided me down the metal steps. Lillian and Violet shuffled close behind me, but I stopped dead after two steps.

Jack leaned against the wall, my folded letter held between two fingers. "Ulysses."

TWENTY-ONE

ADELINE

JACK STRETCHED HIS ARMS above his head, dropping one around my shoulders. "Lovely weather in Chicago, isn't it?"

It was dark and sleeting, and a frigid wind barreled across the platform. Lillian gaped, and Violet scowled. Jack winked at them, then looked at me. "Beloved, do you think we could have a moment in private?"

I implored the girls for help. Violet shrugged. "You're on your own, bitch."

Wonderful.

Jack took my valise in one hand, my own in the other, and strolled down the platform, fighting the current of people angling for the stairs. The overhang ended, exposing us to the elements. He wore his usual gray suit, silver chain, and black coat, a flatcap hiding his dark hair. I'd remembered his warning on the ship and had my own winter hat, scarf, and coat, but it still wasn't very *human* of us to stand in the rain.

Sleet bore down, dotting his hat with icy droplets, nothing compared to the frigid look he wore. "I know the first thing you will ask me is, how did I figure out where to find you? To which I'll say you should be well acquainted with my exceptional intellect by now. Then, I know you will ask how I arrived here so quickly, to which I'll say I may have asked a favor of dear Guinevere, who just so happened to reclaim the New York–Chicago channel yesterday. Then you will likely scowl, tell me this is something you must do and I cannot control you. To which I would give a lofty lecture about how I am aware of this fact, but I still have an underground empire to run, and you cannot run off on suicide missions at your will. To which you will throw back in my face that two weeks ago, I said I may make decisions on my own if it is best for everyone, so why can't you? To which I will have no good counterargument other than you are important and needed at home, and I am incredibly selfish when it comes to you, therefore, I don't give a rat's ass about retrieving this book if it means any chance of your harm. To which we will return to the control argument, at which point you storm off and fantasize about my demise while I ponder why it's so goddamn erotic when you get all worked up like that. And I believe that covers it. Agreed?"

I stared at him.

"Lovely, glad we could expedite that." He exhaled a long cloud of condensation. "So how are we doing this?"

"Doing what?"

"Breaking into the Knights of Templar flagship shithole, what else?"

My eyes narrowed. "What are you playing at?"

"I'm not playing."

I jabbed my finger at his chest. "No, you are most certainly playing because I cannot honestly believe you would hunt me down and come all this way to go along with the plan you just called a suicide mission. So which is it? Learn my plans and sabotage them, or simply drag me back kicking and screaming?"

He leaned in, teeth flashing inches from my face. "Listen to me, and listen to me clearly. I think this is the stupidest thing you have ever done. I could write an epic of all the ways this can and likely will go horribly wrong. But I know whether I sabotage your plans or drag you back to New York by your hair won't matter because you will be on the next goddamn train west to try again. Because you are stubborn, and you want to help, and I will admit this may honestly be our one chance to get inside that place and back out again. I still don't give a fuck, but it matters to you, and you are not going to stop. So instead of sitting home, twiddling my thumbs, and waiting for my wife to return like an idiot, I am here. I am asking what your plans are. And whether you want me to or not, I am doing this with you because if you go down, I am going down with you."

Wherever you go, I will always find you.

I inhaled a ragged breath. "I'm not your wife, Jack. And self-sacrifice doesn't suit you."

"It's not self-sacrifice. And before you say it, I'm not trying to guilt you out of this either. The truth is I can't control you, and you can't control me. So if I can't stop you from doing this, then you can't stop me from helping."

The sleet picked up, melting through our clothes. He rooted through his pocket, furiously lighting a cigarette and pacing in measured steps. The foreign blend tickled my nose, eyes on the scuff marks he left on the platform. "It doesn't matter. This was likely all for nothing anyway. The place is damn near impenetrable, and we don't have enough information to work with."

He waved a hand like those were minor nuisances. "What do you know?"

"We have a layout of the first and second floor from my brother, but we need to enter the sublevel. The stairs are essentially impossible to access, and even if we could, we don't know what we're facing underground. The best we have is a hunch. I think it could be a pri—"

"It's a prison," he said.

My brows pinched together. "How did you know that?"

He leveled with me, throwing his arms wide as if to say, *Because I'm fucking Jack Warren.*

Fair enough.

"It doesn't make sense though. I thought they killed all the fae they came across, and that was that," I said.

"Who knows. To study them, torture them, maybe some of them they can't kill." He lifted the cigarette to his lips, crushing the filter to dust. "It doesn't matter. It's down there, I know it's down there, and if you think security is tight up top, it's even worse on the bottom."

"So it's a lost cause?"

"I didn't say that." He stomped out his cigarette, shooting a glance down the platform. Violet and Lillian stood alone, two little smudges in the distance. Lillian waved.

"So what now?"

He ran a hand down his face. "Right now, you are soaking wet, and I am fucking starving. Come on, we can continue this in a hotel room."

WE FOUND A PLACE within walking distance from the headquarters while maintaining a comfortable enough distance to sleep. The air warmed with the rising sun, turning the sleet into a temperate freezing rain. I folded my knees beneath me on a velvet armchair, watching the gray cityscape below. Jack made use of the telephone behind me.

"Three shipments of pocketbooks, one thousand units each," he spoke to the receiver, rattling a pen against the desk in our hotel room. Lillian and Violet were in the adjoining one beside us, the door closed and locked.

"Umbrellas," I mumbled to the window. "Not pocketbooks. If that's Mr. Costa, he changed the order last month."

Pocketbooks was the code word for whiskey. *Umbrellas* for absinthe. I was learning.

"Fuck, my apologies. Umbrellas." He waved for my attention, mouthing, *Thank you.*

I lifted my middle finger.

He smiled at that.

Rain slid down the window and pummeled the street below. Even in the wan, gray light, Chicago was a thriving city. The skyscrapers rivaled New York in height, restaurants and shops dotting every street corner. People hustled to and fro with black umbrellas. Down the block, a dazzling marquee lit in golden letters, stagehands bustling in and out for tonight's show. Chryslers and Bentleys chugged down the road, tops drawn against the rain, mixed into the fray with much more affordable Model T's. Everyone had somewhere they were leaving and someplace they were going to, but still, it wasn't home. I missed the mango trees, the bright sun, and clay between my fingers—

I shook my head. That was . . . peculiar.

Jack finished his phone call. His shoes made muffled steps across the verdant carpet, and he leaned against my window, arms crossed. I'd shed my wet dress for a dry one, but he'd left in such a hurry he only had the clothes on his back. His shirt, waistcoat, and tie were drying in the shower, leaving him in nothing but trousers and suspenders dangling at his hips.

He was in full human glamour, an irregular sight. He never maintained it when we were alone. I searched his skin like I could find his tattoos beneath the magic, craving that common sight for reasons I couldn't explain.

"I have an idea."

I nodded at the closed adjoining door. "Should I retrieve Lillian and Violet?"

"No, I wish to discuss this alone."

That couldn't be good. "Why?"

"Because they're not going to like it." He brought a hand to his face, swiping his thumb over his lower lip. I traced the movement with rapture.

"The only way past those doors is if you are a Knight or you are with one. No one is breaking through on their own. If it was possible, the Morrigan would have already done it."

I nodded, fixated on his lips. His scent. Glamour disguised the fresh rain and oleander, irritating me.

"Needless to say, we need someone to let us through," he said.

"Someone to let *me* through."

He eyed me. "We'll get to that."

I followed the column of his neck down, tracing the thick outline of the muscles across his chest.

"And they are certainly not going to do it without good reason. I highly doubt their establishment allows conjugal visits, so that means one of us needs to get thrown in a cell, and the other gets passage down. Since they still think you're human and we need to utilize that, it'll be me."

I startled, my trance forgotten. "Are you out of your mind?"

"No."

I rose from my chair, pressing the back of my hand to his forehead. "You're burning up."

He pushed my hand away. "I'm sidhe. We run hot, and I'm not losing my mind. Here is what I propose. You arrive at the headquarters late tonight and ask to speak to Agent Rodney directly—he's the only one I know by name with that kind of authority. Tell him you knew of your brother's plan, but before you could make your escape, I caught on and killed him. Say I dragged you here for . . . something—we can fine-tune that later—and you managed to make a run for it in the night. Act hysterical, ask him a million questions about what he could do to protect you and what kind of precautions they have as a group. This is important. You need to really convince him that you don't trust they can capture or kill me. Wait until he brings up the prison, which he eventually will because they're that desperate to put me away, then double down on everything I just said. Say you won't give any of them my whereabouts until you see the prison with your own two eyes and have been explained all the protocols because if I manage to escape, I will certainly murder you and everyone else. There's no way in hell they'll let you down with a mirror, but . . . but did you bring your makeup by any chance?"

I blinked. "My makeup?"

"Yes, your womanly stuff. The red shit."

"Blush?"

"Sure, blush. No—fuck, the stuff for your eyelids."

I stared at him, mouth agape. "Eyeshadow?"

"Sure, the sparkly one?"

Now I could see where he was going with this. "That won't work."

He fell to his knees, clasping my hands in his. "Whether I like to admit this or not, you are by far the most adept person I have ever seen with the shade. We don't understand it, but you can get through practically anything. They'll remove the mirror from any compact you take, but if you can crush up some of the powder onto the floor, then you can shade back in."

I stared at his hands overlaying mine, thick and strong. Rough calluses brushed over my skin, sending shivers up my arms.

"Addie?"

I shook my head. "Shouldn't we test it first?"

"You already did. I dropped the compact in the Guild. No one should have been able to use it to shade—it's not possible to get through a shattered mirror, but you did. And what is glitter in your makeup but much smaller pieces of shattered glass?"

"I'll wear sequins," I murmured. "That's safer, no chance of it spreading too thin."

"They won't let you in with anything reflective on."

"Sure, fine, but all of this is moot anyway. If I can manage to get down there, there is no need to shade back in."

"I'll need you to get me out. Besides, it would be foolish to go in without another means of escape."

I froze. "Why would I be getting you out?"

His hands slipped from mine. I craved the missing warmth. "Because of everything I just said. Are you listening, Annwyl? You seem out of it."

"I am. You're just not making sense."

"Like I said, you'll have to tell them where I am after they give you access."

"Why would I do that? I'll go down, retrieve what we need, and disappear."

He shook his head. "They won't let you leave without giving them what they want."

"Well, they can't stop me from shading out through my eyeshadow."

"Then they'll know you're not human, which is the only safety precaution we have right now. Besides, you won't accomplish anything with them hovering over you the entire time. There needs to be a re-entry. A stealthy one."

"So I'll give them a false location for you."

Another shake of his head. "There won't be enough time. The moment they realize you lied, they will shut down, and if you're going back in, you will be trapped there."

"For fuck's sake, so we'll make time. I robbed a bank in less than ten minutes. I can manage this."

"Annwyl, I'm not letting you go down there alone."

His declaration hung in the air. My lips parted only to shut again, any thoughts fading before molding into words. He refused to look at me.

"You're afraid," I said. It was obvious now. His frazzled state—forgetting what he saying or saying the wrong things. His endless fidgeting.

He rolled his eyes. "I'm fine."

"Jack, I can do this alone. I was alone with Lorvellian, and I was alone with the Morrigan. Both times, I came back in one piece."

He bounced his hand against my knee. "That was different."

"The Morrigan is far more powerful than these pricks."

"It's not about that. It's . . ." He released a breath, running his hand through his hair. "I should have been there for you both those times. You got lucky, and that's not me underestimating your skill or cleverness because you have an excess of both, but we keep walking a razor's edge with all these close calls, and one of these days, you will make a mistake, or something happens we couldn't have planned for, and that time, you won't return in one piece. Even the Morrigan managed to miscalculate once; they didn't account for you."

I grabbed his hand. "Let's just—let's forget this, okay? It was all too rash, too emotional. We'll find another way."

"No, we're doing this."

"We don't—"

"We do." He squeezed my hand, bobbing his knee against the floor. "We do because I have spent the last twenty-four hours searching for any other option. I've put Arthur to the task, I've put Will to the task, I spoke with your brother, of all people, and another solution doesn't exist. We need to make sure the sisters cannot reach that book. I'm sorry, I wish I could . . ." He swallowed, the thick sound filling the room. "I'm sorry I failed you again. I miscalculated too. I've been doing an awful lot of that lately."

Jaevidan, walking across the meadow. All those thoughts about what he must have done wrong, how Annwyl must have hated him for being useless. It seemed Jack had always cut himself to ribbons for those he cared about. And to this day, he hadn't stopped.

My voice dipped to a hush. "You didn't fail me or any of us."

A sad smile. "I appreciate it, darling, but I can't begin to count all the ways I've failed you. The only reason you're still here is because you can't remember most of it."

It was like the sun no longer shined for him. Eighty years ago, something happened that completely broke him. But the pieces fractured long before that. His brother's abuse, the family who left him, the constant self-flagellation for every mistake. Even as a child, he thought himself a monster.

Something I had called him not that long ago.

Jack and Adeline were two very different people from Jaevidan and Annwyl. We were adults to start, but we had support now. People. We had friends and lives and family those two children never did. All they had was each other. Lillian said even the sidhe may grow and change, but some things remained forever. Violet showed that. And Jack was certainly showing it now, this centuries-old need to appease his favorite possession, terrified of losing it.

And I had too. Because Annwyl liked to dance alone in the forest. She was an outcast. She loved to pick flowers. A woman in India how many years past made her shop into a swaying ceiling of herbs. She hid her face and preferred her solitude.

Even now, I could see the mango tree, could taste it on my tongue. Could feel the sun bearing down on my skin, soft fabric caressing my legs. I could hear Jack—from a different time, a different place. His laugh. And what I felt for him then bled into this moment. It had, too, because all I could think was I loved him so much. So much, an entire lifetime hadn't been enough.

I pressed my palm to his face, swiping my thumb over his cheekbone. His lower lashes caught my fingertips, a delicate brush against my skin. "You're not a monster."

Expressionless, his stare burrowed into mine. "You don't know—"

"Stop," I whispered. "You're doing your best now."

His image flickered, the backdrop changing. Sometimes it was this hotel room, sometimes a quiet meadow. Other moments were a red-clay wall or a lush forest of orange fruit. A scar winked on and off his chin. Sometimes he was a fresh-faced boy, others a man. But no matter what changed outside—around us, on us—inside me remained the same. He was terrified to lose me, and I never wanted to see him hurt.

I leaned forward, brushing my lips against his.

TWENTY-TWO

ADELINE

I REALIZED MY MISTAKE too late.

Emotions from the memories had clouded my mind, bleeding into this moment from another time. What a woman felt two centuries ago and a little girl four were not the same as what I felt now, but when my lips touched his, it no longer mattered.

Those lifetimes had their own thoughts and memories, but this lifetime did too. This body. It remembered how he tasted, the exact sound of his quiet breaths. The euphoric rush from the poison leaking off his lips. I recalled what it was to want him—the insatiable, depthless pool of longing. The anticipation of something I desperately needed and the intoxication of finally receiving it.

Jack remembered, too, because what began as a brush of lips became a press of them, then an envelopment, and then Jack's tongue swept across mine, and he grabbed my dress with two fists. I slipped from the chair, landing in his lap. My back hit the floor, and his weight pressed into me, rough hands combing through my hair.

He groaned, and my stomach tightened with the sound. My legs were squeezed closed between his powerful thighs, my heels clicking against his leather shoes. I ran my nails down his bare back, savoring the heat, savoring the smell of oleander and rain, savoring the familiarity of this moment both from this lifetime and other ones.

"Bed," he growled, already reaching beneath me. But I didn't want to pause this, fearing any space between us would create a chasm. I laced my fingers through his hair and dragged his mouth back to mine.

A low sound in his throat, and the bed was completely forgotten. His hands were everywhere—my face, my hips, my thighs. He grabbed the edge of my dress and pushed it to my waist. When the sash around my hips gave him resistance, he broke it in two and pulled the dress over my head.

His bare chest pressed against me, but there was still too much fabric in the way. He thought the same because my slip was pushed down my hips, and the bandeau beneath immediately followed. He licked a line of fire down my chest, not stopping until he took my breast into his mouth. His teeth nipped at the sensitive skin, and lightning raced down my arms.

I swept away a moment of clarity. I wanted this. I wanted him so badly it ached. Between my panting breaths and fluttering pulse, there was no room for logic or reason or past agreements of what we were. There was only the present, his body pressed against mine and his taste fresh on my tongue.

He kissed a line between my breasts, lips soft against the hardness of my sternum. His hands smoothed over my hips and pinned me to the opulent carpet. He dragged his tongue around my navel, kissing the soft skin just beneath. Before I could question his motives, he ripped the lace gauze of my underwear and rolled down my stockings.

I reacted on the memories seared into my flesh. My hips were already lifting, an aching pulse to feel his tongue on that forbidden place between my legs. There was no time for blushing, no time for propriety, before he hooked my legs over his shoulders and pressed his mouth against me.

God, did I miss that feeling.

He gave me a teasing lick, smirking when I shook so hard he had to hold me in place. The aching became a throb, and I was too weak to ignore it. The bond must have agreed because it pulsed between us with startling clarity. No longer did my own desires burn beneath my skin, but everything he felt as well—his want, his desperation, the ravenous need to be inside me. I gasped for air, wanting—no, *starving*—for more. I let that yearning show, and when his eyes met mine across my body, he obliged every ounce of it.

"Annwyl," he hummed against me, sucking *hard*. My back arched against the floor, a throaty moan falling from my lips. He did again. And again. And again. Then his fingers were inside me, and I was so hot I couldn't think.

My moisture glistened along his lips, walls tightening around his fingers. I wanted him harder, I wanted him deeper, I wanted *him.*

"Fuck me," I breathed. When he didn't move, my demand grew louder. "Jack, *fuck me.*"

Desire hit me so hard it made my head spin. I was reduced to a pinpoint of pleasure, an unyielding thirst. I could *feel* him. How much he wanted me, how deeply that craving ran. The throbbing pain below his belt, the flush of heat beneath his flesh. If I was starving, he was dying, but he didn't waver from his task.

A final thrust of his hand and his stare met mine. His glamour flickered, eyes oscillating between human and serpent ones. Heated breaths and a single word. "Beg."

It was a moment before I comprehended. "What?"

"Beg," he said, dragging the word long and slow. "Tell me how much you want me."

My eyes narrowed. "Fuck you."

He grinned, head tipping with a predatory stare. His hand swept down my thigh, igniting fire in its path. He pressed a gentle kiss to the inside of my leg. "I will, as soon as you tell me."

"*Fuck me.* How much clearer could I be?"

"Do you ask that of all your friends?"

It was like being dunked in cold water. A baptism of reality. My breathing slowed, heart resuming its normal pace. "No, I don't . . . I mean . . ."

He pushed my legs off his shoulders, crawling up to meet me. His eyes settled on their true form, vertical pupils inches from my face. He brushed a tattooed thumb across my lips. "I know what I want," he whispered. "What about you?"

I wanted to return the look in his eyes. I wanted to turn back time to when this was all far simpler. When I was one person instead of a dozen, when there was one enemy instead of hundreds. When we would whisper in bed late into the night, even though it was just the two of us, and I thought for the first time I was in love.

But Jack didn't study me with the overwhelming hunger of the parallel bond nor the infatuated loveliness of a budding romance. His expression spoke for him, that I was his other half and closest friend, and he would do anything for me, and he didn't want to fuck me like a stranger because he'd rather make love to his wife.

I said nothing.

He pressed a soft kiss to my cheek and pulled away.

"Jack . . ." I reached for him, but he was already standing, fixing his hair. Silence filled the room as he stepped into the bathroom. Running water filled the emptiness, and he returned with a washcloth, tossing it my way without a glance.

"You have another pair, right?" he asked, rummaging through my valise. My torn underwear mocked me from the floor.

"Jack." I shifted closer to him, ignoring that I was completely nude. He'd already seen every inch of me a dozen times over. He refused to look at me. I placed two fingers on his cheek, turning him my way.

Desire rippled down the bond, fierce and heated. His stare roamed my body, and for a moment, I was ready to forget the last minute happened. Sadly, reason reigned triumphant in the end.

"I would never make you do something you didn't want to," he said, low enough I barely caught it.

"I know," I whispered, and suddenly, I felt so awful it was a labor to breathe. He had always been this way, right from the beginning. Whether I learned the truth about the bond or not would have never mattered, and while it didn't excuse the secrets and lies, I understood. Lillian was right. He cared for me, and whether it was all the other me's or this me didn't matter. He wanted a spouse, and I wanted to fool around. This wasn't fair to either of us.

"I'm sorry," I said. "I wasn't thinking. I got wrapped up—"

"You're young." His lips tilted without humor. "In a way, but I forget that sometimes. It's fine to make mistakes, Adeline. You should. Now is the time to do it."

"Not when it comes to you." Worrying my lower lip, I said, "I wanted to be friends to simplify things, and I just blew that right to hell. I don't want to hurt you."

"You're not." He kissed my cheek, lips lingering against my skin. Hesitation, and then he pressed a second one closer to my ear. "Believe me, darling, I can handle myself. I've been doing this a very long time."

I thought of Jaevidan and Annwyl in the woods. How much he needed her in that moment, and her in return. And the memories of India, arms around each other and quiet sobs beneath a mango tree.

His tattoos caught the light, the Welsh words scrawled across his fingers. *In this life and hereafter.* Then, the two children on his chest, hugging each other in a violent wind. The little boy lifted his head and looked at me, the little girl still huddled against him. I had never noticed before, but those children, that scene . . .

I love you most.

My eyes roamed to the battle on his side. I always thought the dying warrior was the focus of the piece but never paid much attention to the man looming over him. A helmet covered his face, but the build was Jack's.

And the copse of trees on the back of his hand was identical to the ones in a Welsh wood.

And the woman dancing on a tabletop over his bicep, she looked just like . . .

"When did you get your tattoos?" I asked.

"I didn't," he murmured, still against my ear. Before I could inquire further, he said, "You should clean yourself up and get dressed. I'll speak to the girls, and then we have a long night ahead of us."

He rose from the floor. I stewed in my thoughts.

JACK DISCLOSED OUR PLANS to Violet and Lillian while I put myself back together, though I assumed he left the worst bits out since they had no protests when I arrived. In fact, Lillian seemed delighted. Meanwhile, Violet sat in the corner, wearing an expression that made me squirm. I still had many reservations—if that was even the word, but I knew there would be no convincing him nor stopping him. If he was hell-bent on getting himself killed, it'd take the Bogorans themselves to keep him away from the Knights.

Jack sent Lillian off for a little reconnaissance, and she returned in an even brighter mood. Jack wanted us in public tonight, a clear declaration of his general whereabouts and fodder for our story that he dragged me to Chicago against my will. As it turned out, a senator who purchased hooch from Jack was throwing a party tonight. One phone call later and we were given an enthusiastic invitation.

Lillian and Violet would remain behind—much to the former's chagrin. Jack wanted their presence in Chicago to remain hidden, *just in case.* I practiced shading between our rooms with my eyeshadow while Jack and Lillian went out to gather supplies.

Harold curled around Violet's neck, one squeeze away from stealing her life. She stroked his golden head, watching me appear and disappear before her eyes.

"That shouldn't be possible, you know."

Sweat dripped down my face, breath labored. I'd mastered the skill no less than twenty times, but if it was Jack's only hope of escape, I would accept no less than doing it in my sleep. "You all keep saying."

"For good reason." She patted Harold's head, staring lovingly into his eyes. "Is there any particular reason our Morrigan bond grew a bit *tense* after you were alone with Jack?"

Red flushed my cheeks, and it wasn't from overexertion. "No."

"Sure," she deadpanned, tapping a finger on Harold's nose. "Just a reminder—no matter how often I rant and rave about my brother, he's still just that. If you hurt him, I will fucking end you."

I was so used to her by now I only nodded. "Duly noted."

The other two returned several hours later as the sun began its descent. They had fresh weapons—two revolvers with regular lead bullets, extra knives, and a pouch of something that smelled like magic, but they wouldn't say what. Jack handed me a revolver to stash with my iron-filled one and a neatly wrapped box. "For tonight."

Alone in our room, I removed the packaging. A dress worth its weight in gold stared back at me. Soft silk gleamed in a blue so pale it could be mistaken for ice, sparkling diamonds sewn into every inch of fabric, matching the one around my neck. The dress fit perfectly, loose and sleek over my hips and falling mid-calf. A chiffon scarf went around my neck so both ends draped down my back, along with matching elbow-length gloves. At the bottom of the box waited the *pièce de résistance* of the ensemble—a delicate tiara strung with diamonds.

"I said I would get you one." Jack leaned in the doorway, studying my stunned expression.

That he had. The night we went to the ballet, and he not-quite-so jokingly said I could be the princess of prohibition.

"Still not a princess," I breathed, afraid to snap the thin metal in two.

He smirked, silent as he sauntered closer and gingerly placed it on my head. He smoothed my dress straps, fingers catching on every diamond. "Perfect."

"You didn't have to do all this."

He leaned his head to the side, examining his handiwork. "No, but I wanted to."

I feared I'd crossed a line earlier we soon wouldn't be returning from.

Lillian fussed and fixed my makeup until it met her exceptional standards. Violet didn't bother to say goodbye. Then Jack and I stood in the lobby, him chewing a cigar while the *maître d'* called us a car.

How peculiar—since when did I know so much French?

I shook my head and focused on Jack. He looked unusually elegant himself tonight, his suit replaced with a sleek, black tuxedo, his necktie for a bow, and the flatcap for a bowler. The silver chain now burned into my memory hung from his vest and a silver watch on his wrist. Between the human glamour and sharp attire, one could forget who he was.

He caught my stare, lips lifting. My heels, also studded with diamonds, clicked across the marble floors. If I ever learned the cost of this outfit, I'd surely stroke.

"You seem pleased," he said.

"Don't let your head run with it. Your bow tie is crooked." I made quick work of adjusting his already impeccable bow tie, careful not to brush his neck.

"Too late. As we both already know, my ego knows no bounds."

"An unfortunate truth." I patted his chest. "Remind me, where exactly are we going tonight?"

"I'll explain in the car," he said, pointing his cigar at a Rolls-Royce that rolled to a stop beyond the lobby doors. His hand went to the small of my back, and heat flushed my cheeks. A little lower and we'd be dangerously close to the position assumed in our room this morning.

When that only delighted him more, an idea occurred to me. A terrible one, and it undoubtedly made me a worse person, but it could convince Jack to listen to reason. A little hurt could save his life.

The day's rain came down in thick sheets, scattering the city lights along the sidewalk. The driver came around with an umbrella, opening the door and ushering us into the back. The storm drummed against the roof and windows, deafening in the enclosed space.

Jack smoothed back a strand of my hair. "You got a bit wet, darling."

Giving him my full attention, I lifted in my lips a coy smile. "As I often do around you."

He paused, my blonde lock caught between two fingers. "I thought we agreed my ego needs no stroking."

I ran a gloved hand up his thigh. "I wouldn't mind a little stroking."

Up front, the chauffeur coughed. "Where are we going this evening?"

Glamour flickered in Jack's eyes. He blinked, collecting himself, and rattled off an address.

I pressed against the leather seats, arching my neck and back in a long, slow stretch.

A hint of something profane whispered down the bond, squashed moments later. I faced Jack, head in my palm. "A senator?"

"Something like that," he said, fidgeting with a lighter in his pocket. He'd crossed his legs. "It doesn't matter, really. Just another business associate. This gala is for his wife's birthday."

Nodding with rapt attention, I said, "Anything I should know?"

"They're the usual snakes. Act as we always do when trying to blend in."

I pouted. "As we both know, conversation is not my strong suit."

His stare roamed from my crown to my waist. "I doubt that will be a problem."

"You seem pleased."

"Devastatingly so." The words were breathless and dangerously low.

I shifted closer, the blood heating my cheeks entirely real. Our legs pressed against one another, scorching despite the layers of fabric. He'd removed his hat in the car, and I took the opportunity to twirl a strand of his hair. "So, how will we celebrate this senator's wife's birthday?"

A suspicious look, finally realizing I was up to something. Indecision battled behind his eyes, but whether he cared or not became apparent with, "Surely in a far less interesting way than what you have in mind."

"What do you think I have in mind?"

He glanced to the front seat and the driver staring pointedly ahead. "Perhaps I should guess at a later time."

I leaned in, my lips a hair's breadth from his ear. "Should I beg?"

His foot tapped a methodical rhythm. "What is this about?"

"I was thinking . . ." I said, voice hushed as I played with his hair. "I still have so much to decide for myself, but there are some things I know I want. And I don't know why we should deprive ourselves of them in the meantime."

Against his better judgment, he leaned deeper into my touch. "Like?"

"Resuming our fun from earlier." I glanced up through thick lashes, lips a little grin. "We're very good at it, after all. And I do believe there's some things we haven't tried yet."

"True," he murmured, honed on my mouth.

"But I do have one condition."

"Anything she wants," he breathed.

I leaned in once more. It was now or never. "I don't think I'll relax so much knowing you might get hurt, that I'm dragging you into this mission needlessly. So how about a proposition? You let me handle this nasty business with the Knights alone, and we can spend the rest of the night doing whatever . . . you . . . want . . ." I whispered, giving his hair a gentle tug with each word.

A vicious smile. "Darling, are you trying to blackmail me?"

My hand slipped from his hair to between his legs. "I thought that turned you on."

He made a choked sound, pressing the back of his hand to his mouth to smother it. The chauffeur whistled a tune. Loudly.

Lips pressed against my ear, the guttural tone fried my senses. "The sentiment is sweet, Annwyl, and while I do appreciate your concern, I'm afraid you miscalculated. Like I already told you, where you go, I go. But keep up this little charade and I will bend you over this seat right now, witnesses be damned."

I nearly considered it. Say what you will about the rest of our relationship; there was no shortage of sexual attraction.

"Is that any way to speak to your wife?" I whispered.

Tensing, a tic feathered in his jaw. I wondered if I'd taken it too far, but he grabbed my knee, pinning me to the leather. "How about a bargain?"

"I know by now your bargains seldom work in the other's favor."

"Then a wager?" He pressed a kiss to my jaw. My eyelids fluttered, forgetting whatever we just discussed. "This senator's son has been giving me some trouble of late, trying to convince his father to move their imports locally. He was just elected as a judge, and I'm afraid that new position will give him the ability to shut my business down here. If you manage to win him over, then you don't give my true location to the Knights. But if you don't, not only do we go along with my plan, but I get to fuck you however I want . . ." He ran his thumb across my bottom lip, eyes flashing. " . . . wherever I want."

"We've arrived," the driver said, entirely too relieved. I took in the large circular drive lined with cars. Valets dipped between them, umbrellas reflecting the golden light of a massive estate. White stones formed several floors, columns and balconies overlooking a topiary garden. Through the floor-to-ceiling windows, humans in their finest dress chattered over thin glasses of bubbly. The driver exited and rounded the car. In the brief moment of solitude, Jack whispered, "Deal?"

Winning over a judge, how hard could that be? Jack did it every day.

"Deal."

Magic crackled the air as the driver opened our door. It was supposed to be a wager, not a bargain, but Jack worded it in such a way he could seal it with magic anyway. His devious grin burrowed beneath my skin.

Shit.

TWENTY-THREE

ADELINE

BEFORE I COULD REQUEST a renege, Jack opened an umbrella and helped me from the car. We fell into the crowd of other arriving guests, swarming like ants to escape the rain. Most presented an invitation, but all Jack needed was his name, and a burly doorman waved us through.

Even Jack seemed struck by the excessive splendor of the senator's home. I imagined Henry Foster—the druid whose house had been overtaken by a phooka last summer—had taken notes from this man, though his home had been in horrible disrepair from the uninvited guest. The foyer was split by a magnificent staircase leading to a second-story balcony overlooking the ground floor. Marble statues took residence in every corner, and gilded artwork hung from every wall. On our left, double doors to an enormous ballroom were thrown wide open, each embellished with intricate gold engravings. Two doormen offered champagne to those arriving, directing people inside.

Jack took my arm, snatching two flutes of bubbly with a wink. It was the human variety and therefore safe for us to drink several glasses without feeling any effects. Tables in crisp, white linen and matching velvet chairs lined one side of the room. On the other, three long tables filled with every variety of food. A quartet played strings in the far corner, but the crowd was either too sober or too embroiled in conversation to dance. I was unsure of the standard salary for senators these days but had no doubt much of his wealth came from less savory practices.

We joined a long line to greet the hosts. As usual, Jack garnered more attention than I was comfortable with, from men and women alike. I was introduced as his guest to no less than twenty people before we reached the front, too many names and faces to keep track of.

Though, Jack looked fresh as ever as we approached the family. The senator was a short, portly man with slick, silver hair. His smile was jovial but didn't reach the eyes. A politician through and through.

He aggressively shook Jack's hand. "I am so happy you could make it, Mr. Warren. Your invitation would have come sooner had I known you were in town."

"No need to trouble yourself. It was a last-minute trip. Adeline, this is Senator Belmont and his lovely wife, Clarissa. Miss Colton is my guest for the evening."

"A pleasure," the senator said, kissing my gloved hand. I exchanged kissed cheeks with his wife, who, while lovely, appeared as cold and distant as her marble home. Beside her was a much younger man in equally fine attire, thick brown hair gleaming over chocolate eyes.

"Mr. Warren, I don't believe you have met my son, Frederick."

Jack shook the younger man's hand with decidedly less gusto. "I have not, but I have read of you in the papers. Congratulations on your new position."

The younger Belmont nodded. "Thank you." His attention shifted to me. "And it is a pleasure to meet you, Miss Colton."

I held out my hand for him, fluttering darkened lashes. "The pleasure is entirely mine."

Frederick flashed me a smile, complete with two dimples. He was actually quite handsome, possessing his mother's beauty with his father's gleam. He kissed the top of my hand, lingering a moment longer than required. "What a charming accent you have. From the Appalachia, I assume?"

My smile stretched wider. "Now, how did you guess?"

A sheepish grin. "A friend of mine from university had a hunting cabin that way. Though I'm afraid my skills were severely lacking, the scenery was wonderful."

He just grew more and more charming. "Well, if you can find the time tonight, I would love to hear of it. It's always a pleasure to discuss my home with someone."

Something glinted in his eyes, lingering on my ensemble. "You can count on that, Miss Colton."

Jack gave me a sidelong glance, polite smile cracking in the corners. I beamed at him. "I'll be very welcome for the company. After all, Mr. Warren has a spectacular habit of turning all parties into business ventures. I'm afraid I often find myself alone not long into the night."

Senator Belmont laughed, patting Jack on the shoulder. "And of course, we love him for it. Now, please, get something to eat and enjoy yourselves. We can catch up later."

Jack shot Frederick a humorless smile. "Certainly." He took my hand and strolled across the ballroom.

We stopped at a food table, a tense smile plastered on Jack's face. "Darling, what the hell was that?"

I popped a grape in my mouth. "You told me to win him over."

"I think you did a little more than that." He traced each movement of my lips. "Though he may have other things in mind besides my business ventures, as you so elegantly put it."

"I have no complaints. Next time, add stipulations as to how exactly I win our bets."

He tensed. "Don't tell me you're interested."

I shrugged, nonchalant. "Why not? He's handsome, young, a judge, and apparently not one for violence. It may be a good change for me."

His voice came in a frigid whisper. "No."

"Oh?"

"No," he repeated, stepping closer. "Because when I get what I want, and I *will*, it will be mine and mine only."

My lips tilted. "Jack, are you jealous?"

"Not jealous, simply deciding how I plan to enjoy my spoils." He whispered against my ear. "Tell me, darling. Should I take your mouth or your ass?"

I shoved a grape in his mouth. "I think you should stick to fixing boxing matches. Making bets you can't lose."

He scowled. Victorious, I grabbed a second flute of champagne and decided to mingle.

As predicted, it wasn't long before Jack was dragged off by men salivating over his wealth, power, or general mischievousness. Frederick hadn't found me yet, but I could sense him following me around the room. I played the game, wandering until he made the first move. The judge may not have been a hunter, but if I learned anything from Lillian, all men loved a good chase.

In the meantime, I made work of conversing with the women—another strategy of my redheaded friend. Unfortunately, I found little useful information.

Giulia Mastrodoni, an Italian model from Milan, sighed with flair. "I just don't understand why he hasn't asked yet."

"Because he hasn't left his wife yet." Hazel Whittaker, an aristocrat's daughter from New York, also playing second fiddle to another man's wife.

Giulia scoffed. "The hag. We all know she's only with him for his money."

Hazel raised a brow. "Aren't you?"

Giulia raised her cigarette holder, taking a long drag through the sleek, black metal. "Well, we can't all be as lucky as this one. Congratulations, by the way. I hear Mr. Warren may win a certain contract with the local government. And he's certainly fine to look at."

I took a sip of my bubbly, feigning innocence. "You'll have to remind me which contract. Mr. Warren has so many business associates it makes my head spin."

The women shared knowing smiles. Cruel ones. Hazel took a long sip of her drink. "You're just so endearing. Don't worry, I'm sure you will learn all the ways of society soon."

I smiled back with the knowledge I had three daggers under this dress. "Oh, how sweet of you. Wait—I just had the most splendid idea. When we return to New York, you should both invite your beaus over to Mr. Warren's hotel, and we can all have dinner together. Clearly, I have so much to learn from the two of you."

Giulia in particular smiled too hard at that quip.

Next was a set of sisters from Boston, both well-known artists in the upper circles. Strangely, they, too, offered me congratulations. While they were infinitely better company than the last pair, they were equally useless.

By the third congratulations, I suspected something was amiss.

Jack found me at a quarter to nine, when the ambience had grown decidedly more drunk. Partygoers took to the dance floor, though it was still rigid waltzes for the time being. The tables grew louder, the smiles more vicious.

A moment to stand back and observe revealed exactly who was married to whom and who exactly was their mistress.

Jack ran a light hand down my back. "Not that I am one to gloat, but it doesn't appear you've made much progress."

I scanned the room, finding Frederick exactly where I left him. When I caught him ogling, he dipped his head with a blush.

"Don't worry your little head. I have him right where I want him." I tilted my flute toward Jack. "So, how many men sold their souls to you tonight?"

"Very funny, Annwyl. I'd worry more about your own strategy."

"Speaking of that." I frowned, leaning close. "I have a strange question for you."

"As you often do."

"Do I look . . . pregnant?"

"Not that strange." He took a hardy sip of the drink in his hand. "Is there something you'd like to tell me, beloved?"

I snorted. "No, but people keep offering me congratulations. It's odd."

"How could they not? You arrived here with me."

I gave him a scathing look, smoothing it in a jiffy when another presence appeared. "Miss Colton, how are you enjoying the party?"

I smiled at Frederick. That famous demure, Southern smile. "Oh! I'm just having the best time. Your family sure knows how to throw a soiree."

The food was terrible and the people worse.

"Excellent, very glad to hear it." He studied Jack, smile faltering. "Sorry, I hope I wasn't interrupting."

"Not at all. Mr. Warren was just leaving for cards with your cousins." I reached back, shoving my glass against Jack's chest. "Now, tell me the truth, Judge Belton—it will make my entire night. Do you like to dance?"

"Please, call me Fred," he said, looping his arm through mine.

When I threw a wink back at Jack, he appeared nothing short of homicidal.

"I have to admit something," Fred said, leading us to the center of the room. "While I like to dance, I'm afraid my skills closely parallel my hunting ones."

I giggled, nauseating even myself. "Well, then I say we make a perfect pair. I've been a dancer my entire life. You'll have the steps in no time."

"Truly? What dance?" He took my right hand in his, and I laid my other on his arm.

"Ballet."

"I can't say I'm surprised."

"Why is that?"

Red streaked his cheeks again. "Nothing—I only meant you have the figure for it. Tall and . . . strong."

Stars, this was too easy. "That's very kind of you. I have to say, you are also very tall and . . . strong."

He grinned like I'd just hung the moon. We turned, an inquiry waiting when we rejoined. "You have an interesting choice in companions."

I let my eyebrows furrow, endearingly confused. "Do you mean Mr. Warren?"

"The very one."

"Oh, that's a funny story." We turned. "My next-door neighbor is his secretary. When I first got to town, she helped me find a typing job in his office."

He assessed me, the million-dollar dress and glittering tiara. "Does Mr. Warren make a habit of attending parties with all his typists?"

I grinned. "If I tell you a secret, promise not to share?"

We turned, our arms joining once more. His smile turned conspiratorial. "Of course."

Leaning in, chest inches from him, I whispered low in his ear. "Mr. Warren is a brilliant businessman, but I'm afraid he gets rather shy around company, especially the ladies. Whenever he attends parties such as this, he asks a girl from the office to be his date. It's easier small talk for him and a night out for the women. A win-win."

He flushed a deeper red, and I doubted it was from what I'd just said. "Really? That's quite surprising. I've always heard he's something of a lady's man."

Waving a hand, I laughed like he just told a silly joke. "Mr. Warren? No, never. He's far too pious for that."

"Pious?"

"Oh, yes. A Catholic. Very devout."

"Huh, who would have known?"

The song came to an end. Without asking, he settled into position for a second dance. Across the ballroom, Jack seethed against the wall.

I was enjoying this party more and more.

"It's funny, I've never understood how one man could garner so many rumors."

Frederick frowned. "How do you mean?"

"I'm sure you've heard the most ridiculous ones." I looked at him expectantly, smiling when he shook his head. "Truly? How lovely. You know, I really appreciate a man who stays out of the gossip circles. It's a sign of good character."

He straightened, chest puffing like a parrot. "Thank you, Miss Colton. I pride myself on being a gentleman, both socially and in occupation."

"Please, call me Addie." Another sweeping turn. "I suppose it's poor of me to grind the rumor mill further, then."

His lips lifted. "I promise not to tell."

"Well . . . I already entrusted you with one secret tonight." I slid closer to him, far more than necessary for a standard waltz. "You know, I've actually heard people say he's a gangster."

"Ah, that rumor." His smile strained. "I don't think I should comment. It would be in poor taste to cut a man down not present to defend himself."

"Now, don't tell me you actually believe that too?" I frowned. Panic flickered across his face at displeasing me. "The idea is preposterous, and besides, could you imagine someone like me agreeing to work for a man like *that*?"

He cleared his throat. "Believe me, it's no judgment of you. But there are ongoings that a woman may not be privy to, for her own good. It's men's business."

Ugh, never mind. He wasn't handsome anymore. "Not to say he doesn't dabble in a few unsavory things, but nothing compared to Chicago. I'm sure, as a judge, you have your hands full."

"And how would you know about such things?"

"My brother, bless his heart. He's in the FBI, and we have always been rather close."

Frederick nodded. "Good man. I have the highest respect."

"He would appreciate that. But as I was saying, Mr. Warren is far from a gangster. We all know he makes his liquor and wine, but it's really a closed business. He only sells to friends or locals, and honestly, most of it is imported anyway." I lowered my voice. "I'm not sure if you heard, but there was a recent bombing at his hotel. Quite terrifying, but he has been coordinating with the police to find the culprit. They suspect it was someone from around these parts. I don't know about you, but if I was going to purchase a little liquor here and there for the occasional dinner party, I'd much rather buy from a man with standards, one who works well with the government and local police. Unlike those other rumrunners who call themselves businessmen. With their record of violence, it's such a risk."

We grew silent, his expression thoughtful. Our song concluded. "I have to say you're not what I expected."

Biting my lower lip, I reminded myself of Jack's *mouth or ass* comment until my cheeks burned red. "I hope in a pleasing way."

"Very pleasing," he said, leading us off the dance floor. "In fact, you have given me much to think about. If someone such as yourself can speak to his character, perhaps I should have some more discussions with Mr. Warren."

I looked down with bashfulness. "You hold me in too high regard, Judge Belton."

"As I said, call me Fred." He winked, handing me another flute of champagne from a passing waiter. "But enough of your companion. I'd like to hear more about you. "

I clinked my glass against his. "What would you like to know?"

A dinner fork struck glass. The ballroom fell to a hush, turning to the stage, where the senator stood with his wife. Jack used the opportunity to sidle closer, his presence impossible to ignore behind me.

"Please, don't stop on my account. I simply wished to make a little statement," the senator said, but his expression warned he demanded attention. "I wanted to thank you all for coming tonight. As a family man, there is nothing more important to me than the happiness of my wife and son. Seeing so many of our friends here tonight to celebrate my dear Clarissa is truly a gift."

A polite round of applause. The smile still didn't reach his eyes, nor his wife's. I'd never seen two colder people. I suspected this party was more for the senator's campaign than his loving family.

"Though nothing could ever be more important than the lovely woman beside me, as we are here to celebrate, I would also like to offer congratulations to several others close to us. Firstly, my son, Frederick, on his newly elected position as judge. I may be biased, but I believe he will be the finest this city has seen yet."

Another round of applause, more enthusiastic this time. I offered Frederick a brilliant grin and my own quiet congratulations. The entire room watched him, but his eyes remained glued to me.

"Of course, to our dear friends Governor Powley and Mrs. Powley on the birth of their first grandchild. We'll make a politician of him yet." Genteel laughter, and the senator continued. "Mr. Carson . . ."

I tuned the remainder out, applauding or laughing when appropriate. Jack edged closer, the heat of his body searing my back.

"And finally, a little surprise I was only informed of this evening." The senator grinned, gesturing toward me, or rather, the man behind me. "Though I'm a little offended I couldn't hear it from the man himself."

I frowned. Jack looked equally confused.

"Now, don't be so bashful. It was in the papers, after all." The senator held up his drink. "I would like to propose a toast to my dear friend Mr. Jack Warren and his lovely bride-to-be, Miss Adeline Colton. May you two love and cherish each other as much as myself and my dear Mrs. Belmont. To a happy marriage!"

Everyone remained silent, evaluating our stricken expressions. Seconds passed, the extending quiet intriguing them more.

Jack slid his arm around my waist, raising his glass. "I suppose the cat's out of the bag, then. Thank you for your kind words, Senator, and to the future Mrs. Warren."

The crowd toasted, disappointed with the fizzling drama. Frederick glowered, gave a polite nod, and strode away.

I stared at Jack, too stunned to speak.

He took a long sip of whiskey. "I think that means I win."

"ADDIE—"

"Don't speak to me, don't look at me, don't even breathe my fucking air right now."

I stomped ahead of him, rain careening down my face. The driver noticed our exit, stumbling from the car with an umbrella. "It's fine, thank you," I said.

Unsure, he glanced to Jack. *My fiancé* sighed. "Sorry, lad, could you give us a moment?"

I ripped the car door open. Jack shut it with a slammed hand. My finger shook in his face, sputtering, "To win a bet, Jack. To win a *fucking bet*. This is a new low even for you."

"I am just as shocked, alright?" He ran a hand through his hair, steadying his breath. "I have no idea what they're talking about. What paper, none of it."

"Bullshit," I hissed. "God, I don't know why I always put my trust in you. Every time, I believe you will do the right thing, and it comes back to completely fuck me over."

"*I didn't know*." He stepped closer. "Look in my eyes, Addie. You want me to vow it, swear it, repeat in the Abstruse? I didn't know."

"You know everything."

"I didn't—" He stilled, eyes closing. "Shit."

"What now?"

"The reporter."

It took a moment to catch on. Reporters followed him like flies. "The one from the police station?"

"Yes."

It did nothing to quell my anger. "You told me you would have Violet handle it."

"Well, I got a bit distracted with your missing brother and you blowing up the hotel. He must have run the story."

Seething, I snapped in his face. "Do not put this on me."

"I'm not." His heated breath whispered across my lips. "And we can solve this problem after, but right now, we have a more important task. When this is all done with the Knights, I'll see what I can do."

"Do what? Apparently, half the damn country knows by now. Aren't you the one always saying we have a public image to uphold?"

"Yes, but—" Rain sluiced down his face, glamour flickering. Vertical pupils glowed in the golden light pouring from the house. The driver signaled me through the window, but I held up a finger. My chiffon dress was destroyed.

"What is it?"

"I told you, I know what I want." Crestfallen, the words melted into the rain. "And what I want and what you want are different, that's all."

"What *do* you want?" But I already knew the answer.

"You are all I ever wanted," he said mournfully. The dejected reverse of the last time he'd said those exact words, also in the rain, with my happiness literally lifting us into the air. Like all highs, it was short-lived. Reality always dragged us back to earth.

So it was unfortunate for me to realize I still wanted him too. Not for sex and not because memories from past lives forced me to, but for a simple reason. The conglomeration of his support, his willingness to let me go, his respect for me, the mischievous and thoughtful person I adored all pointing to one thing. Something I was afraid to admit because there was another bitter truth. We had done nothing but hurt one another. Hurt everyone around us.

The driver stepped out with an umbrella. "Is everything alright?"

"Yes, sorry, just another moment," I said.

"Forgive me for being forward, but you two will catch your death out here."

I smiled without humor. "Myself and Mr. Warren are quite hardy, but thank you. Just another minute, please."

He grumbled about young folks but shut the door.

"I care about you. I have for a long time," I said. "But the future is so uncertain. I need to finish the memories and discover more of who you are, who *I* am. And we have a lot to atone for before we find our own happiness." Jack's lips parted, but I continued. "I need to understand you, Jaevidan. So much bloodshed has followed us, and that's not who I want to be. You know damn well that's never been who I am."

"I know." His throat bobbed, eyes refusing to meet me. "And I won't marry you out of societal pressure or political strategy, nor would I ask you to. That was never the case all the times before."

Longing squeezed my heart, more déjà vu of lives I didn't know. Apparently, I'd been married to Jack who knew how many times. It said something if I kept returning.

"Why?" I needed to know. Needed to prove something. "Why did you do all of this to bring me back? Why couldn't you move on?"

"Because . . ." He licked his lips. "Because you don't owe me anything, but I owe you the world."

A frown slashed my lips, head tilting aside. "What does that mean?"

"You'll find out." He gestured to the car. "Let's go. We should get a few hours' rest before all this with the Knights."

I didn't move. "I don't want you to go, Jack."

He sighed. "I won't let you—"

"I know you won our wager, but I don't want you to go. It's not worth the risk with how much depends on you. If something happened, who would guard the low fae? Provide their glamour? What would happen to your sister and our friends?" I paused, letting him mull it over. "I know you're afraid, but you have to let me do this alone. It's a hard choice, but it's the right one."

A drawn moment, his apprehension thick between us. "Is that what you want? To fight the world on your own?"

We weren't discussing the Knights anymore. "Right now, I have to."

Jaw clenched, he nodded. "Fine. Don't tell them where I am." He opened the door for me. "Just know I'll be waiting for you."

TWENTY-FOUR

JAEVIDAN

My hands were full as I slipped through the Veil, the flowers blessedly remaining alive in my leather-bound hands. Though I had long been able to move through the Veil no matter the state of the moon, it was a coincidence the human sky was black and empty tonight. This trip to visit Annwyl was unplanned, but they had all been recently. I spent more nights here than I did in Gerenstad.

It had been four years since I was declared dust-marked. My control over the powers had improved considerably, but whether it was the lower levels of magic in the human world or the presence of Annwyl, I fared better here. The endless ache in my head dulled to a tolerable thrum, and I could even touch the humans without causing them harm.

A discovery I was grateful for tonight with my plans. Both Annwyl and I had been so busy of late our meetings were often short. On the rare occasion I could sneak off during the day, Annwyl tirelessly worked in the castle. The lord had offered full-time work as a scullery maid a few months past, finally freeing her of the convent. She seemed happier, but with the castle farther away from our meadow and the endless work, it was difficult for her to meet me. I often had to sneak through the fortress myself, becoming adept at glamour as I disguised myself as everything from the numerous guards to other humans she worked beside. If it was nighttime, she slept in a large room with the other maids in little straw beds packed close enough to touch one another. In the warmer months, I took her out to the meadow, but she was so tired we talked for mere minutes before she fell asleep in the grass.

So, tonight would be special. I had flowers from Ildathach, a variety of moonlilies not found in the human world. I procured the wine my brothers gave humans when they wished for them to keep some inhibitions and, best of all, a loaf of bread straight from the kitchens with a charm for good spirits. I bartered away my best dagger to the brownies for their food and silence at the strange requests.

The bread remained warm and untouched beneath my arm, but I was already well in good spirits tonight. The bread would provide Annwyl some much-needed energy, and we could finally spend a few hours of uninterrupted time together.

I hid my wares beneath my cloak and disguised myself as Sir Edmund, a lousy drunk of a knight who was found more often beneath tables than his posts. Since he was rarely where he was meant to be, he was the easiest to mimic while not raising suspicion among the other guards. He also had a vexing habit of loitering in the kitchens and flirting with all the maids. Vexing, especially because he had taken a keen interest in Annwyl. All the men had.

At fourteen, she was still a child according to the customs in Ildathach. But humans lived faster, or perhaps they simply didn't give a shit because Annwyl was approached often. With her new station, she was fed well for the first time in her life. Her body was grateful for the sustenance and rewarded it handsomely. While still small in stature, she developed hips nearly overnight—wide ones able to accommodate child or whatever else the rotten bastards had in mind. With that came breasts that too often spilled out of the gowns she had long outgrown. And with the last remnants of child's fat slimmed from her face, she looked every bit the blushing maiden they no doubt saw in her.

It irked me, though I could not say why. Maybe it was her lovely innocence, not yet shed like the childish features from her body. Or that these men did not wish to know or love Annwyl, only to use her.

My own innocence died the night the Poison Prince was born, but at least I treated Annwyl the way she deserved to be. Or I tried my best.

The castle kitchens exploded in a flurry of rushing maids and sweltering fires. Smoke poured from the three burning hearths, all laden with roasts or bubbling stew. The sound of knives chopping through meat or vegetables drummed a steady beat, the melody calls of "more salt" or "bring this tray to the good lord." Brownies flitted between the unaware humans' feet, their non-glamour-touched eyes unable to see. A scullery maid by the name of Drusilla shot me a barely concealed scowl.

"Sir Edmund. I am afraid we have no drink for you tonight, but you may join the others in the great hall."

I frowned. "Where is Annwyl?"

She pushed back a sweaty strand of hair that freed from its coif. "How should I know? The good lord requested her elsewhere, as if we could afford to lose a set of hands." She shooed at me with a rag. "Go on, then. You can see we are up to our elbows for the feast."

Feast?

My heart sank. So much for our few hours of uninterrupted time. But I was already here and desired to see my friend.

I disguised myself as Drusilla to enter the women's quarters, but the room was empty. Next, I tried the grain stores and the barns, but Annwyl was absent from those as well. I wandered damn near half the castle when I caught her scent somewhere on the floor above me.

I made my way up, the scent growing stronger. Humans all smelled the same to me, but the glamour-touched had specific scents. Some effect of the scant magic dribbling through their blood. Each one was unique and easy to identify after one trained their nose to detect the notes beneath their overpowering human smell. Annwyl's was one I knew in my sleep. Strawberries and willow bark.

I found her in a room much finer than her other accommodations. A lady's maid fixed her hair with hot tongs while another tightened a corset around her waist. A real corset, not the flimsy things she sewed herself after the budding of aforementioned breasts. I wore the glamour of Drusilla, gesturing to the ladies. "You are needed down in the kitchens."

"We were tasked with cleaning the scullery maid, not becoming one."

Compulsion leaked into my voice, the air rippling with magic. "The kitchens have fallen behind schedule. I am afraid they need more hands, and mine are not suited to the task. I will finish with little Annwyl. Go on."

They blinked, then, like puppets on a string, dropped their items and scurried from the room. Annwyl smiled. "I know it's you."

I dropped the glamour, bowing. "I could hardly say the same. What is all this?"

She ran her fingers through a delicate ringlet, long, blonde, and beautiful. Her face had been whitened with wheaten flour and lips smudged with pink salve. No cosmetics were needed to make Annwyl more beautiful, and I was bothered by the absurd notion anyone would think as much.

"Is it not wonderful?" she asked, twirling a fresh strand of hair around the tongs. "You will never believe this. Lord Beynon has asked me to perform tonight at the feast!"

An involuntary scowl with the lord's name. "Perform?"

"Yes! You see, he ventured out one night for a ride when I was taking my evening walk to the woods. He saw me dancing and singing with the flower pixies—he could not hear or see them, of course, otherwise I would seem dull in comparison. But he said I was so lovely he wished for me to sing to his guests tonight. He even insisted I wear a lady's dress!" She gestured to a ridiculous gown hanging from an armoire. "I can hardly believe it myself. Me, entertaining the nobility."

"You could never seem dull," I said, assuming a position against the wall beside her. A spotted hand mirror had been propped on the vanity, in which she meticulously curled her remaining locks.

"Forgive me, Jaevidan, but you may be biased." She flashed me a lovely smile. "Is this not exciting? If I perform well, it may just elevate my position. The good lord said as much himself. He may even bring me to court when the season begins next spring!"

That sounded anything but exciting or lovely to me. Not only because I was yet to find a break in the Veil near the infamous Hampton Court, but I was wary of the *good lord*. His interest in Annwyl only grew with each passing month, and it was not like he could marry her. Even if he could, he was a doddering old fool.

"I am happy for you. That is very exciting news, indeed," I lied.

"Jaevidan, dear, could you please come cinch my corset. I am afraid I cannot reach that far."

I stood behind her, perplexed by the complicated set of ribbons and eyelets. She gave me a knowing grin, instructing me. My first attempt while wearing the gauntlets was useless, but I was not afraid to touch Annwyl without them. The single time she touched my cheek and came away scathed had never occurred again.

My fingers brushed her bare back, the creamy, white skin. I had seen Annwyl undressed dozens of times, back in the days of childhood when we went swimming or frolicked through the grasses in the nude. Even after her eleventh birthday, when she insisted on modest garments due to her womanhood. But that had not happened in a long while now, and especially not since she grew into herself. Annwyl was my closest friend, and I always viewed her as such, but even I noticed the changes in her. It was impossible not to when she was so . . . what she was.

Those thoughts came in dizzying waves as I tightened the corset around her waist, then helped her into the gaudy dress. On anyone else, it would be downright hideous, but with Annwyl's full figure and blushing cheeks, it stirred a few thoughts I had never had of her before.

"Why do you look at me so?" She frowned, checking her face in the mirror. "Do I appear ill?"

"No, not at all." I gave my head a shake, clearing those ideas away. "You look lovely, I promise. If you fail to dazzle the court, I will fall on my sword."

"Do not say such things." She laid a hand on my cheek. "May I ask something of you?"

"Anything."

Even beneath the layers of wheaten flour, her cheeks flushed pink. "It is rather embarrassing, actually."

"Even better." I grinned and flicked her ear, to which she giggled and pushed me away. "I am serious, Jaevidan."

"Go on."

"Well . . . there has been a boy, I suppose."

The smile melted off my face.

"He is very handsome. Seventeen years of age and a squire for Sir Benedict. You know the one. They say he will gain full knighthood soon."

I collapsed into a chair, picking at my nails. "Sounds like a yaldson."

"Jaevidan! Do not use such foul language, and he is anything but. In fact, he has been very kind to me these past months." She twirled a golden curl around her finger, suppressing a grin. "And with the prospect of me no longer being a scullery maid, he has been interested in . . . you know . . ."

I stared at her. "No, I do not."

"Well, if I can present a good image of myself, he may ask for my hand."

My vision went blinding red, slowly fading back to Annwyl perched on her stool. "What?"

"I know it is uncommon for knights to take a peasant woman's hand, but truly, Jaevidan, I think Emyr may be in love with me. I have no dowry to offer, but even this does not bother him. He says I am the most beautiful maiden in all of Wales, and this is all that matters."

Well, Emyr could go fuck himself. With a pike. In the arse.

"I always speak of your beauty, Annwyl. And I am a prince."

"Yes, but you are—" She waved a hand. "You are my best friend. It simply does not count."

"It counts."

"Unless you plan to marry me, it does not."

I had not, but I suddenly had half a mind just to keep this simpleton away from my human.

It had occurred to me Annwyl may marry, but human customs were so foreign to me. She was still so young, in my world nothing but a girl. Marriage would be preposterous at her fourteen summers. Drinking, merriment, and fornication, sure, but certainly not marriage. Thinking we had more time, I never gave the concern much attention. It was not that I wished to hinder her happiness, and perhaps it was selfish of me to feel so, but when Annwyl married, she would forget me.

And I knew her. She would swear on her human god and all that was holy she would not. She would reassure me I would always be her friend. But how would I visit her at night when a human man desired her bed? How would she find the time to walk the forest with me or sing faerie songs once she bore children? Annwyl was lovely beyond compare, and any man would covet it all for himself. The days would turn to weeks, the weeks to months, until one day, years went by and she no longer thought of me at all. Why would she, with a handsome knight for a groom and a litter of little humans to keep her occupied?

I had offered to marry Annwyl myself once, but we were children. Children who barely understood what the term meant. It was nothing but a silly joke, a tiny bargain she had likely long forgotten about.

I did not need Annwyl in my bed. I just needed her in my life.

Foolish anger manifested deep in my bones. It had always been the two of us. Me and her, Jaevidan and Annwyl. We had no one, so we had each other. But now she had an elevated position, a lord who took interest in her, and a possible groom on the horizon. All I had was corrupted magic, letters from princesses I despised more than the last, and a family that simultaneously feared and abhorred me. She broke our unspoken covenant by finding a life outside of me.

"Jaevidan, you are leaking."

I looked down. The wooden chair had turned black and warped beneath me. "Sorry." I stood, reminding myself to remain calm. This squire had not asked for her hand yet. "So, this Emyr . . ."

"Oh, yes. Well, it has not been confirmed, but Drusilla heard from Claudia, who heard from Alys, who overheard one of the boys in the stables say that he plans to kiss me tonight."

"Emyr does?"

"Yes, who else?"

I could not say, only hoped the answer would change.

"Anyway." Her expression grew guarded, a concerned look my way. "I suppose this is the embarrassing part, but there is truly no one else I may ask. They taught us so little in the convent, and you know how the nobility are, but I once overheard Drusilla warn the younger girls not to be led into temptation by kisses."

I squinted. "Kissing is hardly a wild temptation, Annwyl."

"Is it not?" She chewed her lip. "She said kissing leads to making babes, and before marriage, that is a terrible sin—"

I held up my hand. "Come again?"

Her throat turned a brilliant shade of scarlet. "Kissing is how babes are made, are they not?"

Slowly, to make sure I did not mishear her, I said, "No, Annwyl. Kissing is not how babes are made."

"Then how are they?"

Unwitting, my eyes fell to her breasts.

Tell her tell her tell her tell her.

I cleared my throat. "Perhaps that is a conversation you should have with Drusilla."

"But you are my best friend."

"Of course I am, but—"

"I can ask you anything."

"Yes, but—"

"Drusilla would only lecture me about the sins of Eve, and if I asked the other girls, they may not know. Or worse, make a fool of me."

"Fine, so—" I stopped. Annwyl stood with bated breath, eyes shimmering.

I shook my head. "On second thought, the best person to tell you would be your husband, after you wed. That is usually who explains everything."

"How would you know? You are neither human nor wed yourself."

True. On the fucking fates.

"Fine, but come closer. I do not wish to say this too loud, nor can I look at you."

She wore a devious grin, wrapping her arms around me as I whispered in her ear. When I was done with my explanation—which, I had to admit, was far more detailed than necessary—her eyes widened like dinner plates.

"Really?"

I nodded, thinking of anything that was not attached to me and below the navel. "Really."

"How vile." She shimmied with a full-body shiver. "Why would anyone want to do that? I thought only animals did."

I rubbed my hand over the back of my neck. "Well, it does feel rather good."

Her mouth formed a perfect circle, matching those too-large eyes. Lower than a whisper, she breathed, "Have you done it?"

"Me? Oh, sure—dozens of times. Many times."

That was a lie straight from the pits of human hell.

Biting her nail, she grinned through a fan of long lashes. "Liar."

"Do I lie to you?"

Now, she looked unsure. Guilt wormed beneath my skin, and I knew I was being childish, but I could not stop thinking of her stupid squire and his stupid kiss. As well as her lord and her excitement at the beginning of her life. I was the older one between us, the magic-born prince who had always been her sage guide. I taught her the ways of faerie and how to read and write and, apparently, how ones makes babes. But she was moving on with her life, moving ahead of me, and I wanted to prove I had options too.

"So you have . . . experience?" she asked.

"Yes."

"With kissing too?"

"Of course."

"Can you show me?"

My mouth fell open.

"Just the kissing part," she stammered, turning pink. "Not the rest of it. That would be . . . well, that would never happen, of course. But if Emyr truly does kiss me tonight, I want it to be perfect. This may be my one chance to woo him."

That would never happen. Those four words bothered me far more than they should have.

"I am not going to kiss you, Annwyl."

"Why not? It would just be for practice. Here, sit." She shoved me down onto her stool, sinking to her knees on the floor. "It is purely educational, just like when you taught me to read. Only this time, I want you to show me what to do. What a boy would like."

Churlish anger resurfaced. "It would be gross, Annwyl, and it is even stranger that you would ask."

She rolled her eyes. "I chewed spearmint leaves just before you arrived."

"That is not what I—"

"Besides, it is only strange if we make it so. You are like a brother to me; it is nothing more than a lesson."

I flinched. "A brother?"

"Of course. We have practically known each other since infancy. Now, stop being silly. How does one kiss?"

I stared down at her, perching pretty on the floor. Her eyes glowed with happiness, fantasies of her handsome suitor and their happily ever after. I could not say why I felt so bitter. Why I suddenly wanted to grab that squire by the neck and run my sword through him.

But her smile was so hopeful, so sweet, I could not be the one to ruin it.

"To start, do not seem so eager."

She squealed and clapped her hands. "Have I ever told you how much I love you?"

Bitterness soured my gut. "Do not move in too quickly—you will knock heads that way. In fact, do not move at all. Let him come to you."

"Let him come to me, understood."

"Um . . ." I rubbed my sweaty palms on my thighs. "Honestly, for the most part, girls just need to stand there and look pretty. You will know when he wants to kiss."

"But how?"

I sighed. "You know, he will cup your face or lean in or something."

She waved me closer. "Show me."

I really, truly did not want to, but I was a slave to my human and her whims. Worse, I had the notion that if I were to do this, I must make it perfect. Like Annwyl, terrified to ruin her one chance to woo the squire.

Maybe if I kissed her well enough, she would change her mind. My poison lips would ruin her and all other squires for the remainder of time. Then this entire marriage business would be dropped, and we could go on as things had always been.

Determined, I lowered myself to the floor in front of her. The torchlight burned hot against the walls but left us shrouded in shadows. I could see fine, but the dim light was perfect for Annwyl.

"Like this." I brushed the backs of my fingers across her neck, pushing a ringlet over her shoulder. I often forgot how nice it was to touch someone, to feel actual flesh instead of leather against it. The fact it was Annwyl only improved the experience.

She shivered. "That feels nice."

"Good." I smiled. "Or maybe he will stroke your hair." I ran my fingers from her scalp to the tip of a fresh curl. "Or lean very close."

She slid forward. I laid a hand on her shoulder. "Not you, him. Remember, you want to make him do all the work."

She frowned. "But what if he does not want to?"

"Then he does not like you enough, and you deserve better anyway." Her lips remained downturned, but I continued. "Trust me. You are a prize to be won, the glory at the end of a hunt. He wants to earn you, to feel like he received something special. Right?"

Nodding, she whispered, "That makes sense."

"Anyway." I shifted nearer, our knees brushing. "You will know he is about to kiss you because he will lean in, perhaps touch your face." I smoothed my thumb across her chin, dipping my own. "Wait for him to get about this far and close your eyes." She watched me with an austerity I had never seen on her before. Her eyes fluttered shut. I was so close now her fevered breaths warmed my lips. "And when he kisses you, move with him. Just purse your lips and enjoy the feeling . . ." I leaned closer, mouth a hair's breadth from hers. My fingers grasped her chin, her neck craned back with a hitched breath. One second more and we would touch. I would feel her warm softness against me. I would *taste* her. Lightning crackled along my skin, mouth tingling. Her lips parted, a gentle sigh passing her teeth and—

She cleared her throat, turning away. My hand remained midair, unmoving as she said, "I think I have it, thank you."

My hand dropped, a scowl stretching my face. "Glad to hear of it. Off to your feast, then?"

"I do think it is about that time." She stood, smoothing her dress and fixing her hair with jittery motions. She was acting strange all of a sudden, the seconds putting more and more distance between us. "Will you come down? You can glamour yourself as a knight."

Why? So I could watch her sing for a room of salivating men, waiting for her to be whisked off on a white horse? "You know I am not one for celebrations."

"Of course." Looking down, she wrung her hands. "Why do you not stay here, then? No one will enter this room, I swear it. And after the gathering is over, I will return and tell you all about it. Perhaps sing you one of my songs."

"Fine." I refused to look at her.

"Good." She nodded. "Well, see you in a few hours."

I gave her a half-hearted wave and spent about fifteen seconds on the floor before deciding I would kill someone if I remained in this castle.

My feet moved before my mind did, shuffling back the way I came. It was not until I stood at the Veil that I understood what I was doing.

Never leave, she told me, yet she was.

You are all I have left, yet that was not true.

Annwyl could be a liar, but that did not mean I needed to be.

I wandered the Darkwood until I emerged on the low road. But instead of following it home, I trekked deeper into the forest. Already, I could hear the sounds of drums and merriment. There were certain groves, gardens, or cliffs where the festivities never ended. We were fae. *I* was fae. And unlike our stuffy human counterparts, we were wild. Free. We did not need marriage or courtship or silly rules to earn our fun. We did not need permission to take what we wanted, and I was tired of pretending to be a human when I was not.

A group of dryads gathered around a fire, sipping wine and dancing to a faun playing the flute. High sidhe scattered the circle, deciding who would be their prey for the night. Sprites flitted through the air, chasing each other on drunken wings. They all stopped to bow at my presence.

I grabbed a sleeve of wine from the nearest creature, a redcap that must have wandered far from home. The creature scowled but did not resist. They all knew who—and what—I was.

"Do not stop on my account," I said, taking a long swig. I had never had the drink, and it tasted foul, but that did not stop me from swilling half the sleeve at once. "Your prince demands entertainment. Entertain me."

They looked to one another, unsure. They heard the rumors, they saw the bodies I left behind, and more so, I had a reputation for being the antithesis of mirth. But as I finished the sleeve and demanded more from a nearby spriggan, they decided a night of ruining the young prince seemed like a good time after all.

I got nice and drunk, which took an embarrassingly short amount of time. When the world tilted beneath me and the fire became a smudge of light, I pointed to the prettiest dryad in the circle. "You. Come with me."

She did not hesitate before rising to her feet. Her skin was birchwood, with hair like rippling sunlight. Offering a coy smile, she ran her hands down my chest as I led her into the darkness.

Only when she moaned beneath me did I realize she looked like Annwyl.

TWENTY-FIVE

JAEVIDAN

I woke up sometime past midnight, head like someone took a stone to it. A birchwood dryad curled up against my body, fast asleep. My naked body.

Fuck.

I sat up and rubbed at my temples, grabbing my clothes from the forest floor. The dryad stretched and gave me a sleepy grin. "Would you like to go somewhere else, my Prince?"

Suddenly, I felt revolting. Unclean. Like a lifetime would not be enough to wash off the stain of this mistake. I could barely remember what happened with her, but I was sure of what did. Too late, I realized having sex for the first time may have been important to me.

Something else I ruined. As usual, the fault was entirely my own.

She reached out to stroke my calf. "Lay down with me."

"No, sorry, I—" Stepped back. Pulled all my clothes back on. "There is somewhere I need to be."

She smiled. "But you are the Poison Prince. There is never anywhere you *must* be."

"My apologies, just . . ." I turned in a circle, feeling like I should give her something. Payment for using her or something, I could not say. "Just return to your tree and live a good life. Thank you."

She frowned, but I left no time for protests before sprinting through the woods.

I wanted to see Annwyl. I wanted her to smile and sing me her song. I would tell her everything. Confess what an idiot I had been and let her hug me and stroke my hair and tell me she thought no less of me for it.

But when I returned to the room, she was not there. No one had been for hours, the stones cold and torchlight extinguished.

I glamoured myself and entered the great hall, but aside from a few straggling drunks, it was clear of life. Next were her usual quarters, but the other maids were all fast asleep and her bed empty. I tried the kitchens, the stables, nearly got caught when a knight asked what I was doing on the balustrade. When absolutely sure she was no longer in the castle, I stalked to the barracks belonging to the knights.

If she was there with him, I would probably kill him.

Thankfully for the prick squire, her scent was nowhere on or around the building. I would have crossed her in the meadow, so that left only one place.

I pushed through the underbrush, no longer needing the will-o-wisps to guide me. It was Annwyl's favorite spot, and I often caught her sleeping there, even in the cold. The copse of trees emerged in the distance, the faerie lights hanging back as if afraid to approach. A group of brownies watched behind a bush, nervously chattering among themselves. Flower pixies stood watch from the tree branches, hugging and drying one another's tears. The sound of muffled sobs met my ear, then the thick stench of blood.

A lot of blood.

A pixie approached with a hasty bow. "Prince Jaevidan, we tried—"

I flicked him away.

Annwyl sat on her knees, fancy dress shredded and muddied. She held her face in her hands, crying so hard her shoulders lurched with each sob. I grabbed her hair, the curls now limp with blood and soot. "Annwyl, look at me. Where is all this blood from?"

She sunk into herself, crying harder. I tried pulling her hands away, but she turned into the darkness.

My heart thrummed against my rib cage, lungs seizing. Panic was unwelcome right now, but the stench of iron and blood filled my nose. I took a deep breath, hoping and praying it was not hers. Each heaving breath drew more strawberries and willow bark into my lungs.

I snatched her wrist. "Annwyl—"

"Do not look at me." She curled into a ball on the ground, knees tucked to her chest. "Please."

Enough of this. I pulled her into my arms. She thrashed the entire way. A million pleas left her lips, but I ignored them all, finally wrenching her hands away from her face.

I stopped breathing.

She sobbed, the sound more a scream. Snot and sweat and blood mixed on her face, dripping into her teeth. I used my sleeve to wipe it all away, but the blood kept pouring forth, crimson tears from a gash across her face. More than a gash. It started at her hairline, cutting across the bridge of her nose to end on the opposite cheek. In some parts, the knife went so deep it cut through to her mouth.

"I'm sorry," she wailed. "I'm sorry, I'm sorry—"

"Annwyl, stop." I tore a strip from my shirt, dabbing at the wound filling her mouth with blood. "Annwyl, please, stop. Just stop crying, you are making it worse. *Stop.*"

It was no use. She fell against me, heaving into my chest. I ran my hands up her back, warm moisture seeping through my shirt. "Tell me what happened."

She shook her head.

"Annwyl, tell me *now*."

She shuddered, and I realized with blinding wrath her face was not the only place blood poured from.

"I did not want to," she said, each word quivering more than the last. "I told him not to. I swear it."

My lungs failed me.

"I let him ruin me." She sobbed, shaking so hard I nearly dropped her. "I told him not to. I tried to get away, but he slashed my face, and I thought he would kill me and—"

Poison leaked from my hands. I willed it away, the pain all-consuming. 'The squire?"

"No." Her muffled scream vibrated against my chest. "No, he never even came. to the weeping pixies and chattering brownies, heads hung low. Only one dared to look back, the pixie who'd approached me before. He gave a solemn shake of his head, mouthing two words I would never forget.

Lord Beynon.

Lord. *Fucking*. Beynon.

Adeline.

I loosened my grip on her dress, tilting her face to me. "Tell me what he did."

Adeline, wake up.

She shook her head, tears streaming down and through her torn cheek. "I tried to fight him off, Jaevidan. I swear to you."

Adeline, it's a fucking emergency. Wake up right now.

I was too angry to think, too angry to stop myself. "Annwyl, tell me what he did."

What's wrong with her? Why isn't she waking up?

I don't know, try the memory diamond.

"I—"

I thrashed against the bed, sweat pouring down my skin. Someone's hands were on me, reaching around my neck. I screamed, but . . .

She cried out. "Please, Jaevidan, don't—"

Addie, can you hear us?

There was nothing Annwyl could do about it now.

Addie—

Blood splattered across my face, the only sound my echoing laughter—

Adeline, wake the *fuck up*.

"Please," she said. "Please, I will do anything."

I cut my knife through her throat. "You know what I hate most in the world? Liars."

TWENTY-SIX

ADELINE

HANDS THREADED THROUGH MY hair, and my head cracked against the head-board.

I screamed, kicking out. Lillian grabbed my arms and Violet my legs. The sheets beneath me were soaked, practically steaming with sweat. My heart thrummed like a hummingbird. A clock on the bedside table said it was past three in the morning, the pitch-black sky outside confirming it.

"What the *fuck* was that?" Violet screeched.

I ignored her, surveying the chaos around me. The hotel room looked like a tornado had run through it, the curtains and wallpaper shorn, the furniture atilt—even the carpet had been lifted in some places. My clothes scattered the room like flotsam on a deserted beach, Jack's watch embedded in the far wall and my valise torn in two. I brought my hands to my cheek, rubbing at a sharp pain there was no source of.

Violet and Lillian stared down, speechless.

"Where is Jack?" I asked. When neither answered, I had to stop myself from screaming. "Where the hell is Jack?"

"We wanted to ask you the same thing." Violet thrust a letter into my face. "This is all we have."

It was my letter, the one I'd left for him when we ran for Chicago. All had been crossed out except two lines of the poem, circled thrice.

One equal temper of heroic hearts,
Made weak by time and fate, but strong in will

Below that was a message written in hasty pen.

Some advice from a long-suffering scoundrel—next time, word your promises better.

And darling, try not to take too long.

- Jaevidan

P.S. The password is Annwyl.

Fuck.

I leapt from bed, grabbing the first dress I could. It was ripped in three places, but it covered me well enough. "He left without me."

They both asked, "He did what?"

"He left!" I pulled my shoes on, hopping on one foot at a time. "I told him not to come along, so the bastard went and turned himself in."

Lillian shook her head. "Turned in to who?"

"The Knights."

Violet pushed forward. "Please tell me that was a fucking joke."

"No, that was his master plan all along. He wanted me to shade him out with the eyeshadow."

"Why would he do that?" Lillian asked.

"Because—" I froze. Why? He said as our cover story, to give me enough time to get in and out, but none of that mattered if he went without me, before I had the chance to bargain access to the prison in exchange for his whereabouts. One could say he was enough of a fool to go and get himself caught, so I had no choice but to let him aid me, but Jack was many things. A fool was not one of them.

I reached for the diamond hanging around my throat, but it was gone. A glint in Violet's hand told me she had ripped it off. What happened at the end of that memory . . . it must have been Violet and Lillian tampering with it, skipping ahead to different scenes. It was only flashes, nothing substantial to grab onto. But I could still hear Jack's voice, his maniacal laughter through a vision of savage red. And that last part. I couldn't tell who the woman was but remembered what he said.

You know what I hate most in the world? Liars.

It must have been Annwyl. There was no one else it could be.

Dread chilled me to the bone. He couldn't have—no, Jack wouldn't.
Would he?

He had acted so erratically, going off to drink and fornicate simply because Annwyl wanted to kiss a squire. He was only sixteen, but still, it seemed extreme. Maybe. The fae were not like us, so it was difficult to say, but what if something happened that sent him over the edge? What if the reason he brought Annwyl back to life was—

No, he had told me Annwyl got married at twenty years old. She was only fourteen in that memory.

But the flashes at the end seemed to be from a different time. Likely a different memory. And Jack could have always lied . . .

"Violet, I know you can't speak of this, but how did I die in my first life?"

She blinked. "What the fuck does that have to do with anything?"

"Just answer it."

She threw her arms in the air. "Even without my vow mark, I couldn't say. I didn't know Jaevidan yet, not until after she died. I never met Annwyl."

On the fucking fates.

Lillian grabbed my shoulders. "Addie, what's going on?"

I shook my head. "It doesn't matter, not now. We need to get to Jack, then I'll get answers." I looked around the room. "Where is my eyeshadow?"

We scoured the room, finding no sign of it anywhere.

"It's not here," Violet huffed. "We can rob a department store along the way. Come on."

It wasn't here.

Everything else was here, so why wouldn't the eyeshadow be?

"Are you coming?" Violet snapped from the hall.

"Jack took it," I breathed. "Jack took it. He got arrested, and he brought the palette with him."

Lillian, "But he can't use—"

I ran for the bathroom before she could finish her sentence. My reflection stared back in the gilded mirror, warping with hellish intent.

I slammed my hand to the glass and entered the shade.

TWENTY-SEVEN

ADELINE

BLINDING LIGHTS CAME FROM every direction. For a moment, I wondered if there had been a mistake. That I had entered the wrong place. Once my pupils adjusted, I could see how wrong I was.

My experience with prisons was limited. As in, I had never been inside one before. But I had seen pictures in papers or heard descriptions from others. I pictured darkness and mildew, cement blocks and rows of bars. This was nothing I could have imagined.

Mirrors glinted from three walls, surely one-way glass. The entire ceiling had been affixed with glowing yellow bulbs. The fourth wall was the barred door I imagined, but wrong. No doubt iron—I could tell from the smell alone—but a waxy sheen coated them. It rippled in the oppressive illumination, shimmering rainbows like oil.

It was disturbingly silent.

I placed a tentative hand on the bars, grateful when they gave way. This cell, as well as the one across from me, was empty. I strained my ears, listening for any signs of life, when my heel slipped.

I expected eyeshadow dusting the floor. Instead, I saw blood.

Large pools of blood.

My breath hissed past my ears. There was no way to tell if it was Jack's, but glimmers of my eyeshadow along the far mirror said without a doubt, he had been here.

If he was dead, I would bring him back just to kill him again.

I ran my hands through my hair, thinking. There was no way to tell what lay ahead, and in my haste to get down here, I hadn't brought many weapons. Only the knife usually sewn into this dress and one I kept strapped to my thigh at all times nowadays, even while sleeping. I could always shade back to retrieve guns and help, but if the blood on the floor was Jack's, there was no saying how much time he had left.

That was my brilliant plan. Find Jack, find the book. Get out.

What could go wrong?

I listened once more, confirming no one lurked around the corner. Pushing the bars, I cringed at the squealing hinges. No footsteps pounded down the hall, nor did any gunshots ping off the walls. With a final glance at the blood, my reflection warbling in the crimson, I slipped into the corridor.

The block was entirely empty, which explained the silence and lack of guards. The long hall ended both ways with an intersection and, presumably, more cells. With any luck, the prison was a circle, and heading in either direction would take me where I needed to go, but I had my doubts.

Deciding left was as good a choice as any, I ran.

It was freezing. Strangely so—even my immortal flesh developed a chill. The fae ran hot and preferred that climate, so it had to be another form of torture, though I wondered how it was even possible. My footsteps clicked against the tile floors, too loud in the empty space. I kicked them off and left them in an empty cell, praying I wouldn't require footwear later.

I padded down the hall, checking the corners before deciding to turn right. Another long stretch of empty cells, chillingly cold.

My hair stood on end as I neared the final cell of this row. The soft patter of dripping filled the air and muffled voices. I searched for somewhere to hide, but with the blinding lights and smooth, mirrored walls, it was impossible. The voices grew louder, close enough to distinguish. I ducked into the nearest cell, flattening myself against the wall. Hundreds of my terrified reflections decorated the mirrors.

" . . . think the others know?"

"Can't say."

Their footsteps neared, coming from the intersection. I pressed against the wall until the mirror groaned behind my head, praying they didn't turn this way.

"It's strange, don't you think? I can't understand—"

"It doesn't matter. Just do what Rodney said, and maybe we can go home tonight."

"Don't you think we should question him more?"

They stopped, mere feet from where I hid. A few inches more, a turn of their heads, and they would see my reflection cast in a hundred mirrors.

"It doesn't matter what I think," the second Knight said, voice gruff and thick with age. An old-timer. "You're given instructions; do them."

"But—"

"Unless you want me to tell Rodney you can't follow orders."

Silence trickled down, heavier than the sweat dripping from my palms. The first Knight sighed. "Let's get this over with."

They continued down the perpendicular hall, footsteps hastened.

He. They had mentioned a *he.* I wasn't one for betting, but I'd put my money on it being Jack.

I slipped between the bars, dipping into an adjacent cell. They turned left at the end, and I followed, running back and forth between empty cells at their backs.

"Soon enough, these will remain empty forever," the first Knight said, running his hands along the clanking bars.

I used the cover of sound to speed ahead.

The second one snorted. "That will be the day."

They turned no less than a dozen times, feet carrying them faster with each hall we traversed. The underground prison was a maze, so many sharp turns and winding corners I soon lost track of how far I walked. It would be a problem for later. After what felt like a lifetime, the smell of oleander and rain struck with a vengeance.

The Knights ducked into a cell, but this was nothing like the others. Two other agents stood outside the door, a padlocked iron monstrosity. No bars on this one. The door was left ajar. I wondered if the door sealed to block out air.

I was never told if fae required oxygen like their human counterparts, but I wasn't waiting to find out.

The two Knights at the door shuffled in place. I flattened myself inside a cell five down from them when they weren't looking, wondering how the hell I was supposed to get past. My immortal strength was good, but even I couldn't stand against two large, heavily armed men. I had no gun—not that it would matter; there were still two Knights behind the door that I would rather not alert of my presence.

I appraised the bare room. There was nothing, not even a bed or sink or toilet.

Two knives. I had two knives and several weeks of Will's training on how to use them. The chance of me throwing each at the guards before one had time to call out and making them both lethal hits was slim to none.

I had no glamour or compulsion either, not that either would help me here. All I had was the shade. Something the Knights must have not figured out how to block yet, hence all the one-way glass.

Racking my brain for something, anything, I gasped when an absolutely terrible idea struck.

The image of my reflection in Jack's blood. My eyes in the crimson red.

I rolled my shoulders. Jack would fucking owe me for this.

Taking one of the daggers, I slashed my forearm until a steady stream of blood dribbled onto the floor. I had a brief moment to panic at how deep I cut, but it would heal within minutes. Immortality had its perks.

When a sufficient pool of blood stretched the ground, I counted my breaths. Evened my pulse. I only had one chance to pull this off.

I took the second dagger, memorizing the reflection inside it.

One of the Knights began to whistle. This was followed by a grunt of pain from behind the thick door.

I stepped out from the bars, throwing the first dagger at the closest Knight.

Before either had time to react, before the knife even struck its mark, I took the second one and flung it at the pool of blood, directing it through the shade and out the reflection of the first knife whizzing through the air.

There were two muffled grunts, then silence. My wound still wasn't healing, but no time. I tore my dress and bandaged my arm as I ran, bare feet splashing through the fresh crimson. The first knife had gone through the Knight's eye, and the second one, his companion's neck. The companion was still alive, sputtering around the blood filling his throat. I froze, watching pain and desperation cloud his eyes. An arm stretched out, fingers grasping air with a plea for mercy. Then, he grabbed a gun off the dead one's hip.

I ran forward, slipping in his blood and falling atop him. Hands circled my neck, pale and clammy. I choked for air, thrashing as he squeezed the life from me with the dagger still embedded in his throat. I slammed my forehead onto the hilt, sending the blade through the rest of his windpipe. A final twitch, and he slumped to the floor.

Air whooshed into my chest, but I couldn't feel it. My skin had gone cold, my mind erasing everything but the dead Knight's eyes. My own wound leaked through its crude bandage, and each breath hurt more than the last. Why the fuck wasn't I healing? I panicked, breath too rapid. If I wasn't careful, I would faint.

Survive, I told myself. *Survive, and you can cry alone later. Just like the Guild.*

That snapped me into focus.

I rose on trembling knees, clutching my forearm. Swiping guns and clean daggers from the dead men, I inched closer to the door.

Muted grunts of pain, of *agony*, whispered behind the iron.

I had both a gun and knife at the ready, but when I slipped past the door, it was another hall.

This one looked closer to my expectations of prison. Everything, from the walls to the floors to the bars, was made of iron, coated in that oily substance. The same oily substance that now coated my fingers and arms. A memory nagged at me, something Tommy had said after Babd kidnapped us. That I was unable to shade right away because they had used formulated wolfsbane and ashwood on me.

No time to dwell on that because unlike the cells behind me, these were occupied. Filled to the brim. At least twenty faeries snapped up at my presence, the nearest clambering closer to their bars. Others were chained with iron manacles to the walls, faces seared from iron muzzles.

A hobgoblin, no higher than my waist in height, leapt forward. "You—"

I put a finger to my lips, nodding my head down the row of cells. It seemed to go on forever. *Jack?* I mouthed.

The creature shook its warty head. *Help us.*

I turned in a circle. Most of the faeries here were weak, dying . . . some already dead and left to rot among the living. They were thin and broken, limbs at odd angles and bones protruding through taut skin. None of them had been given shoes and only a few clothing. Forced to stand, their feet were raw and bleeding on the iron floors. The ones too exhausted to remain upright curled on the floor, skin melting away beneath them.

I recognized these kinds of fae. If the Knights were to hunt down anyone, I would expect the vicious redcaps, the winged sluaghs, or monsters of myth like the Librarian. But all of these faeries were benevolent, creatures like the ones living in Jack's hotel. Little brownies like Charlene, their fur patchy and shorn. Flower pixies contained in iron cages. Spriggan men, whose treelike corpses petrified against the walls upon death. These faeries weren't harming anyone. They could be mischievous at times, but they had long lived among humans, sweeping floors or providing good harvests in exchange for offerings. Even if they had been the malevolent kind, no living creature deserved this.

I can't save them. The thought struck like a freight train. They were sick, injured, dying. They could no more fight the Knights off than I could.

But I could shade.

I looked down the row of cells. How many fae were here, tens? A hundred? A thousands? I could shade multiple at a time, but how long would that take? If I could at all with the Knights' formula seeping into my skin.

Jack and I were more powerful together. The closer our bond, the stronger the magic. If I could find him, I might be able to shade.

I crouched before the hobgoblin, swearing at myself for leaving my shoes behind. "Listen to me. I need to find Jack Warren, then we will release all of you. But I can't break you free without him. Did you see where they took him?"

Fae rushed forward, clambering for my whispered words. The hobgoblin waved them back, demanding silence. "Who may that be?"

Goddammit. This fae must have been new to the human world. "Jaevidan," I said. When that garnered no response, I said, "Prince Jaevidan, of House Valdivia."

The hobgoblin reared back. "But the Poison Prince is dead."

Blood pounded through my veins. No, he couldn't be—

"For centuries," he added.

Centuries?

That made little sense. Jack had been alive, well, and wreaking havoc for many years now. He was banished years ago but hadn't died. Unless banishment was so final to the fae they considered it another form of death.

Still, there were veil-crossers who smuggled in goods, such as the smoke blend Jack was fond of. They were few and far between, as Will had once explained to me. They couldn't be banished folk, as none but a few were powerful enough to override their banishment curse and return to Ildathach, where they would be killed if caught anyway. So all those who smuggled goods into this world were from the faerie side, and I assumed they would bring news back to their world. Though, I had never heard of Jack interacting with them. The one occasion someone did, it had been Will. Presumably because he was the least disliked among the Band of Banished.

It had been centuries since Jack had left his world, and time had a way of warping truth. Banishment became death, and death became myth.

Or Jack didn't want them to know he was alive.

I'd add it to the growing list of burning questions for him. I reached through the bars, pulling the faerie closer. "He's not, and he's here. Is there someone who knows where I may find him, someone who saw them bring him in?"

The hobgoblin cursed, dismissing me with a wave of hands. "Dash your hopes, my friends. This one is touched in the head."

They all slumped in defeat. Some cried.

On the fucking fates. "I will return later, I swear it."

But the hobgoblin turned away, joining a crowd of weeping brownies. I bounced on the balls of my feet. I didn't have time for this, but if one of these fae collapsed and died in my absence, I would never forgive myself.

I tore my dress, leaving the hem damn near my unmentionables. Not ideal, but it would do. "Here, take turns resting on this until I come back. Make sure everyone has a chance."

The hobgoblin stared at the proffered gift.

"Take it," I hissed.

He bowed his head. "Bless you. This—this is a life debt . . ."

I realized he was waiting for my name.

"Annwyl." I dropped the fabric into his hands. "And consider it fulfilled."

TWENTY-EIGHT

ADELINE

TERROR SEIZED ME THE longer I searched the prison.

Either Jack wasn't here, or all of these faeries were fresh from Ildathach because not a single one could speak of his existence. I sped down row after row, block after block. Thankfully, I found no more Knights, but the scores of imprisoned fae were endless. Those cells outside must have been a way of luring them here, trapping them in the one-way glass before dragging them to their final resting place. A thought too nauseating to dwell on.

Stranger, my name preceded me. The fae from that first cell repeated it in awestruck whispers, spreading like wildfire down the rows. Fair folk reached through the bars for me, calling for "Annwyl" like it was a prayer. Two rows past, I'd stopped to question a dryad about Jack's whereabouts. She sobbed so hard she could hardly speak, proclaiming the golden goddess had returned to exonerate them.

Dark fae dwelled deeper into the prison, but they were locked behind multiple sets of bars, too far away to speak to without screaming. It couldn't have been more than twenty minutes of scouring the cells, but it felt like a lifetime. Worse, the longer I searched the prison, the fainter Jack's scent grew. Finally, I could no longer detect it at all.

I stopped, leaning my hands against the wall to catch my breath. *Think, Adeline, think.* If I thought the Guild was a labyrinth, this could have been the end of the world. I'd already wasted so much time, and there seemed to be no indication I was getting any closer. I'd been careful to avoid the bars and felt my power slowly leak back, but the wound in my arm still produced steady trickles of blood. For all I knew, Jack really was already dead.

A thought occurred to me, so obvious I wanted to scream. The pools of blood in the first cell. If it was his, then it stood to reason I could shade to it again. A pool of blood wherever he lay.

My reflection cast through the flat side of my blade. It took longer than usual, but eventually, the metal warped and bent, ready to enter. But when I tried to reach through, there was nothing on the other end.

That meant one of two things—Jack no longer bled enough to form a pool, or his new cell was too dark to cast a reflection. I prayed it was the first and not the second.

What else, what else, what else? I paced. Any reflective items on his clothing would be long gone.

Eyes.

Eyes were the window to the soul. The entire reason one could enter the shade with ease through their own reflection. How many times had I looked deep into Jack's yellow irises, searching for the answers behind a hardened gaze?

Lifting the dagger, I thought of golden irises, the endless black of two vertical pupils. The flash of them when he smiled, my loving gaze from once upon a time gleaming back at me.

I landed in a room. Blood spurted from my arm, and dizziness racked me, like all my magic had been diverted to the task of shading.

For a moment, no one noticed me. Five Knights were present, one of them being the infamous Agent Rodney. They were pushed against the walls, skirting and diving around tendrils of poisonous smoke. Their guns had been coveted in the center of the room, but that didn't stop them from hurling iron daggers or long-pointed spears through the bars of a metal cage.

The fog cleared, enough to catch a glimpse of what lay inside. My heart slammed against my ribs.

His eyes were like beacons in the roiling smoke, two golden orbs that could have been suns. Darkness roiled around him like a shroud, a coat of shadows at his command. The tattoos along his skin were blacker than night, the hue so devoid they seemed to suck in the remaining light. There were more, more than I had realized, and the pictures so vivid they seemed to lift off his skin, gaining dimension.

His canines grew into long fangs, spitting venom as he snarled at anyone reaching too close. The cage kept him contained, along with thick iron manacles around his wrists and neck. They had cut away all his clothing save for boxers, skin red and raw wherever his skin touched iron.

The Knights noticed me.

One cried out, and the rest soon followed. In the space of a blink, one of those iron daggers directed at Jack whizzed my way.

The metal was too dark, too dull and matte to shade anything through. I dropped to the ground, grunting as the air left my lungs, and the blade soared overhead, close enough to scrape along my scalp. I produced the stolen gun, firing blindly into the abyss. A bullet pinged off the metal wall. A vicious shriek followed.

Someone reached for me, but I kicked out, swinging the dagger aimlessly. It struck something soft, another howl of pain. I ripped the dagger out and swung again and again, not stopping until blood splattered my face and the floor. Another Knight neared, but the lingering fog spurred into action, surging down the man's throat and up his nostrils. His face blackened and withered, his dying scream lost as he collapsed.

A spear hurdled my way, but I rolled to the side just in time. Agent Rodney's eyes met mine across the room, a flicker of malice, before the poisonous fog thickened until there was nothing left to see.

It gathered around me, dark and ominous. I flattened against the wall, shaking. "Jack," I called out. Louder, "*Jack*."

The fog edged closer. I sought the exit, but it was no use. I could no longer see more than a few inches around me. Darkness touched the ceiling, blocking out the last remnants of light. I sucked in a large breath and closed my eyes, but that would only delay the inevitable. When the shroud of death touched me, my skin would blacken and burn like the rest.

"Jaevidan," I moaned, a final plea. This is how I would die, saving the man who would kill me. I shouldn't have come here. I should have trusted my gut, allowed myself to accept the truth of what happened to me in my first life, what had killed Annwyl—

The fog brushed my skin, a cool caress of misty rain. With a gasping breath, I shivered, waiting for pain to arrive. It didn't. The poisonous gas swirled along my skin, eerily similar to the shade.

I opened my eyes.

It was pitch-black, a depthless midnight. I lifted a hand before my face, seeing nothing but the dark. Terror conquered my thoughts, wondering if the fog had made me blind. Hot fluid coated my arm and stomach, feet unsteady.

Two lights flickered in the darkness, golden beacons drawing me closer.

I sank to my hands and knees, too weak to walk. Liquid seeped in the lines of my palm, between my bare toes.

Golden eyes blinked, leaving me temporarily suspended in darkness. The vertical pupils narrowed, calling me home.

Come to me, they said. *Crawl to me. Writhe for me. Drag yourself across the stones.*

I slid forward, one painful inch at a time. My wounded arm screamed beneath my weight, dizziness threatening to take me down.

Closer, those eyes whispered. *Be with me. Submit to me. Obey. Fall before your master and kneel as my slave.*

I slid across the floor.

Closer.

Blood gushed down my arm, filling the space between my fingers.

Closer.

Golden eyes hovered a mere foot away. My salvation, little suns in the dark.

CLOSER.

My head cracked open, and nausea sent me to the floor. Liquid pooled beneath my stomach. I hadn't realized I'd been stabbed there.

Sharpened talons scored my skin, sinking into the remnants of my ruined dress. I cried out, but they wrenched me forward. Two hands grasped my face, slick with blood and hard with calluses. I struck out, shaking my head and sobbing curses when a pair of lips pressed to mine.

Euphoria. Sun drifting through the trees, and the sweet smell of peaches on the wind. Cold water rushing past my ankles on a scorching summer day. My brother's laughter and Papa's song, our grins as we scattered salt above our heads. Lillian's fingers through my hair and Violet's approving eyes.

Will's wicked smile and Arthur's ruby blush. The shade—dark and lovely and powerful as I waded through its depths. And Jack. Jack in our grove, singing songs of the snow spirits. Jack on our farm, watching me through darkened trees. Jack beneath the mango tree, kissing my hair. Jack grinning, kissing my outstretched hand in the gardens of Versailles. Jack kneeling across from me, bowing over tea. Jack lying beside me in the forest, stroking my hair. Jack, and Jack, and Jack, an endless loops of memories and moments with different times, different skins, but finally—

His lips left mine. Pain faded, a happy buzz coursing through my veins. I reached blindly but knew exactly where to touch. "What did you do?"

"That will only stop the pain for a few minutes. Get the keys."

I frowned. There was darkness and rolling hills. Jack's youthful face swimming before mine as he dangled a coif over my head. "Jaevidan, what keys?"

"The keys to the cage, Addie."

The image changed, this time an opulent palace. I slipped a key into his hand, red touching my cheeks. "So you may visit me."

"What?" He rattled my shoulders. "Addie, get the keys off Rodney's body. He's right there."

We reclined in a gondola, the hot sun bearing down. I stretched out my legs, grinning as I dipped my feet in the water. "The key to my heart, you say? Well, it will take far more than that, Welshman."

"*Addie.*" He shook me so violently my teeth ached. "I need to get you out of here. Get the goddamn keys. *Now.*"

The setting changed again, melting into a scene where those eyes flashed in the dark.

"Get the keys off Rodney's body," Jack said. My mind locked onto those two circles of gold, the only things left in the world. Voice low, the sound layered on itself like a creature of hell. "Bring them to me."

My ragged breaths joined the darkness, a sense of wrongness. My limbs moved against their will, blood pulsing to the beat of Jack's heart. Compulsion. He used compulsion on me.

Even knowing that, I lurched forward. Sweat tracked my face, leaving salt on my tongue. A klaxon sounded in the distance, a flash of red bleeding through the fog.

I found Rodney. Maybe. My hands moved over his shriveled legs and hips, finding what I sought. What Jack sought, but his desires and mine felt one and the same. I wore the key ring like a bracelet, crawling back to the cage.

"Yes, yes, thank you." He took them from my outstretched hand. The keys dangled from my wrist, melting into the image of golden bangles. I gave them a little shake. "Hello, foreigner."

"Hello, Annwyl," Jack said. "My name is Jaevidan, or Jack, depending on the century. I don't know why this is all coming to you now, but you most probably believe your name is Sujana at the moment." There were several clicks and metal clanging against the ground. "Tell me, are we married yet?"

"No." I shook my head. "I love you, but this is my home."

"I know it is not the same, but I promise you will adore Europe. We can make a new home," he said, smoothing back my hair.

I shook my head, determined this time. "I will—"

"—not return to Wales with you. If you love me, truly love me, you will stay in Chennai."

"I never did win that argument." Strong arms wound beneath my legs and lifted me into the air. "But you were right. Chennai grew on me."

My cheek rested on his bare chest. I startled at the sticky wetness. "You're bleeding."

"So are you." We left the room, fog roiling behind us. Warning lights replaced the dim lantern, dousing everything in eerie red. "Do you remember which way you came? They blindfolded me."

"But what if Samuel hears?"

"Let me worry of him," he breathed, sheathing himself inside me. "Do not speak of him when I fuck you."

"But he is my husband. He—"

"—will know. He will kill us both."

"Don't worry, Lizzie, he's long gone." Jack tapped my cheek, bringing my vision back to the present. "Tell me how to get out of here."

My vision blurred, the prison a streak of iron walls and roiling, red smoke. Alarms blared, pounding against my senses.

"Set me down," I said.

"But—"

"Please."

Jack lowered me. I stumbled against him, willing the world to stop spinning. Other scenes flitted by, times and places that weren't this one. I shoved them away, pain igniting behind my eyes. Clattering echoed down the hall, cries for help and shouts of anguish.

"We need to help them," I murmured.

"Help who?"

"The other prisoners."

Jack stood in nothing but undergarments, form unsettling. Any pretense of humanness must have dropped with all the wards on the prison. How he managed to use his other abilities was beyond me. Everyone said Jack was unnaturally powerful, but I never realized how much until now.

"We have no time." He grabbed my arm, jerking me down the hall.

I dug my feet into the ground. "No."

"Listen to me." He grabbed my face, stared deep into my eyes. I shut them to weaken any compulsion. "We don't have time. Knights are swarming down as we speak. We can draw another plan later, but we must leave *now*."

I understood, could recognize the urgency, but it was the Guild all over again. Us running, others dying. My life saved while so many others fell on my behalf. I would not—*could* not—allow that again.

"We still need the book," I said.

"Fuck the book."

He pushed me forward, but I held my ground. "You were the one who told me the druids didn't die in vain. *You* were the one who said becoming the fate they deserved was the only way to repay them. What about your speech on hard choices, that everyone is perfect when they are on the outside looking in? If we leave now, what does that make us?"

Violet said none of us were good, but that didn't need to be true. I didn't care if it ruined our mission. I didn't care if it killed me. Jack warned me to never lose my humanity. That immortality could ruin us. I would rather die now on the right side than live forever on the wrong one.

He saw it. The determination in my face, the truth that I would not concede this time. He pushed two daggers into my palms, glinting in the chilling, blood-tinged light. "I'll look for the files. Start shading them out, and if you are found by any Knights, don't think, don't look back, just get the hell out of here, and don't return. *Swear to me.*"

I'd made many promises to Jack, and I was yet to break a single one. It was hypocritical to hold him to his honor without maintaining my own, but if he thought I would leave him down here, leave anyone down here, he didn't know me at all.

I pressed a kiss to his cheek. "Go."

He was gone before I could blink. I turned to the first cell in sight, ignoring the wounds and memories vying for my attention. The faeries here were mostly dead, but a few sick remained. Using the keys from Agent Rodney, I rummaged through until I found a skeleton key. The lock clicked open at my touch. I snatched the prisoners and threw a knife to the ground.

There was no saying they would survive the shade in their damaged states, but it was the best I could do. I thought of the hotel room in Chicago, but that wouldn't be enough to house all of them. They needed somewhere safe to go, a room large enough for all the dying. Somewhere someone could help them.

Time to put my skills to the test.

I had three passengers, a large load traveling a few miles, let alone the distance I planned. I reached through the shade, the liquid current resisting me. It thrashed and seethed, a riptide dragging me back the way I came. But I was stronger. I was faster. I was its master.

The four of us landed in the ballroom above Jack's apartment in the heart of Manhattan. A starry nightscape stared back through the skylights, the city pouring through the windows. The faeries groaned, panicked voices rising through the din. "I'll return with help. Stay put." I had one more stop before returning to the prison.

I landed in Will's apartment. It was dark, but his soldier senses must have never left him because he appeared in the living room, hair mussed with sleep and brandishing a sword. Two long, slow blinks before he recognized me. "Addie, what are you—"

"No time." I grabbed his arm, and we returned to the ballroom. "They're injured, and there's a lot more coming. Call for help and heal as many as you can."

He trembled at the naked, half-burned fae on the floor. "What is this?"

"I'll be back." I kissed his cheek and returned to the prison through the discarded dagger.

Another wave of dizziness sent me to my knees. Another memory surfaced, this time of a life I had never seen before. A dusty old tavern—no, a saloon. A man red with perspiration and drink slid an empty shot glass across the bar . . .

No, focus. I found the next cell, filled entirely with high sidhe. They saw what I had done with the last group and clambered at the bars, begging for release.

I brought them to the ballroom and shaded back for the rest. Each time I arrived back in New York, a new fae from the hotel arrived to patch wounds and deliver tonics. By the fifth round, Guinevere had arrived, along with Arthur. I didn't stay long enough to chat. Each journey brought a fresh wave of nausea, each trip taking longer than the last, but I didn't stop. I ran into my first Knight when the block was complete, but the liberated fae took him down for me, their cries for Annwyl blending with his dying screams.

On the next block, I opened all the cells at once. A few rushed forth, but most remained still, too terrified or injured to move. It took far too long to coax them out, but when I did, I found several volunteers willing to watch my back or take the skeleton key and open more cells. The relentless fog persisted, only harming those with human blood. What Jack was doing should have been impossible, but there was no time to question it.

It was chaos. Screaming prisoners, dying throats gurgling, blood splattering the red-tinged air. The klaxon blared on, burning a memory into my eardrums. I opened a cell filled with red caps, offering them asylum in exchange for holding the barrage of Knights back. They agreed with disturbing glee, dragging their cloaks to soak up the blood on the floor.

The memories tormented me, slamming against my skull and demanding entry. At one point, I blinked and found myself on scraped knees, washing a shirt in a pool of blood. Another moment, someone shook me, asking why I stared into an empty cell. I thought I had been in Wales, gazing out across a barren, wintry field. A dagger slashed my arm, but I didn't feel it. A bullet fired through the smoke and grazed my cheek, but there was no time to think. Only move. Only shade. Only get to the next round of prisoners.

The swarming fae overpowered the guards at the door, screaming to run for the stairs. So many knights remained but were soon overwhelmed by the rushing tide. Someone slammed into me, and my head struck a set of bars. Someone called my name, but they were too far away to hear. I slumped to the ground. My muscles ached, blood poured from wounds, but my body was too weak to heal them. Once more. I could shade once more.

A voice cried through the crimson din. The sound of my name lifted above the chaos.

Through a sea of rushing legs, malevolent eyes met mine. A man ambled through the fog, gun raised. His clothes were scorched black, skin melted with dripping fat and blood, but somehow, I still recognized him.

Agent Robert Rodney.

The blaring klaxon faded away, the stomping feet and hum of voices. His voice did not translate to sound, but bloody lips formed seven words. *You will burn in hell for this.*

The gun lifted. A finger that was nothing but bone curled around the trigger. His hatred reminded me of something Jack said yesterday, a declaration he and the Knight shared. *If you go down, I am going down with you.*

But in the end, I still won.

My lips curled upward, blood and iron coating my teeth. "See you there."

A bullet fired. Clutching my diamond necklace, I slumped to the ground.

TWENTY-NINE

JAEVIDAN

ANNWYL, JUST TELL ME what he did.

That time, she had. And with each word passing her lips, with each gory detail, my rage crescendoed. Lord Beynon. Lord fucking Beynon. He never cared for Annwyl. He never believed her kind or hardworking or skillful, though she was all those things and more. He only wanted to use her. Control her. *Rape her.*

He hurt my human. *Mine.*

Releasing her, I drew to my feet. I had only one thing on my mind, and Annwyl sensed it. She cried out. "Please, Jaevidan, don't—" The cries dissolved into withered sobs, fists clutching my legs at my retreating steps. "You cannot harm him. He is my lord and—"

"I couldn't give a fuck less of some lowly human's title," I snapped.

Her sobs died, fingers unfurling from my legs. She trembled, doe eyes craning up. Fear shot through them. Real fear.

She had never looked at me like that. Not once.

I sank to my knees, cupping her face. She winced when I brushed the open wound, but all the blood obscured where the borders began. "I'm sorry. I should not have spoken to you like that."

Her lower lip trembled.

"No one is your lord," I whispered. "No one is your master. As long as I draw breath, all your enemies may answer to *me.*"

Her throat bobbed, hands twitching in her blood-soaked lap. The crimson stain rekindled all my rage. "He provides my work. My food, my shelter. If I do not go back, there is nowhere else to go. Even you cannot protect me from this."

That propelled me over the edge. It was salt in the wound, a stab to my pride within my simmering fury. I was drawn back to all those times I truly couldn't help Annwyl. When I was weak and magicless, her hungry and desperate. If it had not taken so long for my powers to appear, her obsession with the lord may have never happened at all.

"Come here," I murmured. Her eyes still spoke of fright, but Beynon had changed her. He'd molded her into this tiny thing, this little bird bred to obey and please. I ached for the days she threw rocks at my head or called me a fool. She crawled back into my lap, wrapping her arms around my neck. I kissed her hairline, letting the smallest touch of poison fall from my lips.

It was a trick my brothers used on women, but their intentions were not mine. Mine were the opposite. The touch of toxin eased her pain and her mind. She slumped against me, and when I kissed her again, our grove went silent.

I laid her down on the ground. It would keep her unconscious for the night, but we needed more time. Her to heal, and me to act.

Compulsion no longer worked once you were far enough from the victim, but I was dust-marked, and it was possible to hold a spell if the person did not resist. When I told her to stay asleep for the next few days, she would.

I gestured for the pixie with enough balls to approach me. "She needs fresh clothes, and those wounds must be stitched. Pick your best seamstress for her face. She lost a lot of blood, so make sure to drip water and broth into her mouth until I return."

The pixie bowed his head. "We of the Bannau Brycheiniog have always known Annwyl as a good friend of the fair folk. We shall care for her as if she were one of us."

"Good," I said, backing away. "Because if she dies, the rest of you will join her."

In the meadow, my skin leaked poison like a sieve. I could not tame it if I wanted to. The unprecedented rage that followed the dust marking my blood had reached its peak. Somewhere inside myself, I knew I was wrong. I knew I should obey Annwyl's wishes, remain with her instead of seeking revenge. But I could not stop. I could not discipline my anger if I wanted to. The world had let Annwyl down. *I* had let Annwyl down. Now, someone needed to pay.

Donvidan was in Tearachan, a diplomatic envoy to ease growing tensions. People whispered of war on the horizon, and my burned brother sought a way to renew his reputation. This did not matter. He was not who I wanted, anyway. I needed someone stupid, someone violent, and someone just scared enough of me to do my bidding.

I found Kalvidan and Periwen in the gardens, sipping wine to the twinkle of a dryad's harp. Faeries in various states of drunkenness lounged around them, giggling as they ripped the wings from a sprite who wandered onto their path. Fine. The more witnesses to my declaration, the less likely his pride would allow him to back down.

I slapped a hand against the harp, silencing the strings. The dryad hissed at me, jaw slackening when she realized who I was.

"Friends. Brother," I called. The latter watched me wearily, fingers stiff around his chalice. "I have a dilemma, and I am afraid I require some assistance."

They grumbled among one another. I paced the stones, snatching the sprite from a kelpie's claws and returning her wings. "You see, it would appear a human has insulted me. This foul, worthless creature calls himself a lord. Lord of what I cannot say, likely of shit." The faeries tittered. I opened my palm so the sprite could flit away. "I cannot let this slight go unnoticed. If a man thinks he is worthy to speak my name, then I say we pay him a visit." I gestured to Kalvidan, a smile stretching my lips. "What do you say, brother?"

THREE DAYS LATER, I rode a kelpie into the human lands, glamoured to appear a common warhorse. An entourage of sidhe fanned out behind me, each sporting saddlebags filled with the finest gold, jewels, and wine Gerenstad owned. Beside me, I stuck Kalvidan on a fat, white pony, the human jester's costume glittering in the sun. His fingers curled around a ridiculous trumpet, his scowl permeating the balmy air. He'd insisted on playing my role, but after I let my poison burn all our surroundings, he swore to do anything I asked.

It was petty, but that was not beneath me.

Yesterday, I asked Scholar Rindshaw to pen the finest announcement he could. He did not understand my sudden penchant for cruelty, but it did not bother him. In fact, he found my proposed scheme quite entertaining, stating I should use it as dinner conversation at the next Calamity. The letter was sent ahead to Beynon Castle, and the final preparations were completed this morn.

I felt quite good about myself as we strolled through the village. Peasants lined the streets, throwing flowers and cheering as we passed. Feeling extra generous, I produced a bundle of wrapped pastries and threw them to the crowd, along with several shillings I had collected over the years. They swarmed into our path, sobbing and stroking my steed with cries for "the good prince." They could not see what I truly was. Could not detect my horse had eyes of brimstone and teeth sharp as blades. To them, we were nothing more than the richest, most beautiful humans they had ever seen. Only the glamour-touched cowered in fear, watching through slats in boarded windows.

Kalvidan played his stupid trumpet as we approached the castle. The guards I'd become so familiar with lined the drawbridge, suited in freshly polished armor. Lord Beynon, his wife and three sons, a vizier, and several other important enough to attend stood before the main gate.

My eyes honed on one man only. Poison threatened to leave my gloves, but I tamped it down. I'd had three days to let my volcanic rage melt into a cold one. The kind of anger that lay dormant, a bottomless well of patience ready to strike when it would hurt the most. The kind of anger that never left someone.

This man had degraded Annwyl. He had taken her at her happiest, the moment all her dreams were supposed to come true.

I say, let him enjoy the taste of his own foul shit.

Kalvidan completed his fanfare, announcing to the crowd, "Prince Jaevidan of Arabia, first of his name, Son of the Golden King and Master of Swords."

It sounded even more pompous from Kalvidan's lips. Delightful. The way these humans practically fell over themselves to greet me brought an evil joy I could never reproduce.

The lord rushed forward, bowing himself in half. "Greetings, good prince. We received your letter this day past and have prepared for your arrival. It is such an honor to host one such as yourself for this trade envoy you—"

"Do you have wine?"

Beynon blinked. "Yes, Prince Jaevidan, the finest—"

"Bring me some."

A lengthy pause echoed over the bridge. Smile cracking at the edges, the lord turned to one of his maidservants. "Fetch the prince some wine."

"No," I called, mustering my best arrogant huff. Removing my foot from the stirrup, I thumped the lord's chest with a muddy boot. "I asked you."

Cheeks redder than a cardinal's ass, he clenched his teeth and gave a perfunctory nod. "Of course."

Satisfied, I swung down from my horse. The stableboy—his name was Ifan, I thought—rushed forward with a flurry of bows. After asking every question short of if my horse liked to piss facing west, he brought the beast back to his stables. Hopefully, it did not eat the real horses.

With the lord gone, I swaggered toward the gate. His wife was much younger than him, perhaps only five or so older than myself. Pretty enough, but plain. As the sons looked near her in age, she was clearly the second bride after their mother joined the dark.

I took her hand in mine, kissing her knuckles far longer than necessary. "And who may you be?"

Her cheeks turned a dangerous pink. She curtsied. "Lady Beynon, Prince."

"Lady Beynon," I repeated, reciting it like poetry. "Tell me, do all the women of your lands possess a countenance as lovely as yours?"

Beynon's oldest son gave me a sidelong glance. I flashed my teeth at him.

"You are too kind." She curtsied again, but her knees trembled. I pondered if I should fuck this man's wife before killing him.

Fantasies of how he would react ended as the lord returned with my chalice of wine. My distaste for the drink had not changed in three days, but I had an appetite for watching him serve me. Swiping it from his hand, I declared, "The Lady Beynon will give me a tour. Bring my men to their quarters, and we shall resume our introductions tonight."

"But—"

I took the lady's arm, beaming. "I have heard of these so-called English roses, but truly, you are something exquisite . . ."

The lord fumed behind me. In the distance, onlooking sprites chimed with tinkling laughter.

Lady Beynon was as plain as her face, but I listened with rapture to every word she said. She asked me questions, but I feigned more interest in her than myself, answering only a select few. Yes, I was truly a prince of Arabia. Yes, we desired trade. I chose to visit their land because I'd heard tales of Welsh beauty and desired to see the sea before returning west to hold audience with the English king. Yes, I did keep cobras as pets, and yes, they were very venomous.

I toiled the day away with Beynon's wife until the setting sun declared it was time to feast. Kalvidan would play his part and entertain us while my court dined and conversed with the humans.

I managed to slip away briefly, donning the glamour of Drusilla to enter the servants' quarters. The brownies would find Annwyl something acceptable, but I knew she would want her own dress. The scent of humans overwhelmed me, and I stopped in the doorway as voices floated from the room.

The real Drusilla stood with two younger scullions I did not know the names of. One of them whispered, "But she still has not returned."

Drusilla shrugged. "Perhaps she ran off, then, but it is not your concern. You both are needed back in the kitchens."

The second girl chewed her lip, glancing anywhere but at her elder servant. "I know we are not to speak of such things, but I think she was hurt. I heard screaming that night. It sounded like Annwyl."

Blood freezing over, I leaned closer.

"Whatever happened, she brought on herself," Drusilla snapped. "She chose to partake in the sins of Eve. Blushing at every man that passed. You two should take warning of what happens to girls with loose morals. Annwyl got exactly what she deserved."

"Yes, Drusilla," the girls murmured. I retreated into the shadows.

The lord was good and drunk when I returned. "Our guest of honor! I would love to share a word with you."

I would rather gouge out my eyes but took the seat beside him. "You may speak."

He smiled, but his eyes spoke displeasure. Men like him were unused to being talked down to. "I detest politics at the dinner table, but I see you are a very busy . . . man." His expression revealed exactly what he thought of me, the faerie wine inhibiting his control. A petulant boy, one he was forced to cater to. "In the spirit of new friends, I wish to pass you my counsel. Our great King is no fool and will make no trades without gaining your trust. Windsor Castle may be a treacherous place indeed, but with a fellow countryman at your side, I believe an arrangement could be reached that would suit both our fine regions."

He thought me an idiot. A pampered prince incapable of political sparring. "And I assume you propose yourself?"

"I have long held the King's trust. We studied together as boys, and it was on his recommendation I obtain lordship in Wales upon its conquer. My opinion is held in high regard, and my resources may be of value to you."

Hogwash. No one wished for this lordship. Cardiff held all the power. This land was barren, rain-soaked, and limited by the wild forest and mountains beyond. Beynon was either sent here as punishment or because he held no favor in the human courts.

I played along. "What value do you speak of?"

"My land is one of bountiful harvest. Lumber, crops, cattle . . . you need only name your price. Like all lordships, we are subjected to taxes from the crown. As a foreign emissary, the fees for export and the sovereign's own taxes will decrease your own profits. But I am a man who takes good care of friends, Prince, and I see no reason a transaction could not occur silently between men of similar interests. For the sake of diplomacy, I could represent you in an offer to our good King as well. With me, you have more to gain."

And he was a traitor to his crown. Lovely. "You have my interest."

"Good." Lecherous eyes sparkled with mirth. "A toast, then, to the beginning of a grand alliance. Huzzah!"

I held my chalice in the air, smiling myself. "Huzzah."

The lord drank greedily, gulping the last dregs of his wine. I had insisted we finish the drink of my people before a single sip of his. The entire human court was deep in their cups. I could end this all now, but I wanted him to soak it in.

He nodded at an elderly man at the table across us. The man lifted his cup and toasted me. Soon, the news of the lord's successful swindle rippled across the feast. No doubt all these preening idiots had gold in their eyes, plans for how they would utilize the new wealth and status their lord now offered them.

It was Beynon's moment of glory. His court adored and respected him. He would not only gain favor with his king but hold leverage within the human courts. He would be richer than the crown if he worked our trade treaty right. Everything a disgraced nobleman could wish for had dropped on his doorstep. His wildest dreams come true.

There was only one thing left to do. Take it all away.

Drusilla entered the hall with more fruit and meat for the gluttonous beasts. Fruit girls like Annwyl picked, meat the peasants starving in their hovels raised and slaughtered. Not a flick of dust on their clothes or callus on their hands. They thought they were above all others. Their low-birth slaves were mere objects beneath them. Someone should have warned them. No one was above me.

I leaned toward Beynon. "Where I come from, it is customary to provide entertainment to visiting guests."

Nodding like an eager dog, he said, "Forgive me, Prince. That we may provide. What entertainment do you seek?"

"Women," I murmured, grinning. "The finest your land has to offer."

He loosed a barking laugh. "That will be no problem. Drusilla!"

The scullion came our way. "Yes, my lord?"

"Our fine guest requests company. Choose one or two of your girls to clean up and meet him upstairs."

She nodded. "Of course, my lord."

With that confirmed, I stood. "Remain a moment. I have an announcement to make."

She looked unsure but would hardly disobey a prince. The gathered humans and members of my true court faced me. The wine had long since taken effect. There was a reason I never gave faerie food or drink to Annwyl. It had the pesky habit of enslaving humans.

I came for the lord, but they were all culpable. The wretched monsters who grew fat and greedy while the orphans starved in convents. While Annwyl suffered year after year, begging for scraps from their table. Using those beneath them for all they had, then discarding them like waste.

A venomous smile stretched my lips. The fae tittered with glee. Stepping onto the table, I held my chalice in the air. "Friends," I called. "Do you know why I have chosen to visit tonight?"

The nobles frowned. They thought my intentions were made. "No?" I asked. "Well, the reason is simple, really. I have been insulted. Something that belongs to me has been taken." I strode down the wood, kicking chalices and plates aside. "Your dear lord must answer for this. I seek what he stole."

Beynon stood. "What is—"

I turned on my heel, snapping my fingers.

His lips welded shut. Grunting, he clawed at his face with rising panic. I grinned. "Do sit down and shut that shithole of yours." His ass hit his gilded seat, eyes watering. But Annwyl's tears meant nothing to him, and his would mean nothing to me.

"As I was saying before being so rudely interrupted." I stomped on the fingers of a noble. He screeched but made no movements. None of the humans did, enslaved to their chairs like discarded puppets. "It is most unfortunate that your lord must die tonight. I will consider sparing the rest of you, on one condition—find what was taken from me, and you will not meet my wrath. A fair bargain, my friends?"

Kalvidan laughed himself hoarse. I had half a mind to kill him too, but not yet. The human voices rose in deafening clatter. The Knights stationed by the doors stepped forward, but my own court held them back. I raised a hand into the air for silence.

"Do not think me so cruel," I said. "I will make your task simple. Beynon, you wretched cur, why not speak for us? Inform the court what you have stolen from me so they may retrieve it. Your life for theirs."

I snapped, allowing him to speak. Curses spat from his tongue, fury and fear. "What are you, foul creature?"

My glamour dropped. The humans howled, terror rising as the man or woman beside them appeared in their true forms. The faeries reveled in it, joining me on the tables and stomping dishware or hands. Magic tainted the air, metallic on my tongue. I raised my hand. "*Silence.*" Their path of destruction heeled, all eyes on me. I only had ones for the lord. "Tell them, Beynon. Tell them what you took."

He shook his head. "I have stolen nothing from you. Begone, creature of hell. Leave this place."

Blood roared in my ears, the lust for death. I strode toward him, letting my poison leak. Without the pain, I moved faster, more determined with each step. The high of his horror fed into each drop coursing across the table, the deadly nightshade blooming in my wake. I knelt before him, pressing my dagger to the tip of his nose. "Does she mean so little that you have already forgotten?"

He searched for Lady Beynon. "You may have her if you wish."

"Not *her*." I leaned in, not stopping until I saw the pulse of his veins. Until his rancid breath filled my nose. "Annwyl."

Breaths came in ragged pants. "Who?"

I broke.

My hand snatched his neck, skin blackening beneath my fingertips. Blood filled his throat, dying gurgles music to my ears the deeper my poison burned. I broke the enchantment so I could watch him squirm. Watch him kick and claw with desperation as I lifted him into the air. Before he took his final breath, I sent him sprawling to the center of the room. I threw my arms wide. "It would seem unfortunate for the rest of you the lord can no longer speak. Not that it would ever matter. You see, what he stole cannot be returned. Let this serve as a warning to all those who think they can bear the wrath of the fair folk. You cannot." I leaned my head to the side, smiling. "And to my court—no women, no children, no low-born. Do what you will with the rest."

Screams rose as I jumped down from the table. I landed on Beynon's chest, kneeling to pat his cheek. "Fear not. I will return for you in just a moment."

I found Drusilla.

She huddled beneath a table, brandishing a wooden crucifix. Throwing a chair to the side, I snatched her ankle and dragged her out. She screamed, spitting curses as I lifted her to her feet. My teeth snapped inches from her face. "Did you know what he would do to Annwyl?"

"You will burn in the pits of hell." Spit smacked my cheek.

How impertinent of her. "There is a high possibility. Now, answer my question."

She resisted but was no match for my compulsion. Jaw slack and stare like glass, she mumbled her confession. "Of course I did. The lord has tasked me with finding him girls for years. He pays me for the service, and I can cull the undesirables from the kitchens. It works in both our favors." I released her and drew a blade. She fell to her knees, pleading. "No, spare me, good sidhe. I beg you. The girl had already sullied herself. We all saw her sneaking to the woods each night, off to whore with who knows. She brought it upon herself. I have done nothing wrong."

My eyes narrowed, voice softening. "Beg. Beg like Annwyl did."

"Please," she said. "Please, I will do anything."

I cut her throat. "You know what I hate most in the world? Liars."

MY FOOTSTEPS THUDDED ACROSS the grass, a wooden chest heavy in my arms. After the fae finished their fun, we glamoured the remaining humans to think vagabonds had caused the massacre. I searched for a suitable box to present my gift in and ordered Kalvidan and company home. My spirits were high with the ruse's success and all the poison I had released tonight. There was only one thing left to do.

I cursed as blood dribbled into my mouth. It caked beneath my fingernails and stained my skin, darkening my hair. Funny how the nobles acted like swine. They bled like them too.

Will-o-wisps turned in circles along the forest edge, but I no longer needed their light to find the path. I raced through the wood, eager to see how Annwyl fared. A small fire burned ahead, just outside her copse of trees. Brownies tended the wood, and a dryad roasted chestnuts. She reminded me of the last dryad I'd interacted with, setting my lips to scowl. But the feeling dissipated when I spotted who sat beside her.

Annwyl huddled beneath a cloak, holding her hands to the flames. She had been washed and fed, the gash across her face sewn with thread. Nothing more could be done for the wound, but it still looked horrid. The scar would last the rest of her days.

Nerves stopped me before they noticed my presence, Annwyl's gift heavy in my hands. I prayed it would be enough. That she would forgive me when she learned what happened that night.

Deep down, I felt just as responsible. Annwyl had been brutalized, likely waiting for me to come save her, knowing I was within the castle. Meanwhile, I had gotten drunk. Fornicated with a stranger only to promptly forget it because I was angry she wished to kiss a squire. I had explained sex to her that night, only for a cruel lesson of it to follow in my absence.

If I were her, I would never forgive me.

The flower pixie from three nights past landed on the branch above my head. He dipped his head. "You have returned, Prince Jaevidan."

"Aye." Annwyl smiled at the dryad, words exchanged I could not hear from this distance. The dryad played with her hair, weaving flowers and blades of grass through blonde plaits. My human adored when the fae doted on her, but her smile did not reach the eyes, her expression hollow.

"She woke yesterday. We have kept her company since."

Shame slithered beneath my skin. I should have been the one keeping her company. There should have been no need for company at all. Swallowing, I gestured to the pixie. "Thank you. I am in your debts for this. I vow it." Magic sealed the vow on my spine.

He blinked, waiting for the catch. For a cruel smile and another threat to his life. "We are honored, my Prince."

"May I speak to her alone?"

The pixie bowed his head. "We will return in the morn."

I waited until nothing but wind whispered through the trees to step forward. Annwyl glanced up, down, and back up to gape. "Do not rise for me, please," I said, halting her trembling ascent. "The blood is not mine."

She settled to the ground, chewing her thumbnail. "What happened, Jaevidan? Where were you?"

I placed my wooden chest by the fire and bent to a knee. Up close, the wound was worse than I thought. By some miracle, it had missed her right eye but had cleaved the brow clean in half. The gash grew deeper over the bridge of her nose and deeper again near her mandible. It would hurt every time she ate. Every time she spoke.

I bowed, pushing the chest closer to her. "For you."

"Where were you, Jaevidan?"

Bile rose in my throat. "If you can never forgive me, I understand."

Her good brow shifted. "Forgive you for what?"

"For not saving you."

She shook her head. "I only ask where you have been the last few days. I worried for you."

"How could you worry for me?" I stared at her like I could decipher all her strange human notions. Could find the goodness that permeated her soul and forgotten mine. "I left that night, Annwyl. I was angry and went off and acted a fool. I should have been there. I could have stopped this."

Her lips parted, but I pushed the chest forward. "I cannot undo what was done, but I have atoned."

Shifting closer, she slowly undid the latch. Her eyes roamed the offering inside, expressionless. Annwyl wore her heart on her sleeve, but as she took a deep breath, muscles rigid, I could glean nothing now.

"What is this?" she asked.

"An offering, for your forgiveness." I bowed my head. "And so you know he may never touch you again."

She pushed the chest away. My gift jostled inside—Lord Beynon's severed hands, cut off at the wrist, curled into his dying fists before I sawed them off myself.

Her voice came low, a warning. "And you thought I would want this?"

Words failed me. What else could she want? A debt of blood was repaid, her honor restored with the hands that broke her. This was the way of sidhe.

A tear ran down her cheek, catching in the jagged wound. "You foolish boy. What have you done?"

I reeled back. "What do you mean?"

"Do you know me at all?" She inhaled a serrated breath, voice catching. "To commit bloodshed in my name. Do you think this is what I want?"

"What else would you want?"

"I want to forget." Her breath hitched. "And I do not blame you for the horrors another man committed. I never did and never would, no matter where you were. But I do not want vengeance. I want to move on. It hurts."

Her fingers brushed her face. "There is already so much pain. There was no need to inflict more."

"Annwyl, look at what that man did to you. He deserved to die."

"That is not for me to decide."

"No, it was for me," I snapped. I had no right to be angry, but I was. Angry Annwyl simply accepted this. Angry Annwyl was not angry at *me*. I wanted her rage, her vitriol, her poison, because if anyone deserved to have it, it was her. I refused to watch her wilt beneath her wounds and accept her shitty lot. She deserved *more*. More than I could ever give.

"It was for me," I said, darker, slower, my voice taking a tone I did not recognize. "It is for me to protect you, Annwyl. It is for me to be the monster, to love you most. If you cannot be, then I will be your violence."

Leaves drifted on a lazy breeze. She tracked them, little twirls of red and yellow capturing the firelight. "If you are my violence, then what shall I be?"

I gave her the truth. "My everything else."

She was silent for a long time. The fire crackled. A wind soaked with blood and magic drifted through the wood. It was a moment that would stay with me for life, a memory I'd wish to forget. I could not see the future, but I knew everything had changed.

Her words came faint, diffident. "He never kissed me."

"The squire?" I asked.

"The lord." She stared into the fire, the golden light bouncing off her pupils. Endlessly, hopelessly black. "He took everything else, but I still have my first kiss."

"Save it. Give it to someone deserving."

"I know who I want to have it. It will be safest with him."

Jealousy robbed me of air. Her squire, most likely, but I could not say why it bothered me so. Until three days ago, the thought of kissing Annwyl had never crossed my mind. Now, it plagued all my thoughts.

But so much had already been taken from her. My own selfish desires had no place here. So I nodded, taking her hand. "Whatever she wants."

She turned, her expression one I had not seen before. I thought I could read Annwyl like a book, but she was a mystery to me now. She shifted closer, and the blanket fell from her shoulders as she rose to her knees. I froze, for once without words as she held my face and leaned in.

Her lips brushed mine, timid and unsure. The little brushstroke hardly counted, so when she drew back and licked her lips, I kissed her for real.

Soft and lovely, just like her. Notes of strawberry and willow bark, the blood still coating my skin. I circled her waist, holding her flush to my chest as her neck craned back. She sighed against my mouth and broke the spell, pressing her forehead to mine. Her eyes were closed. Mine were wide and consuming her.

"Keep it safe for me, okay?" She breathed deep, pulling away like she had not just ruined me. We spent the rest of the night in bonded silence.

Her gift seemed a blessing from the stars then. In truth, it was an omen. The first time I kissed Annwyl, it tasted like blood.

So did the last.

THIRTY

ADELINE

WHEN I WOKE, IT must have been in hell.

Opening bleary eyes, I pushed myself off the cold, hard ground and rubbed at my head. My body felt . . . wrong. All the proportions were off, my hand passing my temple each time I went to soothe it. My face felt different, eyebrows a smidge off from where they should be, teeth fitting together in the wrong pattern. Pain coursed across my flesh, but all my wounds acquired in the prison were gone.

Even my skin appeared different, the undertones an unfamiliar color. My hands were smaller—stout fingers and bony wrists. I flipped them from back to palm, wondering when I had received so many little scars.

I took in my surroundings. This certainly wasn't the prison, but it was nowhere else I recognized. A cave, judging by the pointed stalagmites and misty dew covering the stone. Rushing water splashed in the background, joining the endless drip of condensation pattering the ground. Clear, white light came from somewhere. I looked behind me. The mouth of the cave waited ahead, a powerful waterfall blocking all but the wan light.

Pushing to my knees, I tried not to stumble as I realized my height was changed too. Shorter. With my center of gravity off, each step was a challenge. My hands dragged along the damp walls until I got my bearings, slowly making my way to the mouth of the cave and, presumably, freedom. I expected a steep drop when I reached the edge, but the smooth ground continued beneath the pummeling water, leading to another room. Where the water went, I could not say. It hit the ground and disappeared into the flat, gray stones.

There was no way around the waterfall, but I sure as hell wouldn't stay in this cave. I held my breath, muscles screaming as the powerful tide beat down on me. It went on forever, my skin burning with the onslaught, before I finally breathed open air.

I pushed my hair from f my face. Long hair. Long enough to reach my waist. My hair had been short ever since moving to New York.

Rubbing water from my eyes, I surveyed the room.

It was large and circular, much like the main hall of the Guild. But here, the walls and floor were made of black stones. Every ten feet was another waterfall, presumably hiding more caves. A ceiling stretched so high and dark it was impossible to see the top, giving no indication of the water's source. A large shimmering pool took up the center of the room. It glowed in the murky, gray light, but there was no source for that either. Not a single window, lamp, or sign of escape.

"Welcome, sister."

Like a veil was lifted, others appeared. At first, all I saw was white. Tens, maybe a hundred women, their clothes and skin and hair the same bleached color. Some wore recognizable clothes, flapper dresses or night shifts. Others had sweeping ball gowns, robes from the East, or garments I couldn't recognize. One of them was mostly nude, breasts freed with nothing but a small cloth around her waist.

The wraiths sat around the edge of the pool, a pile of clothes beside each. They washed each item, silver light pouring from fissures or holes in the fabric. When satisfied, they floated the garments on glass-like water to the center of the pool. Two women stood there with bare feet.

Their robes were also white, but their flesh had the untainted pallor of life. I could see no more than their mouths and ankles with the glowing fabric wrapped around them, but the first was a slight woman, pale as marble with pink lips. The other was taller, her dark skin like midnight on the moon against her robes.

And above them was . . . something.

It stretched nearly as wide as the pool, hanging from the endless darkness above like an unfurled scroll. A tapestry, but I had never seen one like this before. Each thread rippled with magic, giving life to the pictures woven through the strands. There were thousands of them, *millions*, moving within the vivid fabric and taking a life of their own. Near the bottom where the women stood, there were some I even recognized.

A cluster of battle scenes stretched a foot high and took the entire width of the fabric. Fighter planes zoomed past one another, tanks rolling across barren ground. German soldiers with flamethrowers sprayed fire into the pits of a trench. Each inch of fabric brought more scenes of death, soldiers screaming and bombs exploding. Sobbing women receiving letters and boys whispering prayers over gangrenous hands. Millions dead in a single row alone.

Below it were more recognizable scenes. Women cheering as they were given the right to vote. Men playing jazz music on a stage. A movie of a man riding a galloping horse. Interspaced were forgotten moments, little memories I doubt anyone would recall—a woman washing her son in the bath, a drunken man losing at cards, a couple with their lips pinched together, ignoring each other from their sides of the bed.

Another scene I recognized, not because it made the papers or I'd seen photographs. It was me.

Me and Jack, to be specific. In the alleyway outside the movie theater. Rain flattened our hair against our faces, our lips brushing as my toes lifted off the ground.

"Come closer, sister." The brown-skinned woman gestured for me, leaning down to retrieve a dress from the water. She lifted it, and a sharp talon sliced the fabric in two. When all was done, a single thread wound around her finger. Turning to the frayed, unfinished ends of the tapestry, she weaved the single thread with adept hands. The glowing tendril swayed beside the millions of others like it.

Words caught in my throat. I coughed, trying again. "Who are you?"

"They call us *beandishe*. Banshees, harbingers of death. The fates," they answered simultaneously. The pale woman gestured to herself. "I am the Crone, and she the Mother. You may join us, Maiden."

The wraiths ceased working, attention fixed on my frigid form. Though I could not see the fates' eyes, I could feel them on me as well.

"You don't seem like a crone to me."

They both laughed and together said, "These are titles."

"Am I dead?"

"No, but it touches you," they said, voices overlapping and playing off one another. The ring of a child's cry and a widow's rattling breaths. Fresh leaves on the trees and bare branches creaking beneath snow.

"Then why am I here?"

The Mother extended her hand toward me, beckoning with two curled fingers. "Come."

Seeing no other choice, I stepped forward. My feet pressed into the hard stones, growing warmer as I neared the pool. Two wraiths stepped aside, clearing a path for me. My toes brushed the water, and I was surprised by the warmth, as well as the quality. Hot and viscous, nothing like the creek beside my home or the cool water I splashed on my face in the morning.

I eyed the wraith's stolen clothes, the silver liquid streaming from each piece.

Keeping a healthy distance between us, I asked again, "Why am I here?"

"It was time," the Crone said, offering no other explanation.

"But why now?"

The Mother retrieved another garment from the water. An infant's night-gown. Pulling a thread from the fabric, she wove it into the tapestry. "Without all your memories, you were incomplete. We could not reach you, even as you touched the shade. But now completed and this close to death . . ." She let the unfinished words speak for themselves.

"So it was the memories?"

"It was fate," the Crone said. She retrieved her own thread from the water, this one from a man's smoking jacket. "As all things are."

The tapestry rippled in a breeze I could not feel, the pictures shifting around one another. The fates had been described to me in many ways. Death, destiny, determiners, but the implications held no meaning until now. Before me was the world, the entire world, and all the lives occupying it.

"Are you goddesses?"

"No," they uttered, voices blending into one. "We are the fates. We were created by the Varaxes, tasked by the third fallen star. We weave life, and we weave death."

Varaxes. When Jack and I visited Estheria, she had called herself that. It must have meant stars.

My voice came in a hollow whisper. "You determine all of that? If that is the case, why weave this?" I gestured to the depictions of the Great War, then several others below it. An infant passing in their cradle. A car wreck that took the lives of three. With the power to determine, well, *everything*, why not create a better world?

"It is not for us to determine," the Crone said.

"The weavers do not design, only sew the threads asked of us," the Mother added.

"Then who designs?"

Neither answered.

"Bathe yourself in the pool. Release to us your dress." I could no longer depict which one spoke. It was a request, but the urge to be near them grew stronger, the tendrils between us pulling tighter. I pushed my feet into the ground.

"I prefer to keep this on, thank you."

Their mouths turned down in frowns, foreheads pressing together. Whispered words flitted between the two, impossible to hear over the raging waterfalls.

Straightening, they both turned to face me. "It is time, Annwyl."

The use of my name—the name of my first life—jarred me. Jack had called me by it a thousand times, but this was different. I stepped back, catching my reflection in the pool.

My lips parted, but they were not my lips. My hands came to my face, but they were not my hands or my expression. I pulled on the long, blonde hair falling around my neck. Not mine, but Annwyl's.

In the memories, she was still a girl. I had never seen her as an adult but knew it was the face staring back at me now. Her eyes were crinkled in the corners, an awful scar across her face. She couldn't have been older than her early twenties.

Pulling my trembling hands from my face, I whispered, "Why do I look like this?"

The Mother frowned. "You look as yourself."

"No, I look like Annwyl, a girl who died in Wales nearly four centuries ago. I look like Adeline Colton."

The wraiths hissed. Chills scattered down my spine.

"Adeline was not fate," the Mother said, gesturing for the wraiths to calm themselves. "She was never meant to exist, so she does not. Your current body was never meant to join the design."

"But I'm right there in your tapestry."

"An abomination," the Crone said, soothing and gentle despite the content.

"If I am an abomination, why did I become one of you?"

They looked to one another again. Deliberating silence, and then the Mother spoke. "Nearly four human centuries past, you died. A sidhe begged a Bogoran to fracture your soul so you may not move on. The pieces formed a wraith, while the remainder inhabited bodies meant for other souls. These lives were never meant to be woven, but alas, they existed. When the last Maiden made the choice to join the darkness, she was tasked with finding her predecessor. Your wraith desired her position, and as she was not meant to roam this world, the last Maiden agreed."

I looked between them. One of the few things I knew of the fates was they were created from wraiths. Arthur had explained it once, saying a wraith was chipped pieces of different souls that could not move on. They amalgamated, becoming a new being. My wraith was the exception. The abomination. While she was technically made from many different lives, each of those lives had only one soul. My soul. I lost pieces of myself each time I died, but joined with them again, I was now complete.

That meant the two fates before me were a blend of many people, creating something new. They had been wraiths once, and now they were this. But when they became this, they had already been dead, as all wraiths were.

They said they couldn't reach me, not until I was close enough to death. I tucked the information away for later.

"Join the darkness?" I asked, stalling while I planned escape.

"As we all do one day." The Crone produced another thread, working as she spoke. "The wraiths may join when they find their missing pieces and become complete, and we may do so when we feel our thread is done. A new fate takes our place, and we join the darkness as all others in this world do, in our eternal rest among the stars."

It was something else Estheria had mentioned, my father's soul singing for them after he joined the darkness.

Escape forgotten, I breathed, "It's the afterlife?"

"For those of this world," the Mother said. "There, right behind that waterfall." She gestured to one of the caves, as unassuming as the rest. Nothing could be seen behind the thick wall of water, but now that she said it, I could sense something. A beckoning. The promise of everlasting peace and joy, comfort and the warm embrace of the stars.

Her words nagged at me. I turned them over until I discovered what. "What about those of other worlds?"

They froze, two sets of hands rigid around clothing of the dead. "We weave them when we must," they said.

"But where do they go?"

The Crone shifted her head, stopping before she gave something away. It was too late. Her body shifted toward a waterfall behind her. It also seemed familiar. Much more than the liquid pooling around my feet.

"The Bogorans created their own children, different from the ones of flesh and dust made by the stars," she said.

Yes, I knew that. Estheria once called the fae her nieces and nephews, children of glamour and blood. The Bogorans were the star's brethren, according to Jack. The corrupted version of whatever the stars were.

"But their magic was corrupt. Their children too. And so it was not meant for us to weave. Their souls do not join the darkness but are guided somewhere their wretched forms may keep them."

I realized why that one cave beckoned to me, why it felt so familiar.

Breathless, my voice came in a ragged whisper. "It's the shade. That's . . . what, your version of hell?"

"It is where those of glamour and blood may lie," the Mother said. "It is why you were chosen. For the Crone is death and the Mother life, but the Maiden is tasked with all in between. She weaves the paths taken in this world and rules souls of the shade in other ones. A son of glamour and blood defied us to create you, and so your penance will be to weave his strings."

God, and I thought I could be petty. "And if I refuse?"

"There is no refusing," they said. "You were chosen, and so you will be."

A wraith stepped into the pool, her bone-white ball gown rippling in the waves. Another joined her, creeping closer.

"But you don't design," I said. "You don't determine my destiny. I do."

The Mother held out a hand. "We give life, and we call for its end, but souls choose their paths in the mortal plain. You were not meant to be, so destruction will follow if you remain. You must join us, sister. Before it is too late."

I stepped back. "But you can't make me yet, can you? I'm still alive. I still have a body. One needs to be dead to become a fate."

Neither agreed, but the Crone stiffened. "Give us your dress, Maiden, so we may finish your threads."

More wraiths joined the pool, water sloshing with each of their steps. I retreated, noticing something odd about the tapestry for the first time. The entirety of it was human life, all but a small corner of it near the bottom. There lay all images of the fae, some from places that must have been Ildathach. But their corner ended abruptly, the pictures melting into darkness. Nothing but black threads hung from the bottom, scorched and frayed like one had taken flame to it. A candle held to the threads.

A candle.

I drifted closer to the waterfall.

"Do not run from destiny, Maiden." It was the Mother, her work forgotten. She stepped forward, a mass of wraiths surrounding her. "This is the way the Varaxes intended it."

But no, that wasn't true. Estheria had told me herself. *You must trust in Jaevidan. It is the only way to stay in the light.*

A wraith lunged for me, sharpened talons catching my dress. I screamed, kicking her away and yanking the shredded fabric close. It was a dress I didn't recognize, something I had never worn before. A white lace gown, much like—

Another wraith lunged, but I was faster. They gathered around the waterfall I had come from, blocking my return. Any moment and they would swarm me, too many of them to overpower.

"I know the eighth fallen star. This is not the path she gave me," I screamed.

It was useless. The fates floated above the pool, hands clasped as their robes drifted around them. "Join us, sister."

I broke into a run.

It was a hunch, and if I was wrong, I was doomed. The wraiths gave chase, their howls and cries screeching behind me. The fates screamed, rattling the cave.

Stalagmites cracked and shattered on the ground. The waterfalls rippled and sprayed water across the pool. I didn't stop running, not as specters clawed at me and the fates delivered their wail of death. I ran, not fast enough in this different form, but before any of them could grab me, my fingers brushed the darkening waterfall.

I tumbled headfirst into the shade.

THIRTY-ONE

ADELINE

THAT TIME, I WOKE in Jack's bed.

Everything looked the same as I last remembered it, so much I wondered if the last few days had been a dream. A fire burned in the hearth, popping smoke and ash up the chimney. The ever-present vines curled along the walls and beneath the bed. The closet exploded with both our belongings, the items I meant to move still strewing the floor. Dark sheets twisted between my legs, bare with nothing but a negligee to cover me. Jack slept beside me.

Tattoos shifted along his skin, pointed ears peeking through glossy black hair. I reached out to touch him, wondering if it had all been a dream. His eyes shot open.

"On the fucking fates."

Faster than my brain could process, he straddled me and turned my head. "Are you really awake?"

I blinked. "Yes."

"How do you feel? Anything wrong?"

I pushed his hands away. "I feel fine. How did we—"

He cut me off with a kiss, rain and oleander filling all my senses. His fingers wove through my hair, skin scorching against my own. I moved beneath him without thought.

"Never again," he whispered against my lips. "Never fucking again, do you understand?"

I broke away long enough to intake air. "What are you talking about?"

There was no stopping him. He kissed me, running his hands along every curve and dip of my body, whispering things that made no sense at all. I let a minute pass before gently pushing him back. "Jack, I don't remember much, so you need to fill me in. How did we get here? What happened at the prison?"

"It doesn't matter." He leaned in, but I shoved him back.

"Did you get the Dianomican?"

He tensed, this conversation clearly not something he wished to have right now. "Yes, but—"

"And what about the prisoners? Are they freed?"

Eyes softened, the crinkles in the corner revealed his true age. "Yes," he breathed. "You saved all of them, Addie. Every last one."

For some reason, that was the straw to break me.

A whimpering cry left my throat, any efforts to hold it back for naught. Tears burned my eyes and streamed down my cheeks. Jack settled beside me, stroking my bare arm, and kissed them away.

Each brush of his lips left a drop of poison, so little I wouldn't be able to detect it. He was drugging me, little doses of euphoria to ease the pain. It should have been repulsive, but I let him do it anyway.

When I had calmed down enough, I spoke against his cheek. "How are their injuries? Is there anything—"

"It's all been coordinated." He kissed a straggling tear, lips lingering on my skin. "Will and Guinevere have taken over the healing. Lillian has been working with their leaders to determine next steps, but they are welcome here as long as they need. I won't be using my ballroom for the foreseeable future, thanks to you."

A shaky laugh bubbled from my throat. His lips stretched into a smile against my skin.

Mirth bubbled away faster than it came. "And what of the Knights?"

"We don't need to discuss that right now."

"No." I turned him to face me. "I want to know."

Running his tongue over his teeth, he turned away. "It turns out you can overwhelm those wards against malevolent intent. You and I disposed a large portion on our own, but the prisoners handled the rest."

"They're dead?"

He shrugged. "The ones from Chicago, yes. But there are still so many around the world. It will take them a long time to regroup, and I'm honestly not sure how this will be explained to human authorities, but for now, we have no need to worry of them."

There should have been overwhelming joy at that. The Knights had long since been a scourge on the banished fae, an unkillable foe that brought our plans to a screeching halt at every turn. But a man's furious eyes swam into my vision, the gasping chokes as he fought against the inevitable.

On one hand, good riddance. After seeing what they had done to the low fae, it was easy to dispel any notion of humanity they may have possessed. They looked human but were monsters. How else could one justify the torture and cruelty.

But there was Tommy, my own father. I knew so little about Papa's past with them, but he had been one himself. Papa was many things, but I would never consider him evil. His permittance into the Knights had been one of revenge, but love for his family changed his path. And Tommy never wished to be a part of that world. He told me they held a gun to his head and said he was in or out, and the only reason he was able to escape their clutches at all was by aligning himself with the fae through me.

There was no way of knowing if the ones I'd killed believed in their cause or were victims of circumstance. No way of knowing if they had wives or children or friends. If someone sobbed somewhere for a dead man and I was entirely to blame.

Jack tucked a piece of hair behind my ear. "Whatever you feel right now, don't ever forget it. It makes you good."

Maybe not. I couldn't remember leaving the prison, but I remembered what came afterward. First, Jack's memory and the guilt I felt now at suspecting him. He hadn't killed Annwyl, and I knew deep down he never could. He said it himself. She—*I*—was his everything.

Which made what came after hard to say. Like sending the truth into the air would make it so.

The fates had called on me. The fates wanted to punish me for what he had done four hundred years ago. And according to them, Jack and I could not be together.

All it would bring was destruction. As I suspected all along.

Playing with the hem of my negligee, I avoided his stare. "Jack, there's something I need to tell you."

Eyes narrowing, the golden color sharpened. I drummed up the courage to explain, but a knock hit the door before I could.

Will entered, pausing when he noticed our position. Jack with his arms around me, our faces close. Him half-dressed and myself in nothing but a sheer gown.

"You're awake," he declared, scrambling for words. "Am I interrupting something?"

"No." Jack sat up, shoulders rigid. "Coming to check on her?"

Will nodded, tension tightening each of his muscles.

I waved at him, pulling the sheets to my chest, though Will had seen me compromised before. As a healer, it came with the territory. "I feel fine, Will. I'm sure you have your hands full with everyone upstairs."

Sitting on my side of the bed, he shook his head. "Don't worry, love, we have that all under control now. I'm more concerned about you."

"Like I said, I feel fine."

"I'm glad to hear that, but you were shot, Addie. Not to mention, out for two weeks."

Two *weeks*?

Jack leaned casually in the door, arms crossed. The aura of calm was a lie. He was coiled to strike, stare sweeping me like he could order my body to reveal the problem.

"That's impossible. It couldn't have been two weeks. I was only gone for—"

Ice prickled my veins. From the time I saw Agent Rodney's gun to diving headfirst into the shade felt like an hour at best. A full night of sleep at most with the memory I'd seen.

I stared at my blackened fingertips. The darkness had spread. It reached my wrists now.

Jack inhaled, but Will spoke first. "Jack, could I have the room?"

He wanted to protest but nodded and shut the door behind him. Doctor's orders trumped all.

And Will looked every bit the role. In glamoured form, it was impossible to tell his true nature. Tongue depressors and syringes stuck out from his waistcoat pockets, and a stethoscope hung from his neck. "Are all the human items for me?" I asked.

"What? Oh, no." He placed the stethoscope in his ears and listened to my heart, murmuring, "Magic can't solve everything. Sometimes humans have the right idea."

It was more than that, but I didn't push. Thick bags hung under his eyes. It might have been my imagination, but he seemed thinner since I last saw him. Will's affinity was healing, but powers were draining. Even Jack had his limits, once pushing himself until it nearly killed him.

Guilt simmered in my stomach. I'd asked a lot of Will, and who knew how long it would be for him to recover physically. Or mentally. His healing affinity had been a secret, one our group coveted due to Will's past. There had to be thousands of fae upstairs. It wasn't a secret any longer.

Determining my heart was right as rain, he leaned back and wrapped the stethoscope around his neck. "Talk."

I squinted.

He squinted back. "There is something you won't say, and I don't know if it's because of Jack or me, but if it's important, then spit it out."

I shook my head. "I don't—"

"I'm sworn to confidentiality, right?" His lips twitched with an almost smile. "I may have a medical degree, but I'm the best physician you have right now. So, talk."

"How are you feeling?" I asked instead.

"You're stalling."

I was. I didn't have the words yet to formulate everything that had happened, all I'd learned of the fates. The only thing that made sense was my draw to the shade. Supposedly, I ruled it.

My hunch must have been correct, as well. The fates had never encountered something like me, so they hadn't anticipated the small hiccup that I was alive. This body kept me tethered to the real world, inaccessible.

Until they killed me.

If they could. The fates admitted themselves they were nothing but the weavers. But they still determined death and, suffice to say, could order mine.

"I need Lillian," I said.

He sighed. "She pulled your memories while you were asleep."

By his demeanor, I knew there was something he withheld. "And?"

He licked his lips, refusing to meet my eye. "I know they belonged to you, and some part of you may always be incomplete without them, but they're gone. Completely gone. She destroyed them."

Hurt gnawed my chest in a way I hadn't expected. I couldn't recall the memories now, so it was not a longing but an emptiness. Grief for something that was gone and would never return. An opportunity forever taken.

Worry succeeded the emotions. The fates said I needed to be complete for them to call on me, but I wasn't sure what that meant with the memories gone. They said I could not remain in this world without wreaking havoc, but I wasn't sure whether to believe them yet either. If I returned to them, it would be through death, if I could now at all.

"She's right outside if you wish to speak to her," he said.

I did, but not about the memories. "Let me get dressed."

Jack, Lillian, and Will lounged around the fire. Arthur leaned against the bookcase, snapping to attention when I entered. Guinevere was present as well, pacing the back of the room with a pinched expression. They settled onto a settee at my presence, the former squirming and the latter cut from stone. It felt like ages since I'd seen Arthur, and I wanted to ask how he was coping with everything, but I would save it for later. In private. As usual, I couldn't glean much from Guinevere's austere presence or why she was suddenly around so often.

Violet was nowhere in sight, but someone I hadn't expected fidgeted on a chaise. My brother.

He leapt up. Lillian startled beside him, expression plagued. "You're awake," Tommy said.

"And you're no longer in a cell," I countered.

Lillian offered me a weak smile. "Thomas and I had some time to chat while you were recovering. We came to an understanding."

Jack rolled his eyes. "The understanding being he refuses to speak with anyone but Lillian."

My suspicious stare bounced between her and Tommy. He cleared his throat, mumbling, "She's a pacifist."

"She's also a redhead," Jack said.

Pink dusted Tommy's cheeks. "Really? I hadn't noticed."

"Jack, darling, why must you always ruffle feathers?" Lillian stood and squeezed his shoulder, sauntering to me. "You look better."

"But she's still not recovered," Will said, gesturing to a chair. "Sit, if for nothing but my own sanity, please."

Despite my two weeks of unconsciousness, I was exhausted. I sighed. "I will in just a moment, but Lillian, I need to ask you something."

She squeezed my arm. "I'm sorry about—"

"It's not that."

She nodded. "I have some news too, but perhaps later. I need to . . . confirm some things."

The way she said it set my teeth on edge, but one crisis at a time. "We can talk tonight." I lowered my voice, turning us away from everyone's prying eyes. "It will take me some time to explain, but we need to burn all of my clothes. Now."

THIRTY-TWO

JAEVIDAN

THE END WAS NIGH. Scholar Rindshaw confirmed as much, recounting in excruciating detail each of Donvidan's failed diplomacy meetings with Tearach. To attempt such talks was weakness in itself, and the Tearachans were like the Dearg sniffing for blood. They knew the turmoil within our courts, with my mother holding the throne so long without a king. They knew there were no good candidates for the hunts on her passing. Kalvidan had secured his reputation as a fop at the last delegacy, nearly losing his head to a group of bored red caps before Donvidan intervened. Donvidan himself was once considered the strongest, but ever since I marred his face, he'd fallen from favor. The strong did not respect the weak.

As for myself, I'd developed a reputation of being an incorrigible savage who shirked my duties more often than not. It was not my fault I despised my species—they made me this way, after all. But while the other kingdoms respected power, there was such a thing as too much of it. The wider and taller I grew, the more I mastered my weapons, the more agitated I grew with each conniving princess, the more the outside world grew wary of the Poison Prince.

"Where are you?" the scholar asked. It was an odd question. We sat across one another in my parlor, the only place safe from listening ears. Donvidan had moved out after his last failed envoy, taking residence in our father's old rooms. The King's parlor. Scholar Rindshaw had been furious. Said it was an insult to both my promise as king and the traditions of our people. I could give less of a shit, but my advisor feared my inaction made me seem feeble. Or worse, was silent approval of my brother's bold claims for the throne.

"Your brain softens in your skull, old man. I sit before you in my parlor."

He ignored the bait. It was a testament to both his patience and my insolence that I was yet to make him crack.

"And where is your brain, boy?" Impertinence threaded each word, subtle but present. I smiled in victory.

"Am I no longer a prince?"

"Not when you fail to act like one." A long, withered sigh and he regained his composure. "Your mind ferries itself elsewhere. Tearach is one ally away from declaring a war we are not prepared to win. We lack leadership, Prince Jaevidan. With your mother's refusal to relinquish her throne and her sons squabbling for the seat, their armies will march on us and claim the castle within days. Yet, you do not seem disturbed by this. If I were a bolder man, I would suspect you are even pleased."

I maneuvered a glass ball across my fingers, dipping between my digits like silk in water. The armorer claimed it the best exercise for fine dexterity. I found it nothing but a parlor trick. "The queen will burn the bone bridge before she allows an army to cross. The mountains and the great river protect us here on our craggy oasis."

"They will lay siege." He slammed his fist on the table, any semblance of the quiet, restrained man gone. "And that is after they lay waste to the greater lands of Gerenstad. Your people will suffer, my Prince. Dryads burned in their trees, children enslaved, men killed for their powers. All while the higher court suffers a slow, starving death behind these walls."

Let them, I nearly said. *These lecherous swine mean nothing to me. They kill each other for sport. Rip wings off their brethren as a garden game.* But a thought gave me pause. The same thought that worried me in the long days after my awakening, accidentally poisoning my servants and fearing Annwyl's reprisals. The same thought of her displeasure if I forced brownies to do her work for free or when I had threatened the pixie's lives after her attack. She would never forgive me for allowing such atrocities to fall on my people. Even if she had never known them. Even if they would do far worse to her should she enter our world.

"So I ask you once again," he said, drawing out each word, "where are you? Where has your mind been these last months? Because neither your brain nor your body have held much presence, and others are beginning to talk."

I knew as much. My visits to the human world had increased at unparalleled rates, though no one knew where I snuck off each day. Not only did war disinterest me, but it was Annwyl. My fear for her. Since the night of Lord Beynon's demise, she had . . . changed.

We had not kissed again, and I did not think we ever would. She did not smile so often, and as of the last month, not at all. Each day, she grew bonier than the last despite the constant nourishment I provided. The pixies told me she no longer visited them in the forest, and the brownies heard her weep each night in her straw bed. Even my presence had done little to sway her. She no longer taught me the names of flowers in the meadow. Did not laugh at my jokes or jest. A fortnight past, I had presented her with a luxurious gown that put Lord Beynon's monstrosity to shame, yet all she gave was quiet thanks before retreating to the kitchens.

After the murder of Lord Beynon and his court, the Lady Beynon had returned to England. Some distant cousins tried to stake claim to the castle but were quickly usurped by native Welshmen who resisted the King. In turn, the Welshmen were usurped by another poor fool sent to restore order to the lands. Annwyl's new lord was quiet and serious, too occupied with civil unrest to pay the scullions much mind. He was also a man of strict morals and tradition, forbidding the lower classes from intermingling and punishing knights or noblemen who tried. I thought this would please her. She was safer under his rule. But she flinched each time a man entered the room. The light left her eyes each time a child or drunken cretin brought attention to her scar. I thought it made her fearsome and beautiful. The humans did not agree, and as skillful as the pixies were at mending, the reminder remained a clear insult upon her skin.

She did not look like my Annwyl. Her rosy cheeks were wan and gaunt. Her buxom chest and hips whittled to skin and bone, lips flattened into a permanent line. It terrified me, and I knew not how to fix her. To heal the invisible wounds that Beynon had left behind. I lent her my company each day, denying the fear she may harm herself. But even this had unpleasant effects. The other scullions complained she shirked her duties. One contemptuous hag spotted us together outside the castle, and with the lingering rumor she had seduced the late lord, had deemed Annwyl the local whore.

So my foul mood had grown fouler, my patience too thin. Even as Scholar Rindshaw pleaded for my attention, I planned my departure for the human world come morning.

"And what do the people say?" I asked, as disinterested as I felt.

Bold, green eyes scoured me. Scholar Rindshaw was not a simple man, and his assessment rattled me. "They say you depart for the Darkwood near daily. Some fear you cavort with corrupt powers within her brambles. Others speak of the distinct scent you carry with you upon your return."

I snorted. "Pray tell what this scent may be?"

"Human." He folded his hands in his lap. "And for one closer to you—hypothetically, someone such as myself—it is obvious this particular scent belongs to a particular human. Perhaps one who is glamour-touched?"

My blood congealed to an icy sludge. "Then I would deem that hypothetical someone a fucking fool."

"Hold your tongue, boy. You are no man yet." With great weariness, he sighed. "We need allies, my Prince. Kalvidan is a waste of breath, and Donvidan has failed to sway the masses. I will speak with candor in that you curry little favor yourself, but your name holds strength. Your dust-mark as well. Others fear the mysterious prince who seeps poison from his skin and are willing to lend you their swords in exchange for your mercy and power. The throne could be yours for the taking, but compromises must be made. Dinners attended. Kings satisfied. Princesses wooed. Your distaste and reluctance for these affairs are the tantrums of a heedless child. If you wish to speak like a man, act one first. Wars are not won on battlefields; they are won in dinner halls and bedchambers." He produced a scroll from his robes. "This is a letter from King Areignas of Ond. Since you will burn it without a glance, I shall provide the details. He has five thousand swordsmen at your disposal, fifty healers, a guarded road leading to Tearach that could be made a supply line, and three daughters whom you may have your pick of. All he asks in return is the elimination of his rival in the north and for his grandchildren to bear your name. You will meet in his halls in ten days' time to negotiate and choose your bride. You will wed her within a fortnight, secure your lineage in her womb, and prepare to march on Tearach. That is what a man does. That is what kings do."

Poison seeped from my fingers, darkening the table. Scholar Rindshaw did not move from his position, eyes hard as stones. A peculiar comfort. Outside of Annwyl, he was the only one who did not fear me. Perhaps the only fae who truly knew me.

It also made him dangerous, though the scholar had never betrayed me. But he was fair folk, and I was not senseless enough to believe it beneath him.

"I will kill his enemy in the north, but I will not marry his daughter."

"You are far younger than most, but war cannot coexist with tradition. An experienced princess will aid your transition to the throne and bolster your claims as a competent ruler."

"I will not marry or bed anyone," I repeated. The slithering disgust following my last bedding taunted me. I had not repeated the act since and had little desire to. As it turned out, I did not share my brothers' appetite for meaningless affection.

He sighed. "Is it the human?"

"No. There is no human lover or whatever else you may suspect." It was not a lie. Annwyl never wanted me in that way and never would. She thought of me as a brother, a friend. And in her current state, I feared she would never desire anyone again. That her fantasies of romance were destroyed the night Beynon slashed her face.

He drummed his fingers on the table. "A matter of taste? If it is men you prefer, one could be provided in the marriage bed to keep things palatable. It would not be the first time, and once you have heirs, your marital duties can be shirked for preferable ones."

I scowled. "Not that it is any of your perverted business, but I have no taste for males either."

The scholar evaluated me. I squirmed beneath his stare. "Ah, I see the trouble now." A small laugh, and he flattened his palm on the table. "I forget your youth at times. No matter, this can be remedied quite easily."

"What can?"

He stood, grasping my shoulder. "Do not worry yourself, my Prince. Prepare for travel, and I will handle the remaining arrangements." He paused in the doorway, deliberating. "Have I ever told you I once had a son?"

Confused by the change in conversation, I shook my head.

"I did." He nodded, running his hand down the doorframe. "His name was Barnag. You remind me of him, in a way."

"How so?"

"He was . . . better than us. A noble man who made the tribe of soft spriggans proud. He cared for his people and his family. He loved fiercely, even when others deemed him weak for it. Had he lived, he would have made a fine scholar. A just one. Perhaps he could have been something more."

I swallowed, already fearing his answer. "What happened to him?"

"A fire on Lughnasadh. Some sidhe nobles grew bored and wished to see if his green flesh would burn." He looked to me. "I have known you since you were a babe, Prince Jaevidan. I gave enchantments over your first cradle. In all your seventeen years, I have never once seen you harm the low fae, whether justly or for entertainment. You find no joy in it, and I am afraid that is a rare thing indeed."

My hands curled into fists. "I am dust-marked, Scholar Rindshaw. Corrupted and wrong by nature."

"Yes, that is what they claim, isn't it?" He paused. "And some final counsel, I believe you that there is no human lover. Such a union would be beneath you. But I will say this—if there is something you care for, something you love, leave it behind. Precious things do not last long for righteous men. They become the weapons that ruin them." He bowed his head. "Sleep well, Prince Jaevidan. We have much to discuss in the coming days."

SLEEP WAS POINTLESS. I tossed and turned, the scholar's words playing over in my mind. The story about his son. It made sense now why the old man despised the fire holiday as much as myself, but my reasons were different. The human slaves' tormented faces always reminded me of Annwyl, raising nightmares of what sounds she would make burning in flames. How the skin would melt off her bones until she became unrecognizable. So consumed with the plight of the star's children, I'd never taken note of how many low fae suffered similar fates.

I couldn't say what the scholar expected me to glean from his tale, much less what he expected me to do with it. My revulsion for trivial death would win me no respect among the sidhe, nor was it my triumph to claim. I was only who I was because of Annwyl. Without her, I would be as ruthless as the rest of them. Worse, because of the power running through my veins.

I hoped she was sleeping instead of crying. I would have to speak with the brownies before I left for Ond, assuring she had friends and watchful eyes while I was absent.

While I was wed.

I flinched. That would not happen, no matter how much Rindshaw might protest. Besides, it would fracture his precious alliance. My control over the poison was at its best, but there was no guarantee I could tame it in a bedchamber I had no desire to be in. I doubted King Areignas would lend me his swords if I accidentally blackened his daughter on our wedding night.

Someone knocked on my door.

I reached for my dagger, already halfway from bed when it creaked open. I had enchanted the hinges to whine terribly if anyone opened the door. A brief moment of relief when I saw who it was—Periwen, who was so empty-headed she must have forgotten Kalvidan no longer resided here. She smiled and stepped forward. I also belatedly realized she was without any clothing.

"Apologies, my Prince. I did not mean to wake you." She sounded anything but apologetic. It was also impossible to look at her with her breasts on display. Without thought, I pulled the sheets up to cover my bare chest.

"Kalvidan is in the south tower."

"I know."

I gestured around. "Then what the fuck are you doing in here?"

She giggled like I'd told a joke. The hair raised on the back of my neck.

She ran a hand over her bare hip, sliding closer. "You know, just a few hours ago, I overheard the most peculiar conversation. Between that vile, old spriggan always stealing you away and two sidhe women."

Warnings rattled through my skull. "Oh?"

"Yes, he had an . . . assignment for them." She smiled. "But I have known you for many years, Prince Jaevidan. And Talia told me of all the fun you two had a few months past. You are like your brothers in that way—sidhe are just not exotic enough for you." She glanced at my covered lap. Appreciatively.

"Though, according to Talia, you are *very* different from them in more exciting ones."

Bile climbed my throat. "Goodnight, Periwen."

"There is no need to be shy with me." She leaned her hands on the bed. I spread my feet to avoid them. "How long have I known you, my Prince? Guided you? If there is anyone fit for the task, should it not be a woman who has always nurtured you, who has watched you grow into a man?"

Now I really was going to vomit. I tried a different tactic. "What about Kalvidan?"

She huffed with a theatrical roll of her eyes. Climbed onto the bed and inched closer. "Kalvidan, Kalvidan, Kalvidan. We had our fun, but let us be truthful. He will be no king."

"What does that have to do with anything?"

"Everything, my liege." She reached for my thigh. I spread my legs wider, which had the unfortunate result of producing a direct pathway to my groin. "We all know who will win the hunts. Who will soon rule. I have long been in service to the crown. And kings?" She bit her lip, walking her fingers up my leg. "Well, kings can have *whatever* they want."

I leapt from the bed, crashing to the floor in a tangle of sheets. She yelped as I took her down with me. Poison blackened the fabric, but I could not cease its path. Shoving the squirming dryad away, I broke for the door.

"Jaevidan! Where are you going?"

I burst from the parlor, wearing nothing but thin braies. A squadron of soldiers howled with laughter as I sprinted down the hall. Belladonna bloomed with each of my footsteps, but it was contained. At least until I heard Periwen's shrill cry of fury from the floor above. I did not stop as I exited the castle, nor when I crossed the bone bridge in my skivvies. The guards there laughed too, but one scathing look from me and it was all silence.

My feet knew where to take me before I did. One moment, I walked the Darkwood; the next, the barren meadow of the human world. I chanced an attempt at the shade to shorten my walk but to no avail. A year of practicing and I was still horrid with it.

All was quiet and dark at the human fortress. By my best estimate, it was well past midnight, and it dawned on me how ridiculous this was. Periwen was a disgusting creature, but nothing I could not handle. Scholar Rindshaw wanted me to swindle kings, to lead armies and conquer lands, yet I could not incapacitate a teeny dryad? I could have killed her with my eyes closed. Sent a warning to any other women who sought favor through my imagined sexual desires.

Yet, the thought made me ill for some reason. It was not like I had not killed before and in much more gruesome fashion. But my worst sins were in defense of Annwyl. To make others pay for what they had done to her. It felt more justified to protect her honor instead of my own.

I was being absurd. Nothing had happened, truly nothing when compared to the fate that befell Annwyl. She was the one who deserved middle-of-the-night visits. Comforting words and assurances. No doubt she would think less of me if she knew I came all this way because my brother's old flame touched my leg. Meanwhile, she had been literally and figuratively scarred for life.

"Jaevidan?"

My eyes rose, and my heart sank. Annwyl stood at the lone window to the servants' quarters, shivering in her nightgown. Hair unbound and falling to her hips, she wrapped her arms around her chest. Low enough to not wake the other girls, she said, "I thought I heard you. What are you doing here so late? And wherever are your clothes?"

I crossed my arms, teeth chattering. I countered with my own question. "Why are you awake at this hour?"

"Bad dreams," she said, so faint the wind swallowed it. "Stay there. I will bring you my blanket."

"No, Annwyl, it is—" Darkness filled the window before I could finish.

She appeared with a threadbare blanket of wool, shaking from the chill. "Why did you come?"

I shrugged, refusing the blanket even as I nearly cracked a tooth. I'd become more accustomed to the humans' climate, but the air was bitter tonight.

"Did something happen?"

"No, I just . . ." Had nothing to say but had no yearning to return home either. I would suggest we sleep together in the meadow or copse of trees, but her frail state worried me. It would be too cold tonight, even sharing body warmth.

She looked to her empty window. "We could go inside."

So someone could wake and confirm her reputation? "I will go."

"No, come." Tugging my wrist, she led me backward toward the servants' entrance. "Just glamour yourself and be quiet. No one will know."

It was too tempting to ignore. If I were a better person, I would protect her honor, but I wanted to be with her so badly it hurt. Besides, the nightmares plagued her again. She needed me too.

We traversed the damp stairs and slipped into the women's quarters. Ten scullions slept soundly on their straw, the only light from a dying hearth. Annwyl stoked the flames and led me to her bed. The fibers were rough against my skin and the room frigid, the bed too small for my frame, but I would be nowhere else as she climbed in beside me, wrapping the blanket over our heads.

I glamoured us so it appeared she was asleep and alone, warping the air to contain any sound. A full moon leaked light through the thin wool, and I bent that as well, forming a tiny ball of luminescence at our necks. I wrapped my arms around her and massaged each of her frozen fingers, all bone and sinew now.

Her other hand played with the light, eyes reflecting the silver glow. "How beautiful," she whispered.

My lips turned up. There was the old Annwyl. I demanded the light to change shape—a band of horses, manes flowing in the wind across a plain of silvery light.

She smiled, cupping the stallion in her palm. "Every day is a new wonder with you."

"As it is with you." Annwyl possessed no magic, but she gave me gifts others could not. Her smile was a beauty worth more than all the gold, the magic, the power in this world, her kindness a rarity in mine.

The light extinguished as she closed her fist. The horse turned to a couple performing a dance when she opened her palm, moon-lit faces similar to our own.

Her fingers danced over my chest, tracing her letters. Blonde hair tickled my nose as she buried her face against my neck, but I did not move. If Periwen's touch had been ichor, Annwyl's was mead. A euphoric warmth that lacquered all my wounds.

"Tell me what happened," she said. And either because I forced her to speak of Beynon or I was weak to all her whims, I did.

Her lips curled with disgust. "What an awful woman. Why, if I . . ." Her nose scrunched. "I cannot speak my vile thoughts. She deserves worse than hell."

I did not believe Annwyl's version of heaven or hell existed, but her rancor concerned me. It was so unlike her. "Do not worry for me. I can temper the dryad."

"You should never have to. How could someone hurt you so? Try and take you against your wishes? What right does she have? No wonder you came." She hugged me tight, and I felt utterly despicable. *I* had no right. Not compared to what Annwyl went through.

"It is nothing."

"But that is untrue. And do not compare yourself to me. I know you do." She cupped my face. "You are allowed to be hurt, Jaevidan. Even if another's misfortune seems worse than your own."

What had I ever done to earn the affection of such a lovely creature? My eyes watered with shame, both from Periwen and needing Annwyl so. She deserved more than I could ever give. A safe place to call home, a man who could love and provide for her. All the comforts and kindnesses of the world. All I brought was my own misery, my selfish cravings to covet her for my own. I should have heeded the Scholar's warnings and left her behind forever. I had the chance years ago after my awakening. But I was nothing without Annwyl. So when she wiped my tears and held me close, I did nothing but accept the gift.

"Why do you think others wound us so deeply?" she asked.

A woman snored across the room. Another tossed in her straw. I checked the glamour around us and shook my head. "Why do they or why us?"

"Both," she said, voice small. Broken. I would give my life to remedy it.

"I cannot say." My true answer was not one she could afford to hear. In my opinion, because there was more evil in our worlds than good. Hers was leagues ahead of my own, but the humans knew cruelty just as intimately. As for why us, it was simple. I was weak and Annwyl far too good for this existence.

"Sometimes I dream of running away," she whispered. "That a place much better waits on the horizon, far from all we have ever known. But I wake each morning and realize the truth. Such places only exist in the hearts of children and silly dreams."

"Or we have not found it yet." It was fruitless to give Annwyl hope, but I ached for the starry-eyed girl she once was. The one who believed such places existed everywhere. "Perhaps your dreams are premonitions. Tell me of them."

She shook her head. "They are foolish."

"Tell me anyway."

She resumed her letters. "Well . . . I always dream of this cottage. One set between a meadow and forest, with a lovely creek nearby to swim in. There is a heifer for milk to offer the brownies and a garden filled with the most colorful flowers. The pixies sing their songs beneath the windows, and the spriggans dance beneath the moon. And it is you and I and . . . and all the other girls and boys of the world with nowhere to go. We sow our fields, and no one is ever hungry. No one ever grows cold in the winter, and we sleep beside a fire while the snow spirits sing. No one hurts one another. We are nothing but hardworking and happy. At peace." She swallowed, her tears dampening my neck. "How silly is that?"

"Not silly." I combed my fingers through her hair, smoothing the oily strands. "Maybe one day, we will find it."

A breathy laugh. "Do you really believe so?"

No. Possibly. I hoped. The dream was fanciful but not impossible. And now that it had been whispered to life, I craved it more than anything. Not the war in Ildathach or the throne in Gerenstad. Not my visits to the human world while Annwyl slowly aged and died, growing older each year while I remained the same. But the place she described, a warm cottage and a simple life. My darling human by my side as we danced and feasted and sang and taught our ways to all the other children of the world. A family who knew nothing of life's horrors. Except in my version of her dream, we were a little older. And all those children had Annwyl's hair and my eyes. And after they fell asleep around the fire, we tucked them warm into downy beds, and then I led Annwyl into our room and showed her just how deeply I loved her.

I wanted it so badly I forgot how to breathe. Aching filled my chest, a longing so deep it fissured my soul. I understood now why the fae could not restrain themselves. Their lust for bloodshed and depravity was insatiable, and so was my lust for the life Annwyl described. I could know no peace without it.

It was with a heavy heart I realized I was in love with her. Deeply, irrevocably in love with her. No one else could ever compare.

"Let's run away." The words came before I could stop them, before I could acknowledge all the holes in this plan.

She shook her head. "We cannot."

"But we could." I tilted her face toward me. "We could, Annwyl. I will renounce my title. I never wanted it anyway. We can build a life here, in the human world. The first years will be hard, but I have magic. We can build that cottage wherever you wish, and I will keep it safe. We can raise our food and build our fires and invite any we wish to come join us. I believe your dream, Annwyl. We should do it."

Tears glinted along her lashes. "But what of ten years? Twenty? You cannot renounce your throne, Jaevidan. I will grow old, and so will all the other humans. Then you will be alone."

"But . . ." Annwyl was glamour-touched. She could be made a druid. They would happily take Annwyl into their fold.

Of course, we would need to find a Bogoran to change her. There were so few left. Some believed none at all.

Then I would take her back to Ildathach. Nothing aged there, even humans. But if I renounced my title, if I had no means to protect her . . .

She patted my chest. "Do not trouble yourself, Jaevidan. Maybe one day."

"I will find a way." I silenced her impending protests. "I swear to you, we will make it happen. I only need a little time to prepare."

Her wan smile did not believe me, but I would prove it to her. I would not travel to Ond and speak with their king. I would not battle against Tearach. I would find a Bogoran to transform her, and we would hide on the farthest reaches of the human world where no one could ever find us. Annwyl would heal, and I would have everything I always wanted.

That was our dream. That was my plan.

But war arrived the following day, and fate had other ones.

THIRTY-THREE

ADELINE

After we burned my clothes, the plan was to meet at the Silvertongue Speakeasy to discuss next steps. Lillian, Tommy, and Will would fetch Violet, and Jack and I agreed to bring Arthur, who had left the study shortly after I did. I thought Tommy and Lillian would prefer to wake our druid instead of poking the beast, but Will was insistent he get Violet.

We took the shade, landing in Arthur's shambolic apartment. Checkered tiles ran beneath my feet, chipped and shimmering with an unknown substance. Dust swirled through the air, and discarded clothes spotted the floor. A lone green lamp had been left on, illuminating the chaotic disarray of worktables in lieu of normal furniture. Most of the lab equipment had been swept aside for dozens of journals open to marked pages. One table held the chalice and Knight's helmet as usual, and another contained a bowl of smoking herbs that smelled suspiciously like reefer.

I raised a brow. Jack sighed and shook his head. I had seen so little of Arthur since the collapse of the Guild, and worry gnawed at me. The apartment was disastrous, even for the druid's standards.

The kitchen was empty of life, unless one counted the mildew growing in the sink. Or the suspicious rattle from a canister I dared not peek inside. His bedroom as well. My heels clicked across the tiles when a low noise drifted from his office down the hall. I rapped twice on the door, pushing it open. "Arthur, are you—"

I yelped. Blood rushed to my face, and Jack howled with laughter behind me. Arthur was in here, alright. So was our new druid ally, Guinevere.

And she was naked.

Arthur jumped at my scream, glasses askew. Half-dressed, he reclined in a thick, leather armchair with a nude Guinevere straddling his lap. The motion sent her tumbling to the ground, scowling.

"Sorry, sorry. Goodness gracious, I didn't mean to—"

Guinevere rolled her eyes. Jack still chuckled behind me, and Arthur turned redder than myself. "This better be important," she said.

Jack finally got his bearings, snapping his fingers. A silk robe appeared before her. Too shocked to say anything, I looked between the druids and wondered when this development occurred.

Arthur pulled himself together, buttoning his trousers and standing from the chair. His pale chest gleamed against a dim lamp. Guinevere tugged the robe around herself, not bothering to tie it closed. The tawny skin between her breasts—and everything below that—was on full display as she produced a cigarette in a holder, pacing the room.

"Sorry to bother you," I stammered, cheeks cerise. "We're all meeting at the red room."

"Right, of course. Just let me find some . . . you know." Arthur glanced around, finding no clothes. Fidgeting, he shimmied past us in the doorway for his bedroom. Jack laughed under his breath again.

Guinevere fell into the chair, legs crossed. Neither she nor Jack seemed bothered by the nudity, but I was still more human than I realized.

Attempting to fill the silence, I said, "So, you and Arthur are . . ."

"Divorced."

I stared at her. "Come again?"

"We are divorced," she said slowly. "As of about five hundred years or so ago. Though, we still have our fun from time to time, don't we, sweeting?" Arthur blushed as he re-entered the room.

"Oh." Stupidly, I asked, "So you were married?"

She shrugged. "He makes me laugh."

Arthur shot me a panicked look. "She scares me."

I had never seen Guinevere so much as crack a grin. Arthur being terrified made sense. "On that note, we should be going."

"You coming along?" Jack asked, gesturing to, apparently, Arthur's former spouse. How Lillian had never drunkenly declared this gossip to me, I was floored.

Guinevere blew out a puff of smoke, bare skin golden beneath the lights. She scrutinized him. "I still despise you."

Jack grinned. "Funny, my own ex-wife does as well. Perhaps you two can discuss it over tea."

Now, she scrutinized me. After a long moment, she extinguished her cigarette. "Arthur, find me something to wear, would you?"

"Yes, darling." He scampered off like the room was on fire.

"I don't despise you," I said. The Silvertongue Speakeasy was in full swing tonight. After Jack gave our password at the door, the four of us entered the hall of smoke and debauchery. As usual, it was an eccentric mix of all things modernly human and anciently fae. High sidhe wore dresses of sequins and fringe, the hems cut far above their knees. Men in long coats and bowlers puffed cigars of roiling vermillion smoke. Brownies darted between our legs with flutes of absinthe—or, around these parts, faerie wine. Trumpets and drums filled the energetic air with jazz, spriggans jumping to the melody around a lone dryad in a ritualistic dance.

"Then what?" Jack mumbled, pushing a woodland troll aside.

I had no good answer, but shame consumed me. With all the warnings and Jack's past transgressions, I had been looking for any reason to condemn him. Any way to prove all the assumptions were true, that he was as evil as I thought. It hadn't occurred to me until the second-to-last memory, the one I saw unconscious in the prison. I'd been so convinced he killed Annwyl I'd considered no other options.

Was he all good? No, far from it. *I can be your violence.* But he wasn't wrong either. Deeply flawed and deeply admirable at the same time. Ironically, it made him more human.

We stopped outside the ruby drapes leading to the red room, allowing Arthur and Guinevere to pass. Hands shoved in his coat pocket, shoulders squared, all the doubt beneath his stoic expression was masked. But he could hide from others. He couldn't hide from me. In so many ways, he was still that insecure boy, self-flagellating over and over again because all the ruin in his life had to be his fault.

"I don't despise you." My hand brushed his cheek, savoring the warmth. The familiarity. "I'm just learning who you are."

He turned and kissed the center of my palm. An intimate gesture out of place in all this madness. Without further word, he stepped behind the curtains.

I hadn't realized how good it would feel to see everyone here again, my family complete with Tommy bouncing his knee nervously beneath the table. He looked relieved to find me standing there, shifting down the booth so I could take the space beside him. Arthur and Guinevere sat side by side across from him. Will paced back and forth, swatting at rose petals falling from nowhere above us. Lillian reclined cross-legged in the corner chair, smelling of wine. And Violet had decided to lie on her stomach across the wooden tabletop, feet bent to her bottom as she read a book and absently stroked Harold.

"Took you long enough," she said, slamming her book closed. My faerie common tongue wasn't very good, but I could discern the title read something erotic.

Will pounced on me. "You need to be resting," he scolded, guiding me to the open space beside Tommy. His attention was fixated on the snake curled around Violet, flinching whenever it hissed his way.

"I'm fine, Will. For the hundredth time." Jack leaned against the wall, and the healer joined him. Lillian hiccupped loudly in the corner, murmuring something incoherent.

I glanced around the table. "Is she well?"

"Physically, she will recover. Emotionally, I doubt she will forgive you for burning your wardrobe," Violet said. She laid her chin on folded arms, grinning. "Now, why the fuck did you drag me from bed?"

"We have a problem."

"We have many," she countered.

"The Fates called on me."

The room plunged into a silent abyss. Even Violet's evil grin melted away. "And?"

I looked to each of them. I wasn't sure how to explain this, how to put all my thoughts into a cohesive sentence. So I said, "They're even bitchier than you."

She cackled. No one else did. Guinevere leaned forward, a druid on the hunt for knowledge. "What are they?"

I started from the beginning, waking inside the cave and then finding the great hall they called home. The pool of wraiths washing bloody clothes and the enormous tapestry above the banshees' heads. Then what they told me about the design, how they were mere weavers, not deciders, finishing with the worst part of all. "I think the shade is hell."

No one spoke for a long time. Then Violet rolled onto her back, shrugging. "How disappointing. I thought it would be more creative than that."

"And you're all going to it. Except for Tommy," I added.

Will chewed his thumb in the corner. "As . . . disheartening as that is to hear, it's not surprising. Fae rarely speak of death, knowing either nothing or nothing good comes with it. The price of immortality."

Jack nodded his silent agreement.

"Besides," Lillian added, rocking like a ship at sea, "if you're queen of the shade now, just make it good. If you're taking requests, I'd love a hot spring and river of wine in the afterlife."

Arthur released a nervous chuckle. "Throw in a library for me while you're at it."

"I like it just fine the way it is," Violet said.

"Maybe I could, but only if . . ." I tapped my fingers on the table, unsure if I should reveal this part. I'd intentionally left out the reason for my escape, burning my clothes, and relief at Lillian reclaiming the memories. There was no telling how they would react, and I didn't like either of the two most likely possibilities. There could be anger—believing me selfish for running back to reality when I could have helped us. Finding me selfish for valuing my life over the destinies of everyone. Or there could be relief, which was somehow worse. Plans drawn and executed to keep me from their grasp forever. Placing me above everyone else, again, for the sake of my existence. Making me the useless burden, again, so I wouldn't be gone forever.

I knew how Jack would feel.

And I knew it would destroy him. All the lengths he went to bring me back, to protect me, to reunite with his beloved Annwyl were all for naught. Violet's harsh words to him from a lifetime ago floated through my head. *You've had your time.* But Jack wouldn't see it that way or be any more grateful for it. He wanted me to have a life. He wanted to redeem whatever happened in my past by giving me the opportunity to make choices now. It had become his greatest obsession, and if he failed once again—failed to keep me from enslavement of a different kind—there was no telling what he would do.

At sixteen, he killed an entire court and chopped the hands from a human lord for harming me. So much of that anger was at himself, for being a rash teenager and storming off in anger instead of staying behind in case the worst happened. The decision to make me a fate was one of punishment. A punishment for an insult he committed against them. I didn't feel it was his fault, but he would. Forever that young man who hated and blamed himself for everything.

I didn't want to hurt Jack, but this was bigger than us. Right now, all I had was the shade and a fickle scream of death, but if I joined the fates permanently, I would have real power. They claimed no part in the design, but I didn't believe that, not entirely. And with the shade as my own dominion, I really could add a river of wine or a library or anything else that didn't subject all my friends to a cruel fate when their immortality came to pass.

And pass it would. The possibility of defeat loomed heavy over all of us. Our luck was running thin. If we failed to bring Babd and Nemain down, the entire banished world down, we were doomed. The humans were doomed.

But not if I could change their destinies.

I looked at each of them. Drunken Lillian giggling to herself in the corner. Arthur, failing to hide his nervous tics, clutching the pensive Guinevere's hand beneath the table. Will's brows furrowing with concern. Violet's silence as she ran a hand down Harold's sleek body. And Jack. Always Jack, calculating every move, stare burrowing into me like he could glimpse straight to my soul. The way he coiled and tensed with each of my breaths, watching, waiting, for the sun to stop shining.

I couldn't tell them.

I finalized that decision in my heart when Jack said, "Don't lie to me."

"I didn't say anything."

"But you are withholding the truth. And the last time you did that, you ran off to go infiltrate the Knights. So forgive me if I'd rather know your next suicide mission ahead of time. We don't need a martyr, Annwyl. We need a plan."

Violet looked sidelong at me from the tabletop. We weren't connected the same way Jack and I were, but she was still my sister in our Morrigan, and we had come to an understanding with one another. *Is this a price you are willing to pay*, she'd once asked. She would defend all my hard choices.

"You're all so macabre," she drawled. "And this conversation is boring me. Listening to dear old Adeline blather on and *on.* How about we all scamper off to bed now or, better yet, have a drink since we're all fucked, anyway?"

"I want to know what Addie's thinking," Will said. I glared at him. He returned a scathing look that said I was still his patient.

"You know how the druids feel about banshees. We are always on your side," Arthur added, nodding at Guinevere. Her silence was agreement, even with all I had taken from them already.

My brother was noticeably silent. Violet released a long sigh. "All you men and your cock-measuring contests. Who can win the damsel in distress this time? If she doesn't want to share, then fuck off. Addie earned her big-girl panties; she can handle herself."

"Violet," Jack warned.

She pointed at him, darkness leaking from her skin like fog. "You most of all."

Tension vacuumed the air from the room. Whatever poured from Violet, she reined back inside in a blink. Will stepped forward, then, thinking better of it, let her be.

It was Tommy who cut the deepest. His voice came soft, faded like the lullabies we used to sing in my room. "I can't do this without you."

I refused to look at him. Tommy had always been the chink in my armor. The variable that led me down all the wrong paths because I loved him too much to care for anything else. If anyone could talk me out of it, it was him.

"I can't do this without you, Ads," he repeated. "I thought I could. It kills me I can't, but I don't know what the hell I'm doing here, and I won't survive long without your help. You've got all the power now. So whatever you're thinking, remember who you're taking with you."

Violet scowled at him. I sighed. "Violet's right. We can cease with all the melodrama. There's nothing to say."

"If you think I will simply let it go, you don't know me very well," Jack said.

No—I knew him too well. That was the problem. That was the difference between us. I would burn myself to save the world. Jack would burn the world to save me.

And he would never let this go, so I relinquished the truth with the framing he wanted to hear. "I'm not a true *beansidhe* right now. This has never happened before, and they weren't prepared, but I can't truly join them or make any substantial changes to fate because I'm still alive. I have a body. It keeps me tethered to this world and separate from their domain. I didn't want to tell you because that means I can't actually help. There's nothing I can do."

He wasn't satisfied. "Unless?"

Feigning ignorance, I threw my hands in the air. "I'm not sure, Jack. I suppose unless I die."

"Well, that isn't an option," he snapped.

"Did I say it was?"

They all watched with various expressions, unease to weariness to relief. Those who thought I considered it versus those who believed I hadn't. The latter group was smaller.

"This conversation isn't over," he said.

"It is. Like I already said, there's nothing else to say."

Lillian laughed from the corner, making even the seasoned among us jump. She giggled like a woman possessed, more hysterical by the second. "On the fucking fates, I can't . . . I can't believe . . . my darlings, could one of you be a dear and find me another drink?"

Bloodshot eyes and snot dribbling from her nose. I'd never seen her like this. How much did she drink? Will shook his head, disappointment creasing his face. "I think you've had enough, Lillian."

She swayed, glass tipping dangerously from her fingertips. Mania pulled her lips into a feral grin. "Oh, no, I haven't. There aren't enough drinks in the world. Certainly not in our old one."

Violet scowled. "Oh? Do share with the rest of us, why don't you?"

Lillian shook her head, giggling. "Why do that? I think we have had enough misery for the night. I'd rather drink."

Curiously, it was Tommy who rose from the booth and kneeled in front of her, clasping her hands. "You know I have the utmost respect for you, Miss Carter, but Will's right. That's enough for tonight. Why don't we get you home, and we can talk in the morning?"

"*Miss Carter.* That's not my real fucking name. Your human tongue couldn't pronounce it." Her smile turned cruel and mocking, every bit the murderous royal she used to be. She leaned forward, rubbing her nose against Tommy's like he was a naive little boy. "But no one will soon enough, so why don't you give it a try, Thomas? Here, I'll whisper it in your ear, though I should warn you no mortal has heard it and lived long enough to repeat it."

Wordlessly, Jack snatched her empty glass and passed it off to Arthur. The druid sniffed it, frowning. "Nothing odd about it. Just wine."

Will grabbed Tommy by the collar, wrenching him back from Lillian's clutches. He was a soldier, once Lillian's soldier, bound to her by an awful vow her parents made him swear. He'd despised her for years, and his eyes now showed two centuries of atonement and trust completely unraveled. The first time I'd seen her vicious and the first time I'd seen Will angry. "What the hell is wrong with you, Lillian?"

"Come on, play with me. We were all gracious with Addie when she acted out." She winked at me. "You still love me, right?"

"I do, but not like this," I said.

"Addie was a pathetic, blubbering idiot. Not a fucking lunatic," Violet snapped. "And if you remember, *darling*, I don't make exceptions for anyone."

Softly, leaning against the far wall, Jack murmured. "I have always been gracious with you, Lillian. Always. But you will hate who you are in this moment when you wake up tomorrow morning because you are better than this. It's the only reason I have ever allowed you that grace. So if you won't talk to the rest of them, at least talk to me."

Smile fading, eyes shimmering, she stared at him like he had all the answers. Like he had always been the answer. She swore she no longer loved him, but I believed a part of her always would.

"I figured it out," she said, lips twitching between a smile and a grimace, giggles punctured by sobs breaking free. "I am your perfect, little spy. Tell me how perfect I am, Jaevidan."

Colder than ice, he replied, "What did you figure out?"

"What the Morrigan wants. What they plan to do. Why." She listed each item without a hint of emotion, like she had drained her well of it dry.

"Start with the first one."

"But don't you want to know the story? You just *adore* tall tales, Jack." Her savage grin returned. "There I was, continuing all my talks with the prisoners you and Addie saved. I hope you have a lot more room at the hotel, by the way. Anyway, we have peace treaties and fealty and all the usuals from most, but I could tell there was something they were all hiding from us. Many of them recognized me, you know. They call me kinslayer. It sort of has a ring to it, but I do find it so fucking ironic that when men murder each other in the hunts, no one bats an eye. But I digress. So I did a little espionage, and I found the information I was looking for. One of our refugee leaders has been a rat, siphoning secrets off to the Morrigan. There is nothing left of his mind now. You should be proud. I learned to kill without breaking my vow. Your mentorship has served me well."

Jack's eyes honed into daggers, arms crossed and voice low. "What did you see?"

"What they want," she said, ticking off a finger. "They want all the Dianomicans, and they want to kill the three of you. They know your own Morrigan carries the power of a Bogoran, and with the Dianomican complete once more, they can steal that power from you. They have six of them."

We already knew they wanted to kill us. That was nothing new. But collecting all of the Dianomicans? Putting the books back together?

Jack didn't miss a beat. "Go on."

"What they plan to do," she continued, ticking a second finger. "I suppose I already revealed half of it. Put the books back together, kill us all, do whatever the fuck you did to Adeline and bring back their dead sister, then, after they are the closest thing to our dead gods, rule the world."

Violet yawned. "We already deduced they want to rule the world, Lillian. Give us something a little more useful for once."

"Not this world."

No one breathed. You could hear a pin drop. Jack pushed off the wall, arms uncrossing. "Why do they give a shit about Ildathach? They were banished a millennia ago. Once, humans worshipped them as goddesses here."

She ticked off a third finger. "Why? Well, that would be the funny part." Her string of giggles dissolved into sobs. Awful, racking sobs.

Tommy looked to me, then shuffled forward. For someone so distrustful of the fae, he sure put a lot of stock in Lillian. Especially now. He swiped his thumbs across her cheeks, gently lifting her chin. I couldn't say if it was the alcohol or her emotional state, but something broke inside her. Softer than silk, she asked, "How old are you, Thomas?"

"Thirty-two," he answered, no hesitation.

She nodded. "When I was your age, I killed all my brothers. One of them was only two years older. For us, that's practically twins."

He shifted but didn't drop her face. "Well, when I was twenty-one, I killed a lot of people too. Two of them were fathers. They had pictures of their kids in their uniform pockets. All of them were someone's brother or son. I'm still making up for it, but it doesn't make me evil."

"This is why I love humans so much." She looked at me. "You don't have time, so you learn to forgive. You always move on because you lack the luxury not to." She turned back to Tommy. "But my kind doesn't forgive, and they never forget. We had gods once, and we killed them all. Jack and Violet killed the one. But in immortality, my species forgot foresight, thinking we would never need it. A world created by gods cannot live without them."

Violet stood. All her vitriol was gone, a warning. "What are you saying, Lillian?"

"Ildathach is dying." She pulled away from Tommy, like her penance was speaking this alone. "Actually, most of it is already dead. Nothing. Everything from the western stars to Gerenstad has been leaking away. Four hundred years, our world has slowly drifted back into darkness, and they were all too proud to admit it. So they've been watching it crumble until it all became too much and disintegrated all at once. The mountains and Jaevidan's territory are all that remain. Everyone from my home is dead. Not a single one escaped. The few survivors living near the Veil have fled here. Why do you think all the prisoners were new to this world?" A tiny laugh bubbled from her, devoid of humor. "And that, my dear friends, is why we will lose. Because the Morrigan has the books, they have a following, they have the unseelie, and they do not have the hatred we do. They don't have a kinslayer among them, or the two people the fae hold responsible for destroying our gods, or the Fate who assassinated one of the holy sisters. The other banished haven't rallied behind them because they want to keep their enemies close. They wave the Morrigan's banner because they believe them when they say they will restore Ildathach with the power they have and will obtain from the three of you. And when all is done, even the banished will be allowed to return. Their plan was never to kill all the humans and take your world for ours. Their plan was to destroy technology enough that when the time came, they would have the power to save everyone else and leave the humans alone forever. And all this time, we have been hindering them, thinking technology was the sole reason our powers dwindled, not that the source was going extinct. That the Morrigan sisters were power-hungry goddesses wishing to rule, not that they have been trying to save everyone. You were right all along, Addie. We're the bad guys. I'm sorry for misleading you."

No one spoke. No one but Jack. "If Ildathach dies and the source with it, what happens to us?"

Guinevere answered. "The undercrofts where Bogorans died in this world, including the one beneath your hotel, would likely continue on forever. Power is energy—it cannot be destroyed. That energy flows back into undercroft reservoirs after it's used. And the Stars' presence here would provide some as well. You would all be much less powerful than before, and I cannot speak to the effects on immortality, but we would still exist."

Jack looked to Violet. There was a question in his eyes, one I didn't understand until she rolled her shoulders back, eyes on the exit. "Then I say let it rot."

She strode out. Noise poured through the brief opening of the curtain, laughter and music and joy. None of us moved, and all were silent. Eons passed before Will sighed. "On second thought, I'll get you that drink."

THIRTY-FOUR

JAEVIDAN

JUNE THE FIRST, 1548

Dearest Jaevidan,

I received your letter from Parsna (and since I know you have already forgotten, she is the brownie from the village you employed). I cannot speak to the joy I felt when I read it. I pray for you every night, to my god and yours. I hope you are being fed well and kept far away from the violence. Your mind and leadership are needed, not your sword. I know you have more important duties than I, but I worry so much in the weeks or months of silence. Every day, I fear Parsna will return with devastating news. My heart could not go on if something happened to you.

But you said in your last letter you wished to hear of happier things, so I will write those now. The lord has been good and the castle quiet. I spend most days in the kitchen. Alys married last month and is now with child, which we are all excited for. With the summer approaching, the fields are prospering and our bellies full. If you are given leave soon, we must celebrate your eighteenth birthday. I have the most wonderful gift for you.

Most importantly, please be safe. Now is not the time to be a hero. I know it makes me selfish, but all I care of is that you return in one piece. Until then, I love you most.

Yours Truly,
Annwyl

The war tent buzzed with chaos, but I found a quiet corner to read her letter. Parsna waited outside for my response, but I would need to pen it quickly. The battle set for tomorrow morn still required much preparation.

Tearach had declared war the day after I'd promised Annwyl we would run away. The castle had been in disarray when I arrived, plans made, letters drawn, and soldiers armored. We met Tearach in the Fields of the Unsung, a short distance from our borders and, despite the ambush, had won.

I had no taste for war but had little choice in the matter. I'd debated abandoning my country and running for the human world, but it was Scholar Rindshaw and Annwyl that convinced me otherwise. Not with words but with stories and dreams. Worse ends than what befell his son fell on our people who were caught on the war fronts. I saw forests and villages crumble and my brothers unable to stop them. Annwyl's dream was of a happier place, where all the children of the world could be safe. But the children of mine were burned in their beds, so with her blessing and the promise to return, I became the man they expected me to be.

Since then, my mother's army had been working tirelessly to push back the battle lines. The military had been split in three, one army given to each of her sons. Kalvidan fought Tearach's allies on the southern front. Donvidan took the western borders of our land. And I pushed their army farther north, securing victory after victory along the very road once promised to me by King Areignas of Ond. He was killed in Silasar three months past, but his son, Detres, agreed to a tentative alliance with me.

Detres paced the war room now, barking at the scholars pouring over the map table. It had been enchanted to move with us, showing the positions of my brother's armies, turning kingdoms black that had been captured and glowing gold on ones we claimed.

Tomorrow, we would march on Petuaria, a small kingdom along the bi-continental road that was vital for our supply lines to continue north. They raised Tearach's banners six months past. Now, they would pay with their blood. I would join the front lines as I had done for every battle we fought. My men were weak in mind and spirit when I found them. It was Donvidan and Kalvidan who remained behind while they sent our charges to their deaths, but my army had been so successful for one simple reason—they rallied behind the Poison Prince, who fought by their sides.

Swords sharpened and men swarmed as I retrieved a pen.

July the eighth, 1548
My Beloved Annwyl,

I miss you more with each day, and it is only your words that provide reprieve. I also pray to the gods, and even yours, that this war may end swiftly. As promised, the first thing I shall do is squeeze you half to death and buy all the marzipans in Wales for us to eat.

I am overcome to hear good news. I will return this letter with a tonic for Alys that promises a healthy birth. I have also enclosed a ring for you that once belonged to the Great Queen of Ferasha. It is customary to gift these spoils of war to our queens and princesses. As you rule my heart, it shall be yours.

I paused over the drying ink.

And please, do not worry yourself so much. This war has been terribly boring for me, in truth. All the excitement happens on the fronts while I am forced to debate scholars and generals far from the battle lines. If I am recommended one more scroll on shield tactics we should utilize, my eyes may bleed.

I long for the day I hear you sing again, and I promise it will be soon. Until then, dream of our happy place and be sure to eat the provisions Parsna sends. They will help rebuild your strength. I love you most.

Yours Truly,
Jaevidan

January the twenty-second, 1549
My Mischievous Prince,

I am beginning to exhaust of places to hide your gifts. First a queen's ring, then a tiara for my birthday. What am I to do with a tiara, you foolish boy? And all the charms and trinkets afterwards. I wish I had something to send, but all I have is my love. I must remedy this when you have a chance to visit. This year has been so empty without you.

I am glad you continue to remain safe. It sounds like the war may be over soon. I pray both night and day now for this news. Until then, be well, and I love you most.

With all my love,
Annwyl

MARCH THE NINETEENTH, 1549
My Sweet Human,

If all goes well in the next battle, I will return soon. There is a break in the Veil outside the territory that leads to not far from you. It is with this knowledge I promise a victory, and you will be overwhelmed by the gifts I have to bestow.

I have been well. Harthon (the commander, if you remember) got into a bit of trouble with me last night. You will laugh yourself hoarse when I tell you the tale. The other men fare fine as well, and Draaph once again sends his regards to my mysterious letter girl.

In fact, all my commanders sent regards—and some cruder messages—to my mysterious letter girl. Not that I would ever repeat those to Annwyl. Draaph, a sidhe I'd grown unfortunately fond of these past months, leered at me while a healer patched my leg. Some bastard Tearchan caught me with an ashwood arrow last night, so I used the time to write Annwyl while it was patched. Whenever I produced pen and ink, all the boys had taken to howling like banshees until I told them to fuck off.

Perhaps one day you will meet them all. I believe they will adore you as much as I do.

There was no telling how my sidhe soldiers would react, but it was a concern for another day.

And your love will always be the greatest gift I could receive. But if you wish to send me something, provide a swatch from your dress. I miss your scent, and I would like to fold it into my armor for good luck.

I love you most.

Dreaming of you,
Jaevidan

"LOOK WHAT ARRIVED FOR the princeling!"

We all rested beneath the shade of an elder tree, tallying our damages. I was still coated in blood from the fighting a night before. Tearach had come full force, pushing our lines damn near back to Petuaria. We lost six thousand men, half our supplies, our best battle mages, and still, all I felt was the sweeping disappointment at not making it to the break in the Veil. Not getting to visit Annwyl.

Corin, Draaph's brother and equally my bastard in arms, dangled a letter in the air. Also dangling from the air was Parsna, who nearly tore the letter in two from her furry grasp. Our sour moods lifted with the arrival.

"It's alright, Parsna." She scowled and fell to the ground. I produced bread for the brownie, the last I would have to eat for the next day. She'd earned it and then some over the last year and a half.

"And I must say, it smells *horrid* today." Corin cackled, fanning himself with the folded parchment. "On the fucking fates, what swamp does your mystery girl hail from?"

All the men howled.

I swiped the letter from his fingers.

April the twentieth, 1549

My Other Half,

I dreamed of you last night, just before your letter arrived. We were at our cottage, but it was different. The walls were red, and flowers I have never seen before dried from the ceiling. I painted a vase while you lay beside me, and we spoke a language I have never heard. You seemed very happy.

You have spoken of premonitions in the past, so I believe it a sign of good fortune. That at some time, someplace far away, we will be together and never again leave each other for so long.

I sent a piece of my dress, as requested. But what of this armor you mention? Seems quite silly for all your battles fought over war room tables. Though, your customs are always a mystery to me.

Send word as soon as the battle is won, and you may visit. I wait every day at the window for you to arrive I am so overcome with excitement. But until then, here is your second gift since you claim it to be the best.

I love you. I love you. I love you. I love you. I love you. I love you today and tomorrow and forevermore. I love you most.

Soon,

Annwyl

Cloth fell into my lap. I dropped the letter, clutching the fabric in a fist caked with dried blood. I held it to my face and breathed deeply. Strawberries and willow bark, just as I remembered.

"What is an Annwyl?" Harthon asked. They all leaned over me to scour the letter. It was in our language—Annwyl knew some, and Parsna helped translate in the event a letter was lost so no one would know it came from a human. There was nothing incriminating in her words, but their silence unsettled me. I'd grown close with these sidhe brothers, more than I ever thought I could with my own kind, but they were not human. They would not understand.

Scholar Rindshaw had been pushing me of late. Whispering ideas of a better world, an Ildathach with a ruler who allowed no cruelty. A place where the low fae and sidhe lived in peace, gratuitous violence a thing of the past. I thought it a fool's dream, but Annwyl thought that of her own. I never wanted to be king, but if this war was won and my place secured before the hunts, if the scholar was right and this new order could exist, then it would be safe for Annwyl. We would need no Bogoran to be together, and her cottage of good children could be a castle. It was that dream that drove me into each battle.

But it was still too early to share it. I leaked poison into the paper until it was nothing but crumbling dust. The men were silent. Draaph spoke first, and the unexpected words filled me with hope, both for Annwyl and Scholar Rindshaw. "Must be nice."

Destres, officially crowned king of Ond now—though we all forgot to call him it—chuckled. "No wonder you refused to marry my sister."

Corin, Harthon, and my last commander, Frae, all laughed. But the sound was thoughtful, perhaps a bit envious. Unlike most would, they did not find weakness in it.

Parsna bowed. "Will you be returning correspondence, Prince Jaevidan?"

I had nothing to eat, let alone pen and parchment. The remainder of my army stretched down the hill. My mother and the war council back home would want answers for what happened, answers I could not provide. We were hungry, wounded, and had lost all the progress we had made in nearly a year. I could not speak to human wars, but faerie ones could last a lifetime. There was no saying how long this ebb and flow would last, fighting for kingdom after kingdom, pushing ourselves farther up the supply road. And that was all if we survived the coming weeks. If Tearach did not bear down on our broken army and wipe us from the soil once and for all.

Parsna wrung her hands. "I could tell her what happened. That it may be some time before you return."

I shook my head, wary of my friends listening with rapt attention. But we all needed hope right now. Good fortune. "Tell her . . . just tell her that I love her. And I always believe in her dreams."

She gave me a sad smile. "Of course, my Prince."

"And Parsna?" I called, halting the brownie's retreat. She turned. "How does she seem nowadays? Honestly."

The brownie shrunk with discomfort. "She eats more, but not much. We do what we can . . ." She looked across the commanders, choosing her words. "The village and forest are different without you. She will be our girl again once you come home."

Not Gerenstad or the castle of my birth. Not even my own world. Home was an impoverished village beside a dank castle, bordering the Bannau Brycheiniog forest in Wales, where a human girl of golden hair loved to dance. That was my true home, not this soil where my own blood fed the earth.

But I could not have Annwyl without this place. I could not protect her. I could not be the man she deserved without pursuing her and Rindshaw's dreams. So I would fight for this kingdom like it was the barren meadow across the Veil I longed for.

I dismissed her and wasted little time after that. We had plans to draw, battles to win, and I would think of nothing else until we besieged the land that would allow me across the Veil.

Standing, I looked to my commanders. My brothers in arms. My friends. "I want to reach Hearel within one month's time, and I want a plan to do it within twelve hours."

IT TOOK US NINE months to reach Hearel.

Annwyl and I wrote extensively. It was difficult with Parsna needing to travel back and forth so often across war-torn territory, but others helped me now. When I'd first come here, my army needed spirit, but even I had not understood how sorely my fae brethren lacked it. It was weak to love in our world. Weak to care. Even Scholar Rindshaw had once warned me to leave anything precious behind.

But the fae, and even the sidhe, vied for stories of my letters and the mystery girl who wrote them. While my brothers' armies made no progress in the south and west, mine advanced with purpose. They did not fight out of fear of their queen or simply because they craved the violence. They fought because I sowed seeds of Scholar Rindshaw's dream among them.

And I told them stories. None had ever heard the name Annwyl before, so I painted her as a woman of myth. A fierce and gentle soul who took a scar across her face in battle. A maiden of woven gold hair and a beauty that made men weep. How she sang with the snow spirits and left offerings to all who showed her kindness. That one day, she would bless all the good beings of the world and reward them with her love and shelter.

One day, a general from an allied army asked in earnest what Gerenstad would be like with me as king. I told him it would be like Annwyl.

After that, her name became synonymous with hope. Tales spread of the Poison Prince, who wished to burn the world and raise it anew from the ashes. Soldiers defected and joined my ranks. Most of them were low fae, but we gathered our sidhe as well. When their voices rose on our marches, they did not chant for Gerenstad or my family's name. Their battle cries were for Annwyl.

I knew I had done right when Scholar Rindshaw took me aside one night, laying a hand on my shoulder. We had just won Leonta. In the golden halls behind us, my soldiers sang songs of the Golden Goddess.

"You have made me proud, my boy," he said and, in a moment so unlike his stoic nature, squeezed me in a tight embrace. "You have made an old man very proud."

Then he told me stories of my father. Not the kind I was used to, hushed whispers of fear. But good stories, humorous ones. "There was more to him than you will ever know," he said, patting my arm. "But it is time for me to retire for the night."

But none of this compared to the joy I felt the morning after we conquered Hearel. While Destres managed his own men and Corin directed mine, I slipped through the break in the Veil. I found myself on the other side of the Bannau Brycheiniog, but my immortal legs could carry me fast, effervescence igniting my veins. Three hours later, I arrived in Annwyl's village. It had not changed in the three years of my absence.

I smelled something terrible but had not wished to waste time cleaning my armor. My longsword dangled from my hip, and my hair stuck at odd angles from my helmet. I glamoured myself to appear human but was too exhausted to hide my foreign attire. The dirtied silver reflected a midday sun, so dull compared to the one in Ildathach. Dung and piss infiltrated my nose, the decay and sweat of humans. I had never relished a scent with so much joy.

It was a balmy spring day. On the south face of the castle, the scullions rimmed a stone pool with lye or hung fresh washing along weathered lines. Annwyl laid a bedsheet over the twine, the breeze wrapping the damp cloth around her willowy frame. Her blonde hair was dark with ash, dress a dingy gray from dust and too many washings. She was gaunt with chipped finger-nails, frown lines around her mouth at only eighteen summers, her scar a purple slash of fury across her face. She was the most beautiful thing I had ever seen.

She looked up—looked down and up again. Those large eyes swallowed her face. Her hands trembled around the sheet. An inhuman sound left her throat, capturing the other maids' attention. Then she ran, dress catching around her shins, arms pumping at her sides, and I did not care they watched with wary eyes as she leapt into my arms. As I spun her around, her laugh filled my ears, and I kissed her hair and her cheeks, and I could have died right there a happy man. Her scent filled me, and her arms wrapped around my neck, and if her human heaven existed, that moment would be mine.

"You came back." Tears streaked her face. She held mine like she needed proof I was real.

"Of course I did." I brushed my nose against hers. "I will always come back to you."

The visit was short. With Hearel as our last obstacle before the Kingdom of Tearach, there was much to do, but I made the most of our time. We visited the forest, and I recounted tales of my adventures, leaving the goriest details out. She described her quiet life in the castle and all the plans she had made for us when the war was done. Darkness fell too soon, and I had to return. I kissed the top of her hand, kneeling like the knights did in all her stories. Her token for me was a lock of hair. I kept it safe behind my breastplate.

Only one battle left. This would all be over soon.

But the siege of Tearach went on for months, and Annwyl's letters stopped coming.

THIRTY-FIVE

ADELINE

THEN I SAY LET it rot.

Violet's cold words haunted me as I lay in bed. Jack's bed. Despite the Abstruse being repaired in my weeks of unconsciousness, it didn't feel right to return. There was no particular reason. It all led back to the emotions I couldn't explain.

No one stayed long after Violet's departure. Barring Tommy, we each sipped a glass of faerie wine and silently agreed to end the night. Since emerging from the dungeons, my brother had been staying at Will's. He insisted Lillian take the sofa so they may keep an eye on her and nobly claimed the living room floor. Jack offered him the Abstruse or a hotel room of his own, but I had the feeling my brother still held a grudge. I couldn't entirely blame him. Guinevere returned with Arthur to do Bogorans-knew-what, and Jack and I returned home. He said he would be in shortly, but that was hours ago. I woke from the short stretch of rest I managed, and his space on the floor remained empty.

I stared at the tangled mess of blankets and pillows beside the fireplace. How inconsequential it all felt now. My anger with Jack, my worries about the fates, the memories visiting me when I slept. Who knew how many had died in their home world. Who knew how many more would still.

Violet hadn't been in Ildathach since hours after she was born, abandoned and discarded to the human world for being a girl and a twin. So I couldn't say I was surprised she felt no nothing now that it was gone. But I didn't entirely understand how she felt. All her guilt and anger lay in what she did to the Bogorans. She took a personal vow to never use her abilities due to the shame. Where was all that passion for her fellow fae? Then again, the Bogorans were not the ones who'd rejected her.

How Jack felt, I didn't know. He had no lost love for his home either, more apparent with each memory I watched, except perhaps for the last. But he was also the one who chose to slowly kill himself to protect the low fae. The one who took them all under his wing, as long as they agreed to live peacefully among the humans.

In the aftermath of Lillian's admission, my status as a fate had been completely forgotten. For now, at least. I was equally terrified and relieved. If I were honest, some part of me hoped Jack would convince or coerce me out of it. My flesh was new, but my mind was human, and all our primitive senses desired was survival. The thought of being confined to that cave for eternity brought no happy thoughts. The thought of leaving my life behind, the one I'd been fighting so hard for, felt more like defeat than anything.

But there were millions of souls suffering inside the shade now. All alone in the icy dark. Someone needed to champion for them. The fates said my role was a punishment for Jack's sins, something I thought hilariously petty at the time. It wasn't. Jack's destruction of the last Bogoran brought this down on us. On everyone. If anything, the punishment was merciful. So I would go, just not yet.

There was a strange quality of peace with admitting it. I no longer needed to toil in my guilt and shame, asking all the right questions and denying their answers. We were wrong. We failed. We destroyed more than we created. So if the worst had already come to pass, then nothing was at stake anymore. Nothing left to lose.

For me, at least. My time was done. I knew it the moment the fates called on me, even if I didn't understand it yet. But I still had lives to protect. Jack would go down swinging, and so would everyone else. Heroes always died in the stories because they sacrificed themselves for the greater good. But I didn't fall in love with a hero. I gave myself to something else.

Trusting him didn't matter. Atoning for his sins didn't matter. Nothing mattered anymore. I wouldn't let the sisters kill him or anyone else I loved. Jack and Violet had the power of a Bogoran, and with the Morrigan gone, they could collect all the books, and everyone else would have no choice but to follow them. The twins brought down their world, so they would be the ones to fix it. They didn't want it, which made them the most deserving. They could start their world anew, creating a better existence for the living just like Scholar Rindshaw once dreamed. And somewhere far away, I would do the same for the dead.

That was my plan. My fate. Convince Jack and Violet to begin again in Ildathach themselves. Rid the world of Babd and Nemain so they could. Then take my place beside my sisters in the dark.

A hero would sacrifice themselves and everything else they loved. A hero would allow the Morrigan to do what must be done, avoiding a war and countless more deaths in the meantime. But my sentiment echoed Lillian's. We were the bad ones. Jack had mentored me well.

If days among the living were numbered, I would enjoy them without regret, without overthinking it all so much. That's what I told myself as I rose from bed and shimmied out of a brand-new nightgown and threw it in the fire to burn. It would be my new routine until I stopped fighting destiny. Everything I wore had fresh tags or didn't belong to me, and it all turned to ash the moment I was done.

I had no undergarments. I didn't need them. I pulled one of Jack's dress shirts from the closet and slipped my arms through. The soft, white fabric ended near my knees, and the sleeves were too long. I left them dangling, not bothering with the buttons either.

I wrapped the open sides around my chest and padded into the study. Vines slithered beside my feet and coiled out of the way. The fire was massive tonight, dousing the room in its orange glow. Jack sat in an armchair like a man possessed, legs splayed and so close to the fire it must have burned. His fingers clutched a lowball glass, and judging by the empty decanter beside him, it wasn't his first. His glamour was gone, how I preferred him. His stare remained on the burning hearth, empty, but the moment I stepped into the room, all his attention snapped to me.

He watched me like I were a phantom, the ghost of an aching desire long withheld from his grasp. I drifted closer, footsteps soft against the stones. He followed me with the rapt attention of a predator, the preternatural stillness raising my flesh. Only his eyes moved with my steps, the remainder of him coiling to strike. It was these moments—these simple, unexpected moments—I remembered exactly what he was.

Standing between his spread knees, I let the shirt fall open.

Heat licked my back from the fire, rivaling the warmth wherever his eyes touched. All his emotions were dammed up, walled behind the bond. No sound. No words. He simply leaned forward, grabbing my calves with calloused hands. They roamed higher, the rough skin sweeping the back of my knees, my thighs, pulling me closer until my shins pressed his chair and his fingers dug into my bottom.

He rested his forehead on my stomach. His long, ragged breath heated the skin below my navel. We had done this before. Even no longer possessing my memories, I felt it in my soul. I wound my fingers through his hair, tenderly smoothing it back.

Red laced his eyes as he pulled away. I knew him, so I would pretend it was from drunkenness. Jack never asked for what he needed, and I was often too prideful myself. So I left no room for interpretation as I let the shirt slip from my shoulders, whispering, "Mouth."

He shook his head.

"Our wager," I breathed, sinking to my knees. I ran my hands up his strong thighs, fabric smoothing beneath my fingertips. "I choose mouth."

"Forget the bet, Annwyl."

"I don't want to." His waistcoat and tie were gone, only a buttoned shirt similar to the one I discarded behind me. I undid his belt, taking my time to release the clasps beneath. He didn't help me but didn't stop me either as I tugged his clothes down to reveal what I wanted. This time, he didn't ask me if I was sure. If this was what I wanted. It was only me and the devil here.

Tattooed hands gripped the armrests while I grabbed his cock. Any struggle to mute the bond dissipated, and all at once, it flared heavy between us. His skin was soft, length hard, heat filling my face as a drop of moisture beaded at the tip. My eyes found his and remained there as I licked it away.

Still frozen, nothing but a serrated breath passed his teeth. Warm moisture gathered between my own legs. I could feel his want. Feel his need. Visualize the tainted thoughts swarming his head. I licked him again, slowly, a little grin pulling my lips at his responding shiver.

Stroking him with one hand, I took him fully into my mouth. Rain and oleander filled my nose, the taste of salt and man along my tongue. A dark pleasure rolled through me, and he snapped.

Rough fingers twined through my hair, raspy voice demanding, "Take it." He pushed into my throat, then slowly pulled back. Again. Tears stung my eyes, and I choked for breath, but heat clambered along my skin. Pooled low in my stomach. My knees dug into the carpet as he fucked my mouth just like he promised to.

"You're so good for me, getting on your knees." He thrust his hips, my throat numb. My watery stare met his blackened one. He pulled out, spit forming a little string between his cock and my lips, his thumb brushing over them. "This is mine," he rumbled, a promise and a threat.

"Yours," I breathed. Always had been. He'd claimed my lips for his nearly four hundred years ago, sealed with a kiss of blood. Jack was the first man I'd ever tasted. He would also be the last.

"All of you," he said, pushing into my mouth and silencing any protests. "You are mine. You have always been mine, and I do not fucking share, Annwyl. Do you understand?"

I knew. The reason I ran from him in the Guild, why I ceased fighting it now. I was his. I had always been his, and he had always been mine. Centuries of bloodshed and pain sealed our covenant. For all the ruin we left behind, there was one guarantee in the end. Wherever I went, he would always find me.

My answer was not with words but stroking him harder, taking him deeper. I wanted to feel him break beneath me. I wanted the taste of his come on my tongue. But it wasn't enough. One moment, I knelt before him on the carpet; the next, I knelt on stones.

He'd shaded us but not to the bed. His enormous three-tier mirror had shattered when I destroyed the apartment, the identical replacement not yet hung on the wall. Violent hands grasped my waist from behind, our reflections in the mirror propped against the bookshelves on the floor. He wrenched my head to the side, teeth marking the skin at my neck as he shoved his trousers to his knees. All his clothes were still on.

"Look at me," he demanded, gazes colliding in the mirror. My lips were swollen, hair askew from his brutal clasp. His knee shoved between my own and forced them apart, heaving breaths pushing his chest against my back. Ink swirled his hands and coiled along his neck. Those terrifying eyes, the mark of my dark prince, claimed every inch of flesh mirrored back. "Who can touch you, Annwyl?"

His hand flattened against my stomach, skimming lower. Breath pushed through my clenched teeth. "You. Only you."

He rewarded me with two fingers, slipping inside the wetness between my thighs. "Who can be inside you?"

"You," I gasped. The bond had no mercy now, too hot to breathe.

His hand fell away, replaced with something else. The length of him pushing against my wetness, but not inside. "You're mine," he repeated, pupils a black abyss, darkness kissing his skin. "I fuck you. I worship you. I pleasure you. I love you, and no one else can. Swear this to me."

My eyes fluttered closed. Nothing mattered anymore. There was no longer a future to decide between the two of us. With all bets off, I could have him, and he could have what he wanted until there was nothing left to give. "I swear."

He pushed inside me. A startled gasp, muscles clenching as he stretched and filled me. I'd forgotten the feeling, but my body remembered how to accommodate. Painful ecstasy rippled across my skin and tightened my stomach. My head fell back on his shoulder, a breathless moan off my lips.

He grasped my jaw. "I want you to watch, Annwyl. Watch me take what belongs to me."

I did. Dark eyes met mine as he slowly, torturously unsheathed himself, the truth of how much I wanted him glinting against his skin. He thrust in, my knees buckling as I struggled to remain kneeling. His hand slipped down my waist and grabbed the soft underside of my thigh, holding me up and locking me in place. I couldn't move, couldn't stop the savage way he claimed me even if I wanted to. I was reduced to pinpoints of feelings. Desperate moans and endless pleasure. Scorching heat and depthless desire. Always begging for more, more, more. He watched me in the mirror, a smirk touching his face. Lips brushed my ear, and hot breath demanded, "Come for me."

Magic filled my mouth, the sharp metal of compulsion. Shock waves coursed across my skin, walls tightening around him. My mind fractured apart, my body his slave. A deep and twisted euphoria cut through to the bone. I forgot to think, forgot to breathe as he continued fucking me into a trance.

A low, poisoned chuckle, and he tugged my earlobe with his teeth. "Harder this time."

Vision darkened, I writhed against him with sounds I didn't know I could make. He groaned against my ear, holding me down so tightly it hurt. "*Fuck*, Annwyl." His panting breaths matched my own. "Do you know how tight you are?" he rasped. "How fucking good you feel finishing around me?"

My only answer was a throaty moan. I had a moment to catch my breath before he murmured, "Again."

It was all too much—the pleasure, the pain. I was a mess beneath him, a whimpering pile of ruin. Still, he kept on kissing, biting, touching, fucking, and when his lips parted to make another demand of me, I turned my head and kissed his lips instead.

"Come on, Annwyl," he murmured.

"No, I can't—"

"Nearly two months, darling." He tugged my lower lip between his teeth, groaning at my answering pout. "We have a lot to make up for. One more time," he whispered. No compulsion laced the words, but my body tightened in anticipation. "You can take it. One more time for me."

Magic wasn't necessary. Despite my exhaustion, despite the overwhelming sensations, he did something to me. Something deep and inherently wrong, a mark on my soul that ached for him. I slumped against him as I finished, energy sapped. The noises I made, half bliss and half a plea, were only drowned by his wild moans as he finished inside me. I shivered as he filled me up, hot liquid coating my inner thighs. He laughed and kissed my cheek, the corner of my lips, pulling out and scooping me into his arms.

"I'm done," I lamented against his chest. His shirt scratched my cheek. I thought he would take me to the bed, but we entered the Abstruse and its adjoining bathroom. It had been completely remodeled after the explosion, the bathtub nearly double in size.

He caught my look and chuckled. "I told you I would remedy the bath only fitting one." He snapped his fingers beneath my knees, and it filled with water, the scent of lavender and eucalyptus drifting from the steam. Gingerly, he set me down in the tub and removed the rest of his clothes.

The warm water was just the balm I needed. Of course he would think of that. He joined me as I ran water over my shoulders, snapping once more to dim the lights.

"Why do you always do that? The snapping?" I asked.

"Helps me focus. Especially with more complicated tasks or if the reflections I'm using for the shade aren't very good."

He snapped again, a candle appearing on the rim of the tub. He hadn't used the mirror, all his attention on me.

It made me wonder. I closed my eyes, breathing deeply. Reflections were gateways to the shade but theoretically didn't need to be visualized in order to use them. I snapped my fingers once, grinning when I opened my eyes to no less than twenty candles scattering the room.

Jack smirked. "Show-off."

"I can't use compulsion or glamour."

"Because you're not fae. You are something better." He drifted closer. Running his hands through my hair, he whispered, "Thank you."

"For?"

"Coming back to me." He pressed two light kisses to my cheeks, the space between my eyes. All I felt was shame. Regret. I wasn't his to keep.

He whispered against my skin. "Let me wash your hair."

"What for?"

"I want to."

I didn't question it, putting my back to him and dunking my head beneath the water. My hair had grown out halfway down my neck without the time or means to cut it, a reminder of how chaotic our lives had been since that dreaded night everyone's lies came crumbling down.

Slowly, he ran his fingers across my scalp, smoothing each lock of hair. I hummed with the feeling, savoring the warmth. The gentleness. It could be so rare with him.

"Where I come from, it's a sacred act to wash someone's hair. It means you care for them deeply."

Lillian had washed my hair once. I hadn't thought much of it at the time, but it made my heart break for her even more. The news of her homeland had wounded her deeply. Unlike Will, she hadn't come here by choice. And neither Violet nor Jack had much to miss. Part of her may have always hoped she could return one day and redeem herself to her people.

"I'm surprised you had gestures like that," I said. "I thought the sidhe in Ildathach didn't know what love was."

"Of course we did, but love was a rare thing there. Something special. It was hard to grow it when surrounded by so much cruelty." His voice softened. "And declaring it was more a danger than anything. So we had our rituals, our gestures instead of words. I always like this one, the vulnerability in it."

"How is it vulnerable?"

He lathered soap into a gnarled knot, no doubt from our gesture of vulnerability minutes before. "You have to put your back to someone if they wash your hair. Close your eyes. Trust they mean you no harm and let them touch unguarded parts of your body."

Another reminder of the differences between us. Violet said fae could not love like humans do, and she was right. To fae, love was the ultimate sacrifice. A weakness. Even their practices to declare it demanded submission, the risk of letting someone use your trust against you.

Let it rot, Violet said. Because in her mind, there was nothing worth saving. But there was still Jaevidan and his letters. The hope that brewed among the low fae and even the sidhe that someone could build a world where love existed without fear.

He finished his task in silence. It was late, and Jack hadn't slept yet, but when I went to stand, his arms held firm around my waist, each rise of his chest warm against my spine. His thumb made slow circles over my stomach. A soft kiss to my cheek and a low whisper. "I love you."

I stiffened. Not for the reasons he thought. Our reflections bounced back in the vanity mirror, low in the candlelit bathroom. Jack looked the same as he always did, chin resting on my shoulder. It was me. Not my face, the face of Adeline Colton, but that of Annwyl. Her high cheekbones and sharp jaw. The scar across her face. The only difference was the eyes, a pure eggshell white without pupils or irises. I brought my hand to my check, brushing the spot Jack bequeathed those three words to my skin. The mirror's vision reflected the movement. I blinked, and it was Addie and Jack once more.

"You don't have to say anything," he whispered. "I just wanted you to know."

"I know." One could argue until the cows came home whether it was love or obsession, but the result was the same. Love was dangerous, especially now. We both had roles to play in the coming future, and love had no place in either scenario.

"I know what you are thinking."

He settled back against the tub's edge, bringing me with him. I laid my cheek on his chest, tracing the battle on his side and the warrior raising his sword. "What am I thinking?"

"The fates cannot have you," he said.

I glanced in the mirror again. Still Addie and Jack. "I don't think we have a choice this time."

"I will find a way. I always do." His hands smoothed over my stomach, dipping lower. But sex wouldn't be a distraction this time. I laced my fingers through his, stopping his descent. He squeezed tightly. "We can speak with Estheria," he said. "You can choose another predecessor, and this will all be forgotten. With the parallel bond, you will still be immortal. You may lose your command over the shade, but it seems a small price to pay. I told you this life would be yours, and no one will take that away. I swear it."

Because Jack would burn the world. I'd suspected it the moment we met. There was a reason he set every room on fire.

"What if you fixed it?" I asked.

"I plan to."

"Not my status as a *beansidhe*." I angled my head to look at him. "We form a Morrigan, Jack. We have the Bogorans' power. If we had the books, we could right this wrong ourselves. Ildathach doesn't need the sisters. It has us."

He didn't speak, wearing an expression I'd seen few times in this life but felt many times through his memories. He was my violence, and I everything else. The reward at the end of a long, hard battle. Reverence held his eyes, respect. And for some reason, I already knew what he wished to say when he dipped his chin. "What if Ildathach doesn't deserve it?"

"How could you say that?"

"What's done is done. Restoring my world will not return the dead already lost. The remaining survivors are here, and those who wish to stay made their choices."

"I know how you feel, but—"

"I'm tired, Annwyl." The words rumbled deep in his chest, heavy and empty. "I'm not like you. I do good things for the wrong reasons. All I've ever cared about was carving out a life here. Granting those same protections to my friends and being with you." He stroked his fingers across my cheeks. "There is nothing left for me there and, to be completely frank, little worth sacrificing more for. We had thousands of years to progress, right our wrongs, stop killing our own gods, and we did not. This was the natural evolution of our choices. This is what we deserve."

No, this was what Jack thought *he* deserved. He placed me on a pedestal, but humans as well. In mind and heart, he became one himself, renouncing his true nature for his idea of what was better.

But Estheria gave me a choice. She gave me warnings and insinuated I had a path to decide. The fates may not have been designers, but the stars couldn't be either. They gave us free will, otherwise they would never allow such atrocities to be woven. That free will was what made us good, made us deserving of joining the darkness. Everyone was perfect until they made a hard choice. Those defined us.

"Love exists. You just told me." Jack shook his head, but I continued. "You said yourself that cruelty made it hard to cultivate, but what if it had room to grow? I've seen your memories. Your life. I know what has always been in here, what the others dreamed of." My palm flattened on his chest. "Even before me, all you wanted was a family and friends. The world you lived in took that away. But this is a chance to begin again. To start fresh with those who share your vision and all those who have lived among humans like you have. We don't need to restore Ildathach to what it was. We can make it better."

I felt out the bond, scouring his eyes for the answers. Emotions slipped through. The pain and enervation, longing and remorse. It was easy to forget how old he was. How many centuries had passed him by. How many wars he had witnessed in this world and the other one, how many bodies buried, how many sacrifices made, just how much one could carve of themselves until there was nothing left to give. That was what Jack did. Filleted himself one piece at a time, sloughing everything away. It didn't matter if it was for selfish reasons. That result was the same.

"Don't look at me like that," he said.

"Like what?"

"Like I'm good." His hand coasted down my stomach, settling against my hip. "Because I am not, Annwyl. Finish the memories, and you will understand. There was only one thing I ever wanted. And now that I have it, the rest can go to waste."

"But you don't." I sat up to face him. "You don't have me because I am choosing a different path. I can help as a fate. I can make the shade something good and have a hand in changing the course of everything. It's not what I want, but it's what I will do. And say what you will about yourself, but I know who you are too. You almost died holding the glamour to protect the low fae. You refused to let the sisters hurt humans or this world. So maybe you should give yourself more credit for things you create and less for things you have destroyed."

"I'm tired." A sad smile pulled his lips. "I can't do this anymore, Annwyl." He'd said that not long ago in his bedroom, but this time was different. Warning bells chimed around each word.

I held his face in my hands. "You're Jack fucking Warren. You can do anything."

"There is a reason the stars made humans mortal." Pulling me closer, he brushed his lips against mine. "You wanted me to be honest with you, so I will be. I've been doing this a long time. Too long. I never wanted any of it, but I have done it. And not because I am good or righteous, but for you. Because you always made me better. You have always kept me honest and forced me down the right path." He kissed me again, deeper. Warmth cascaded down my body, a heady fog. "But without you, I would have been doing none of those things. I would have turned into everything I hate."

"That's why you are needed so much now," I murmured. "You can be the opposite. We have a chance here to save them in more ways than one."

"But I don't want to. I want to end this once and for all." He kissed my cheek. "So I am going to free you from the fates. I am going to kill the sisters. I am going to destroy the Dianomicans so they can never be used again. And whatever happens to the fae will happen, but it is no longer my burden. Nor is it yours."

"We can do better, Jack."

"I can't." The way he said it, devoid of all things that made him so utterly *Jack*, set my teeth on edge. My plan had been to run away, to join the fates and let Jack's role fall into place afterwards. But I saw the cracks in that plan now. I saw how much weight he held on his shoulders, and my decision would be the one to crumple him. He wouldn't save the fae without me, maybe not even with me. And despite what he said, I knew this was more than about me. It was a lifetime.

"Talk to me," I said.

He evaluated me. Long enough for the bath water to turn tepid, the candles to fade down. I ran my hands through his hair, across his shoulders, expressing in any way I could that I was here. But in the end, he only said, "I cannot lie to you in the Abstruse."

I nodded.

He nodded back, swallowing thickly. "Maybe one day."

Leaving no room for a reply, he scooped me into his arms and shaded us to the bedroom. Another snap of his fingers and we were dry, but our clothes were long forgotten. He slipped into bed beside me, forgoing the pillows and blankets on the floor. I let him. All the time, my mind brimmed with questions. One day, what? He would lie or tell me what I needed to know? But within moments, he was fast asleep, arm tight around my waist and cheek pressed to my chest. Those answers would have to wait.

THIRTY-SIX

ADELINE

WE SLEPT FAR LONGER than we should have, but I felt Jack needed the rest. I also thought he needed what came after we woke—his face buried between my legs, then my own taste on his lips as he kissed me. He fucked me hard, every stroke a reminder of the vows he made me take. I was his to please. His to keep. His to love. Even if I had not yet promised to love him back.

I was so sure of myself last night, but everything had changed after speaking to Jack. I already knew what he would destroy to have me, but it was different thinking it and hearing the words aloud. My entire plan depended on him, on his willingness to pick up the pieces after I was gone and do what he must. It hadn't occurred to me I may break him in the process.

Estheria once said Jack would do anything for me, that it was a wonderful and terrible responsibility. How right she was.

That was frightening enough, but there was another reason I feared the final memories. Not that they would push me away from Jack, but that they would draw us closer. That they would tear down the last wall, and I would want him the way he wanted me. Because if I allowed that to happen, I wasn't sure if I could do what I needed to when the time came. There was no place for love and selfish desires with so many lives hanging in the balance. Jack already had too many for the two of us.

So I let him touch me. I let him kiss me. I let him make me come before finishing between my legs, only to flip me over and begin the process anew. I lay on my back, him on his knees as he thrust inside me over and over again. I scoured his tattoos, wondering again how he got them. His hands smoothed over every inch of my skin, gaze feasting on the sight of his cock pushing into me, my bare body beneath him, when a strange thought arose. The memory of him drinking in the sight of Annwyl the night of the feast. How he had salivated over her breasts and hips, things I was born in this life without.

"What is that look on your face?" Jack leaned forward on two elbows, slowing his rhythm as he kissed up my throat. I shook my head, not wanting him to stop.

Even as I mewled against his lips, rolling my hips for some friction, he wasn't deterred. His expression said I would receive nothing else until I answered his question. I sighed, annoyed by the ache he wasn't fulfilling as much as the embarrassment of my insecurities. "I don't look much like Annwyl."

Lillian may have taken my memories away, but I remembered the names he'd listed off in the prison. I doubted I looked much like Lizzie or Sujana either.

Groaning, he pushed deep and mumbled against my neck. "Does that bother you?"

"Does it bother you?" My mirrored reflection from last night haunted me. Annwyl on his chest but with the eyes of a wraith.

"I'm most concerned with what's in here," he said, bending down to kiss over my heart. "And these," he added with a devious grin, giving each of my nipples the attention they deserved.

"But hasn't there been some kind of . . . preference?" Surely, he couldn't have been attracted to every body I had inhabited. At least one version of me had to be less than desirable. Or, at the very least, there were qualities he preferred I didn't have now. Judging by his teenage memories, large breasts were one of them.

He kissed me long and slow. Cupping my face, he stared into my soul. "You are more beautiful each time I find you. I mean that."

I smirked. "Liar."

He tugged my lower lip between his teeth, moaning as he rocked into me. "Want me to prove it?"

He proved it. Afterwards, I donned one of his shirts as he took a shower. It was nearly eleven, but it had been too long since I had a famous Charlene-made breakfast.

The last button slipped into place as I entered the study . . . and nearly jumped out of my skin. Will sat at the dining table, sipping tea.

No glamour, which was unusual for him. His pointed ears stuck out from his dark hair, head cocked in that distinctly fae way. "Funny. I'd heard you two were just friends as of late."

My cheeks burned red as he surveyed my attire, bare legs on full display. He'd seen me in far worse, but the context had been more . . . medical.

"I had to burn all my clothes."

"Uh-huh." His sly smile said he didn't believe a word, only made worse by Jack entering a moment later, shirtless. Wet hair flopped onto his forehead as he pulled his suspenders over his bare chest. "Oh, Will. I wasn't expecting you."

Will raised a brow. "You're in an uncharacteristically cheerful mood this morning."

It was true. Jack grinned like an idiot, attention ravenously on my legs. "It's a beautiful day."

"Our dear Adeline here was just saying you two have been enjoying your lovely, platonic friendship."

"Of course we are." Jack wrapped his arms around me, dipping me low into a heated kiss.

When he came up for air, Will shook his head. "You never kiss me like that."

Jack beamed. "Come here, then." He only got a step forward before Will threw a spoon at his head.

"I always suspected Jack was a little sweet for him," Lillian said, sporting a little smile despite the bags beneath her eyes. I hadn't noticed her slumped in an armchair. Her clothes were bedraggled, hair askew. I could only imagine the headache as she rubbed at her temples, shielding her eyes from the lamps.

I sat beside her, folding a blanket over my lap for some decency. She kept her distance, lowering her voice so only I could hear. "I need to speak with you."

"You don't have to apologize," I said. Her mouth crumpled, tears coalescing on her lashes. I wrapped an arm around her and stroked her hair.

"Jack was right. I do hate myself," she whispered.

"It was a bad day for everyone," I murmured. "I know who you really are. We all do."

She nodded, wiping her cheeks. "Your brother gave me a nice tongue-lashing this morning, I'll tell you that."

"Where is he, anyway?"

"Stayed behind. His burns were bothering him again." I knew Tommy got bad pains from his old battle wounds, but I'd not once heard him mention it. I wondered again when the two of them had grown so familiar.

"Anyway . . ." She lifted her head from my shoulder, nodding at Jack. "We all need to discuss this new development."

Like the end of the world hadn't been announced twelve hours earlier, Jack settled into a dining chair and picked at a pastry. "Nothing to discuss."

"But—"

"I know what I need to do. I'll inform you when you are needed."

Even Will flinched. I knew he wasn't being cold to Lillian because of the way she acted, but she wouldn't. I rose and wrapped my arms around his chest, whispering in his ear, "She thinks you're angry with her."

"I am not angry with you, Lillian," he called out. I sighed. "I have everything handled. For now, we continue as we have been."

Will tossed an apple in the air and caught it. "Care to share, then, darling?"

"No." Jack gave me a pointed look and sipped from his cup.

Lillian joined us at the table. "But what about home?"

"This is home," he said gruffly.

Will frowned, treading carefully. "Not everyone agrees with you, mate."

"Do you?"

"Haven't decided yet, but the fact is we can't just let it rot." Lillian's eyes narrowed at that. She and Violet had really been at odds and ends lately.

"We have enough at the moment. We kill the sisters and help Addie first," Jack said, tone clear that this discussion was finished and his patience with it.

The other two looked to me. As if I could ever persuade Jack from his warpaths. But when they continued imploring me for answers, I realized it was something else. Not the expectation of swaying Jack to their side but of giving my opinion. Forming a decision. I wasn't sure when I became as much a leader as Jack.

"We still need to explore our options," I said. "This news changes everything. I don't know the sisters like you three, but have we ever considered a more diplomatic approach? We have the same objectives now. Maybe they will work with us."

Unfortunately, even Lillian shook her head at that. "You killed their triplet, Addie. Even without that, the sisters are not ones to share power. They have an opportunity to rule everything and will eliminate any threat to their goals."

"Even if it means saving their world?"

Will's lips thinned into a sad smile. "We're lucky to have someone who thinks less . . . fae, but the sisters are not like us. They would sooner see the world end than relinquish the hold they have. Had it been purely for noble reasons, they would have sought you three out instead of trying to kill you in the first place."

I'd already suspected that, but it was worth a try. "Then Jack is right. We need to worry about the fates and taking down Babd and Nemain first."

Jack didn't look up from his drink, mumbling. "As I already said, I have it handled."

"Not the fates," I said.

"Them too." He leaned back in his seat, closing his eyes. "I already spoke with Estheria."

Surprise flickered through me. "When? You said last night you planned to."

"It was a long day. I meant I already had." He made himself busy with picking a thread from his suspenders. "While you were sleeping after the Silvertongue, I made the trip. She told me what I need. We kill Babd and Nemain, and the rest will fall into place."

I glared at him. "Why didn't you tell me?"

"As I told you, it was a long day."

"Well, according to you, it's a beautiful one today, so what did she say?"

He gave me a pointed look. "Not now."

All the dread I felt yesterday piled back. "What aren't you telling me?"

"Do you trust me?" He reached across the table, taking my hand in his. A plea circled the bond, the desperate favor of not having this conversation with witnesses. "I'd never put you or anyone else in harm's way, so please. Let's eat." He dropped my hand and pushed a plate in front of me. "Besides, it's not me you need to convince. It's Violet."

It sounded an awful lot like he was the one needing convincing last night, but I respected him enough to make it a private matter. "She'll never budge. If we do this, it would be me and you."

He shook his head. "You need her." I didn't like his use of *you* instead of *we.*

Will nodded. "I can speak with her."

"It needs to be Addie," Jack said, rising from the table. "In the meantime, I have some errands to handle. Lillian, keep your ears open for any new developments. Will, do whatever it is you do all day."

Will grinned. "Torture Charlene? Gladly."

AFTER JACK DEPARTED FOR the-lord-only-knew, Lillian offered to bring me to Violet's residence. Out of all the Band of Banished, she was the only one whose home I had never been in. She'd spent most of the past decade living in the hotel but moved down the block shortly after I arrived in the spring. No one quite understood why, but no one much understood Violet.

Lillian was quiet as we stepped onto the sidewalk. With the holidays approaching, the city had been transformed into a winter wonderland. We tucked our faces into our coats, arm in arm as humans bustled past. The thick gray sky warned of inclement weather arriving soon. Wreaths decorated doorways and holly in shop windows. Bells rang from the harnesses of police horses, and a group of nuns stood on the street corner, calling for donations to the local orphanage. I left them two dollars and Jack's business card with the promise that J.W. Enterprise would purchase toys for all the children this year. With our absurd wealth, it felt the right thing to do, and besides, Jack's reputation could always use some bolstering.

"What do human children usually receive as gifts?" Lillian asked as we walked away.

"It depends, but most enjoy books or games. New shoes or hair ribbons. My father once bought me a porcelain doll. I brushed her hair every day for a year."

Lillian nodded. "When we return, we should keep that tradition. For our own children."

For our better world was what she meant. A place where children could be just that, not subjugated to the cruelness of the adults around them. Where there were no more wars or constant threats to mature them before their time. It was a nice notion but not a realistic one. Rome was not built in a day, and neither would Ildathach be. If we could succeed in our task at all.

Ten minutes later, we passed through a ramshackle neighborhood. The spirit of St. Nick failed to touch these parts. Men smoked in cluttered alleys beneath boarded windows. Women hung frozen wash on frayed lines, and dirty children sat on stoops, faces black with soot from the factories up the road. Hungry eyes and gaunt cheeks followed our steps. Once, I was one of them. It was still surreal to look on the remnants of a life gone by. To remember being one of those dirty children, scared and alone.

I wondered why Violet chose to live among them. If it was the familiarity of her own lost and lonely years before finding Jack in this world or the penance she consistently brought on herself. My thoughts edged to a darker place as we stopped before her building, perhaps the most dilapidated of them all. The wooden foundation canted at a dangerous angle, threatening to topple the buildings beside it. Scorch marks claimed the first floor from a past fire. Garbage and soot layered the sidewalk, and broken glass framed each window. Icy wind barreled through the large slats of the outer walls. Some inhabitants had covered the walls in blankets to stave off the chill, but others had not bothered, giving a peek into the poverty lying inside.

"She's on the top floor," Lillian said.

"You're not coming in?"

She shook her head. "Not today."

I squeezed her arm. "Did something happen between you two? You seem rather odd with one another lately."

Lillian shrugged, producing a cigarette from a silver case. It was unlike her to smoke in public. "We all come and go with one another over the years. It's inevitable when you live so long."

It felt like more. We had all been so fractured of late. It was presumptuous to assume I was the reason, especially with the centuries of history they all shared, but I knew Jack and I had a role to play. They all looked to him, but he had been so preoccupied with me. My initial arrival had brought everyone together, the common goal of assimilating me to the fae and preparing to take down Delsaran. The sisters should have been the same, but something had changed.

"I'll wait for you," she said.

"Are you sure?" An uneasy glance around the neighborhood. "I can shade home. This doesn't seem the best place to loiter."

"I need the air." I nodded, squeezing her arm before ambling up the rickety stoop.

Stairs groaned beneath my feet as I made my way to the fourth floor. Smells wafted from beneath the passing doors, unwashed bodies and smoldering fires. The building was one untamed hearth away from erupting in flames. The final staircase did not lead to a landing but a single door with peeling green paint. I could sense Violet's presence behind it, a flood of darkness and misery that set my teeth on edge.

She opened the door before I was halfway up, a cigarette dangling from her lips. Hair in finger wave clips, she wore nothing but an ivory brasserie and a satin skirt slip that fell mid-thigh. Golden eyes raked me up and down, laced with bulging red vessels. "What the fuck are you doing here?"

Knowing anything I said would be met with ire, I pulled a bottle of wine from my purse and held it to the light. A human variety from Italy that Will let slip was her guilty pleasure.

She scanned the label. "How manipulative of you." She opened the door wider. "I admire it."

"I thought you would." She stepped from the doorway so I could enter. Midway through removing my coat, I stilled. Despite the state of the building, I presumed Violet's own abode would be a little corner of paradise atop the misery. I couldn't be more wrong. Wooden walls and floors weathered to a soul-sapping gray. The slats in the walls hadn't been covered and, worse, were riddled with holes that allowed the draft and leaking moisture in. Her possessions were of a finer nature but recently destroyed—a rose-colored futon shredded into a feathery explosion, picture frames with broken glass, the wrought frame of a single bed twisted into frightening angles. But none was so shocking as the woman herself.

I'd never seen her so bare, and now I knew why. Jack had scars. Will and Lillian and Tommy had scars, but none quite like hers. Deep grooves circled each bicep like cinching armbands. Another around her neck, forming the halo atop a ghastly one down the entire column of her spine. Two more circles of poorly sewn flesh ringed her thighs. Like she was the creature of Shelley's novel, a beast pieced together with mismatched body parts. Or someone had flayed her with an iron dagger, one surgical section at a time.

She turned to glare at me, revealing another thick scar down her torso. A dark fog leaked from her skin, pulling the endless shadows from the corners. Her eyes grew wider, alien and unnatural. I stepped back, and she grimaced, shaking her head and returning to normal. "If you expect better accommodations, piss off."

"What happened to you?" I asked.

A cruel smile. "As if I would pour my heart out to the sweet, little farm brat."

With enough wine, I hoped she would. "Shall we drink, then?"

She waved her fingers like I was her servant. Searching her cabinets, I only found two chipped bowls and a molding sack of flour. The icebox was empty too. What in the hell did she eat?

I joined her on the ruined bed. We slid into the center from the twisted frame, taking turns swilling directly from the bottle. A rat skittered across the floor. Harold appeared from a hole in the wall to chase it.

When the bottle was halfway gone, she declared, "I don't give a fuck."

"I didn't say anything."

"That was my preemptive response to whatever you were about to prattle on about. Why do I live here? Because I don't give a fuck. Why did I tear apart my chaise? Because I don't give a fuck. Why do I not want to save

Ildathach? Because I *really* don't give a fuck. I don't give a fuck about your holier-than-thou approach to the topic either."

"Which is?"

"Obvious. That's what it is." She snorted. "Unfortunately, I know you well. The druids'[SD1] untimely demise, killing Macha, the prison, it's all just eating away at that fragile morality you have, isn't it? So this is how you redeem yourself. Let me guess, your final wish before departing this world for the fates is convincing me and Jack to take up the mantle ourselves, saving faekind while you nobly accept the burden of responsibility bestowed on you." She shook her head. "Fucking pathetic, as usual."

"And you aren't?" I asked. I'd never be so crass with anyone else, but this was Violet. She didn't need nor respect soothing words. "Look at you. Pretending none of this is bothering you. Destroying your home and locking yourself away in squalor because obviously, you don't care. As if you aren't the one who vowed to never use your powers from an act committed three and a half centuries ago. And don't think I haven't noticed how you push Will away. That man adores you, and all you ever do is use him."

She dropped the bottle, pinning me to the mattress with a ferocious hiss. Her teeth gnashed in my face. "Don't fucking presume to know me. You don't. You don't know *anything*."

Her eyes flickered from gold to black, endless and consuming. Sweat lined my brow, heart pounding with her canines inches from my face. The darkness coalesced around her, but she laughed, and it dissipated. She laughed herself hoarse, then shoved off me and paced the room with her wine.

"Leave Will out of this." Her shoulders hunched forward, curving her spine at an odd angle. Like her bones itched to break free of her skin. I blinked, and she straightened.

I pushed up from the bed and leaned against the wall, searching for a reflective surface if the atmosphere continued to sour. "Fine, no Will. But I stand by my point."

She turned in circles, the bottle's neck dangling between her fingers. "Hypocrite. Like you aren't using my brother. Or me."

"I'm not using anyone. I'm trying to convince you to think beyond ourselves."

"Pardon me. I forgot I was speaking to the perfect, altruistic princess."

"Would you get over your fucking complex for once?" I snapped. She glared at me. "You're right. I feel guilty. I feel like all we have ever done is make things worse. I don't think Jack and I are deserving of happiness because look at what it has done to the world. Look at what we've sown." I gestured around the apartment. "Complete fucking destruction. But that doesn't change the fact we have a chance to redeem ourselves. You are powerful, Violet. I'm not sure how much, but if you're anything like Jack, you're damn near unstoppable. You judged me endlessly for being useless and pathetic, but look at you. The world at your goddamn fingertips, and you'd rather wallow in your own misery."

She pointed a finger at me. "Stop making presumptions."

"Then help me understand."

"What have the fae ever done for us, hm? What did they do besides forsake me, abandon me from the moment I was fucking born? You think I have these because of humans?" She gestured to her gruesome scars. "And look at your life. You spent two decades fearing us. You saw our evil, our violence, everything the Bogorans made us, and a few kind sidhe show you the way, and now all of a sudden, we're poor sods that need your help? That you got a few druids killed, slit a couple throats yourself, and now you understand us, that with your loving guidance, we're fixable? The worst partner for naivety is arrogance. Congrats, you've managed both."

"But that's not true. There were others who dreamed of a better world once, one that can be made again. I know your past, Violet. I know how badly the world wronged you, but—"

"No." Shaking her head, she gritted her teeth into a gruesome smile. "Only Jack does, and that secret is ours to share. Ours to take to the grave. You have everything else, but you can't have that."

Wind whistled through the pockmarked walls, the only sound. Time doesn't heal all wounds; some just become more complicated. How right Lillian was.

"All he ever gave a fuck about was you," she hissed. "*I'm* his sister. His twin. His *blood*. I was left behind with nothing, even less than he had, which was fuck-all. He made vows to me too, you know, but what do those matter anymore? He has what he always wanted. Do you think he ever would have given a shit about you had I found him first?"

"Yes." The answer came without thought. After weeks of scouring his memories, seeing what we shared, I knew Jack would have wanted me anyway, and not just because he was lonely or desperate. Because I gave him something else he needed. Goodness, hope, love. Because through our cruel worlds and cruel lives, he was my violence and I his happiness. We completed one another in a way Violet was too broken herself to understand. She didn't need Jack's penchant for cruelty or vendettas. She needed the Wills and Arthurs and Lillians of the world.

And we needed them. The ones who took responsibility even when they didn't want to. Who were willing to make the hard decisions and speak the truth so the rest of us could be the people able to help in return.

"Love isn't finite," I whispered. "It's not a limited resource, Violet. There is more than enough for everyone. And we're all willing to give it to you, but you have to want it. You have to accept you and all the others deserve more."

"They deserve nothing." The words circled us, empty and cold. "Get out."

I bit my lip. "Violet—"

Her eyes darkened again, black from corner to corner. The foil to my reflection in the mirror last night, the eggshell pupil of a wraith. Like the universe wished to show us just how opposing we were meant to be.

The flesh raised on my arms. Her head cocked to the side, a trembling finger pointed to the door. I hated to leave her like this, but Violet was so impossible to permeate. She only trusted Jack, Jack only trusted me, and I only trusted her. A vicious cycle that led to nowhere.

"Should I call for Will?" I asked.

"No." Her voice layered over itself, the hellish twin of when Jack used compulsion. She blinked, and her eyes returned to normal, her shoulders slumped. "I don't have the fucking patience anymore. Just leave."

Despite my better judgment, I squeezed her shoulder. "I'll come back in a few days."

"Don't," she said, but it was sapped of her usual bite, utterly exhausted.

I paused in the doorway, wondering if this was a bad idea. Before I could insist on her at least speaking to Will, I froze. Darkness circled her once more, gathering at her fingertips. For a moment, I could see images in the roiling depths—flashes of her life, of times unknown, the dreary glint of a starry night sky.

"Violet?"

She didn't turn.

My voice wavered, a primitive fear I could not explain. "Violet . . . what exactly is your affinity?"

She craned her neck, just enough to shoot me a vicious grin. "Pray you never find out."

THIRTY-SEVEN

JAEVIDAN

IT WAS THE TWO-HUNDREDTH and eighty-ninth day of our siege on Tearach, and my mother had decided to pay a visit.

I had not seen her since my departure from Gerenstad nearly four years ago, and I feared what had brought her to the battlelines now. When word of her arrival circled the camp, I sent Draaph to find more information. I was sent back his first and third fingers.

I tore through the line of tents, riddled with mud and misery. The Tearachans fared far worse, but our supplies had begun to dwindle here. Allie[SD1] s to our enemies attacked at random, threatening to destroy all the progress we had made with each ambush. My soldiers were weak and exhausted, and the Queen's arrival had done their temperament no favors.

Neither had the dwindling letters from Annwyl. It had been six months since I heard from her last, even with others volunteering to ferry the letters from Gerenstad to Tearach. I had not seen Parsna in that time either, though it was expected now to get the letters across the Veil. I had grown desperate enough to bargain with a brownie from home, forcing a vow mark on them for their silence, but they had not returned either.

There was a break in the Veil on the other side of this valley, in a stretch of barren land where magic and arrows rained in shifts from the sky. We had not been able to cross it, the distant warbling image of the human world taunting me each day. Half a mile from where I stood was the means to find Annwyl, to see what brought forth her silence.

I refused to believe the worst.

Two sentries stood at the entrance to my war tent, Gerenstad's crest on their breastplates. The Queen's royal guard. They moved their spears to stop me, but poison blackened my footsteps. I shoved past them.

Behind the golden fabric were the usual sights—the map table and scattered chairs. My second set of armor cleaned and ready to replace the one I wore until it needed repairs. Draaph—alive, thank the stars—slumped against the wall, cradling his wounded hand. My scholars, Corin and Destres, were present as well. But at the head seat sat my mother, donned in an armored dress of depthless black. Six royal guards flanked her.

I did not bow. Her lips curled in a sneer.

Scholar Rindshaw came to my side, bowing at the waist. "Prince Jaevidan, I—"

"Silence, you idiot." The Queen snapped her fingers, ordering Scholar Rindshaw aside. He shuffled away with a pleading look, a warning behind green irises. I gestured for him to stand back and faced the woman who birthed me.

We looked nothing alike. Her long, white hair was that of Kalvidan's, her eyes a striking violet. In the four years of my absence, she had not changed, but I had. How strange immortality could be. Though she was centuries older, we appeared roughly the same age.

It made her no less intimidating. Only time and destruction could create the depth of her eyes, a frigid austerity that chilled my blood.

"I received word one of my sons was dead. I had hoped it was you."

I felt nothing, neither for the news one of my brothers was gone nor her hatred. I knew what she felt for me since the day I was dust-marked.

"I apologize for your disappointment."

She smiled, absent of joy. "Do you not care your better was slain in battle?"

"You have not told me which of my brothers joined the darkness."

"Kalvidan," she said, and I felt my own disappointment. He was a cruel idiot but not the one I shuddered from, shamefully, even after all these years.

I bowed my head. "May the Bogorans guide him into the dark."

"Do not act as if you care." She rose from her seat, rounding the table. "Kalvidan was my sweetest son. My poor, little fool. It was not his destiny to die in such a way."

My lips pressed together.

"The Bogorans, the fates, they laugh at me," she said. "They took my favored away and laugh and laugh as I stand before you. My abomination. My only true regret."

Draaph shook his head. Caution permeated Scholar Rindshaw's posture. She wished to get a rise out of me, but I was no longer the rash teenager she sent away to war. My anger was exactly what she wanted, so she would not receive it.

"My condolences," I said flatly.

"You mock me too." We stood nose to nose, her guards inching closer. "You mock me with your corruption. With the eyes of your vile father. With this fruitless campaign you waged in my name, bringing shame on our land as our army withers away during this cowardly siege."

I bowed my head. "If you observe the map, you will see my army has met more success than Kalvidan's and Donvidan's combined. We lay siege to reduce our own casualties and assure our army is not—"

She slapped me. Blood filled my mouth, poison leaking through my boots. She eyed the black inching closer to her but did not retreat. "Do not speak his name." She seethed. "Do not dishonor him with your offensive tongue. I should have stabbed you in your fucking cradle."

I spit blood to the ground, cracking my neck. "If I do not speak his name, then do not speak of my father."

Grinning, she stepped back. "There are whispers of you. Lies I could not fathom until I saw them myself." She raised a hand, motioning a guard forward. He delivered parchment to her outstretched hand, and she read aloud, "My Beautiful Annwyl . . ."

Every fiber of my being screamed.

"Beautiful . . . Annwyl . . ." she repeated, a mocking singsong. "I have not heard from you in some time, and I grow concerned with your silence. Please assure me you are well and received my last letter. I tried to visit you a fortnight past, but enemies circle us constantly. It is my sincerest hope this correspondence may be snuck past."

She circled the room, the leather dress slapping her shins. "Please know I will return to you soon. It is this hope that drives me into each battle, which keeps me warm in the cold nights and fills my heart when all seems lost. And know I am not the only one. It is you alone who gives us courage. Who brings a dream of better days to the men around me. They sing songs of the Golden Goddess, of the merciful Annwyl who one day will usher in a better world. They believe in you, darling. They love you. They love you as much as I do." She glowered. "When I am king, I will make your dream truth. I will give you all you desire, show you the place you once imagined exists, but I must know you are alright. Please respond and assure me all my fears are the nonsense of a troubled mind. I love you most." She crumpled the letter into her fist. "Tell me, boy, does she exist, or is this another of your games?"

Silence ensued. I could have cried with relief. She had found the letter but not Annwyl.

Or had she?

Draaph snarled from the corner. "You will address my king with respect."

A guard pushed a knife to his throat. Both my mother and I signaled for him to heel. She turned on him, expression cold. "You call him king when he has not earned the title. Why?"

He looked to me. I shook my head, but he held a deference I could not sway, a stubborn bastard to the end. "He is more a ruler than you have been in all your reign. More than your elder sons could ever hope to be. I choose no longer to follow a wicked queen who slays her own husband, boys who reflect her insolence and lead us into ruin. I follow the Poison King and his Golden Goddess. Long may they reign."

My mother stepped forward. "Then die a traitor."

"No—" It was too late. The guard cut Draaph's throat with an iron dagger, leaving him to bleed on the floor. Corin gripped the table with bleached knuckles, bloodshot eyes on his dead brother.

"Leave his body to the crows," she said, a flippant wave dismissing the guard.

Rage filled my voice, a demonic sound I did not know I possessed. "Touch him and I kill everyone in this room."

The guard halted. The Queen glared, a warning, but he did not move. I strode closer to her. "Go on, touch him. See what happens."

My mother turned. "I would sooner die than see you become king. You were never meant to survive the hunts."

"There will be no hunts," I snapped. "No more bloodshed. Brothers against brothers. This is not the world I choose to live in, and you cannot stop me from making it so."

She laughed, the sound like spikes in my soul. "You think yourself strong? Clever? A king of what, exactly? Starving, foolish soldiers." Her head cocked. "Your dust-mark taints your mind. You know nothing of our ways, of how to lead. They follow you here, but no one else will. It was always Donvidan meant to rule, the only son to heed my counsel. To protect the throne of the woman who made him, a man of unwavering loyalty. A true king of Faerie." She ran a hand down my face, the feeling like ichor. "And you will die like you were always meant to."

I had not noticed. The dagger she held, the sharp point of it as it plunged into my abdomen, carving through soft flesh. Blood stained the front of my shirt, the pain unbearable. But I did not fall. I refused to do so in her presence.

She stepped away. My mother, my flesh and blood, my enemy. "Tearach meets you in the field at dawn. My spies have assured me. The rest is your choice. Die on the battlefield with some honor or return home to my wrath." Guards circled her, exiting the tent. "Choose wisely."

BLOOD LEAKED FROM MY crude field stitches, the iron wound refusing to heal. This stopped nothing. I donned my armor beneath the stars dancing over my death, leaping atop my horse.

Scholar Rindshaw ran beside the steed. "What are you doing?"

"Scouting before the battle." Not that there was much need. Whatever my mother had done to assure my demise, to put her loyal puppet of a son on the throne, was despicably thorough. A full moon shone overhead, illuminating the Tearchan soldiers gathering on the field. They outnumbered us five to one.

"You are not fit for battle, Jaevidan."

"I see no other choice." I kicked his hands away, tearing more stitches. He latched onto the beast's mane, jerking the warhorse to a rearing halt.

"If you fight now, you will die."

"If I do not, we all die." I motioned toward our camp, the sorry state of our men compared to the field ahead. "What would you have me do? There is nowhere to retreat, nowhere to run. I make a final stand here or in Gerenstad."

"You do not fight." He grabbed my legs, clawing at the fabric beneath my greaves. "You let the men go forward and stay behind. This is their battle, not yours."

"I do not send those beneath me to die alone." I ushered my horse onward.

"What of Annwyl?"

I stopped. Scholar Rindshaw breathed hard behind me. "I do not know if she exists, if the letters and the stories are a strategy, but I know whether or not her essence inhabits a body or your mind, she is truth, and you must live for her. She is the only hope we have left, and you are her messenger."

I swallowed, finding the break in the Veil. It glowed in the vicious night, a passage lying between two monstrous trees.

He stepped forward. "But she is real, isn't she?"

Slowly, I nodded.

"You can see her." His voice took a desperate edge, a plea. "We can secure this victory, and you two may be together again. She can be queen, Jaevidan, but not if you do this." He broke on the final word, anguish lacing the crack. "I already buried one boy. See reason for an old man, I beg you."

But I had no reason left. There was no place for it here. The others would not fight without me, and I would never see Annwyl again without pushing forward.

"I'm sorry," I said, kicking my horse into a run.

Corin found me later in the night. I directed others from the war tent, telling them to prepare to fight in the morning. I had repaired my sutures three times, but each twist or bend of my body tore them open again. Blood dribbled down the front of my trousers, darkening the black fabric.

He assessed my wounds, eyes rimmed with red. His flesh and blood had died tonight. If I were a better man, I would give him comfort. Instead, I stoked the flames.

"When the battle is done, I want you to lead a hunting party for the Queen."

He bowed. "And what shall I do once we capture her?"

I would not deliver the orders to murder my own flesh and blood, as wretched as she may be. But the Queen had long held a throne that did not belong to her, that she could not if our better world were to exist. So I handed Corin my dagger and said, "Do what you may."

His fingers curled around the hilt. A promise of vengeance.

Come dawn, we gathered on the valley's crest. I gave a great speech, though I could not remember a word. It hardly mattered—most would be dead before they could repeat it.

Assuring my bandages were still in place, I unsheathed my sword and took to the front.

Pink sunlight barely brushed the treetops before blood turned the valley red.

There was no time to think. Only move. Slash my sword this way, dodge, strike. Poison the fields around me when too many soldiers charged at once. Duck from an ax, avoid the battle mage compelling men to fall on their swords. Shove my guts back in my stomach. Keep moving. Keep killing. Wipe blood from my eyes and throw my shield to the sky against a barrage of arrows. Frae died, body blending into the red and gray pile of them. The sun fell once more, and I listed sideways from blood loss. Someone struck me, but I raised my sword. Day ended, but the fighting raged on. Men's screams sounded so much worse in the dark.

I dropped to my knees, willing myself to stand. To stay on the ground meant death, either trampled or slain. If I fell forward to the mud, I would never rise again. But I was so tired. My throat burned. Hot moisture seeped through all my clothes, and I feared my intestines had fallen through the stitches again. An arrow landed beside my feet. I could only blink at it, knowing I should raise my shield but not possessing the strength to.

Get up.

My eyes closed, chin sinking downward.

Get up, you bastard.

My fingers squelched in the mud. My sword clattered against my greaves.

You foolish boy, another whispered, an apparition I wished were here. *You promised you would never leave. You swore to always come back to me.*

My blood-tinged gaze found the Veil. I rose to my feet, dragging my sword in the grass. Harthon's legion cheered—they had breached the battlement, men pushing the castle gates wide for our invasion. They swarmed around me, leaves swept on a rapid current toward the mouth of our victory. It would be swift now. I may not live long enough to see it.

I could stay behind and lead the others to honor and glory, or I could leave now and cross the Veil.

I chose the Veil.

And in the death-soaked night, no one saw one dying soldier slip between the trees.

THIRTY-EIGHT

JAEVIDAN

I STUMBLED THROUGH THE human streets, a hand clutched to my stomach. Stars winked between the sloped rooftops, and salt perfused the air. Voices rose behind me, harmonizing with the roil of an angry sea.

I dropped pieces of my armor, not caring who retrieved them. Finding a quiet alley littered with waste, I slumped to the ground and sewed my wounds closed.

When that was done, I leaned my head against the stones of an empty cottage. A cool breeze picked up, an impending storm. But there was something else, so faint only I could detect it. Strawberries and willow bark.

Wherever I was, Annwyl was near.

I followed her call down the alley. Sea salt strengthened and overpowered it, sending me down three dead ends. But when I caught it again, it led me to a small stone establishment near the shore. Torches flickered beside the door, casting orange on a rocky beach. Ships lolled on black waves in the harbor, their masts swaying like pendulums. Weathered men with blackened teeth roamed outside, lifting wooden cups and singing songs of shipwrecks past. Above the door, a name had been etched into the stone: *The Warren.*

Heart clambering up my throat, I pushed through the door.

Torches and a roaring hearth washed the open room in warm colors. Worn tables and chairs scattered the mud-packed floor like discarded toys, each filled with a rowdy sailor. Tavern girls wound through the labyrinth in corsets and stockings, some less. Ale fermented on the wavering notes of minstrels playing a crumhorn and drums, the patrons belting a bawdy tune about maidens and mariners. Besotted seafarers grabbed the barmaids round their waists, throwing farthings between their cleavage and before them up a set of rickety steps.

Strawberries and willow bark coated my senses, drawing my eyes to the center of the room.

Men flocked to her like insects seeking the light. They turned in their chairs, inching closer for a better view. I pushed through the crowd of them, blood roaring in my ears. A drunkard fell facedown to the floor, allowing me to see.

Annwyl stood on a table, bare feet stomping and turning to the music. Her arms floated above her head, and blonde hair fell down her back. Her skirts were short and caked with mud. Despite her joyful smile, the dance she performed for the cheering sailors, her eyes were empty. Hollow. She was the thinnest I had ever seen her.

She also had her top shoved down, breasts fully on display.

They reached for her calves and threw farthings on the table. Her eyes closed, a pulse shuddering through her body that I knew was for her and her only. She did not hear the pounding drums or unruly seamen but the song of the snow spirits. The quiet words we sang as children.

The song ended, and she gave a ceremonious bow. They jeered and called for another dance. Her eyes sparkled with fabricated mirth, a smile stretching her pink mouth as she turned in a circle. When her gaze found mine, the smile faded away.

We stared at one another.

The music began again, the men roaring a new ballad. Her feet pressed flat into the wood, arms coming up to hide her chest. Her nose twitched, and brows furrowed around the scar now white with age. Patrons noticed, following her line of sight to what disturbed their plaything.

She recovered her breasts and held a hand in the air.

The minstrels silenced, the gathered crowd dying to a hush. She rocked on her heels, a devious smile taking her lips. She gestured around. "Worry not, for I will dance again soon. But first, I must deliver news. There are two things I must say to you fine men, one good and one bad. As tonight belongs to you, I will let you choose which to hear first."

"Good news, Annwyl!"

"No, you always hear the bad first."

"Agreed, tell us the bad, Annwyl."

She raised a brow. "Bad news first, then? Well, if you all insist." She extended a twirled hand toward me, feet sweeping across the wood. "You see, it would seem my lover has arrived."

Their attention found me, my black armor stinking of blood. Some stepped back at the longsword on my hip. Others assessed me, gold in their eyes.

Annwyl grinned. "And now for the good, but a story is required first. What do you say, mariners, would you like to hear my tale?"

Raucous cheers rose with the stench of beer, the minstrels playing jaunty notes. A barmaid shoved me into a seat, whispering low in my ear, "The tavern keeper wants no trouble tonight. Keep your sword on your hip and you may remain."

I nodded, all my attention on Annwyl spinning atop the table.

She began. "Once upon a dreary summer, two lonely children met in a meadow. A little girl of golden hair and a little boy with eyes the same. They had no one else in the world, so chose each other. And thus they swore on love and blood that nothing would keep them apart."

A sailor laughed from the back of the room. "Annwyl, do not say it is a romance! Tell us a tale for men. Or better yet, show us your tits again." A few others agreed, but most shushed him.

Waiting for silence, she gestured to the minstrels. Her next words came with the music, body swaying as she wove her story. "But the little girl knew something of this boy, had suspected he was not a boy at all. She was raised with warnings of the fair folk, mischievous creatures who roamed the wood. It was not long until she received his confession, that he was not only a boy born of the fearsome sidhe but a prince of all fae."

My hands clenched, but the sailors only laughed. The same lewd sot from before called, "A prince? Prince of the privy, perhaps!"

I scowled, and Annwyl continued. "But the little girl was clever of mind, not easily fooled by his faerie tricks. So when he asked for her hand in marriage, she proposed a bargain instead. She would not return with him to the land of magic yet but offered him friendship. Enough time to make the prince fall deeply in love with her so when the time came, he would keep her safe. Only when that girl turned twenty years of age could the prince once more seek her heart, take her hand in holy matrimony, and make her a princess of his wicked people."

Longing choked me of breath, for simpler days and childish ideas. When we met in the meadow each full moon and no war lingered in the world left behind. When Annwyl was discontent but safe in her convent, not entertaining leering men from dirty tabletops. Truthfully, I had forgotten of our bargain so many years ago. I thought she had too.

"Life went on for the little girl, and her handsome prince visited each full moon. They grew older, him more fearsome and her more beautiful. Many sought her favor, but she could never forget her fate. That one day, he would come to retrieve his prize, and no force in this world or his could stop him. But one bright night, the prince did not come. Nor the next month, nor the next. She wandered the forest in search of news, bargaining her soul to the creatures she had come to know. The prince sent letters, reminding her of his affections. Of his promise to always find his way back to her heart. But even the letters stopped arriving, and the girl, now a young woman, believed her prince to be dead and her bargain no more."

The room was silent, all but the hearth and shifting barmaids. I wanted to scream, to explain what had happened, but Annwyl was not finished yet.

"The girl was cast from her home, sent to roam the wilds of her land. Soon, she came across a city filled with ale and the finest sailors on the rocky shores." The crowd laughed, stomping their feet. "But in all her cleverness, she had forgotten. Forgotten the ways of the fae, their magic. That no bargain may be complete, even upon death. So when he arrived in Cardiff one stormy spring night, she told him this tale, lest she face the wrath of not returning the dark prince's favor." Her eyes found mine, riddled with grief. Even the barmaids listened now, wondering what this strange yarn would weave.

"So at twenty years, I will be his forevermore. Banished from this world to another one, a princess of all wicked creatures and the Poison Prince who seeks my soul . . . but my fate is not all for naught. And now for the good news." Her lips pulled into a guileful smile. "It would seem Lady Luck blesses her mariners tonight, for I am only nineteen."

Laughter and applause burst forth with clamorous delight. The seamen banged their cups on the table, beginning another tavern song. She bowed.

"And for only sixpence, I will call you prince of whatever you desire." They howled, the tavern erupting into chaos. The minstrels played a jovial song, and the other barmaids clapped along. Beer sloshed, and fists flew. Annwyl hopped down from the table, crossing her arms as she met me.

I could only watch her, this withered husk of the girl from last year. Wan lips pressed into a line, the perpetual sadness stitched into her frown lines. I rose to my feet, ignoring the sharp pain in my gut. "I am your lover now?"

A smile without humor. "Well, I do love you. Even still."

"Annwyl, the letters—"

A buxom woman of gray hair charged forth, hands on hips. "Annwyl is working tonight. You want her time, you pay for it."

I prepared a great speech ending in *fuck off*, but Annwyl spoke for me. "He was just leaving."

The old wench looked me up and down. "Looks like he would rather pay. And judging by that armor there, he can afford it." She sniffed. "What do they call you, knight? The tavern keep don't like too much having men around without any name."

My thoughts dissipated, wondering why Annwyl wished to send me away. Before I could think of an acceptable human name, she sputtered, "Jack."

The wench waited. I raised a brow.

"Jack . . ." Annwyl looked around, finding the tavern's name scrawled into the stone. "Warren. Jack Warren of Wales."

The wench hacked spit onto the floor. "How original. Either pay up or get out, Jack Warren of Wales."

I reached for a coin purse if only to satisfy Annwyl, but she laid a hand on my arm. "Just wait for me in the alley. I shall finish here soon."

Men leered at her, waiting for this conversation to conclude so they might approach. There was no question as to what sort of work she performed here. Protests rose to my lips, but her expression stopped me cold. She did not want me to intervene. Not anymore.

I nodded. "Try not to take too long."

IT WAS HOURS BEFORE Annwyl appeared in the alley beside the Warren, clutching a shawl riddled with holes. Biting wind barreled off the sea and swept her hair around her face. Knobby fingers turned white in the cold, her forlorn look stating she would rather retreat inside. But I needed to understand what happened. Why she looked at me so.

"Let us sit by the water," she said, turning before I could suggest somewhere warmer.

We settled onto the craggy shore, the moon glinting in her dark eyes. Before I could utter a word, she whispered, "Do not judge my choices, and I will not yours."

"What choices?" I inched closer to her, ignoring the scents emanating from her body. Sickness and old wounds, the odor of other men upon her skin. "Did you really think I was dead?"

"No." Lips pinched, she stared at the sea. "But you may as well have been after your final letter. I had already suspected, anyway."

"Suspected what?"

"Do you respect me so little you now make me repeat it?"

"Repeat what?" My teeth gritted with the booming laughter behind us, men tempting death by calling for Annwyl to keep them warm. "The last letter I sent begged for your response. The last ten. I have not heard from you in nearly a year, Annwyl. I tried finding Parsna, but—"

"Parsna died in Ildathach. The others told me." She pulled the shawl tighter, teeth chattering in the cold. "And I prefer you not to lie. The letter came eight months past, declaring I was nothing to you. That you had found a princess worthy of your title and would marry by winter's end. Not to wait for you anymore." Impassive, she looked to me. "So what lies will you speak to me now? What fanciful words will leave your lips, promises you do not mean to keep? Because if it is more of the same, you may leave."

Rage sunk into my bones. "I sent you no such letter, Annwyl."

"It came with your seal, written in your hand."

"*I sent no such letter.*" I suspected what had happened, but all my fury could not be directed at the woman responsible. How witless I had been speaking of the letters, letting others know Annwyl's name. How I ever thought it would not come back to hurt us was senseless. I had been nothing but a fucking fool.

She stood. I pulled her back down beside me. "Listen to me, Annwyl. The Queen intercepted one of my letters. I enchant most to burn if opened by anyone but us, but she must have broken the spell. I have sent countless letters to you, have worried for you every damn day. I fought an uphill battle with half my intestines pouring out just to come here and find you. I cannot say where this letter came from, but it must have been the Queen. You have become a legend to us, a beacon of hope that threatens her power. Someone must have betrayed me and replaced my words with fake ones. But I swear to you, I swear on all that is good, there is no princess. There is no wish in my heart to lose you. You are the only one who occupies my thoughts. Every day, I have fought to come home to you."

Annwyl shook her head. "I am not a little girl anymore, Jaevidan."

"Why are you here?" My voice broke, the scent of her customers burning my nostrils. Her scar gleamed in the moonlight, a pale reminder of men's cruelty.

Tears dripped from her lashes. "Do you really care, or do you only wish to confirm your thoughts of me?"

"I care, Annwyl." My voice rose, battling the raging sea. "I care so fucking much it hurts me to look upon you right now. To see you like this. So tell me, what brought you to Cardiff, to this—this horrid place."

She turned away. "That letter destroyed me, Jaevidan. I was foolish, not so careful with all the others and the gifts you sent. A scullion found them, telling everyone I wrote in tongues and cavorted with darker powers in the wood. I fled before they could have me burned." She drew a long breath. "And before you ask, there is little employment for a scarred woman fleeing the pyre. Speak ill of my life at the Warren, but it was that or to starve."

"Why not ask the fae for help? Those of the forest would have cared for you."

"Parsna died for me. I could ask no more of them." She coughed, a bone-dry sound that rattled her frame. "Besides, it would not be so long before the knights found me. The entire village hunted for the witch among them."

The hacking cough went on, the scent of her illness rising in the chilled air. Her lungs wheezed to my fae ears, heart weakened. How long had she been in this state? Her human body was not meant for such conditions.

Blood splattered her palm. She smeared it on a rock, trying to hide it. "I should retire soon."

I refused to let her back in there. "Let us find an inn."

She shook her head. "They will charge me double room and board if I do not return."

But I could not be swayed. I lifted her into my arms despite my screaming wound, striding down the shore. It was a testament to how poorly she felt, for she said nothing.

I found a quiet inn on the edge of the city, golden candles flickering in the windows. Horses knickered at a post, and hens slumbered in their pens. I pushed the door open with my shoulder, frowning at the salt circle lining the entryway.

A white-haired crone slumbered before a fire. A bell chimed above my head, sending her to her feet. Rubbing sleep from her eyes, she stumbled to the entry. She stopped.

Her scent was that of a human but with notes of magic. Cinnamon and cloves. I wore glamour, but I knew it meant nothing as the old woman surveyed me, glamour-touched eyes seeing through the thin illusion, understanding what I was.

She bowed her head. "I hope my salt did not insult you, good sidhe."

Another human, a little girl with hair like fire, peeked out from a stairwell. The old woman followed my look, voice lowering. "If you must punish us, spare the girl. My granddaughter does not have the sight. I swear this to you."

I swallowed. "I am not insulted, nor do I mean you harm. All I ask for is a room."

She hesitated, taking in the limp woman in my arms. Annwyl's breath came in feeble rasps, eyes shut tight. In a brazen move, she asked, "What do you mean to do with her?"

"I mean her no harm either."

"This place will not be used for evil."

"No harm comes to this woman. I would sooner die." The little girl trembled, running up the stairs like they caught flames. I sighed. "She has taken ill. We need room and board and your silence."

The crone evaluated me. Tension stewed the sweltering room, but I must have passed her test. She bowed once more. "Mared! Prepare a room upstairs for our guests." She trudged into the living area. "I will heat bathwater for her. She will need fresh clothes and food to regain her strength."

"Thank you," I murmured, settling by the fire with Annwyl in my arms. She stirred at the heat, twisting deeper into my hold.

The crone worked around us, heating water for a copper bath at my back. She knew the ways of the fair folk and filled it with flowers and oils common among our remedies. I tried to wake Annwyl, but she was either too sick or exhausted to do more than blink and swiftly return to her dreams. I removed her clothing, praying she would not find fault in the action as I lowered into the steaming water.

The first time I saw her, I thought her unclean. A dirty little girl caked in mud. Now, she was a dirty woman, bearing all the marks of a miserable life. Chapped skin covered her hands and feet, broken nails crescent moons of black. Her chest rose and fell softly as I cleaned her skin, taking care not to harm tiny, pus-filled wounds along her arms. I left her hair for last, conscious of the rituals from my home and what they meant.

I set to her work on her gnarled roots. The bath had grown cold by the time I completed the task, only to realize she had been infested with lice. I used magic to heat the water once more, working layer by painstaking layer to remove the nefarious insects.

Halfway done, her despondent voice met my ears. "Do you think less of me?"

So focused, I had not realized she'd woken. The crone had set food and ale beside the bath, now cold. I handed bread to Annwyl. She refused to take it.

I resumed my post on the stool at her head, combing through her hair. "Why would I?"

She ran her hands down her bare body, skimming lavender petals stuck to her thighs. "Because you are an immortal prince. And I am nothing but a lice-ridden whore."

"You are a survivor," I said. Guilt sucked the air from my lungs, words wavering. I hated myself. I hated my kind. I hated all I had done, that I had ever met Annwyl at all. It was my presence that made the others fear her a witch. My love that others weaponized to wound her. I should have never gone to war. I should have run away with her when I had the chance, and now look at us. Look what came of it.

"You are a survivor," I repeated. I laid my cheek on her hair, folding my arms around her bony shoulders. "You are Annwyl, the bravest and kindest and strongest woman I know. If anyone should think less of another, it should be you scorning me."

Tears fell down her cheeks, dripping onto my forearms. "But I am weak. I am so weak I cannot survive without you."

"But you are surviving," I whispered. "And what would I have done? Where would I be without you, Annwyl?"

"In a castle, or in the forests of your own world. Enjoying feasts and entertaining princesses. Anything besides cleaning the sweat and muck off a lowly human."

"If I wanted those things, I would have them." I grasped her chin, forcing her to look at me. "I do not want princesses. I do not want castles or glory or gold. I want you. I have always wanted you and nothing else. I *love* you, Annwyl. I love you so fucking much, ever since the first day I laid eyes on you. How many more ways can I say it? I would have nothing, be nothing, without you."

Her eyes fell to my lips, empty of want. Empty of joy. "You foolish boy," she whispered, trembling with unshed tears. I let them fall and washed them away. I finished her hair and helped her from the bath, wrapping a thick robe around her shoulders. Her teeth chattered, and her spindly legs were weak. I lifted her into my arms and carried her upstairs.

Annwyl coughed the entire way. I would have to consult a healer in Il-dathach, and soon. The room was warm with a raging hearth, but with the way she shook, one would never know. I laid her in the downy bed, drying her as well as I could. When even the thick blankets and heated brick at her feet did nothing, I shed my clothes.

"I will dress if you wish me to, but you need body warmth, Annwyl."

She said nothing, gaze vacant as I climbed into bed beside her. "There are no ulterior motives. I would never use you," I said, though she had requested no assurances. But wicked men had wounded her all her life, and I would not let her fear I intended the same.

"I know." She pressed against me, her breasts on my chest, her breath on my neck. I encased her legs in mine, running my hand up her jagged spine. In another life, we would lie here and be content. I would make love to her throughout the night and all the morning, kissing her unscarred flesh until she was sick of it.

But in this life, she pulled the blanket over our heads. I glamoured the firelight, spelling two flickering children into the space between our faces. A little boy and a little girl, holding hands as they ran through a meadow.

She cupped the girl in her palm, red and orange glinting in her pupils, the silent tears clinging to her cheeks like golden crystals.

"There is truly no princess?" she asked.

I shook my head, ageing the boy and girl into adults. Us, when I visited her castle and swept her into my arms. "There has been no one, Annwyl."

"Surely, there must have been at least a pretty girl or two."

"No." The glamour flickered, becoming the image of us lying in bed. "I know what I want."

Her tears came faster, staining the sheet beneath our heads. "I do too."

She kissed me.

She did not taste of blood this time but salt and oils. Unspoken words and endless regret. Her lips moved against mine with measured practice, the thoughtless motions of someone who did this night after night.

"It's me, Annwyl," I whispered. "It's Jaevidan."

Her throat choked with tears, the kisses frenzied, desperate. I tried pushing her away, but she clung to me, the remaining raft in a merciless sea. Her hand wound through my hair, and mine cupped her face, her back, the steep slope of her waist. She reached between us, fingers brushing my cock, but I snatched her wrist and rolled on top of her.

"Not like this," I breathed. My skin flushed so hot I could hardly think, my throbbing erection aching for more. Being inside Annwyl was a late-night fantasy I had pleasured myself to often. But not like this. Not with her tears dampening the mattress, her hollow breaths rasping with fevered lungs. Not with stitches tearing in my abdomen and hot pain sluicing through my thoughts. When I took her, it would be the happiest moment of both our lives. Not a means of escape from our dreary existence.

"Is it become I am ruined?"

"No," I said, too sharply. She flinched. I smoothed back her hair, admiring her face. Those too-large eyes and the fearsome scar. The smattering of sunspots atop her cheeks. "I want you more than I have anything before, just not like this."

"You swore never to lie to me."

Taking her hand, I pressed it between us. I nearly caved as her fingers stroked my cock, desire clambering so fiercely it caused physical pain. But I only said, "Obviously, I desire you, Annwyl. I cannot explain how much, but not when you are ill. Not with tears falling from your eyes." I kissed the corner of each, murmuring, "I will never take you while you cry. While you are hurt."

She looked away. "Then when?"

I kissed her cheeks. "When you are twenty, as you said."

Silence ebbed between us, the taste of her tears on my tongue. "But that can never be."

"It can. It will." A thought occurred to me, one so awful it chilled my blood. "Unless you do not want it to."

Maybe I had been presumptuous. I fell in love with her years ago, but perhaps she had never felt the same, content with our bond and friendship. Maybe she still desired that silly squire or another man more deserving than I.

"It is not a matter of want," she whispered. "This was always our destiny, Jaevidan. We only have the present."

Despite my trepidation, I spoke the truth. "I want to marry you, Annwyl. I want you by my side, now and forevermore."

"But there is no forever," she said, a fresh wave of sadness dampening her skin. "You are an immortal prince of the fae. I am human. When will you understand there will be no happy ending for us? I will grow old and die, and you will always remain the same." She laid a hand on my cheek, her tremors vibrating across my skin. "A thousand years from now, you may forget I ever existed at all. That is the difference between you and I. You will be my entire life, but I will only be a moment in yours."

"You are my entire life," I said.

"In a few short years, I will not be."

"But that is not true." I leaned closer, my nose brushing hers. "We conquered Tearach, Annwyl. Their threat to my land is gone. My Queen will soon follow, and Donvidan stands no chance against me in the hunts. I will bring you back to Faerie, where you will never grow old and never die. I will marry you and make you my queen. Forever is just on the horizon. I know I have asked so much of you, but I only need a little more time."

"I cannot be your queen," she murmured.

"You already are. My people believe in you. They believe in your dream. They sing for the Poison Prince and his Golden Goddess. They want you on the throne."

"Because they do not know what I am." She shook her head, a bitter smile stretching her lips. "You call me the dreamer, but I always knew they were ones of fools. They will never accept a human. I will die in Faerie like I will die here, only if it is in Ildathach, I will take you with me."

"I will prove it to you," I said. "I swear, Annwyl. I will vow it on my skin. I will always protect you, and they will come to love you as you are. Everything is falling into place now. We are so close to that better life, and we will have it. Please be strong a little longer. I will not fail you, never again."

"You should never make promises you cannot keep."

"And I never will." I kissed her fingers, her palm, the tip of her nose, and between her eyes. "Starting with this one—you will never return to that brothel. Everything you want and need will be provided here, and as soon as I can, I will return for you, and we will never be apart again. All you need to worry of is what color you desire your wedding gown."

Her lips curled into a smile, a phantom of what it used to be. But she would see. She would fall back into herself with time and my love for her. There was nothing but good fortune ahead, her dreams of the cottage finally real. She would have it all and more, one day wearing her scar like a badge of honor.

"White," she whispered.

"White?"

"For my gown. I have never had the means before to keep such a pure color clean."

"Then you will be dressed all in white." I kissed her, a long-suffering weight lifting off my chest. Even with the broken flesh of my wounds, with Annwyl's long road to recovery, I felt the lightest I had in years. Perhaps in my entire life.

She assessed me. "And you will take my hand, truly?"

"I will take your hand, I will take your heart, I will take your womb, all of it. I will make you my wife and queen, the mother to my children. I will love you until the stars come down from the skies and not a moment sooner. I make few promises in life, but I give you this one."

Her voice came timid and low, terrified yet hopeful. "And I may have you, in heart and body and soul? Even after everything, after all this time?"

Tears formed in my eyes, but these were not like hers. They were the good kind. "If you will have me, Annwyl, then I am yours."

THIRTY-NINE

ADELINE

I WOKE ON THE settee to Jack gently shaking me. After my visit with Violet, I had returned to an empty apartment, taking to the study to review one of Arthur's journals. Apparently, it had bored me to sleep.

Yawning, I stretched my arms. "What time is it?"

"Late," he whispered. "Are you up for a walk? There's something I'd like to show you."

I blinked. " I suppose. Let me dress."

He took my hand on the sidewalk, leading us down the empty street. A clear winter sky stretched overhead, glittering frost coating iron lampposts. Jack was silent as we traversed the city, only pausing when we reached Central Park. Lanterns flickered at the entrance, lining a snow-covered path.

"Will your feet be warm enough?" he asked, eyeing my stockings and heels.

I gave him a sleepy smile. "I rarely feel the cold anymore."

"Doesn't mean it can't hurt you." He sighed and pulled me aside anyway, forgoing the pavement for our path into the trees.

The park was quiet, muted in the way only a snowy night could be. The farther we walked, the more others appeared—not of a human nature, but Jack's kind. Cerulean will-o-wisps bobbed in the cold, little eyes peeking from bare branches and snowdrifts to watch us pass. The longer we traveled, the more metal filled my mouth, the taste of magic sharp on my tongue. The city may have been for humans, but in this oasis of nature, the faeries found home.

We continued until we came upon a clearing, the snow so thick it reached my shins. Jack snapped his fingers and plucked a blanket from the shade. Laying it down beneath a towering evergreen, he sat and pulled me with him.

It was only us, but something about this place demanded respect. Quiet reverence. I whispered, "Why are we here?"

"You will see." He wrapped his arms around me, and I leaned back against his chest. *It's because we're cold*, I told myself. Why I bothered lying, I didn't know.

His thumb made slow circles over my forearm, leather gloves hissing against wool sleeve. "Before you came to New York, I spent a lot of time here."

"Why?"

He paused. "It reminds me of you. Better days."

Surveying the empty grove, I could see why. The trees were evergreen and the circle wider, but it was reminiscent of another clearing from long ago. A Welsh forest where a girl liked to dance and a boy of golden eyes loved her terribly.

"It's a good place to think," he continued. "I've had a lot of that to do lately."

"Have you thought about what I said?"

He nodded, chin resting on my crown. "That, among other things."

I squeezed his arm. "We should do something, Jack. We wanted to in the 1500s, but maybe we didn't have the means then. We do now, and we can make the difference we once dreamed of centuries ago."

Pensive for a long moment, he finally said, "You didn't say Annwyl."

"What?"

"You always refer to that time as Annwyl and Jaevidan. Their actions, their thoughts." He paused, swallowing. "What changed?"

I wasn't sure and hadn't noticed the slip myself. When *had* I begun to think of Annwyl as myself? Not a separate entity, a girl long lost to the past, but a former version of who I was now. One with similar hopes and dreams, wants and desires.

Deep down, I always knew. The memories resonated, even from Jack's point of view, because I was within them. I looked different, sounded different, but where it mattered most, it was me.

"I suppose I finally relate to her."

He held me tighter, breathing a long sigh into my hair. "How far did you get?"

"An inn on the edge of Cardiff. And I know why you took up the name Jack now." It was another reason I felt more connected to Annwyl. I recognized that inn. It had changed much over the centuries, hardly recognizable anymore, but I knew it was the one Tommy and I had found after fleeing Ildathach. I didn't believe in coincidence, not anymore. Something inside me knew I could find safety there. A memory that had lasted through time. Even death.

His fingers tightened on my forearms, a tremor entering his voice. "Oh."

"That's all you have to say?"

There was no explanation, only a change in conversation. "I've been thinking about it. Ildathach, the sisters, everything. As much as I'd love to forget it all, that was never a true option."

I tried to turn, but he held me steady. "But it's complicated, Addie."

"When are things ever simple?"

"This is different," he whispered. "But that's not why I brought you here."

"Then why did you?"

"Look to the trees." Tilting his head, he hummed in my ear. It took a moment to click in my mind, the lullaby one I'd heard a thousand times before but never with words. It'd been too difficult to pronounce then, my human tongue mixing all the letters. But I had sung the melody a thousand sleepless nights, twirling in a forest for an audience of wild creatures.

The first of them appeared with Jack's low voice. Neither man nor woman, nothing discernible, with a shapeless body and golden veil over its face. A glittering hand reached from an evergreen's branches, fingers curling as if to coax the song near. Golden light washed the snow like a miniature sun, splashing the frost-ridden grove in a luminous glow.

Jack hummed louder, prompting the snow spirit to enter the clearing. Another joined it, much smaller and much less graceful. It hopped from foot to foot, excitedly shaking to the whispered song. I laughed, watching the older one place a hand on its tiny shoulder, showing them how to move.

More joined, lulled in by the song. They filled the little clearing, twisting and spinning in perfect synchronization, the whirring gears of a clock all turning harmoniously. Their veils lifted in the breeze, and their fingers reached for the sky. They spun and dipped one another and interlocked hands, a story through the movements not meant to be understood. For no one but themselves to rejoice in and others to revere.

Before long, I hummed the tune myself. I remembered it now. Every single note, the feeling of my lips going numb in fear of stopping, not wanting them to leave. Tears touched my cheeks, reflecting their golden light. I wanted to go on, but my breath hitched, and the spirits stopped. Jack had gone quiet a long time ago. I was the only one left singing.

They all turned, even the little one, and bowed.

And with that, they formed a line back into the trees. They drifted into darkness one by one, an ethereal parade of shimmering light. The little one disappeared last, stopping to jump and wave goodbye before fading into the wind.

Nothing but the moon remained to illuminate the night. A cold breeze blew through, hollow in a way it hadn't felt before. Jack kissed my cheeks, carefully catching each tear before it fell.

I held tight to his wrists. "I'm sorry. I don't know why I'm so emotional."

"They always made you that way," he murmured, lips pressed to an escaped droplet. "You're the only person I've ever met who can make them appear."

"You just did."

He shook his head. "They only dance when I'm with you."

Closing my eyes, I drew a long breath. "Is that why you brought me here? To prove my soul hasn't changed."

"No," he said, "It's much simpler than that. I just wanted you to remember there are always good things in the world." He kissed the corner of my lips. "That no matter how hard things get, how bleak the future may seem, for every death, there is a life. For all our suffering, there are still golden spirits that dance in Central Park."

Emotion choked my throat, finding no words but "Thank you."

His voice softened, a gentle caress. "You never owe me your gratitude."

"Why do you say that?"

His thumb ran over my cheek, rough and tender at the same time. A paradox, much like everything he did. "Like I said last night, I already owe you too much."

I stared at him. At the golden eyes dim in the dark woods, the bronzed skin wan in the cold. His lips, the lovely taste one I could never forget. The soft feeling that beckoned me forward, begging me to touch him, breathe him into me, fall without abandon, and never look back.

He leaned away before I could. "There is something I need to tell you."

All my warm, subdued feelings dissipated, replaced with something sharp and cold. "What is it?"

His answer took a long moment to come, each passing second stealing more of my breath, bringing more of a chill to this frigid night. "There is something I must say about the fates and about Ildathach. A choice I want to make. And I want your opinion on it, but only after you've finished the memories. You're at the end now. I can sense it."

I shook my head. "Why?"

"Because I want you to understand before you give me your answer." He caressed the dip of my chin, the curve of my throat. "I want you to know how that life ends before we decide the fate of this one."

Cold leeched beneath my skin, deeper than the winter air could ever reach. "What happened, Jack?"

"You'll see," he whispered, kissing my lips. It didn't feel like a comfort. It felt like a goodbye.

He shaded us home after that, quietly retreating to the study. I could have followed, witnessed this last moment with him beside me, but some primitive sense warned I should do it alone. That he had, and I needed to do the same.

I settled into his armchair, warm beside the fire. With the diamond between my fingers, I drifted into the last of his memories.

FORTY

JAEVIDAN

THE NEXT FEW MONTHS went by achingly slow, knowing what awaited at the end. I made good on my promise to care for Annwyl, speaking with the fae of the Bannau Brycheiniog. They were distraught at Annwyl's hasty departure and more than happy to aid her return. Together, we constructed a little cottage deep in the mountains where no humans could find her. The flower pixies enchanted the soil to always grow food, and some brownies, displeased with their masters, stole hens and a heifer from the village. The hobgoblins promised to keep it warm, and the dryads promised to defend the land. It was not much, but it was clean, quiet, and, most importantly, safe. Annwyl smiled like a child again when I showed it to her, kissing me so deeply even the spriggans blushed.

Corin and my other commanders hunted my mother across Ildathach, finally facing her in the Fields of the Unsung. The fight lasted three weeks, but they reigned triumphant in the end. Corin kept her left ring finger as a prize. They offered me her head, but I had no stomach for it. I gave her a proper burial beside Kalvidan, vowing to be better than she was. To create the world she wanted to kill me for.

Donvidan could not be found, disappearing deep into the wildes with the call for the hunts. Though I was not technically king yet, I was treated as such. Scholar Rindshaw guided me through the politics, securing my throne both at home and abroad. They still called me prince, but the scholar assured me this would change soon. Donvidan would have to appear sometime, and with his death and our borders secure with my victory, he anticipated a long period of peace and prosperity.

We stood in the throne room one night after one too many cups of wine. I would visit Annwyl in the morning after meeting with my treasury council but gave him my attention now. Somehow, the scholar and I had gotten on the topic of his son again. It made me desire to see my father. My first order after reclaiming the castle was ordering all his portraits be hung once more.

"You are doing well, my Prince," he said, tipping his chalice toward the portrait. My father's cheerful eyes looked down, reflecting the look in my own these days. "His spirit smiles on you from the dark."

I nodded. "But there is still much to do."

"That there is." He looked to me. "The priestesses approached me again today. They wish to know when you will choose your queen."

"Soon," I said.

"It makes a dusty, old scholar wonder what exactly you wait for."

I grinned into my cup. "I was foolish enough to make a bargain."

"Ah." He laughed, taking a long sip of wine. "Women make fools of us all, but it would aid me considerably if you provided a timeframe for which there will be a wedding. Good tidings are a necessity after war, and we could all use something to celebrate."

"There will be no wedding. Just a private ceremony with Annwyl, myself, and a priestess." I would have done something more grand—my bride certainly deserved it. But I still had not revealed her human nature, and doing so in a hall filled with fae was short-sighted. Besides, with Donvidan still eluding capture, I would hardly announce when and where we both would be.

But Scholar Rindshaw was wise and knew my desire for privacy was not sentimental. "Because she is human," he said.

There was no point in lying now. "Because she is human."

"Then I think your choice is wise." He clasped my shoulder, stepping away. "I will find you a trustworthy priestess and make security preparations for after."

He was halfway down the hall when I turned. "Scholar Rindshaw?"

He stopped.

Suddenly, I felt like a boy again. Writing my sentences while he patiently guided me, heeding his advice lest I face his disappointment. Learning from him, respecting him, not realizing how much he had done until I was too old to cling to his robes. It was an odd thought with my father's portrait above me but the reason I asked what I did. "When the day comes, I would be honored to use your dagger."

Marriages were rare among the fae, but it was a long-held tradition. Sons used their father's blade for the ceremony.

His eyes glistened, lips twitching into a watery smile. He bowed at the waist. "Then it is yours."

The months went on. I cursed myself for declaring Annwyl's birthday in the summertime but was prepared when Lughnasadh finally arrived. Scholar Rindshaw found me a priestess. I had Annwyl's dress made, hoping she loved the surprise. And I spoke with Corin and my other former commanders, the most loyal of my men, asking a favor of them for the ceremony.

Annwyl was knitting socks in the garden when I arrived at the cottage. She had regained all the weight she'd lost, sweeping curves and slopes once again. Her complexion regained color, and she smiled again—often, and it only sometimes failed to reach her eyes.

I had planned to woo her, as I'd promised I would fourteen years before. But the moment I saw her, hair bright in the sun and pink flushing her cheeks, I stupidly said, "We should marry tonight."

She raised a brow, a slow smile forming. "Is that so?"

I rubbed the back of my neck, a bout of nerves drawing moisture to my palms. "If you would be agreeable, that is."

She tapped her chin, considering. "Do I have something to wear?"

"Of course."

"And someone has been procured to oversee the ceremony?"

"A priestess, yes."

She tilted her head, all the love in the world bursting from her expression. "Then why not?"

I paced the gardens while she readied herself. The local dryads insisted on dressing her but agreed to my one condition—no cosmetics or charms. Nothing that would make Annwyl look like anyone but herself. The sun began its lazy descent behind the mountains as she emerged, glowing in the radiant light.

The dress was white as promised, a simple gown of silk with a running train behind her. Matching silk slippers, secured with ribbons that would allow her to roam the forest comfortably. And my favorite part, a lace veil draped over her head and secured with a golden circlet. I had overseen the creation of it myself, a circular band molded into a vine blooming with belladonna. A crown worthy of a queen. *My* queen.

She clutched a bouquet of primroses, pink blush rivaling the falling sun. So beautiful, for a moment I forgot what it was to breathe.

Her gaze cast down, the sunset blush turning ruby. "Do you approve?"

I kissed her cheek, the corner of her lips. "You are the most beautiful thing I have ever seen."

We shaded to the meadow. I had gotten better with it and practiced with Annwyl several times so she could become accustomed to the feeling. She swayed on her feet, but I took her waist, guiding us forward. In all these years, Annwyl had never seen my home. Worry slowed my feet, but Annwyl pulled us onward, her delighted smile enough to light the darkened sky. We stood at the gate, one step from her new world. I hoped she loved it. I hoped it loved her.

"Are you ready?" I asked.

She nodded and, without hesitation, stepped through the Veil. We appeared in my meadow, the sky dark without her moon. But the stars provided enough light, iridescent and shimmering closer than in her own world. Emerald grass swayed beneath our feet, and ivory petals drifted through the air. She turned, a smile permeating her face so deep her teeth glowed in the starlight.

A disbelieving giggle burst from her. "Is this real?"

"Of course." I swept my hand across the air. "And soon, it will be all yours."

She held a hand to her lips, attention roaming from the bobbing will-o-wisps to the sprites chasing one another on the wind. The lullaby of a melodic breeze and ancient voices singing from the mountains. But I had eyes only for her, the way I had never appreciated the beauty of this place until her presence blessed it.

I took her hands. "Come, there is someone I want you to meet."

None but a select few knew what would happen tonight, a precaution for both our safeties. But I trusted my sidhe brothers in arms and had asked if they could patrol the perimeter of where the ceremony would take place. One stood at the end of the meadow, hand on the hilt of his sword. I placed Annwyl behind me, striding forward until Corin came into view.

He bowed with a sly grin. "You seem well tonight, Jaevidan."

"How could I not be?" Annwyl peeked out from behind me. Though a rambunctious fool, he would be an intimidating sight to her. Taller and wider than most humans, iron scars dotting his face, and wearing the black armor of high fae. His sword alone was more than half her length, but she clutched my arm with a friendly smile.

"This is Corin, commander of the first legion in my army and the head of my guard." I acknowledged him. "And Corin . . . this is Annwyl."

He dissected her with his stare, a small furrow appearing between his brows. This was the first test. If he could not accept Annwyl for what she was, then no one could.

"Annwyl," he said, pronouncing it like a question.

"The Golden Goddess herself."

Annwyl turned red, shaking her head. "He comes up with the most ridiculous things." She bowed her head, dropping to a curtsy. "It is a pleasure to meet you. I have heard many stories from Jaevidan's letters."

Another long, dubious moment, and then he bowed in return. "Hopefully, not the humiliating ones."

She laughed. "I suppose you will find out. But I must warn you, he has always been rather forthcoming with me."

"The rotten bastard." Corin smiled, observing her dress. The golden circlet around her head. "And there is no need to ever bow, Princess Annwyl. We are at your service, now and forevermore."

I nodded at him, gratitude wound through the gesture. Annwyl shifted at the title, but she would become accustomed. She would learn our ways and traditions and, with myself and Scholar Rindshaw to teach her, would become a fine queen one day. The path would not be an easy one, but nothing had ever been for us. I wanted her here all the same.

With that thought, we bid Corin goodnight and ventured deeper into my land. Not the Darkwood but the green and gold forest outside it. The journey took hours, mostly from Annwyl stopping to admire every new wonder we passed. Low fae noticed and, once they heard me speak her name, flocked to us like sheep to their shepherd. The guiding light that would lead them home. Pixies played with her veil, and will-o-wisps illuminated her path. The dryads whispered of the new princess, brownies and trolls and goblins peering from behind rocks and trees to glimpse her. Annwyl smiled at them all and offered kind words to the few with enough courage to approach her, requesting her blessing. We had accrued a sizable gathering by the time we arrived. I quietly dismissed them back to the wood, with the promise Annwyl would introduce herself soon.

A priestess stood before a grassy cliff, overlooking the wildes and kingdom beyond. It would be too dark for Annwyl to see, but come morning, she would appreciate its beauty. The terrifying and beautiful world that now belonged to her. The priestess wore robes of emerald and gold, crafted from the forest we now stood in. Her low hood obscured her eyes, a silver candle melting into her palms. She bowed before us, stiffening only a moment with the sight of Annwyl. But my human did not notice, and the priestess soon relaxed.

I took her hands, and the priestess began her rites. I could not recall a word of them, something about the rare beauty of these unions and blessings from the Bogorans. They did not matter. This was mere tradition, all my true words for Annwyl and myself only. How beautiful she was, how perfectly her slight hands fit into my own. The curve of her neck as she swallowed, the twinkle of her eyes as they found me in the dark. These were the things I worshipped, my Golden Goddess the only deity I prayed to.

The priestess produced a chalice of wine and I the dagger of Scholar Rindshaw. Annwyl and I kneeled in the grass, taking turns cutting each other's palms. She was so nervous she nearly took my hand off, but I laughed and guided her. When it came to her turn, I made the cut as shallow as possible, vowing in her ear it was the first and final time I'd ever hurt her.

We dripped our blood into the wine, alternating sips until the chalice was empty. The priestess continued her words and songs, producing a long strand of golden ribbon to bind our hands. My wound pressed to hers, the mixing blood dripping down our wrists. But I had anticipated this and, knowing what her white dress meant to her, enchanted it to repel any stains.

The priestess bowed. "My ritual is done, Prince Jaevidan. You two shall remain here and, come dawn, will be known as husband and wife."

"Thank you. You may leave us now."

Still on her knees, Annwyl grinned. "Are we to stay like this all night?"

"It is tradition." I brought our bound hands to my chest, kissing her brow. "To kneel together until dawn so hardship is overcome early and the remaining union may be a pleasant one." I kissed her lips. "But most use this time to sneak off for more pleasurable things."

I had about three hundred on my mind, starting with removing every white piece of fabric she wore. Annwyl had not approached me again for sex, and I had not suggested it. I was happy to wait until we were wed and do things properly, but now that the ceremony was complete, it was all I could think of.

"No, we should remain here," she said. "If it is your tradition, we shall do it right."

So we spent the night in the grass, hands bound together. We spoke of happy things, all we had to look forward to. I described the castle and the rooms we would take, all the fae she would meet, and gave the subtle suggestion of where any future children would reside. She spoke of memories, giggling at how stiff I had been during our first kiss. Exhaustion set in several hours later, and we laughed ourselves hoarse over the absurdity of kneeling here all night. Annwyl sang for me, and I stroked her hair beneath the veil until her voice grew quiet and the first rays of sunlight broke over the hills.

Then I pulled her into my arms and took her to a quiet grove of trees. We would not be bothered here, and my patience met its limit as I laid her down in the billowing grass. The golden sunrise ignited her hair and brought forth the green flecks in her eyes. I kissed her deeply, and tenderly, and with fourteen long years of love and wanting. Our crowns fell to the grass, and the veil slipped from her head. I tugged the white dress down her body, fumbling with the silk I was so eager to remove it. She laughed as I cursed an impertinent ribbon, removing it herself as I shed my clothes.

I wound my fingers through her hair, breathing hard against her neck. "Are you sure? We can wait longer if you need." I wanted her so badly it hurt, but not if she was not ready. Not if sex brought nothing but haunting memories.

"I trust you," she whispered. "And I want my husband to make love to me now."

I did. I kissed her hair and the lovely curve of her throat. Her beautiful breasts and the soft flesh of her stomach. I wanted her to enjoy this, to know we had a thousand lifetimes of such joy. So I kissed between her parted thighs, blood rushing downward as her back arched against the ground. As she dug her fingers into my hair and breathed my name. And when my wife—my lovely, golden wife—writhed and finished beneath me, I brought my chest to hers and slowly sank inside her.

I had not known true happiness until that moment.

Annwyl held tight to my shoulders, moaning against my lips. I rocked into her, over and over, a pleasure I had not known before destroying my civilized mind. There was nothing but her, body warm and tight around me. The blissful noises she made and her nails stroking my back. I fucked her deeper, harder, showing her how much I loved her, how much I wanted her as poison leaked from my hands and scorched the grass. I could not control it but had no need to. This was Annwyl, and even the deep magic feared my reprisal should it touch her.

"Annwyl," I groaned and, just because it sounded so good as I thrust between her legs, said it again. "My beautiful wife. My Annwyl. I am yours."

"And you are mine," she breathed. "You always were."

Once was not enough to satiate me. A lifetime—a dozen lifetimes—would not be, but when the sun reached its peak and the grass turned hot beneath us, I helped her back into her wedding gown. She laughed at her reflection in a pool, the wild mess of hair and swollen lips. The delightful sound went straight to my cock, and I pulled her back to the grass again.

The sun began its heavy descent when we finally broke apart. It pained me to do so, but I needed to return to the castle. Politics did not stop because I was wed, and there was much to do before announcing our union. Annwyl would return to the cottage for a few days to gather her things and say her goodbyes to the fair folk of Wales. In three days' time, I would retrieve her, and we would never be apart again.

I kissed her beside the Darkwood, desire overcoming rational thoughts despite our audience. Corin howled from a tree branch, Harthon yelling for us to breathe air before we suffocated one another below him.

Annwyl pulled back, scarlet in the face. I smiled at her, tucking a strand of hair behind her ear. "Pay no mind to the rotten bastards. I never do."

Corin leapt down from his branch. "Is that a smile I see? One day of marriage and the poor sop has gone soft."

"Fuck off," I drawled. He and Harthon laughed like madmen.

My voice lowered so only she could hear. "You are a princess now, soon to be a queen. I will wait to make formal announcements until you return, but some already know. Keep your wits about you, and do not leave Corin's side for anything. He will keep you safe."

The man in question fell into an overzealous bow. "No harm will come to our beloved Annwyl in my stead. This I assure you." He took her arm, grinning like an idiot. "I must admit I have never visited your world, Princess. Tell me, what can a rotten bastard find to drink behind the Veil?"

"Water," I said. "Do not make me regret this."

Annwyl returned to my side, holding my cheek. "You worry too much." She kissed me, stirring a few more regrets at her impending absence. "Focus on your duties, and try not to fret so terribly. Corin and I will fare just fine."

"I always worry for you."

"We spent four years apart. Three days will go by quicker than you know it." She kissed me once more, hand over my heart. "I love you most."

My lips brushed hers. "I love you most."

ANNWYL HAD NOT MEANT to be but was a horrid liar. The days dripped by slower than sap, each one more torturous than the last. I fell behind on all my tasks, hardly listening during council meetings, bouncing my knee like an impatient child. I prayed for sleep, if only to pass a few more hours, and completely broke by the second night. Surely, it had been enough time for Annwyl to pack her belongings and say her goodbyes. At worst, Gerenstad would survive a single night without me. I dressed and departed for the Darkwood, breaking into a full run when I reached the meadow.

Across the Veil, the human moon was a slim crescent. Still, there must have been a festival, for the village was bright with golden flames. I stalked forward, looking for the first reflection I could.

"Hello, runt."

Ice crept down my spine. Even after all these years, even with my dust-mark, that voice haunted my dreams, made me cower like a small child again. I turned, spying Donvidan resting on a boulder. His leg hung off the side, lazily swinging. His stance was casual, but the coil of his muscles was not. A dagger glinted in his hand.

Eying the blade, I asked, "What are you doing here?"

He shrugged.

"Mother is dead. They called the hunts," I said.

"I am aware." His eyes hardened like iron, ruined face scrunched with disgust. "We both know how this ends."

Regret coursed through me, despite everything. Donvidan was awful and cruel, had been my entire life, but he was still my blood. My brother. It was childish to hope he could change, but without our mother's influence, perhaps he could. There was a place for him in my new world if he would accept it.

"I can kill you," I said slowly. "But there is another way. I have plans, Donvidan. Big ones. You could be welcomed back to court as my brother and second, if you wished it. There is no need to shed blood tonight."

He scowled. "And you think this would satisfy me? Heeding to a corrupted churl, accepting second place while a runt takes my throne." He laughed, devoid of joy. "Even death is preferable to that."

"It does not need to be this way."

"But it does." He leapt down, feet squelching in the mud. "You took everything from me. My throne, my family, my *face*." He twirled the knife between his fingers. "My reputation was ruined, my dignity. There is only one thing left to do." He held out the dagger, handle up. "At least do me the honor of not using your corruption."

I shook my head. "I refuse to kill my kin. If this is the fate you seek, you may do it yourself."

His lips formed a ghastly smile, the village's firelight reflected in his eyes. "Do not think me so pathetic, little brother. I still die with my honor. I would never go down without a fight. Without my revenge."

My blood curdled. "What do you mean?"

"Congratulations on your nuptials, by the way." The smile stretched wider. "As short as they may be."

I grabbed him by the shirt, poison sieving from my hands. "What did you do?"

But he only laughed. And laughed and laughed and laughed. The sound shredded my soul. Blood roared in my ears.

I snapped his neck.

And before the horror of it could settle, I used the flat of his blade to shade to the cottage.

The windows were cold and dark, the door hanging on its hinge. "*Annwyl.*" I ran inside, taking in the destruction. The curtains had been torn, the scant furniture upturned. Blood splashed the walls, and broken cups littered the floor. My voice layered over itself, the repetitive cry of her name. But I could not scent her, could not hear her—

Someone groaned from the bedroom.

Annwyl was not there either, but Corin was. Blood leaked from his mouth, and his eye was swollen shut. He had been pinned to the wall with knives, embedded in his wrists and feet. Blood waterfalled to the floor.

I pulled the blades out, grabbing his shoulders. His empty eye found me, words mumbling from broken lips. "I am so sorry, Jaevidan."

"Where is she? Where is Annwyl?"

He inhaled a ragged breath. "I tried . . ." But there was nothing else. His gaze went cold and empty, head lolling aside. He had gone to join Draaph in the dark.

Tears burned my eyes, but there was no time. Panic set fire to my chest. Maybe she'd run; maybe she'd hidden somewhere. None of the other fae were around, so perhaps they'd spirited her into the woods. But Donvidan's laugh filled my ears, the fire burning in his stare. The village.

No.

I shaded as close as I could, running like I never had before for the muck-filled streets. Cries and chants met my ears, the haunting sound of women's screams. Fire filled my lungs, and pain shot down my legs. The crowd thickened ahead, villagers with torches held to the sky. I shoved through them, nostrils flared for her scent. All I found was smoke, the char of burning flesh.

A man screamed beside me. "Burn the witches!"

Another, "Send them back to hell!"

No, no, no, no, no.

A group of women prayed, heads bowed over a rosary. "*Our father who art in heaven . . .*"

"Annwyl!" I turned in a circle, the crush of bodies overwhelming, the smoke clogging my nose. "Annwyl, where are you? Please . . . please answer me . . ."

A brawl broke out, sending a group of men to the ground. In the rupturing chaos, I saw her.

Six pyres had been erected, crucifixes engorged in flame. The women strung to the first four were nothing but blackened husks, but the final one was lit most recently. The fire reached halfway up her body, her screams echoing into the night.

I had spent the past decade trying to control my dust-mark. My corrupted affinity. I did no such thing now.

Humans fell around me. I cut a warpath through them, letting the darkness destroy anything it touched. Women howled, and men choked on their blood. Shouts rose on the ashen wind, cries that Lucifer had arrived to take vengeance. I did not care what they called me, what fake human god they mistook for me. I killed any who dared get in my way.

I felt no burns as I stepped on the pyre, slashing Donvidan's dagger at the ropes around her feet. It was not enough, and the flames soon consumed her dress. She sobbed and screamed, kicking as I crumbled the ropes with poison. Blisters bubbled on the backs of my hands, and my clothes had taken to flame, but I did not stop—feeling no pain, feeling nothing but anguish and rage as I finally cut her down.

The humans screamed. Pitchforks and blades came our way as I rolled us in the grass, extinguishing the flames. There was blood, so much fucking blood. Annwyl's whimpers filled my ears.

A knife stabbed into my calf, a man's cries to abolish the devil. I growled, serpent eyes on full display. Poison exploded around me. The circle of death pushed them back, creeping onward and corroding all in its path. All but the small patch where we lay. I gathered Annwyl into my arms.

"Annwyl—Annwyl, look at me. Try to breathe." Her eyes met mine, wide with pain. Lips trembling, she tried to speak, but I silenced her, not wanting her to waste her strength. A pitchfork stabbed into the grass beside us. I ignored it, surveying the damage. Her white dress had been burned away, her beloved wedding gown, abdomen a bloody mess of blistering burns. And her legs, they . . . they were . . .

I removed my shirt, though there was little of it left. My wounds were already healing, skin smooth and gold once more. The humans cried at my warping flesh, declaring black magic, dark magic, I had no fucking idea. I dabbed at her stomach, the breasts I had kissed just three days before. Blood dribbled from her lips. She shook hard enough for me to drop her.

"*It's okay. It's okay. It's okay.*" For each wound I dabbed, three more bled. The dull thud of her heart echoed in my ears, the choking sound of her lungs. But I refused to believe the worst. I could get us out of here, take her to a proper healer. They could fix her legs. She would walk again. She would sing again. She would be fine. *She would be fucking fine.*

"Jaevidan." It took a moment to realize the raspy sound came from her, the rattle of dead leaves scraping rocks. "Jaevidan . . ."

"Do not waste your strength." I kissed her cheeks, imbuing her with just enough poison to ease her pain. "Just keep your eyes open. Look at me."

She shook her head. The poison faltered around us, the humans edging closer. Stones hit my back. I crawled over Annwyl to protect her from them. Another knife embedded between my shoulders, a grunt hissing past my lips. The roaring fire and melting screams were the only sound, Annwyl's serrated breaths beneath me.

I was crying. The tears fell off my cheeks and dripped onto hers, streaking pink as they fell through layers of blood and soot. If I had not let her return here, if I had stayed by her side, if I had not wasted time trying to reason with Donvidan, if, if, if.

"You . . . need to . . . go," she said.

A stone hit me in the temple. Black cornered my vision. "I am not leaving you."

"They will . . . kill you."

"*I am not leaving you.*" My teeth ground together, salt and sweat and blood fierce on my tongue. I gathered her into my arms, concentrating on sending the poison outward, cutting us a path back to the Veil. She only needed to hold on a little longer. I could do this. I could do this.

"Please . . . go."

"Everything will be fine, Annwyl. I promise." I kissed her, the strawberries and willow bark overpowered by blood. "Repeat it, Annwyl. Swear it. Tell me everything will be alright in the end."

But she only stared at me. Color faded from her cheeks, the light dimming behind those too-large eyes. "You foolish boy."

"I promise—" The words caught in my throat. Her neck went limp against my arm, eyes clouded and empty.

Annwyl, I said. I thought I said. I could not tell if it was aloud or in my head. *Annwyl, stop.*

I rattled her, a ringing piercing my eardrums. *Annwyl, this is not funny. Look at me.*

Look at me, Annwyl.

Look at me.

The ringing grew louder, drowning out all other sounds. The screams, the cries, the thunderous flames roaring above my head. I shook Annwyl, anger mounting. *Stop fucking with me, Annwyl. Look up.*

My chest heaved, muscles locking. I closed my eyes. *This is not real. This is not real.* This is not real.

We are asleep in the meadow. Lying beneath a wool blanket on a bed of straw. Safe in the warmth of a Cardiff inn, her skin pressed to mine. Lying in the grass and making love. This is nothing but a bad dream. Only a bad—

A rock struck the back of my head.

My eyes opened, and Annwyl was dead.

My closest friend. My first and only love. My wife . . . was dead.

I stood, and I do not remember what came next. I only know I killed them all.

I know the pyres burned out sometime in the night, leaving nothing but crumbling ash.

I know when I woke the next morning, Annwyl's corpse beside me, the village was quiet and empty. Bodies curled on the ground in a mandala around us, their homes hollow and gray.

I know I folded Annwyl into my arms, stroking her hair as I screamed.

And I know I found my brother's blade in the ash, using it to join my wife in the dark.

I SHOULD HAVE REMEMBERED human souls and faerie ones were not destined for the same place. But that hardly mattered as I opened my eyes, taking in the bleak surroundings. Gray stone walls and gray stone floors. Like ash. Moisture filled my mouth, and I remembered something else too late. I had cut my own throat.

I reached for my neck and found a row of stitches.

Apparently, I did a shit job.

Scholar Rindshaw appeared in my vision, batting my hands away. "Can you hear me?"

I stared at him.

"I will take that as confirmation."

"Why am I alive?" I could barely get the words out, my voice an undulating mess of cracks and whispers.

"Because you are far better with a sword, that is why." His tone was flat, but his eyes were not. Neither was the tremor in his hands as he rubbed a salve onto my throat.

I shoved him away. "Where is Annwyl?"

He hesitated. The night came back in flashes, like my mind could not yet piece it together. Donvidan, Corin in the cottage, something about Annwyl and her burned wedding gown. My head felt stuffed with straw, memories clawing for entry, but I barred them passage. Right now, I felt nothing but numb. Numb was good. Numb was preferable.

Until the scholar spoke. "We brought her to the priestesses. They prepare her for burial."

There was nothing. Not a single emotion as I reached up and tore at the stitches.

I got through three before Scholar Rindshaw struck me across the face.

Blood filled my mouth. I bit down on a broken tooth. "Just let me die."

"You will do no such thing." His hands shook so hard he dropped the salve, giving up on the venture entirely. He sat on a stool beside my head, resting his face in his palms. "I have requested the full rights of Annwyl's title, and the priestesses have agreed. She will be laid to rest in your family's garden, buried with all the honors of a queen. With your brother slain, you are officially king now, Jaevidan. Your coronation will be in six days, directly following the funeral."

"No. My wife is dead, and I would like to be with her now."

"You are young," he pleaded. "You have so few years behind you. It feels like your existence has ended now, but I swear to you, Jaevidan, you have a future even without her. One day, you will recover from this pain. A thousand years from now, it will be nothing but a memory."

I shook my head. "You do not understand."

"*I lost my son.*" He breathed hard, green eyes screaming with wrath. With pain. "I lost the most important thing in the world to me. I know exactly how you feel, but I have forged on. I found other things to care for, and I have protected them. I have done my best." He smoothed back my hair, much like a parent would a child. But my parents had given me no such comforts. Only Annwyl had.

"You do not understand," I whispered. "I'm sorry."

He saw it then. The look in my eyes, the truth behind my words. Everything I was was because of Annwyl. Every dream I had was shared with her. I did not want a crown. I did not want honor or glory. I did not want riches. I did not even want a family anymore. All I wanted was her, and now that was gone.

For the first time in my twenty-two summers, I watched Scholar Rindshaw cry.

Even his tears were green. My childhood self would be delighted.

He shook his head. "You are all I have left. All so many of us have left. You were supposed to change things, Jaevidan. You were supposed to change the world."

My eyes burned, but I shed no tears of my own. I had none left. "I renounce my throne."

"*No.*"

"I renounce my throne," I repeated. "I am no longer king. I choose you as my successor. You are far more accomplished at politics anyway."

He laughed. "Is that supposed to bring me comfort? Is that supposed to ease my broken heart?"

"I do not know," I said. "But I cannot. I cannot do it without her."

Silence. A dryad entered then, one who worked for him. She carried fresh bandages and water, but Rindshaw sent her away. We stared at one another. The light shifted along the wall, the sun descending behind the mountainside. Descending on my short and pitiful reign.

"In the mountains of the human world, a Bogoran still lives," he said.

My stare narrowed. "What good will they do me now? She is dead."

"It has never been done," he continued. "I cannot say if it is foolish to try, but as the sole inhabitant of a Bogoran's power, you will have the will of a god. The ability to change, to create, to make life."

I blinked. "What are you saying?"

"Take my dagger," he said, placing it beside my face on the bed. "If you wish to die so badly, then use my blade to do it. Make me carry your death for the rest of time. But if you are willing to fight, to seek another way like Annwyl would have wanted, then take this risk. Return to the human lands and find the Bogoran. Kill it and bring her back."

"That is not possible."

"Just because something has never been done does not mean it is impossible."

I knew what this was. A fool's mission. A way to distract me, to give me hope so Scholar Rindshaw could buy time to convince me to stay. To become king. And not just any king but the most powerful one in centuries. Perhaps the most powerful to ever exist. A smarter man would see through the lie and refuse. A simple man would believe him and agree. But I was a desperate man, the most dangerous kind of all.

"What will you tell the others? If I leave now, they will declare I abdicated."

"I will tell them you are dead." He sneered, but his eyes filled with tears. "Since you are convinced you are anyway. And when you return with the power of our gods, with your queen, they will believe anything. That the Poison Prince can cheat all, even death."

The offer lingered in the air, tasting like poison.

In another life, I would refuse. I would assure the scholar, the only father I'd ever known, that I would move on. I would live. I would take this throne and continue our dream and Annwyl's dream, even if it killed me each day to do so. I would save the low fae and bring justice to this world. I would if I were selfless. If I were kind. If I were good.

But I was none of these things. Annwyl was.

I was nothing but violence.

FORTY-ONE

ADELINE

THE MEMORY DIAMOND RADIATED, a final burst of light before it went dull and gray in my palm. Tears dampened my lashes. My breath came in feeble pants. Before I knew it, I shook with full, body-racking sobs.

Not just for the boy who'd lost his closest friend, the man who'd lost his wife, but for the other gift Estheria must have imbued in the diamond. Because as soon as Jack's last memory finished, I remembered pieces of my own.

My feet in the frozen mud, waiting beneath a full moon beside the Veil.

Sucking on my finger after pricking myself on blackberry thorns.

A skinny squire speaking to me in the kitchens, leaning close as I chopped carrots for a stew.

That revolting night with Lord Beynon, closing my eyes and waiting for it to end.

Sleeping with Jaevidan in the meadow, snuggling close for warmth.

The first time I kissed him and how I knew I would love no one else.

Those long days in the castle and the fear gnawing at me day in and day out. Those long nights at the Warren, wondering what I had done to make him hate me. Why I wasn't worthy of him anymore. The joy of receiving one of his letters, the scent of rain and oleander wafting from the page. The way his arms felt around me in the cottage garden and star-flecked midnights I lost sleep without his presence. The beauty of Ildathach. How quiet I was during our wedding ceremony because I still couldn't believe he loved me back, that my greatest wish had come true. The fear when Corin told me to run for the forest. The hands in my hair as the villagers dragged me across the grass. Fire, and burning, and a pain so deep I wished for death's release. Had begged for it all to end, my only regret that I would never see Jaevidan again.

The tears didn't stop, my aching sobs echoing throughout the room. The door opened with a crack, and Jack stood there, shirtless, searching for a threat. But there was only me, the memories rushing back like a river after a storm. His eyes found me, the dead diamond in my hand. Wordlessly, he took me in his arms and carried me back to his room.

We lay in bed, the only sound the crackling fireplace and my muffled tears. He stroked my hair. I held on to him and inhaled his scent, the rain and oleander I had known for four hundred years.

"Where did it end?" he asked, the hushed words deafening in the silent room.

"After I died. With Scholar Rindshaw."

He nodded. "I'm sorry you had to see that."

"I'm sorry you had to live it."

His fingers paused in my hair. I shifted to my knees, appraising him. The tattoos across his chest and arms, all from that first life. Us in a violent wind, him raising his sword in the battle for Tearach. Me dancing on the table at the Warren, the copse of trees covering one hand and a burning pyre atop the other.

He took my hand, thumb playing over each of my knuckles. "I want to tell you that something now."

"What Estheria said?"

He nodded, refusing to look at me. "Let's speak in the Abstruse."

There was no time to ask why before we stood in the room, gossamer curtains flowing around us. I ran my fingers over the sheer fabric, Jack's image swimming in and out of view.

"I can't lie to you in here," he said, sitting us down on the bed.

"I know."

"That is the magic of this place. No one can speak an untruth, and the power is strong enough to overcome all others. Even bargains. Even vow marks."

My heart slammed against my ribs. "You can speak of my past lives in here?"

Swallowing, he said, "Yes, and I deliberated it many times, but I wanted you to see the memories first. It's one thing to be told but another to understand.

And I wanted you to understand. So I will tell you three things now, and I ask you to let me finish before saying anything back."

Tears, memories, four hundred years forgotten, I nodded. "Okay."

"First, everything I said the other night—in the bath." He shot me a knowing smile. "All of that was true. It has to be in here. So I do feel deep down my kind doesn't deserve redemption. I know you are safe and happy, and that is the most important thing to me. I'm truly tired of all this, and I can't do it anymore.

"But not because I refuse to," he said. "Which brings me to my second point. I spoke with Estheria, and there is something I haven't told you or any of the others. There is a way to free you from the fates, but what the *beansidhe* desire most of all is penance. Even Estheria cannot deny them this—they are too powerful now. Their hatred is because I defied them, not with you, but as they are unable to reach me, they chose the next best thing. We reached an agreement that satisfied all parties. You may keep your abilities, power, and immortality, but in exchange, I must give them mine. For all intents and purposes, making me human."

I blinked. "And you told them no, right?"

"I told them I needed to think about it. I have until the stroke of midnight on New Year's to make my decision. If you have not accepted your role as a fate by then, the bargain will seal."

I shook my head. "Jack, you can't—"

"Please, let me finish," he said, taking my hands. "I have one more thing to tell you, and this is the longest part, so bear with me." He drew in a long breath. "As you know by now, four hundred years ago, I was a scared, lonely child. I had nothing, but I had you." He tucked a loose strand of hair behind my ear. "I was too consumed by that to understand then, but in hindsight, I found other things too. I made friends, I had followers, and . . . and I had Rindshaw. But for so long, you were the only thing that mattered to me. He was right—I *was* young. We both were. And in youth, it's too easy to lose sight of everything else. So when you died, I did many things I shouldn't have."

My vision blurred once more.

"I have asked myself no less than a thousand times if I was wrong. If I should have let you rest that first time and moved on. If I should have accepted my title instead of running away. Ildathach is undoubtedly a worse place because of my actions, long before this collapse. I had the power and means to change everything and chose not to.

"When you first learned you were reincarnated, you worried that I only loved past versions of you or that you were so far removed from them it hardly mattered. In some ways, you were right, and others, you're still the exact same girl I met in Wales. But I've changed too. I've had four hundred years to grow up and not always be a better man, but certainly a different one. I am no longer that scared, lonely child. I found my sister, who, despite her nature, will always mean the world to me. I met Lillian and proved to both her and myself even the worst among us can redeem themselves. That we can choose whether or not to be monsters. I found a best friend in Will. Arthur came into my service, and I realized there could be a place for anyone in life, even those who had failed before. And I had you, in many different times and in many different ways. Some good, some bad, some where I wished I never met you, and some where I remembered why I fell in love with you in the first place. I've traveled the human world for you, experienced ten lifetimes of joy and sadness and everything in between. And I would have none of that without you either, because if it was not for your death and what came after, I would have stayed in Ildathach and lived a very different experience. I made my own family, taking in all the lost girls and boys just like you once wanted me to. I've helped countless fae find a safe and fulfilling existence in the human world. I've had more time with you and have seen you as everything from a duchess to an artisan to a *beansidhe*. For these things, I have no regrets.

"But the past is coming back to haunt me now." His thumbs smoothed beneath my eyes, salty wetness streaking across my cheeks. "Everything has a price, and I'm finally seeing mine. The truth is, even with killing us, even with the books, Babd and Nemain will not be able to recover my home. I already suspected this, and Estheria confirmed as much. And neither you nor I will be able to do it either. We need Violet." He chewed his lip, looking down. "But Violet can never be convinced. As much as I love her, I understand her faults. And you must understand she is not like us. She's not like any of us, and her life is not one I would wish on anyone. She won't agree to help, but her hand may be forced. She will hate me for the rest of my life, but Will and I are the only ones she will break her vows for. So if I lose my immortality and staying here means to grow old and die, she will do anything to prevent that. Even returning to Ildathach and restoring our world so I can stay with her."

I shook my head. "If you tell her what you plan, she'll see reason. There's no need to go through with this."

"But there is." His thumb ran over my empty left ring finger. "I renounced my throne, Annwyl. I left and took the last Bogoran with me. I abandoned someone who loved me the way I always wanted. I made my choices a long time ago, but I want to take responsibility for them now. The fates want you because they want me, and I couldn't live with myself if you suffered that destiny in my stead. I can't go on knowing all the work I've done with the low fae doesn't matter because they will never have a home of their own. I don't want to see my family fracture and fall apart over this. I want to see you become the Golden Goddess you were always meant to be. I want to try again now that you know the truth, and there's no hiding what I am or who you are like in all the other lives. But if that's not what you want, I understand that too. You're right, you are a different person, and you don't owe me anything. And while all marriages endure change over the years, the hope is to change and still love one another. But if you don't, I can't fault you for that."

I shook my head. "Jack, that's not—"

"I'm almost done." A forlorn smile, filled with shame. "The other truth is this—I am a selfish man. There are good and noble reasons I will agree to the fates' bargain, but if I will be honest, I still want more time with you. I've always been a greedy bastard, and thirteen lifetimes wasn't enough, because even at its worst—even when you hated me, when we fought all night, when you died again and I had to bury you once, twice, twelve fucking times—I still loved you most. I always have. I've seen you at your worst, and I've seen you at your best, and there is no one else who has come close to you. There is no one else I have done the things I have with you. You taught me what love was. You were the first to treat me like more than a monster. You were the only first kiss I have ever taken, the only one I've ever fought a battle for. I wed you because I loved you, and I did it three more times because I never stopped. I've stolen you from a wicked husband. I've sailed the ocean with you. I've sipped wine in the canals of Venice and visited the jungles of South America with you by my side. I've made love to you in gardens and ship holds and royal bedrooms. I've learned a dozen languages so I could call you beautiful in all your native tongues. I've laughed with you and screamed with you and cried from grief and cried from joy. I've kissed you under a thousand skies and watched other men do the same. I've held your children that weren't mine, I've held your hand as you died, and I've let it go as you walked away. And while all that is still not enough, it will be if that's what makes you happy. That's all I ever wanted for you."

I couldn't stop the tears if I wanted to. They rushed forward, charged with too many things to say. We were a mess, perhaps the most convoluted one to ever exist, but I had both our memories of Wales now. I knew without me, he would have become the worst version of the Poison Prince. Without him, I would been bitter and broken. He showed me love, and I dreamed, and in turn, he made that dream real. Our better world would have existed had I not died, and it was only through being separated that all else suffered.

And even in this lifetime, I feared and abhorred the fae, but Jack showed me them in a different light. He wanted to save humans and the low fae, and it was only through our parallel bond he was able to do so. His love for me may have destroyed his world, but now it would be the thing to save it. The love he and Violet shared, the love he shared with all our Band of Banished. That all existed because we taught each other what it was in the first place. And his dream for Ildathach couldn't exist without both of us in it. Without us making each other people deserving of it.

I'd spent so much time convinced all Jack and I ever did was destroy, but there was a reason Estheria wanted us together. Not because we were destruction but because we made each other better. We kept one another in the light.

"Even after everything?" I asked. "After all this time, all we have been through, you still love me as I was and as I am?"

He smiled. "That's the funny thing about marriage. You promise to love someone forever, and sometimes you do."

That was all I needed. All I ever had. I threw my arms around his neck and kissed him with four hundred years of love. Of wanting, the good, the bad, and all in between. He was mine, and I was his, and together, we could stay in the light.

His arms came around me on instinct. His lips moved with mine like they had a thousand times before. It never got trite or tiresome, a truth he revealed as my back hit the sheets and he climbed over me. He kissed my face, my tears, my neck, the feeling the closest to godliness I had ever reached. I wanted him so badly it hurt, now and forevermore.

"Annwyl," he groaned, slipping my dress down my shoulders, pushing it down my waist. Our arms tangled together as we rushed to remove one another's clothes. Our foreheads smacked, and I laughed, rubbing at the spot on his skin. He smiled, so full of life I didn't know how I ever thought he truly smiled before.

I watched that grin transform as he pushed inside me. As he showed me how much he loved me, how much he wanted me, just as he had done the first time. I reciprocated all of his movements, the look in his eyes, repeating all the vows he'd made me take last night.

Only this time, I promised to love him back.

Dawn broke by the time we stopped, lying in satisfied silence in the Abstruse. Jack stroked my hair, murmuring, "Is it safe to assume we're no longer friends?"

I laughed. "Yes, you idiot."

"I must warn you, I won't always be easy."

"Like you are now?"

"Oh, it gets much worse." Grinning, he kissed each of my cheeks. "As we both know, I'm quite prone to poor decision-making."

"You know I'll keep an eye on it."

"I've discovered that whiskey is my favorite human invention, and if we ever return to this world, I refuse to watch romances at the cinema."

I pursed my lips. "I'll get you on a double feature. Continue."

"I swear far too fucking much, my family is rather bizarre, I will never allow a cat in my house, and I'm afraid I possess the unfortunate habit of forgetting to replace the toothpaste once it's empty."

I shook my head. "The cat may be a deal breaker."

He sighed. "Fine, one cat. But I won't like it."

"I'll settle for a dog. They are man's best friend, after all." My smile faded, another thought occurring to me. "You're really doing this? Letting the stars make you human?"

"You know, I think I was always meant to be one." His lips pulled into a wistful smile, fingers sweeping my hair aside. "Like I said, I'm a bit tired, darling. It'll be nice to wake up without pain for once, to never worry about the poison again. And we can have a good life in Ildathach, even if I'm a little less than what I once was."

"You're sure?"

"I've never been more sure of anything." His nose brushed mine, a slow kiss to the corner of my lips. "But it's been a long time since I've been with my wife, and I'd really like to pleasure her again."

"Technically, we're only engaged. According to the papers, that is."

"That can be remedied." He nipped at my jaw, breathing in my ear. "What do you say, darling? Fifth time's a charm?"

Rolling my eyes, I huffed, "Well, when you put it like that . . ."

His lips lifted in one corner, eyes dancing. "I love you most."

I pulled him close. "I love you most."

FORTY-TWO
ADELINE

THE PLAN WAS FAIRLY simple from there. We had a few more weeks until Jack's bargain set in, meaning all I had to do in the meantime was stay alive. There had been nothing but silence from the sisters and other sidhe, even according to Guinevere and Lillian, who were both on the hunt for information.

We kept the plan between us, agreeing the best time to tell everyone would be after the bargain was complete. That way, no one else could intervene beforehand or, more importantly, let anything slip to Violet about what Jack had in store. I didn't love the idea of scheming behind all their backs but understood the necessity. And it was nice to be let in on Jack's secrets instead of discovering them when everyone else did, for once. I gave him one of my own, telling him I now remembered my time as Annwyl. I would let the others know in time, but for now, I was happy to reconcile both my lives in private. It was strange, to say the least, but Jack was nothing less than diligently supportive.

With the faeries from the prison now settled in, Jack and I focused on the business and readying everything for our departure. J.W. Enterprise would officially go completely public come January 1927 and would be run solely by an executive board. We would still hold around a third of stocks, guaranteeing income for us when or if we returned to the human world and for anyone who decided to stay behind. Jack and I married in a discreet civil ceremony shortly before Christmas, just the two of us, a county registrar and Lillian as witness. She was distraught when she learned there would be no formal wedding for her to plan—and asked if I was right in the head even as we approached the courthouse—but I assuaged her concerns by promising she could plan a large event after the New Year, conveniently leaving out where it would take place. I asked Tommy to walk me down the proverbial aisle. He was far from thrilled about the rushed marriage to Jack but agreed when I said how important to me it was he be there on my wedding day. Even if he was only a brother in this lifetime, he was still every bit my blood, and I loved him no less than I did before.

I wore a simple white gown and my mama's pearl necklace. Jack donned his best suit, and we bought rings along the way. It was nothing but a formality, an announcement to temper the gossip papers and give me legal rights to Jack's enterprise. His lawyer, Mr. Theodore King, nearly had a stroke when Jack refused a prenuptial agreement, then developed chest pain and took a handful of pill capsules when we signed papers granting me equal ownership and decision rights to Jack's businesses, properties, bank accounts, and all other assets. Only time would tell if other industry men would honor my status, but with Jack losing his immortality, it would be risky for him to visit the human world for any extended period of time. When upkeep was required, it would be me traveling back to handle it. I asked him if it should go to Violet, as she had already partnered with him for years. But Jack insisted Violet wouldn't be able to leave Ildathach for long either. I asked why, but he only vaguely referenced the promises he had kept to his sister about her affinity and past. As it was their secret to keep, I asked no more questions.

As we stood for a justice of the peace, he stroked my back and hair. I rested my cheek on his shoulder, barely hearing the magistrate's standard vows. I had my own for Jack that no human could understand, but as he placed a ring on my finger, Lillian burst into tears. Tommy shook his head, but his small smile said he was happy if I was. The magistrate declared us legally man and wife, and my husband kissed his bride.

I beamed at him. "Until death do us part?"

Jack winked. "Not even that."

When not sorting through endless paperwork or making rapid arrangements for management, we enjoyed Jack's final days of being fae together. We visited the cinema often and quickly realized I had no stomach for the horror pictures, but we both adored the comedies. We attended *The Nutcracker* ballet at the Paramount, and I purchased new pointe shoes to take to Ildathach. We drank in speakeasies and returned to the Cotton Club to hear that Ellington fellow play piano once more. We gathered our entire family together for Christmas, or Yuletide as the fae called it, exchanging gifts and getting zozzled in the study. Even Violet attended, though she was uncharacteristically quiet in the corner for most of the night.

And after everyone had fallen asleep or returned home for the evening, he led me into our bedroom and stripped my dress. He kissed my hair and my neck, and though it was only a few feet away, we never made it to the bed.

Honestly, I wished we could spend the rest of our lives in that semi-carefree state, but the morning of New Year's Eve arrived, and all my fears rushed back. That Jack would regret this, that he would come to resent me, that Estheria was somehow wrong and Violet and I would make no difference in Ildathach. That Violet would never forgive Jack for the deception or me for allowing him to go through with it. That whatever was broken inside her would become irreparable when she learned our plans.

I knew Lillian would be happy to return home and felt Will was rather indifferent about the matter, happy to go either way. Arthur and Guinevere may choose to stay behind in the human world but might change their mind if we offered them space to rebuild the Guild, safe from both other humans and those in this world who hunted them. My brother was another complication entirely. He was more than welcome to come along, and it would probably be smartest in case the remaining Knights of Templar discovered him again, but I knew he wouldn't be happy about it. He would feel like I was abandoning him. In a way, I was.

There was also the aftermath to contend with. While everyone would be ecstatic when the day was saved, it stood to reason it wouldn't be long before others were none too happy with me, Jack, and Violet in charge. Fighting would break out to claim fallen thrones, protests would be met at many of the laws we planned to enact, and some would simply be unsatisfied with the change.

But I tried not to let those thoughts dwell as Lillian and I got ready in the Abstruse. Jack had planned a New Year's Eve ball for tonight, a last hurrah before all the chaos of the next few years. I wore the dress Jack bought for me in Chicago, painstakingly repaired by a group of brownies living on the eighth floor. I'd burned the rest of my wardrobe but thought the dress had changed enough to be considered a new item. The brownies had rooted through my belongings, sewing in Estheria's diamond and the coin I'd received from the Atlantic queens for luck. The chiffon scarf went around my neck, and the tiara glittered from my head. Lillian rushed home to retrieve a brooch to match her dress when Jack appeared in the room. "Ready to head upstairs?"

I nodded, trying and failing to hide all my nerves. Jack never said, so I wondered how much this bargain would change him. If he would still appear fae without magic and immortality or would seem as human as the glamour he wore. If the tattoos on his skin would continue to writhe and dance or lie flat with normal ink, if they remained at all. I loved him just the way he was and preferred him to remain the same, but it was a small sacrifice compared to what he would give.

He kissed my cheek. "What's the matter, darling?"

"Nothing." I smiled but knew it wasn't convincing. "Come on, we have guests."

The sun was just beginning to set, but the party was already well underway. Humans and fae disguised as them roamed the floor, drinking flutes of green bubbly and dancing to the band belting energetic jazz. We received dozens of congratulations and even more inquiries into the "rushed" and "unexpected" nuptials. I'd received so many scrutinous glances at my stomach I finally declared I wasn't pregnant at the beginning of each conversation.

The fae were no less curious, just in other ways. Most came from Gerenstad, and the older ones among them knew the sad tale of King Jaevidan and his Golden Goddess. Our sudden reappearance sparked curious questions and a respectful, weary sort of reverence. They asked endless questions about what our plans were for Ildathach, to which we replied all would be known soon. It did nothing to satiate them and only made our mythical presence more arcane.

Around nine o'clock, the band slowed down with a romantic tune. The Band of Banished all drank at a table, laughing and conversing with an ease I hadn't seen in months. Even Tommy joined them at Lillian's insistence, forgoing alcohol but smiling at a theatrical story Will recounted. Guinevere arrived and sat beside Arthur, a small smile permeating her severe exterior. Violet was noticeably absent, but Jack didn't seem concerned as he took my arm and led me to the dance floor.

"I need a break from small talk," he said, taking my hand in his. I agreed. Between the posh humans and posher sidhe, I was exhausted.

I eyed the family table as he turned me. "You know, I still haven't heard the story behind Arthur and Guinevere's names."

Jack laughed. "Oh, I'll let him tell you that one. It's quite the tale if you have the time for it."

And no doubt would take a lifetime with all his forgetfulness and back-tracking. I grinned. "We'll have time, eventually."

"We will."

We swayed to the music. It was too late now, but all my earlier concerns swarmed to the surface, namely the ones pertaining to Jack. I still couldn't quite believe he accepted this path wholeheartedly, without regret. I feared he only did outwardly so I wouldn't feel guilty.

I pressed in close to him. "You're sure about this?"

He spun me in a circle. "My answer hasn't changed, Annwyl."

"I know, but—" I chewed my lip. "Not that we have much time to debate it anymore, but I want to know you're absolutely sure. You're about to give up so much, your entire existence as you know it."

"And you haven't done the same?" His gaze settled on me, solemn. "You've lived a dozen different lives and chose to transform into something else in this one."

"Yes, but my transformation gave me power and immortality. It didn't take it all away."

"Like I said a few weeks ago, I think I may be pleasantly surprised. No more pain, no more constant attention to withholding my abilities. And let's be honest, far less responsibility."

My brows touched. "Am I to run this kingdom myself?"

A devious smile. "I wasn't going to let you, but now that you say it . . ."

I swatted his arm. He laughed, continuing. "Too late, Annwyl. You've put the idea in my head. I think I will rather enjoy retirement."

"You're not retiring," I deadpanned.

"Why not? Lay around and do nothing all day, watching my gorgeous queen handle all the big problems. Nothing to worry about except my next shipment of whiskey and where to lick when she gets home for the evening."

I rolled my eyes. "You would spend about five minutes enjoying peace and quiet before losing your damn mind. I can see it now, hovering on the edge of council meetings declaring you want no part, but if you may make one teensy suggestion, you *really* think things would go smoother if etcetera, etcetera, etcetera."

He waggled his eyebrows. "What gives you that impression?"

"That you're intolerably mischievous and restless." I kissed the corner of his lips. "And I love you for it, but I'll be driven halfway out of my mind if you don't just help me take charge of the whole damn mess."

"I'll do my best." He kissed me, long and slow. "It's a shame we didn't get much of a honeymoon. I have a few restless and mischievous things on my mind."

I grinned. "How mischievous?"

"Well, let's just say . . ." He whispered the rest in my ear. My face turned red, toes curling in my diamond-studded heels.

Someone tapped my shoulder. A cold sensation swallowed me, a premonition of dark emptiness. I snapped to attention, but it was only Violet dressed in her usual black.

Jack blinked at her. Lips turned down in a frown, she said, "Let me have this dance."

I stepped away, but she shook her head. "With Annwyl."

Unease trickled down my spine. Neither Jack nor I had told her I'd reclaimed those memories, and she'd never called me by my first-life name before. Perhaps it was coincidence, but something about her seemed . . . off.

Jack nodded, taking the peculiar request with stride. "I could use a drink anyway." He kissed my lips, then kissed Violet gently on the cheek. "Are you alright?" he asked her.

She nodded, gesturing for him to leave.

I'd never slow-danced with a woman, and we got our fair share of amused glances. While stunning as always, Violet's black dress was rumpled, a small tear running up her matching stockings. Wrinkles made a choppy sea of her black silk gloves, and I was fairly sure she hadn't combed her hair. Harold was absent, likely hunting for rodents or terrorizing the human guests. I took her hand, leading in the male position though she was taller.

"You look like shit," I said, skipping pleasantries.

A tremor set into her hands, mouth pinched. "I feel like it."

"Have you taken ill?" I'd never seen her so discombobulated, even the evening I'd spent at her apartment. I'd tried returning several times, but she barred the door from my entry. Besides her muted presence on Yuletide, I hadn't seen her since.

"Something like that." She glanced around, as if searching for demons within the dark spaces between bodies. "There's something wrong tonight."

"What makes you say that?" I wondered if she could sense Jack's impending bargain, their Morrigan and twin bond warning he was about to change. I'd felt no such thing, but she was his blood, and perhaps her magic was alarmed as well. I'd raised concerns to Jack about his transformation technically breaking our Morrigan, that Violet and I would no longer hold enough power to restore Ildathach. He'd only said Estheria assured him it could be done.

Quietly, in a tone of voice so unlike her, she whispered, "It's the air."

"The air?"

"I think I'm fucking losing it."

She stepped away, but I grasped her tighter. "Tell me what's wrong."

"I can't—" Her eyes glistened, teeth gnashed together. Her eyes turned that unsettling black again. "I don't know why it fucking hurts so much."

My voice softened, turning us so no humans saw her face. "What happened with Ildathach?"

A long, tattered exhale. "I don't understand. It wasn't supposed to be like this."

Jack and I had agreed to reveal nothing to the others—most of all Violet—but her expression sounded alarms in my head. She was handling this worse than we thought. Besides, midnight was only three hours away. There was little time for her to intervene.

"We didn't want to say anything yet, but Jack and I have a plan. It won't be the same, but we're going to fix it. And we will all return, and you will have a chance to live in your home, your true home. Only this time, you will be accepted in it."

"They'll never accept me."

Will caught sight of us, a frown stealing his mouth as he slowly rose from his seat. I shook my head, mouthing, *Not yet.*

"Not all of them will accept me either, but enough will. And your family will always be here for you."

"My family is dead," she said, cold and lifeless and so disturbingly unlike Violet.

"Your elder brothers and parents are, but you always have Jaevidan. And me, as much as you deplore it." I smiled. She didn't smile back. "And our ragtag group is your family now. We're all doing this together."

She skidded to a stop, eyes returning to normal but the tremor moving up her arms. "I . . . I . . . don't," she stuttered, heaving breaths like was she starved for air.

Something was seriously wrong. "I think you're sick, Violet. Let's sit."

She shook her head.

"Is it your powers?" I tried. Jack's affinity caused him physical pain; perhaps hers did too. "Let me get Jack. He can help you."

"He can't. I need you." Her nails dug into my shoulders, leaving little half-moons in my skin. I shimmied from her grasp, but she held me tighter. "Bless me. You can do it as a fate."

"What's wrong with you? You're not acting like yourself."

"Just listen to—" I didn't hear the rest, all my attention welding to a strange scene in the corner of the ballroom. That feeling of doom resurfaced, the gathered energy before lightning struck. The music faded to the background, the sharp colors melting in dreary black. I stepped from Violet's grip, tilting my head.

Two birds somehow ended up in the ballroom. Massive, black crows with shimmering feathers. They stood side by side on the molding, black eyes roaming the floor. They found me, and though it was absurd, I swore an intelligent malice swarmed in their eyes.

"Are you listening?" Violet screeched. Couples jumped back around us, the music dimming to a hush. Will stumbled from his seat, and Jack rushed over from the bar.

"Annwyl, I need—"

"Where did those birds come from?"

She turned, scowl slipping from her face. "Fuck."

The room plunged into darkness.

Not the black of a midnight bedroom or a forest glowing beneath the moon, but a true, endless dark. Violet disappeared from sight, the dancing couples and Jack crossing the room. For a moment, I thought I'd gone blind.

Then, the humans screamed.

Glasses shattered as people stumbled for an exit, no lamps or candles to guide them. Instruments screeched dying notes, dropped to the ground or tripped on by panicking guests. I held on to Violet, fighting the crowd for the general direction of the group's table. But we were jostled and turned around until I could no longer tell which way to face.

The screams rose in a swelling tide, a deafening white noise that cleared my thoughts. I felt the air for Jack, using our bond to guide me back to him. Violet shivered against my spine. "And God said, let there be light."

Fire erupted around the perimeter of the room, contained to the walls, but the humans wouldn't know. The orange flames burned my eyes, pupils accommodating to the blinding scene. I reached for Violet, but she was no longer there.

"*Fuck*." The curse was lost to the chaotic room. When my eyes finally adjusted, I understood why.

Nemain stood before me, white dress drifting on a phantom breeze. Her claws snatched the front of my dress, ghastly smile filling my view.

"Hello, Princess."

Those claws lifted and slashed my throat.

We entered the shade before I could react. The darkness curled around us, biting and cold like it used to feel. I reached for the blackness, but it refused to concede to me, my fingers finding nothing but sticky blood.

I screamed, but my voice no longer worked. I kicked and thrashed, finally finding a hold in the shade's depths. I tried to wrench us back to the ballroom, but we landed on an icy dock instead.

The moon winked down from above, stars scattering the clear winter night. Snow seeped into my silk dress, and frost crept along the dock's wood. I grabbed my throat to staunch the bleeding, hot liquid leaking through my fingers. It was deep, but not enough to kill, only to ensure I couldn't use my voice.

To ensure I couldn't scream.

A ship rolled past, horn blowing in the crystal night. Golden lights washed us from the deck, chattering people preparing for the New Year. Nemain grabbed me by the hair, fury twisting her expression. She wrenched our faces close, hissing, "You want to die now? Be my guest."

I reached for the dagger beneath my dress, but it was too late. She kicked my ribs with enough force to snap them. I plunged into the Hudson River.

FORTY-THREE

ADELINE

THE GOLDEN SHIP AND silver moon became nothing but streaks of color. Frigid water encased me, chilling me down to the immortal bones. Her claws weren't iron, but that didn't matter. I could be killed by any kind of sharp object.

Blood poured from my neck, and my broken ribs screamed. I knew how to swim, but my feet might as well have been lead. My dress collected water and dragged me farther into the murky depths, the chiffon scarf a noose around my throat. Fluids filled my chest, a combination of river water and blood. I screamed, nothing but a gurgling drowning by the roaring current.

Jack, but he wasn't here. No one was here, all left behind in the fiery ballroom where Babd would slaughter them all. The thought gave me a burst of strength, but I was losing blood too fast. The current dragged me to the riverbed, and I tumbled over rocks and debris. Suddenly, there was no light at all, nothing but darkness and the deathly chill consuming my flesh.

Jaevidan, I wept. Silent, pathetic tears. I was going to die. He was going to die. Everyone was going to die. Everything, four hundred years of searching, all for nothing.

A hand clasped my arm, slimy and coated with scales.

Bubbles erupted from my mouth and throat, feet kicking at the creature tugging me back to its lair. My foot struck soft flesh, followed by a blood-chilling hiss. Four more hands replaced the one I kicked away.

No, get away! But my throat produced no sound, nothing but another stream of curling red. I sobbed and thrashed, fighting harder when the moon returned and I caught a glimpse of my captors.

They vaguely looked like women, but the resemblance ended quickly. Long hair of kelp twisted from their heads, soulless black eyes darker than the surrounding water. Their skin shimmered with iridescent scales, chests flat and smooth compared to their land-dwelling counterparts. Their waists tapered into billowing, black fins, soft and curved, unlike the jagged talons of their nails, the serrated edges of their teeth, three rows each.

I kicked away, but another came behind and held me in place. A smaller one tore my dress open, running its hands along the ruined fabric. My vision darkened, the edges closing in. My lungs burned, and pain shot through all my sinew. The creature ceased tearing my dress, reaching up and tearing at my mouth instead.

I clenched my teeth together, swiveling my head as it pried through my lips. Exhaustion came over me, sudden and unrelenting. Another moment and I would be dead. No more oxygen left to fuel my brain. Gold flashed in my vision, and I melted into the darkness, praying the water took me before those serrated teeth could.

Something clinked against my teeth, filling my mouth with the taste of metal. I took a deep breath, a slippery hand pressing against my lips.

I took a deep breath.

I took a deep breath.

I opened my eyes, salt burning my retinas. The creatures' voices raised around me, a melodious singsong that demanded attention.

"What is she?"

"I cannot say, but she possessed a coin of the Whydah Gally."

I nearly laughed, then cried and laughed again. That's what they had shoved in my mouth. The ridiculous offering from the Atlantic queens, sewn into my dress for luck by the brownies. That's what allowed me to breathe.

If I ever saw Grillow again, I would kiss them right on the mouth slits.

"Rather ugly, do you not agree?" A third creature brushed my hair aside, startling at my open eyes. "It awakens."

"Do not speak," another instructed, hand squishing my lips together. "Your flesh still bleeds."

I placed a hand around my throat, useless with the water thinning my blood.

"I will take you to the surface now," she sang. I blinked, and we shot through the current.

I was unceremoniously thrown on the dock, hacking the coin to the frost-coated wood. *"Thank you,"* I croaked, in no way audible.

Three sets of black eyes watched from the water. Silent, they slowly retreated beneath the surface.

From my limited experience, I preferred land-dwelling fae.

But that was suddenly the last thing on my mind. The cold set in, licking my wet, exposed skin. *Just because you don't feel it doesn't mean it can't hurt you.* I shook too hard to stand, red gushing from my throat. So much I couldn't believe I was still alive. I needed to get back to the hotel and find Will. I needed to—

The sisters. Babd and Nemain had arrived.

My chest heaved, breaths burning as I entered the shade.

I spilled onto the ballroom floor, littered with broken glass and debris. The room had emptied and the fire extinguished. Tables and chairs lay on their sides, portraits shredded and facedown on the floor. The band's bass drum had been kicked through and a trumpet half melted. No signs of life, either here or on the floor below me.

I shaded to the apartment, stumbling into our room for dry clothes. My blue fingers couldn't affix buttons, so I settled for a loose dress that required no ties. Grabbing a thin scarf, I wrapped it around my neck tight enough to keep the wound from bleeding.

Too tired to stand, I slumped to the floor. Reaching for the bond, I searched for any sign or hint Jack was still in the hotel. Either him or Violet, but I could feel nothing.

It was quiet, unnervingly so.

I felt . . . wrong.

I staggered to my feet, the rug squelching wet beneath my toes. The Abstruse was safest but also had a window overlooking the street. Maybe the fire department had been called, human guests evacuated to the road. I leaned heavily against the wall, brushing a gossamer curtain aside.

The street was empty, devoid of any and all life. Even the partiers roaming the sidewalks, the bustling taxis, and those rushing home late from work. All the windows in the building across were dark and empty. In fact, all the windows down the entire block were dark and empty.

Snow dusted the ground, falling gray like ash through a roiling fog. It coated the ground, tinged a strange color between black and green. Flickering within the haze were candles. Hundreds of them, topped with tiny silver flames.

I stumbled back and ran from the room.

Fumbling down the stairs, I slid no less than three times and crashed onto a landing somewhere near the fifth floor. No people walked the lobby below, nothing but the fog crashing against the doors and consuming silence. Rasping breath pushed through my teeth, a wet rasp from the wound to my throat. I shoved open the glass doors and stood barefoot on the sidewalk.

The fog retreated at my footsteps. Now taller than me in height, it parted like the Red Sea and guided me down an empty section of street. A traffic light blinked from its post on the corner, red flashing in and out of view.

No people, only candles. They melted onto the asphalt, wax spiderwebbing out from each flame. The white candlestick was carved with red runes, all but a single, rectangular space. Just like the candle I'd stolen from the Guild. But the rectangular space was carved on these ones, each one with a name in black.

Helen Cross.

Solomon Levy.

James McNally.

I reached for the last one, breath faltering in my lungs. But instead of touching wax, my fingers brushed something cold and soft. When my hand retracted, blood coated my fingertips.

What the fuck was happening?

"*Annwyl.*"

I snapped to attention, ramming full force into Jack. His arms circled my waist, wild stare taking in the scene around us. His black coat was dusted with snow, shirt tattered and stained with blood.

"Lillian is down the block with Will. I can't find anyone else, but we need to get you out of here," he said.

Ringing punctuated my eardrums, distant screams and muted snarls. *What are you talking about?* I asked, but the words refused to leave my throat. Nothing but choked gurgles and a scratching hiss.

He yanked us to the side, but nothing was there. Distantly, I heard the call for more ammo.

"What's wrong with your voice?" He ripped the scarf off, turning to stone at the sight of my injury. "On the fucking fates," he breathed, dragging me back inside the hotel and furiously dabbing at my neck.

What is happening? I mouthed, but he was too busy frantically attending to me, sputtering curses from wan lips. Maybe it was worse than I thought.

I grabbed his hand, pointing to my mouth. *Why is no one here?*

He shook his head. "What the hell are you talking about? There's people everywhere. It's fucking chaos."

The lobby stretched empty and silent around us. Several candles dotted the floor, silver flames dancing in the draft.

I shook my head. *No people. Only candles. Fog.*

"What?" He paled, grabbing my face. "How much blood did you lose?"

I pointed at the door. *Only candles and fog. What do you see?*

"The sisters unleashed hell on everyone. The whole city block is scattered with bodies. We glamoured the police to barricade the streets to try and contain it, but they're killing everyone. Humans, fae—you don't hear the fucking gunshots?"

I shook my head. *No one out there.*

He wound his arm around my waist, drawing me to my feet. "I'm getting you to Violet. She'll take you to Ildathach."

Bells chimed in the distance, eleven strikes. How did so much time pass? I ground my feet into the marble, shaking my head. *You turn human at midnight. Come with us.*

"Not if you die first," he snapped, kicking the glass doors so hard they shattered.

This time, it wasn't fog and candles. I gasped, taking in the cataclysm.

Broken glass sparkled in the snow, fires erupting from automobiles and blackened buildings. Shots rang out around us, the deafening clang of swords and daggers. No candles carved with names but twisted, bloody bodies facedown in the street. I searched for the traffic light and the candle underneath. James McNally. A dark-haired man lay on his side with his throat torn out instead.

Humans hid beneath vehicles and screamed from dark allies. Metal pierced the air, the taste of magic so thick I could hardly breathe. Fae I was familiar with and creatures unknown battled against one another in the streets, some using weapons of long ago, some with iron-loaded guns, and others with dark affinities, setting fire to their opponents or collapsing the air within their lungs.

My limbs locked, head swiveling. I stumbled back against Jack. He grabbed my arm and ran for an adjacent building. An office.

More bodies littered the lobby. I blinked, and they were replaced with candles, names carved in midnight ink. Another blink and they were bodies again. I didn't understand what was happening, but it must have had something to do with the fates. The artifact gifted to me by the druids. But something about the fog seemed wrong, corrupted in a way that repelled the *beansidhe*. I only had a moment to reach out and touch it before it disappeared from view, replaced with the real world once again.

I knew what was happening.

I was dying.

My feet stumbled beneath me. Jack dragged me around the waist and ran for a back door, dumping us into an ally. A phooka looked up from the sidhe it was eating and charged. Jack's poison reached it first, and it collapsed to the ground. The next block was no better than the last one, swarming with more terrified people and battling fae. A flash of red caught my vision. Ginger hair. The dark-skinned man beside her wielding a sword.

Jack dumped me beside Lillian and helped Will kill a pack of red caps. Her skin turned ivory, trembling hands going for my throat. "Oh my god . . ." She pulled a first aid kit from her purse, the kind the Red Cross gave to army medics. A needle and thread shook in her hand, eyes scouring for a place to start.

"*Will*! Will, we need you here!"

I blinked, and Lillian disappeared. The fog gathered around me, thick as paint. A thin path opened to my left, leading around the corner to Park Avenue.

Will swam before my face, bloodied and dripping sweat. His hands went around my throat, voice shaking. "My fucking god, Addie. How are you walking?"

I stared at him, wondering why his eyes sparked with silver flames.

"Why isn't it working?" Jack screamed, narrowly missing a dagger that flew his way.

Where are the sisters? I mouthed.

Will shook his head. "What the fuck is she asking?"

An automobile burst into flame, causing us all to duck and cover our heads. Blood dribbled down the front of my dress, the wound no less than it was before. Strangely, I felt no pain. Nothing.

"Addie, look at me," Jack said. "Keep your eyes open, darling, please."

Will tried again, throwing his hands in the air. "I—I don't know what this is. I've always been able to heal her. I don't know why it's not working."

Someone screamed, and a bullet pinged off a lamppost. Jack ran down the block, a sword glinting in his hand. It drew a line of sparks along the pavement where the tip dragged along the ground.

The fog returned, more insistent. It prodded against my face until I looked toward Park Avenue.

I have to go, I mouthed.

Lillian sobbed. "We can't understand you, darling. Try not to move. You're losing a lot of blood."

I stood. *Find Tommy. Keep him safe.*

Someone reached for me, but I slipped away. A scream quickly faded into the ether, nothing but the candles and fog left for company.

The silence was comforting, the fog more. I couldn't say why it felt so familiar, like an old friend guiding me home.

From Park Avenue, I turned left on Twenty-Sixth Street, following it down to the East River. The night was silent, the candles fewer. An empty warehouse stood beside the water, windows brown and warped from an old factory fire. The front door opened on squealing hinges, the fog beckoning me inside.

It used to be a meat-packing plant. How . . . diabolic, though I knew I could trust the fog. It guided me across the factory floor. Metal hooks glinted in the moonlight, chains rattling against one another in the breeze. Tables scored with knife marks scattered the floor, like a strong breeze had blown them any way it pleased, all but one table in the center, covered in dripping, rune-ridden candles, hundreds of them forming a floor of waxy stalagmites across the weathered wood. In the center of the silver candle's glow, cross-legged and naked for all but a brassiere and skirt, was Violet.

She cocked her head, black eyes roaming from my crown to my feet. "Took you long enough."

I waved my hand across the barren factory, a question.

She straightened, the movement all wrong. Instead of one smooth motion, she jerked up in fragmented pieces, like clock hands ticking into position. Black fog coated the floor, so thick I couldn't see my feet.

Her lips twitched in and out of a smile. "You look like shit."

I stepped back, wondering if I'd been wrong to come here.

"Though you often do." If her eyes weren't a smooth black, I imagined she'd be rolling them.

I pointed to her bare stomach. *Run out of clothes?*

It's just flesh, she replied, voice swarming inside my head. I smacked my temple, rubbing at the skin like I could push the sound away. Fire erupted behind my eyes, and my knees buckled.

"Pathetic," she huffed, snapping her fingers. The pain left like it never existed, replaced with a strange feeling in my throat. I reached up and brushed my wound, feeling nothing but smooth skin.

"How . . ." I cleared my throat, blood splattering my mouth. "How did you do that?"

"It doesn't matter. The wound is still there."

"What?"

"The wound is still there," she said, drawn and enunciated like I was slow to catch on. "I simply created a new version for this conversation."

"What the fuck are you saying?" I breathed, looking around. "What the hell are we doing here, what's happening?"

The fog coalesced around her, a black cloak of scintillating stars and rolling waves. The silver candles brightened, turning her skin a sickly white. "Babd will arrive in eight minutes, twenty-three seconds."

"How could you possibly know that?"

"No—forty-nine minutes and seventeen seconds." She grabbed her head. "*Fuck.* Eleven minutes, thirteen milliseconds." She growled, staring up at something—or someone—I couldn't see. "Would you fuck off?"

I searched for the nearest reflective surface. Her head snapped toward me, so abrupt she should have broken her neck. "I wouldn't do that if I were you."

My feet rooted to the floor, some primitive sense screaming from the back of my mind. That I'd walked into a predator's den, and my only hope now was a quick death.

She dropped to the floor, stalking closer. Her limbs jerked like a broken puppet, spine rolling and snapping straight. I backed away. "Violet, what the hell is wrong with you?"

She jerked to a stop like someone yanked her strings. "If we kill her in nineteen minutes, Will and Jack may live."

Deciding to play along, I asked, "What about the rest?"

"Lillian always lives. The bitch." Violet laughed, the sound skittering down my neck. "And your dear brother, who was quickly escorted away by Arthur and Guinevere to the new Guild. They'll rally troops and make Thomas stay behind. Guinevere dies in the nineteen-minute timeline, but Arthur carries on another century or so."

I released a shaky breath. "In what scenario does everyone live?"

"None. The interfering cunts." Twin middle fingers were held to the ceiling.

I backed away. "Okay, and in which scenario do *I* live?"

Violet frowned, jerking her head toward me. Her chin canted at an unnatural angle, hair sweeping into her eyes. "You're already dead."

I blinked. "What?"

"You . . . are . . . already . . . dead." She grinned, shrugging like this was a silly mistake. "Sorry to disappoint. It was *fate.*"

"I'm pretty sure I'm alive right now."

She pouted. "But are you?"

A shiver ran through me, a cold so deep it iced my blood. My head slumped forward, the muscles of my neck refusing to work. I brought my hands before my face, pale and riddled with purple bruises. I reached for my throat, feeling the flesh hanging over the collar of my dress.

I tried to scream, but no sound came out.

Violet laughed, wagging her finger at the ceiling. "Not yet, you contemptuous hags."

She snapped, and I returned to normal, gasping for breath. "What *the fuck* did you just do?"

"Calm down. I only showed you as you truly are. Dead as a doornail, unfortunately. You really think you would have survived losing your throat and drowning in the Hudson? And I thought I was full of myself."

My knees knocked together, feet stumbling as I backed another step. "I'm standing here talking to you, Violet. I'm alive, and you're fucking insane."

"Only because I'm keeping you here." Her lips stretched in a gruesome smile. "And I'll tell you, the banshees are *pissed*."

"What are you saying?" I gasped.

She twisted her long arms above her head, the flesh stretching to uncanny lengths. "So here's the skinny. You are dead, technically. That's why you kept seeing the candles, a view from another plane and all that. But I'm keeping you here a little longer because you know what they say: work doesn't stop because your heart does." She laughed. "I'm so fucking clever. Anyway, we still have seventeen minutes until Babd arrives, so why don't you tell me about your day?"

I leveled with her, holding my palms out. "I don't know what's wrong with you, but you're sick. Your affinity is messing with your mind or something, I'm not sure. But I'm not dead. And even if I were, there's no possible way you could *keep* me here. Nothing is capable of power like that."

"But Annwyl, I can do anything." Her smile melted into a grimace, hands thrown to her side like a petulant child, screaming to the ceiling. "Just *not* in this *fucking flesh*."

I felt for the bond, sending all my fear down the channel. *Jack, I need you* now.

"Jack, I need you *now*," she mocked. "Did I not teach you better? Down with the patriarchy. Women can vote now and all that."

I gaped. "You read my mind?"

"I told you, I can do anything," she snapped. "Anything but control the fucking timelines. Why that job was ever given away is beyond me. We have fifteen minutes and five and a half seconds."

"Violet," I whispered, voice wavering on each syllable. "Violet, what the hell is your affinity?"

Her face scrunched. "Really? You haven't figured it out yet? You did thrice before, and you barely understood then."

Something exploded in the distance, sending a warm wave of air across the factory floor. The chains chimed against one another, dust and soot scattering the cement.

"Almost there," she hummed. "There'll be another one in fourteen minutes. That's our cue."

"*Your affinity*," I screeched.

She huffed. "That's where you're going sideways, darling. Trying to shove a square peg into a circular hole. Never thinking far enough outside the box. *I* never said I had an affinity. You did. Who's to say I have sidhe powers at all?"

But what else could they be? She *was* sidhe, Jack's twin.

It made no sense, wasn't even an option, so I wasn't sure why I asked. Why I changed my question just enough to defy reality. "Violet, what are you?"

She grinned. "Now, isn't that the question? You know, that conniving little twit Estheria gave you one more memory of Jaevidan's. I conveniently removed it when you left the diamond with me before the prison."

My blood ran cold. "What *are* you?"

She shrugged. "What the hell? We have thirteen minutes left anyway." She snapped. "Enjoy the show."

FORTY-FOUR

JAEVIDAN

IN THE MOUNTAINS OF the human world, a Bogoran still lives.

With Scholar Rindshaw's final words to me, I descended into the crypts. Priestesses prepared Annwyl's body for burial, just as he promised. I sent them all away, avoiding her death-stricken face as I wrapped her in an ivory shroud. Her clothes had been removed, but a single bluebell remained in her hand, as crisp and beautiful as the day someone had placed it there. Unlike her, it would live forever, frozen in time as all things were here. I left it in her palm, securing the funeral wrapping around her head with her wedding circlet. A faceless corpse in white, crowned with gold.

Then I tucked her against my chest and departed for the human world.

There were several ways to kill a Bogoran, but I knew of one. They were gods, created from stardust and matter with no corporeal form. Their existence came from belief, from the power their worshippers bequeathed to them. That energy sunk into the earth, rooting them to one place for all time. One could be moved elsewhere if they requested it of their acolytes, but the ritual was long and slow, often taking many lives. Most remained where they were created or fell from the sky.

Which made them easier to kill, another long and arduous process. One had to remain with the Bogoran for weeks, months, sometimes even years, ignoring its presence and refusing its commands. Convincing it that it did not exist, that its power was nothing, that it *meant* nothing until eventually the energy dissipated. A gut-wrenching, soulless way to die.

I repeated the process to myself as I crossed the meadows, as I strode through the ashen village and into the slumbering forest beyond. To shade would alert the god of my presence, so I would walk. I would carry my bride through the mountains, lay her before the feet of my creator, and return the life that was stolen from her.

I repeated my mission in the empty, bitter nights, with nothing but a pitiful fire and my cold, dead wife for warmth. In the long days, I traversed the Bannau Brycheiniog, stumbling over rocks as I carried her in my arms. When the biting rain became pallid snow. When the rocky mountainside bore less food, then none at all. When my ribs pushed against my skin, when even the poison lost its strength to fight, when I shivered in caves and beneath a slate-gray sky, chewing on grass to convince my mind I'd eaten.

Annwyl did not suffer in those weeks. Only I did.

Metal tarnished the air the closer I drew. I sensed the power beneath my feet, undulating like the tides surrounding Cardiff. It beckoned to me, a hypnotic call to enter its web.

There was no telling how many days it had been when I came upon its cave. A darkness leaked from the entrance, an endless midnight pockmarked with stars. An acolyte stood at the entrance—

A druid, gold robes bleached pale from the sun. His fallen brothers scattered the ground, frozen hands still clutching iron spears. There was no dignity in this barren, frozen land. The living and dead lay together like old friends.

I stood before him. The point of his weapon prodded my neck. "No sidhe shall pass me."

"I mean you no harm," I said. "I only come to ask a favor of my god. Let us through."

Teeth gritted, his frostbitten hands trembled around the spear. "I am the last acolyte of the last Bogoran. None shall pass while I still draw breath."

My remaining poison gathered between my fingers, blackening Annwyl's shroud. "Do not make me kill you."

He may enter, a voice said inside my mind and echoing to the wind. Neither young nor old, woman or man, containing the power to move mountains and burn bright as the stars. The acolyte trembled, spear wavering at my throat. *Allow the child of glamour and blood to pass.*

The spear lowered. His eyes narrowed, a terrible fear turning them red and rotten. There was nothing more to be done; both he and the Bogoran knew this. If he were wise, he would accept the gift of mercy his god had given him and leave.

There was no light in the cave, even from the mirage of stars. But it was warm. Water dripped from the ceiling with endless percussion. The smooth floor continued beneath my feet, but I walked blindly. When I had come far enough the fog thickened, a wall of black permitting me no farther. I laid Annwyl on the ground, falling prostrate on the floor.

"I come to ask a favor of you."

You lie, the voice said. *You know I grant no such favors. You know what you seek has not been done. You wish to steal my power, forgetting you are nothing but glamour and blood.*

The fog rippled, showing scenes in its murky depths. Annwyl and I meeting as children, the many nights spent in the meadow.

These things are mere deception.

The images changed, my bloody face as I killed Beynon. As the court howled and fell around me.

My children are savage. They know no sickness or death. They were created to rule the lessers, divine acolytes to worship their masters. This is what you are, not the child of flesh and dust you insult my presence with.

"She is a queen."

The voice laughed. *It is in rotten meat in a crown.*

The fog condensed, forming the shape of a sidhe. I recognized him from a portrait, a long-dead king of Tearach, once thought to be the most powerful sidhe alive. An aura of darkness surrounded him, eyes completely black. The voice spoke from his maw, an empty void leading to nowhere. *Tell me what you truly seek, what you believe this human creature may bring you. Is it power?* The king smiled, placing the ruby crown of his land upon his head.

Glory? The king melted away, replaced by Corin in his armor. The cheers of men echoed throughout the cave, calls to open Tearach's gates.

Revenge? It was me, eyes black as pits as I slashed Drusilla's throat.

Or maybe something more . . . primitive, the voice said, a perfect mimic of Annwyl. The Bogoran took her shape, everything down to the differing shades of her hair. Completely nude, the apparition stalked forward with swaying hips. It dropped before me, lifting my chin. A demon used her voice, but I leaned in anyway as she murmured, *I ache for you, Jaevidan.*

"*Enough,*" I snapped.

The false Annwyl smiled. *I can take your memories of me. You will never crave this flesh again.*

"It is more than flesh," I said.

Nothing is. Annwyl disappeared, fracturing into a starry fog. *Nothing but me.*

"You are nothing," I hissed, each word lower than the last. "You do not exist."

I know, the Bogoran said, but the sound was no longer nothing and everything. It took a quality too real for its form, sadness bleeding in from every side. *For I am the last, and soon, I shall die. If not by you now, then before long. I have no kin left. My acolyte will soon succumb to the cold. I will fade into the mist, no rotten flesh to be carried and returned to the soil. What is existence but confirmation you are real? There is no one left to confirm mine.*

The hollow words reverberated against the walls, bouncing and repeating inside my skull. Annwyl's body lay on the ground before me, a husk as empty as the Bogoran's thoughts. But she was kindness, understanding, all good things in this world. If she could hear this god's misery from the darkness, she would weep until the end of time. She would scream for me to stop. I swore to be her violence, but Annwyl tainted me. I killed those who wronged her and nothing more. I fought in battles, but all was fair in war. I thought I could take an innocent life. That my love for Annwyl would drive me to do anything.

But for this, she would never forgive me.

Salty wounds dripped from my eyes, joining the pattering water. The shadows reformed, a creature of darkness on two legs, neither man nor woman, sidhe or human, a ghostly silhouette of a soul not born. It walked a circle around me, a vulture observing its prey.

Why do you weep?

I remained silent.

Answer me, son of glamour and blood.

"Because I cannot," I said. Annwyl's body rocked in the wind.

You cannot what?

"Kill you," I said, so weak the words formed no sound.

What is different about you? the shadow asked, its circle shrinking like a noose. *All others before you killed my kin. Why do you come here and say you may not?*

"Because of her," I whispered, reaching for Annwyl. "Because she would rather remain dead than let another take her place."

But what of your wishes?

"They do not matter. She no longer suffers, so I will in her stead. I am her violence. This was always our destiny."

But how could you choose this? The shadow stopped before me, leaning so close its chill caressed my skin. *Children of glamour and blood are not meant to sacrifice. Not meant for the selfless whims of the stars' children. You were not created this way.*

"Perhaps your children have finally learned the mistakes of their parents."

The shadow recoiled, glassy face somehow appearing stricken. *I see. This is a trick.*

"It is no trick," I said. "I will leave you to die as you may now." Folding Annwyl into my arms, I stood and made for the exit. If I used the shade, I would survive the journey home. She would be buried as a queen like Scholar Rindshaw promised. I would prepare a grave beside her. Like the last of my gods, I was already dead anyway.

Do not yet turn from me, son of glamour and blood.

I froze, the blinding white morning just ahead.

I do not wish to die, but I will if I remain here.

"You will be found eventually, no matter where you go. We both only delay the inevitable."

Not if I can hide, it hissed. *Not if I am given feet to walk, legs to run.*

I shook my head. "I cannot help you."

What if I bring her back?

Breath stuttered in my throat, blood pulsing in my ears. "Can you?"

Return to my side, and we may see.

A trick, a foolish trap laid by an ancient god, most likely. But I had nothing left to lose. Nothing more to live for. Annwyl took her dreams with her to the darkness. She took me too.

The shadow sat on the floor beside me, mimicking all my movements. An uncanny doppelganger of hazy black. When I lifted my hand, it did the same, coiling its fingers when mine fell to my palm. But the shadow held no form, or perhaps the Bogorans were too different from us. Each of the movements was staggered, either too fast or too slow, a poor imitation of the very thing it created.

Have you heard of soulmates?

Shaking my head, I loosed a long breath. "You cannot deceive me. I know of soulmates. They only exist through a parallel bond, something Annwyl and I never had."

The shadow cackled. *How foolish my children are. The parallel bond does not exist, not as you understand it to. But that is a matter for another time. Soulmates are real, not given or innate, but made.* It gestured to Annwyl, arm snapping in the wrong direction. *It is what makes humans so weak. What feasts on their life, shortening their mortality. The deeper they love, the more they share, the more they give away. Pieces of their essence belong to others. Give enough of oneself to another, they give enough of themselves back, and at some point, their souls are mixed. Equal halves of each other's originals. It is why parents cannot return to their former selves when their children perish. Why when one lover dies of age, the other soon follows. A human may live if their essence does within this plane, but not for long when so many pieces of them join the dark.*

It pointed to my chest. *I cannot say how, but you have given, as has this human. Much of her remains in you, but you gave too much away yourself, son of glamour and blood. When she left for the darkness, the pieces of you she carried departed with her. It is why you wish so much to die. Why you feel only half a man, for now you are.*

But, it continued, *this may serve your purposes now. Enough remains in you to keep her tethered here. She cannot fully join the darkness. With so much of her soul trapped behind your chest, her own will become a wraith. But fear not, for it is only wraiths I may speak to. Once the fates take hold, or my wretched siblings of the stars, there is nothing I can do for humans.*

So my proposition is this—we both may leave this cave with what we want. I can bring this Annwyl's soul back, assuring it finds another body in due time. It will not remember you, but it will still be here. Deep down, at least. I will do this twelve times, giving you thirteen lives to spend with her. I can offer no more than this. She is still human, so she will still die. And each time she does, more will leave her. More pieces of her soul will go to you, and more pieces will join her wraith. When she dies a thirteenth time, there will be too little left to bring back.

Hope blossomed behind my rib cage, tiny and unsure now but steadily growing. I could have Annwyl again. I could hear her sing, hold her in my arms. She would look different, perhaps even act so, but she would still be her in the end. A soul of kindness and good. We had a chance for another life, many lives.

And if I brought her back to Ildathach, she would not die at all.

"What do you want in return?"

*A body, for I cannot make this from nothing,*it said. The air trembled as if in protest. *And you as my acolyte, now and forevermore. You are strong, son of glamour and blood. A dust-mark corrupts your sinew, power no child of mine should possess. But you will have the means to protect me with this, to hide me, and to make the body that I seek.*

"I will serve you?" I asked.

Yes, the Bogoran hissed, voice strengthening with each word. *You will remain with me, sworn to always be my protector. We will be as kin, forever remaining in this world lest your brothers and sisters detect what I am.*

I shook my head. "I need to return to Ildathach."

So your human may live forever? Do not be greedy. I offer you thirteen lives. This and nothing more. You will accept this blessing with gratitude and revere the power bestowed by your god. Either this or nothing at all, and if you defy me, I will take what I so benevolently offer.

I would find a way. I would defy a god if it meant keeping Annwyl, but I wanted to be sure it did not mean to deceive me. "How will I know when she is reborn?"

The shadow seemed to think for a moment. *A picture of ink will appear on your flesh. When she dies once more, the image will move.*

"And how will I find her?"

It shrugged, the shoulders uneven. *It will be your task to find her. Consider it a quest to prove your love. And before you ask, I may be of no help. I cannot choose which bodies she inhabits or where, only assure she returns once more.*

I nodded. It was a fool's bargain, but I would do it. Anything to bring Annwyl back. Anything to prove I did not lie, that I would always protect her. I would, now and forevermore, despite what this Bogoran warned. I would never fail Annwyl again.

I can tell you are satisfied. We will begin now. It extended a jerky wrist to the mouth of the cave. *I shall send my acolyte to retrieve you nourishment, for you will need it. In the meantime, you may bury your queen. There is nothing left of her in that flesh, and it is too degraded for our purposes now. Once my body is complete, I will call back her wraith. And you and I will remain together until the end of time.*

"How will we make this body?"

The Bogoran laughed, its shadowed flesh twisting into a ghastly smile. *Do not ask questions you desire no answers to.*

Metallic magic filled the cave, stronger than I'd ever tasted before. It took form, hardened inside my throat, choking all remaining air. It left as swiftly as it came, a fresh bargain mark sealed on my flesh.

The Bogoran retreated into darkness, leaving me alone. I buried Annwyl as instructed, breaking my fingers clawing the frozen earth. The acolyte returned the next morning with a feast. The Bogoran's shadow form watched with pleasure as I consumed it all.

Then, it created a dagger from its inky depths, the black blade sharper than I had ever held. *We shall start with hands.*

A set of hands took the entire night. The Bogoran needed flesh, so this I gave. My right hand sawed off at the wrist, a poetic justice to my crimes against Lord Beynon. My sidhe powers did not let me die, and the Bogoran crafted me a new right hand from the wound. It requested a matching pair, so I gave it my left next. As I lay screaming by the fire with a bloody wrist, it morphed and mutated my old set until it was satisfied.

It healed my flesh sometime in the night, long after the pain plunged me into unconsciousness. Its shadow form woke me the next day, its only words, *Today, you will give me arms.*

So I did, spending another agonizing day and horrid night succumbing to the pain, breathing through it as I offered pieces of myself, my soul to Annwyl and my body to a god. The acolyte returned with more food, but it tasted like ash. Sleep eluded me the next three nights.

I tire of your screams, it said after a week. *So today, you give me your tongue.*

On it went. The days blended into each other, the darkness of the cave resolute. Time was only measured by the parts I cut from my body, the Bogoran molding them into its desired form. The perverted flesh lay across from me by the fire, the Bogoran's shadow standing over it when I woke in the night. Its spasmodic shadows stroked the arms, the hands, lovingly caressing it when it thought I did not watch.

I want eyes, it requested yesterday.

And I will need teeth, it said today.

Tomorrow will only be your hair, it said beside the fire, only the acolyte able to enjoy the food. My bare gums filled my mouth with blood, the only thing I would consume tonight. *You cannot recover without sustenance, and you will need your strength for the day after.*

It wanted my heart. I protested it would kill me, but the Bogoran assured it would keep me alive long enough to replace the beating organ it stole. I only believed it because its body was half-done. It would not let mine perish without its own being complete.

When I stabbed myself between the ribs, it was the exact feeling of seeing Annwyl die.

She was the only thing that allowed me to wake. At first, it was the bargain, knowing the powerful seal on my skin would not allow me to give up. But the longer we remained in the cave, the more I wished for death instead. My thoughts grew twisted, warped by the endless dark and only the silent druid and wrathful god for company. Too many times, I woke convinced I was dead already, that Annwyl's human hell existed and I now lived in it.

With that reality, memories of Annwyl became the only thing left. If I gave up now and succumbed to the darkness, she would remain forever as a wraith. So I wept and cut. I screamed and offered my skin.

*Legs,*it snapped one morning, growing impatient as the body neared completion.

Does one require a liver? it asked the next. I sobbed and quietly answered, "Yes."

Then one day, I woke up, and the Bogoran did not speak to me at all. The cave was empty, the fire cold. I shivered in the early morning air, rising and treading slowly toward the light.

It had been summer when I found the Bogoran. Now, it was spring. The icy mountainside remained as it always did, but flowers and grass bloomed on the hills below. A welcoming sun beamed from above. The acolyte was nowhere in sight, but the Bogoran was. Not in shadow form or the blink of hazy stars but the flesh it stole from me. Its new body crouched on a rock, nude and shivering with knees to its chest. It had grown my black hair, the dark locks cascading down to its waist.

"Join me," it said. No longer the voice of a god, a whisper from beyond time itself. Disturbingly, it sounded like nothing more than a normal woman.

I sat on the rock beside it, offering my blanket. The Bogoran was no use to me if the body it made froze and died before it made good on its bargain. I asked once if it would die if its body did once it inhabited it, but it refused to say. The truth lay in its silence. It was neither god nor sidhe now, but something in between. Something that never existed before, an aberration that repelled the air around us.

Gathering my courage, I assessed it. I had refused to do so anymore months ago, not wanting to see what my old flesh had become. I already knew it would change things, an odd relief that we wouldn't be identical, but we still looked eerily similar. If not born of the same flesh, then close relatives. The only thing that truly separated us was an odd choice the god had made.

"Why a woman?" I asked, taking in the lithe body, the soft curves, and smooth skin, all but for where it had sewn my old limbs back together.

"It felt . . . right." She held her hand before her face, turning it from back to palm. "Why does the cold hurt?"

"You tell me. You made us this way."

"I did not make you," she whispered. "My elders did, those who came before. I was born of the same gods who made the first of you, a child of gods, but a god all the same."

"You had parents?"

She nodded. "Five, but they are all dead now. They asked me to hide here, and their acolytes took them to a faraway land, one the humans here refer to as the new world. They perished shortly after reaching those shores."

"How long ago was that?" I asked. I did not wish to know, not truly, but knew I should glean more into this monster I had created.

"Sixteen summers," she said. "Shortly after I was made."

I stared at her. "You do not—you cannot mean to say you are a child?"

She leaned her head aside, following the arc of a soaring bird. "If one is a child at seventeen summers, then yes. But do not confuse your notions of maturity with mine," she continued. "We are not the same and never will be. I am a god, the last one left. You are a sidhe and my disciple, only made to protect and worship. You swore to me you would." She tried sounding fierce but either could not modulate her voice yet or could not mask fear. She claimed to be different, but a child was a child, and she was a scared one. A lonely one.

I had met one of those once.

"I will," I said tentatively. "But if you wish for me to aid you, you must be my disciple first. You do not move like sidhe, talk like us. They will know there is something different about you. We need a story for your existence and for you to hide in plain sight."

It made me cruel, but there was an ulterior motive as well. The Bogoran wished to always remain with me, but if I could teach her enough, help her blend seamlessly into the culture of her enemies, with enough time, she might not need me anymore. I would no longer be of need or use to her, having all the means to protect herself.

"The humans say there are those of their kin always meant to protect. Mothers and fathers, mostly."

"I will not tell others I fathered you." The very thought made me shudder.

"I did not ask you to." Her neck snapped aside to glare at me. She slumped at an unnatural angle, not used to the muscles yet, I supposed. "We will be twins."

I shook my head. "That breeds dangerous consequences."

"But that is what we are," she insisted. "What else? My power flows through you now, shared with another and enhancing both. We were reborn together of the same flesh, emerging from the same womb." She gestured to the cave. "And elder brothers are meant to protect, the very task I gave to you. So you will be born first, and I second. We may say we were banished from our world for our birth, and as long as I never use my powers again, none will ever know what I used to be."

"But you will," I said, promising consequences. "You swore to bring Annwyl back."

"I will make exceptions from time to time." She poked her knees, frowning at the little half-moons stippling her skin. "So it will be you and I. And Annwyl, as she comes."

A golden snake hissed from the snow, prodding at her foot. I hissed at it, but the Bogoran laughed. "And of course, you too, Harold."

I blinked. "Harold?"

"My acolyte," she breathed, lifting the massive creature into her arms. "He refused to part with me, but others would recognize him and know what I am. So I gave him new flesh too." She stroked the creature's nose, blinking in confusion when its snout brushed hers in return. "This body feels strange things."

"You will get used to them," I said, standing. I needed to find the Bogoran clothes, then hoped to get as far from this cave as possible. Now that I'd stepped outside, only death would convince me to return.

"Because you will teach me, Jaevidan?"

"Do I have a choice?" It was harsh, but I had no love for this . . . thing. She had served her purpose, and that was all. Even if she claimed me now as her brother. I had far too much experience with brothers. It was not something I desired to repeat.

"No," she said, "You do not." There was no way to know if she sounded dejected on purpose, but I felt guilty all the same. Annwyl would treat her with kindness. At least give her the chance.

"If I am to protect you, I cannot call you god or Bogoran. You need a name," I said. A peace offering.

"A name?"

"Something to call yourself, yes."

She scanned the colorful hillside, the wildflowers growing in indigo groves. A smile touched her lips, whether cruel or delighted, it was hard to say. The god looked at me, so like my reflection I nearly believed we were true twins. The spring sun bore down, a breeze bursting with new life touched the mountaintop, and the last Bogoran declared her name.

"You may call me Violet."

FORTY-FIVE

ADELINE

Violet whispered in my ear, "We have four minutes."

I blinked. We lay on the wax-coated tabletop, curled up beside one another. Silver candles flickered around our heads, between bent knees and crooked elbows, our bodies the last pieces of a twisted jigsaw puzzle. Her black eyes scoured mine, face so close I could hear her breath.

Blood pounded against my skull. "You're a fucking Bogoran."

She grinned. "Surprise!"

I rolled off the table, not feeling the candles burning my flesh or the smack of my head when I hit the floor.

She jumped to her feet, hands on hips. "Come on, Annwyl. You always say there's something wrong with me."

I scrambled back on my hands. "You're a corrupted god, the malevolent version of the stars. You cut Jaevidan up for your body."

She picked at her fingernails. "Technically, he did that himself."

"You're not even fucking twins."

Her eyes narrowed. I blinked, and she was on the floor, all convulsive movements as she crawled closer. "He's my brother. We claimed each other."

"He was disgusted by you. You practically enslaved him."

"Jaevidan got over it. I grew on him." Her smile stretched like a puppet's, a vile recreation of the living thing. "But here's the problem, Addie. I grew a little too fond of him too. So when he defied my *one fucking order* not to piss off the fates more than I already had, I let it go. And he made you . . . this." Her fingers twisted in my direction. "So what did those vile cunts do? They burned it."

"What?" I breathed.

"The candles," she hissed. "The one you took from the druids. Every fate has one, all but the last. Your predecessor. She refused to use hers, knowing it was wrong. So what did the other two do? They destroyed her."

I shook my head. "She chose to join the dark."

"*Lies*," she snapped, voice taking the quality I heard in Jaevidan's memory. The voice of a demon, something that shouldn't exist. "They destroyed her. The only good one left. And then used their candles to burn the tapestry, to destroy my fucking world. *Mine*."

The tapestry in the hall of fates. I had seen that black scorch mark in the corner, had wondered what that meant myself. But that explained nothing about the demon in front of me. "You never even visited that place, Violet. You admitted you created nothing yourself. You were the one that said to let it rot."

"Does a throne cease to be yours because you never sat on it?" She inched forward. "Is a child not made by fathers who have never met them? I have no love for the sidhe that killed my race, and they may rot, as I said, but not my land. Not lower fae. Not my birthright."

My pulse hammered in my throat. "So all this because Jack made me immortal? The fates want to destroy an entire world to what, get back at you? I thought Ildathach was dying because the Bogorans were gone."

"Do I look gone to you?" She grinned. "There is more to their goals than that, but we're running out of time. Even the Stars have been unable to stop them, their children forsaking them just like the Bogorans did. Why do you think Estheria begged you to stay with Jaevidan? She knew what they planned for you, knew what you could become. It had nothing to do with her admiring your grand love. Only one thing remains between the fates and destroying the stars, only one thing between them and absolute power over everything."

Her crawling ceased at my feet, chin coming to rest on my knees. "Me—" She cocked her head. "—and—" Shadows gathered around her. "—you."

I froze, all but the heavy breaths lifting my chest. "How?"

"First, we kill Babd and Nemain. It is the only way destiny works in our favor."

"Why haven't you already?"

"So others can know what I am?" Her lips twisted into a horrendous sneer. "So they can hunt me and kill me for my power? Destroy me like they did the rest of my kind?"

My family is dead, she had said. I thought she meant Jack's.

"The only reason I've survived so long is this." She gestured to her gruesome body. "I thought of every other way. I instructed Jaevidan when to act whenever destiny blew a different course, but all for fucking naught. The fates have plans of their own. Delsaran was Babd and Nemain's puppet, and so they are the *beansidhe's*. They thought they could use you too, but they underestimated me. They thought burning my world would reduce my power, but all it did was weaken this flesh. Make it harder for me to hide, to remain within the walls of what hinders me." She laughed. "I'm the most powerful I've been in three hundred and fifty years. If they leave me with no choice but to reveal what I am now, then I will drag those bitches to hell with me."

"What do they want?"

"First, they want to see Ildathach destroyed. Fae wiped from the face of all worlds. They want to rule in the stars' stead, dictating all things, not just life and death. They want what I have."

"But why?" I asked. "Better yet, what do *you* want?"

She frowned. "Have I ever led you astray before?"

I stared at her. Violet, who killed a band of red caps on a train to save me. Violet, who forced me out of my shell, demanding I stand up for myself. Violet, who admitted it grew tedious burying me, something telling me she didn't just let Jack keep me because she cared for him but because she begrudgingly cared for me too. It had been me, her, Jaevidan, and Harold for hundreds of years. Violet, my sister-in-law. My grumpy and rather awful friend. Someone Jack loved very much, despite their horrifying past. Someone who obviously cared for Will, a sidhe, for no other reason than she wanted to.

Jack was destined for something terrible but grew and learned to be someone better. With centuries together, she could have done the same. Time does not heal all wounds; some just become more complicated. But Jack trusted her. My family trusted her. I always had.

I had a feeling I would regret this, but it didn't stop me from asking, "What do you need me to do?"

A wicked smile swallowed her face. "Your soul is still fractured, too much to become a full fate. Lillian destroyed your memories and too much of your soul with it, but there's someone else who holds pieces of you."

"Jack," I said.

"And me." Her lips turned down. "I'll return what I have after we kill the sisters. I can fix this with you, restoring as much as possible while still locked in this flesh. But I can't reach the fates. Only you can."

I nodded. "And what will I do when I get to them?"

She winked. "You'll know."

"Jack will never allow that to happen. He won't let me die again."

"You're already dead," she whispered. "I told you. The corpse you inhabit pumps enough blood to move, your heart only beating because I command it. I did it once with Jaevidan, but he is sidhe. I can't restore children that aren't my own. A human death can't be undone by a Bogoran. Only the stars could do that, but they gave the power of death to the fates."

My heart shattered, more than it apparently already had. "Will I ever return?" I ask.

"I don't know yet."

My eyes burned, mouth pinching tight. "But everyone will be safe? They'll live?"

"If we do this, yes." She rose to her feet, taking my hands to lift me with her. The walls shook around us, the second explosion Violet anticipated. Our cue.

But apparently, I feared death more than I thought I would. I was so ready to accept this position before, but something had changed. I had changed. I remembered so much of my past now. I'd finally got my soulmate back. "I don't want to leave him, Violet. I know that's selfish and wrong, but I can't. I can't do this. I just got him back."

She leaned in close, lips brushing my ear. "Want to know a secret?"

The ceiling rattled, dust and debris falling on our hair. The silver flames performed an erratic dance, the clinking meat hooks muting all other sound. Her nails dug into my forearms, power rushing into my veins. My reflection stared back from a window, eyes completely white in the broken shards. My feet lightened, then lifted off the ground. Violet came with me, both of us floating toward the ceiling.

She whispered low into my hair. A secret, the most important one of all. One that changed everything. "Promise me, and swear you will tell no other," she finished.

My white eyes shimmered with tears, mirroring back in the glint of her black ones. I nodded, wearing no vow mark but feeling it on my skin. "I promise."

"Then I'll give you power," she said, nails digging deeper. A slow trickle at first, and then it poured into my veins. "We can fix what has been done. Then you will find the fates and answer to my call. Never forget what Estheria told you. What keeps you in the light."

Teardrops ran down my face, little wounds dripping onto her hands. "I won't."

She nodded. "Then let's fucking do this."

I blinked, and we were no longer in the warehouse but floating a dozen feet above a city street. The fighting had only gotten worse, more of Babd and Nemain's followers swarming the asphalt. Others held them back, but barely so. Their screams echoed into the frigid night. Blood coursed in a river of red. Below us, Jack fought a pair of sidhe, black coat billowing in the wind. His sword arced through the sorrowful night, moon glinting on the edge of his blade. He danced, ethereal and powerful in a way that stole my breath. Will stood beside him, protecting Lillian. She couldn't kill but stole the memories of all those who dared touch her. But none could see what Violet and I could, our vantage point showing what waited down the street—Babd and Nemain cutting through fae like paper, slashing a path of death straight to our family.

Darkness gathered around Violet, but for me, it was light. Not the gold of the snow spirits, not the sweet softness of buttercups or an infant's dress. Blinding light, a sigil of death. The silver of the fates' candles and the glint of cold steel. It erupted from my skin, fueled by the power Violet scored into my arms. Silence ensued beneath us, the clanging of swords replaced with fearful gasps, all stopping to watch the divine sight above them. Even Babd did at the end of the street, mouth curled into a vicious snarl.

I convulsed in Violet's grip, the power flooding me with unspeakable pain. Worse than the pyre, worse than the flesh Jaevidan hacked away. She laughed, the screech echoing into the night. I tried wrenching away, but her nails cut through my flesh.

Blood trickled from my nose, filled my throat with a retching gag. It was too much, her power not meant for mortals. Not meant for this body, even as a fate.

"You can do it," she screamed. "This is your destiny. Not what your father told you, not what the fates told you, not even what Jack told you. *This is.* You promised me."

I shook my head, vision darkening.

"You are Annwyl of Wales," she roared over the wind. "You took a scar on your face in battle. Men found glory in your name. You have died a dozen ways and returned a dozen times. You are my sister, and you can do this."

Promise me, Violet said.

Tommy, *I can't do this without you.*

Will, *We're lucky to have you.*

I missed you too, Lillian laughed.

We're always on your side, Arthur said. Guinevere nodded beside him.

I'm more concerned with what's in here, Jack whispered, kissing over my heart. *I love you most.*

I opened my eyes. Nothing but the black and green fog—Violet's power circling around us. Stars winked in the darkness like thousands of candles, the night sky where her species hailed from. She pressed her forehead to mine, gritting her teeth.

"You are fate, and I am god," she whispered. "Now, let there be light, Empress of Everything."

There was no need to scream. Not anymore.

Silver exploded from my skin. There was no pain, no feeling at all. Nothing but complete, world-ending silence, blinding light consuming all but Violet hovering with me.

Then, she was gone. Nothing but the silence, the white, and me.

Me and Violet's secret.

The power she gifted.

And *everything*.

EPILOGUE

THE LAST BOGORAN

I OFTEN FORGOT I was alive.

Mostly when I slept, my dreams filled with the night sky. The others' darkness melted into my own, the power clashing into bursting light, nebulas, and galaxies. But I woke again to this imprisoned skin, the flesh tethering me to the ground, inhibiting all I could be. It was hard work keeping a body alive. One had to feed it, but not too much. Bathe it, but not too often. Listen to strange sounds and pains that may indicate somewhere beneath the surface, something went terribly wrong for no good reason. It was weakness, a stinking corpse waiting to rot. I hated it more than I hated my children of glamour and blood.

All too often, I forgot.

Not now.

Annwyl's light exploded across the city. Blinding, deafening, *powerful*. I released her hands and fell to the street, the asphalt shifting and groaning beneath me. The fires extinguished, and the toppled cars righted themselves. The dead humans rose from the ground, blinking into the eerie white. Glass rose from the sidewalk and reformed into windows, blood lifting and returning to rightful owners. She was fate, and I was god, but only fate could control the timelines.

Only fate could turn it back.

"Want to know a secret?" I had whispered into her hair.

She was terrified. I could smell it on her, feel the energy pulsing against my own. It gave me strength. Devotion gave us strength, veneration, but nothing fueled a Bogoran like fear. Her eyes turned the white of the *beansidhe*, her power reacting to my presence. Her terror was good. Her terror meant I could trust her. I would anyway, but it was always nice to have collateral.

"Promise me, and swear you will tell no other," I had said.

She had. Then I took her back to the city and gave her the power of a god. And when that light burst across everything, it changed it. Reordered things back to the way they were. Blessed all the kind and loving people of the world and guided them home, just like she was always meant to.

Jaevidan had created a golden goddess.

But I made a silver one.

Eons passed to me, but to others, it was a flash in the dark. The light burned out, and Annwyl fell to the street. The power I loaned flowed back into me, giving new life to my darkness. Fog roiled around my flesh, delighted after being trapped for so long. My brother's eyes flashed gold in its mist, but I didn't want him to see what came next.

Annwyl fixed. I destroyed. Bogorans were corrupted stars, after all.

Any who raised a sword to us met their death. Not in blood or iron, but simply at my will. Simply because I was grouchy and their sedition pissed me off. They blinked from existence, all but Babd and Nemain down the block. I saved them for last. The sisters' eyes widened, their thoughts swarming my mind.

A Bogoran lives.

If we take its power—

I silenced them.

Gods make, and gods destroy. My kind brought these children into this world, and I took them out.

My useless flesh screamed, not meant for this kind of power. I collapsed to the road, panting for breath.

Stupid. Fucking. *Body.*

A car honked. Humans swarmed me, asking if I was alright. I reordered things in my own way, willing them all to forget me and leave, for the entire block to return home and shut their doors. The prayers of millions of souls flooded my mind, causing a headache. I rubbed at my temples and told them all to fuck off.

Then I rose to my feet.

Quiet sobs echoed down the street. I knew who made them. Lillian and Will surrounded them, the Poison Prince and his precious Annwyl. Then they stared at me, at the black consuming my eyes. They would know what I was, figure it out soon. It was destiny, unfortunately. Lillian would lose her shit, but Will would accept me anyway. He would say he was still in love with me, that he didn't know what this meant, but he would always remain by my side. He always did, every time he discovered the truth and I made him forget. Every time I regretfully pushed him away. Those short bursts of power were dangerous, drawing all those who could sense it near, but the knowledge was far more menacing. The knowledge would get him killed—it did in every timeline. Only Jaevidan could know what I was, and now Annwyl.

I flicked my fingers around the strings of their minds, their physical forces. They would return home, drift to sleep, and not remember what happened here. All they would know was that Babd and Nemain were dead, and Annwyl with them.

I looked around. Life threads swarmed through my vision—mind threads, physical threads, a million pesky fucking threads, all the possibilities of a changing world. But this one was not mine to rule. This one belonged to the stars. The vexing bastards.

A blink sent my Bogoran vision away, replaced with the standard one of a sidhe. I preferred it most days, just as I preferred the silence. The living never knew when to shut the hell up.

Twelve chimes of a church bell. People screamed for a happy New Year, everyone but Jaevidan. Annwyl was a fate and him still a sidhe.

He hated me. I could sense it.

He kneeled, clutching her broken body to his chest. She died with a fate's eyes but wore human ones now. They stared empty and unblinking into the night, her torn throat leaking the last of her blood. Not that it mattered. Her neck had snapped to a lifeless angle with the fall.

I tilted my head. Actually, she didn't look half-bad like that.

"Why?" he asked, rocking her like a madman. His soul winked beneath his bloodied shirt, half-gone now with Annwyl's death, just as I expected it would be.

"*I had a plan,*" he growled. "I spoke with Estheria. We knew what to do. Why interfere? *Why?*"

"You know why," I said.

He produced an ungodly sound, something between a scream and a sob. His soul flickered to a depthless black. It'd corrupt soon. Too soon.

I sighed. Corporeal beings were so fucking dramatic. "You know I'll get her back."

His prayers flooded my mind, reigniting the headache. He did it on purpose, knowing how much it bothered me. The impudent twit. "Don't fucking lie to me, Violet. Even you can't get her back now."

"Would you stop whining? It's *so* irritating." I crouched before him, staring into our matching gold eyes. "I promised to hunt those vile fates, and I will. If you think there's a chance in hell I'll let them keep her, then I'd get your head checked. It's always been the three of us, and as you damn well know by now, I don't like change. And if you remember, you made me promises too. I have a plan for you. Always have."

He gritted his teeth. "No."

"Oh, yes." I smiled, tapping his nose. "Come on, big brother. Get up. Time doesn't stop for anyone, even me."

Instead, he broke into tears. Pitiful, soul-destroying tears. Fingers threaded through Annwyl's hair, his sobs muffled against her frozen cheek.

This was why my elders desired an unfeeling race to worship them. Love was such an inconvenience.

Emotions were new to me, even after all these years. I didn't always understand them, couldn't make sense of why my brain produced them. They were messy and complicated, causing hurt where none was warranted. There were sensations I liked—using swear words, sex, the weird bubbling when Will laughed at his own jokes. But most I hated. Right now, this body told me I should be sad. I should be soft. I should feel guilt. But these things wouldn't fix our problems, bring Annwyl back, or heal Jaevidan's fractured soul. Only action would. This was why brains were stupid and useless.

I lowered my voice anyway, mimicking the soothing tone Lillian always wielded. "I swear to you, I will bring her back."

"She's all I asked for," he said. "I've done everything you've wanted. I've protected you, I've hidden you, I've even loved you like a true sibling. Annwyl was all I asked for in return."

Did he understand what a bitch it was to fracture her soul? To constantly thwart the fates and bring her back? And he knew from the start I'd offered thirteen lives. He got all of them. So fucking ungrateful.

I groaned. *Be nice, Violet. Think like corporeals do. Use* emotions *and* feelings. Fucking bullshit. "I haven't broken my promises. Trust me."

"You swear?"

Thank fuck, we were finally getting somewhere. "Do you trust me?"

He didn't. He never truly had, even after I *grew* on him. After I learned his ways and adapted to this life. He wanted to trust me because despite his reservations, he loved me. Too much. We'd spent centuries together, so it was inevitable. He forgot what I was because I was so good at hiding it, days and weeks and months passing where he completely forgot I was a Bogoran. Thinking of me as nothing but his twin, his friend, until he woke cold in the dead of night, remembering the year he spent ripping out his organs.

I terrified him, though he would never admit it. He didn't know I knew, didn't think I could sense these things no matter where he was, could hear his echoing thoughts through the walls even if they weren't prayers. He wanted to trust, wanted to love without reservation, but deep down realized I was not like him. Knew I could never be. That there was always a chance his dance with a god would come back to screw him.

But he didn't know I would never hurt him. This brain produced too many chemicals, too many signals causing me to feel what I shouldn't. He wasn't the only one who cared too much.

I straightened. "Come along, darling. Let's head back to the hotel. Take your precious Annwyl with you. I know you like that body, and besides, it would be a pain in the ass to find a new one."

Jaevidan scowled but obeyed. "Then what?"

I cracked my knuckles, another sensation I enjoyed. Oh, so satisfying. A grin stretched my face, a *wrong* one if his grimace had anything to say about it, but nothing could bring me down now. All the pieces were falling into place, my long-awaited plans coming to fruition. I strode ahead, heels clicking on the icy sidewalk.

"Then you and I have some fucking work to do."

Acknowledgements

First and foremost, thank you to everyone who has taken the time to read this series and follow Jack and Addie's journey. While not always easy, their story is one that is close to my heart and has been for a long time. I hope you enjoyed this book and to see you back for book three!

Thank you to Sandra at One Love Editing for as usual, doing a wonderful job cleaning up my terrible spelling.

Thank you to Rin Mitchell for the beautiful cover and amazing interior artwork. This book featured several of my favorites and I'm so excited the world now gets to see them.

Thank you to my agent, Susan Velazquez, for all the help with getting these books out into the world and answering my many ridiculous publishing questions.

And thank you to my family, especially my husband and sisters, for all the support, phone calls, late night plotting sessions and all in between. I couldn't have done any of this without you.

Also By Marilyn Marks

The Prince of Prohibition
The Veil of Violence
The Empress of Everything – *coming soon!*

Dark Romance by Mallory Hart

Hit
Marked
Second Son

Printed in Great Britain
by Amazon

37686129R00270